Irlandais

Dennis McCann

1663 Liberty Drive, Suite 200
Bloomington, Indiana 47403
(800) 839-8640
www.AuthorHouse.com

This book is a work of fiction. People, places, events, and situations are the product of the author's imagination. Any resemblance to actual persons, living or dead, or historical events, is purely coincidental.

© 2005 Dennis McCann. All Rights Reserved.

No part of this book may be reproduced, stored in a retrieval system, or transmitted by any means without the written permission of the author.

First published by AuthorHouse 08/17/05

ISBN: 1-4208-6809-8 (sc)

Printed in the United States of America
Bloomington, Indiana

This book is printed on acid-free paper.

Madame Cuvier bent to her turnips. She had been working at them since midmorning and was now sighing with the tedium of it. On this overcast warm day during the late summer of 1943, Madame Cuvier tended her crop in earnest. There were the wartime shortages to deal with and palatable food was scarce in her little village of Couderouge. As with most French people, the Cuviers went without much and longed for the day when the damned Boches no longer trod on their soil. Yet, she thought, there was always work to be done, occupation or not. She leaned back with both hands atop her long spade, stretching her aching back and looked down the road toward the south. A figure on a bicycle caught her attention. It was a man pedaling north toward Couderouge perhaps returning from Privas, the department capital. Madame Cuvier's gaze lingered on the figure as he drew near. She liked men and hastily adjusted her blouse and skirt at his approach. She felt a small rush of pleasure as she finally recognized the man. It was the *Irlandais*. The Irishman.

As he drew near, Madame Cuvier again bent to her turnips. Prodding the soil at her feet, she positioned herself, raising and slowly swaying her ample rump toward the road for the appreciation of the Irishman. She waited for the time it would take for him to pass then, while still bending, she glanced coquettishly over her shoulder toward the road. The Irishman was looking back toward her grinning and holding his tweed cap in an extended arm of salute to her gesture. She flushed hotly with embarrassment and stimulation. She stood as he turned from her and continued north toward the village. Madame Cuvier sighed once more, but not from tedium.

Sergeant Claude Poissy of the *Milice Française* was now more at ease as his truck left the wooded areas around Couderouge and met open country to the south. The mountains of the Massif Central and the French Alps to the east were hiding places for the Resistance and the possibility of ambush was ever in Poissy's mind whenever he traveled the countryside outside of Privas. The *Maquis* came down often enough to strike at Germans, the Milice and French collaborators. Had they not killed several *Miliciens* outside St.-Etienne just last month?

Poissy had spent most of the day in Couderouge seeking information concerning foreign Jews hiding among the rural French attempting to escape roundup by the Milice and the Gestapo. Most of these unfortunates had escaped to France before the outbreak of the war when persecution in Germany had become savage. Poissy had cannily developed the technique of casually engaging people in conversation at random listening for traces of a foreign accent. Without fail, he would choose those who avoided eye contact with him. His job had become more difficult when the German Army had moved into Vichy following the invasion of North Africa by the Allies. When the Gestapo appeared in Southern France, these frantic refugees went into deeper hiding with the help of French sympathizers. Yet, it remained easier to detect these foreign Jews than Communists.

Poissy lit a cigarette. He did not offer one to his driver but scanned the horizon off to his right imagining that he was searching for telltale signs of tactical importance. Looking out over the Rhone-Saone River Valley he saw nothing but landscape and sky. He reminded himself that one day soon he must return to Couderouge to investigate the residence of a certain prominent citizen. That young fellow, whose name he could not remember, had told him while outside the local *tabac* that there were foreigners in the employ of the man. When the informant mentioned that the man was of a landed family and a war hero, Poissy decided he would visit the residence when he had mentally prepared himself for a proper investigation. Yes, he thought, that would be wise of him, wise indeed.

Poissy considered that he too was a war hero of sorts. Had he not stood with other Frenchmen against the German onslaught in the spring of 1940? It was certainly not their fault that the German Panzers had artfully flanked the Maginot Line to the northwest thereby avoiding French valor. It wasn't their blundering but the generals' that had caused the Maginot debacle. He had done what one could only do in such circumstances. Indeed, it was his reporting of his soldierly conduct at that time that had helped him in becoming a sergeant relatively quickly with the Milice. Luckily, no one in the Bureau de Police had attempted to verify Poissy's claims on his formal application. He had stretched the truth on them somewhat. He hardly remembered that, in reality, he had been a quartermaster's clerk in the rear area and had only heard the guns in the distance.

No matter, he was still fighting for France. He fully supported Laval's Vichy Government and agreed with its policy toward Communists and the displaced Jews infesting his nation. He mused on his future in a new postwar France. No doubt, he would be an administrator of some importance with access to real political power. He would choose to be stationed in Paris with an office high above the Champs-Elysees. He would attend crucial meetings and opulent social affairs. Officialdom would rely heavily on his political acumen and instinctive knowledge of the *paysannat*. He guessed that although at some future time the gray at his temples might spread a bit, it would probably give him a distinguished air. He certainly would retain all of his hair as his father had. Claude wondered if he would be wearing a uniform. Perhaps he should have tailored suits. Maybe he would alternate.

Poissy was pulled from his reveries as the driver nudged him and jutted with his chin to indicate the approach of a cyclist moving toward them in the opposite lane. Although hungry and anxious to reach the relative security of Privas, Poissy decided to check him. "We'll stop him," he indicated casually.

As the truck slowed to a stop, he drew on his cigarette, got out and took his official pose before the vehicle's grille. As the cyclist drew near, Poissy raised his left hand from its thumbed position in his wide, black belt and indicated with a palm up gesture that the cyclist should stop. The cyclist, an older man, braked obligingly and came to a stop. He straddled the frame of the bicycle. Poissy stood, legs apart, both thumbs hooked in his belt, scrutinizing the man. He was of medium height and build. Although badly in need of a shave, he had good features with blue eyes that looked out from under heavy eyebrows. Poissy noted that his clothes and his shoes, although thoroughly worn, were of good quality. The man's hands did not indicate that his work was that of heavy labor. The Sergeant said nothing. He waited for the man to show those familiar signs of intimidation and break the silence with a few shaky words of submission. The man, however, said nothing but returned Poissy's gaze with apparent expectation. Poissy surprised himself by speaking first. "Your papers, Monsieur," he commanded.

Still straddling his bicycle, the man reached within his *veston* and withdrew his papers. Poissy did nothing, expecting the man to put down the bicycle and walk toward him. The man remained in place with documents in hand still looking directly at Poissy. The Sergeant knew his driver was watching the encounter and therefore reluctantly stepped toward the cyclist. He stopped before him waiting for the man to hand him the papers. The cyclist remained motionless. For some reason, quite unknown to himself, Poissy asked politely, "Your papers, *s'il vous plait, Monsieur.*"

At this, the man lifted the documents to Poissy. The Milicien opened them, inspected them for signs of forgery and proceeded to read their information. The papers seemed in order. Poissy read aloud the man's name, "Marcus McQuillan, eh?"

On Poissy's tongue the name became Marcooz Makeeyon. The man nodded. "You are a citizen of Ireland?" Poissy queried.

"I suppose I'm a citizen of Ireland," the man replied.

Poissy furrowed his brow. "What do you mean 'suppose'?" he asked.

"Well, back when I left, there wasn't an independent Irish nation," came the answer.

"Oh yes, yes, I see," responded Poissy, not really understanding at all. "Hmmm, well, why is it you left, Monsieur?" the Sergeant continued.

"Trouble," Marcus answered.

"Trouble? Trouble you say. What kind of trouble?" Poissy pressed further.

"The Tans," Marcus said. As he lied, Marcus had the amusing thought that, at this moment, he was dealing with something similar to the paramilitary police force active in Ireland when he was a younger man, the Black and Tans.

Perplexed, Poissy pushed ahead with his interrogation. "The Tans? What are the Tans, Monsieur?"

Marcus smiled. "The bloody English."

"The English were trouble for you, Monsieur? How were the English trouble?" The Sergeant asked.

Marcus squinted into the sky not knowing how to explain this ancient ethnic antagonism to the Milicien. "Well, they were in my country," he simply said.

At this a vague recollection from his school days came to Poissy. Ah yes, the historical enmity between the Irish and the English. It also occurred to him that the Irish were not formally with the Allies in the war. They were also a Catholic people. Had not their émigrés fought in French armies against the English? Poissy suddenly adopted a relaxed demeanor toward Marcus and reached into his black tunic for his cigarettes.

"A cigarette, Monsieur Makeeyon?" he smiled, extending the pack.

"Mercy byoocoop," replied Marcus.

"Pardon, Monsieur?" asked the Sergeant.

"*Merci beaucoup*," Marcus said without explanation.

Oddly, Poissy found himself beginning to enjoy this small respite from the usual tension involved in his duties. He wanted to converse amiably with this fellow without causing wariness. "You understand, do you not, Monsieur Makeeyon, that I must ask these questions as part of my responsibilities."

Marcus shrugged and picked a bit of tobacco from his lower lip. "You do, eh?"

The two men stood and smoked in silence for a few moments.

"Yes, to be sure. France has her enemies," Poissy offered as he handed Marcus his papers.

"That she does," Marcus seemed to agree, then added, "but you know, Sergeant, the English eventually had to leave Ireland."

Poissy was momentarily caught off guard by Marcus' reference to the occupation and the hint of a sardonic smile on the Irishman's face. He nodded reluctantly in agreement while being slightly confused about the willingness on his part to share this sentiment. He was happy his driver had remained in the truck out of earshot. "Well Monsieur, I am presently involved in seeking out those foreigners who have come to France uninvited and are living surreptitiously among us."

Although Marcus did not understand the word *subrepticement* he knew full well that the Milicien was referring to the Jewish refugees. "Well, it's true enough, Sergeant, that I wasn't invited, but I'm behaving myself as best I can," he replied with a slight grin.

Poissy was amused by the Irishman's waggery. "Ah, but you are different, *mon ami*," he smiled.

"Really'? Marcus responded, "Well now, how am I different?"

The Milicien grinned broadly, "You, Monsieur Makeeyon, are not a Jew."

Marcus continued the small farce, "How do you know I'm not a Jew?"

Poissy laughed at what he considered his truly clever riposte. "Because you do not have the large hooked nose."

Marcus, no stranger to the old Gaelic skill at bantering asked, "Do you suppose then Sergeant, that your man, General de Gaulle, is a Jew? He's a hell of a beak on him."

Poissy stood for a moment seeking an appropriate witticism of his own. The expression, "your man, General de Gaulle", like Marcus' earlier reference to the German occupation had slightly flustered him. Rather lamely he remarked, "Well perhaps he is, Monsieur Makeeyon, perhaps he is."

The driver, having noticed the amiability of the exchange between Poissy and the cyclist, cut the engine and got out of the truck. He hoped the Sergeant would not mind if he joined the palaver. Poissy noticed his approach and quickly assumed a more serious affectation. "Well Monsieur," he said officiously to Marcus, "it seems your papers are in order. You may continue on your way."

Marcus, amused by the change in Poissy, responded graciously, "Well, thank you Sergeant." He flicked the cigarette on the roadway, nodded and began pedaling toward Couderouge.

Poissy turned to the driver and commanded irritably, "Privas."

On the return to the department capital, Poissy did not scan the horizon. His mind remained on his encounter with the Irlandais and how he had enjoyed his short time with him. He assumed Monsieur Makeeyon lived in or near Couderouge. Perhaps he would meet him again when he returned to the village. He regretted not asking about the particulars of the man's situation. It occurred to Poissy that he, himself, might be lonely. He had thought he was immune to such considerations. He had no close friends in the Milice and other Frenchmen kept him at a distance. But were not his duties and career the most important elements of his life? He reached within his jacket for the pack of cigarettes and held them in his hand. He should have given them to Makeeyon. Yes, he should have.

Madame Cuvier was coming to the end of the last row of turnips. As she stood leaning on her spade, she saw the truck approaching from the direction of Couderouge. She scowled slightly as she recognized that incomprehensible insignia of the Milice Française on the side of the driver's door. "Rotten bastards," she murmured to herself.

Keeping both hands on her spade, she thrust out her arse in contempt as the truck sped by. "Shit on you," she hissed. Poissy's driver, looking lasciviously at the woman bending over in the field, nudged the sergeant and nodded his head to the left. Poissy looked but saw only crows against the eastern sky.

The young man, Maurice Fleury, casually leaned against the high stone wall next to the *boulangerie* wishing he had a cigarette. When not on errands delivering baked goods for the little shop's proprietor, he stationed himself here observing the comings and goings of the people of Couderouge. He particularly liked to ogle the women. He was hoping that someone he knew well would come by after leaving the *tabac* down the street. That would provide him an opportunity to ask for a cigarette. Sometimes he would loiter in and around the tobacco shop when his yen for a smoke was acute. At midday he was in the *tabac* when the Sergeant of Milice came in. He had waited while the sergeant conversed with the owner hoping that he too, might become a subject of inquiry. The Milicien sought information regarding foreigners living in the area. The owner of the tobacco shop was not helpful. He said he knew of no one in that category. Maurice knew he was lying. When the sergeant glanced his way, Maurice nodded toward the outside indicating he would like to speak to him without the tobacconist's overhearing. Maurice left the shop first and proceeded up the street several yards. Shortly thereafter, the sergeant exited the *tabac* and walked to his vehicle. When he saw Maurice he indicated with a crooking of his forefinger that the young man should come to him. As Maurice drew near, the sergeant pointedly asked, "You have something to tell me, young man?"

"Yes Sergeant, I have information that would be of interest to you," Maurice said in a low voice while looking up and down the street.

"And what is that?" the Milicien asked in a flat tone betraying no apparent interest.

"There are foreigners working at Monsieur Deschaines', Sergeant, at his residence outside of the village," Maurice offered eagerly.

"Oh yes? And who is this Monsieur Dechene?" Poissy continued almost indifferently.

"He is a wealthy man who owns a small estate. He has several foreigners working for him," the young man answered intently.

And where exactly is his residence?"

"It is a few kilometers west of the village," Maurice replied, "on the Ormeau Road."

"The Dechene residence on the Ormeau Road, eh? And Monsieur Dechene, he is an important man?"

"Well, some think so, Sergeant. Some say he is a war hero."

"Is he married?"

"Yes, Sergeant"

"Is there any other thing that is noteworthy about him," Poissy added maintaining an air of indifference.

Maurice thought for a moment then said with the faintest trace of a grin, "He is a cripple."

The Milicien noticed this expression of Fleury's sentiments toward Monsieur Deschaines. He guessed there was something quite personal in the young man's willingness to supply this kind of information. His experience in the Milice had taught him that it was primarily for blatant self-gain or petty revenge that informants were motivated. He looked at the young man with the watery blue eyes and bad complexion and was quite uninterested in what motivated him. "Is there anything else, young man?"

"Well, it is said that Monsieur Deschaines dabbles in the *diablerie*," Maurice pronounced gravely.

"So, he involves himself in the occult" the sergeant flatly commented. He knew he would get nothing more from the questioning. He looked at his watch and said, "*Merci*, young man" putting his hand to the handle of the truck's door.

"My name is Maurice Fleury," Maurice volunteered assuming the Milicien wished to know his name.

"We'll talk again, Maurice," the sergeant responded curtly. He opened the door and swung into the truck.

Maurice saw Poissy pull a pack of cigarettes from his jacket and stepped to the open window. "Sergeant, will you give me a cigarette?" he asked weakly.

Poissy looked straight ahead and after a small pause said, "N*on*," casually pointing ahead with his finger as an indication for his driver.

Alone against the wall in the late afternoon, Maurice was glad he had given the information about the Deschaines. Had they not had wronged his mother several years ago when she was employed as their cook? She had worked for them a few short months before they had dismissed her. They had falsely accused her of stealing silverware and household items. Madame Fleury explained to her husband and children that these things appeared in the Fleury household because they had been given to her by Madame Deschaines in gratitude for superb cookery and excellent maintenance of the kitchen. The false accusations, she maintained, were manufactured to allow Madame Deschaines to hire that slut Madeleine. Madame Deschaines was, after all, a lesbian.

Maurice remembered that as a teenager when his mother was working for the Deschaines, he had frequently visited her in their kitchen. There he ate well and now and again he had a word with Monsieur or Madame

Deschaines as well as their man, the Irlandais. Well, those days were gone, he thought. Some time ago he had heard that the Deschaines had taken in a refugee family. The local gossip said they were German Jews in hiding from the roundups. On those relatively rare occasions when he returned to the Deschaines residence making a delivery of bread, the refugees were nowhere to be seen. When he bicycled out there Madeleine ignored him and although Madame Deschaines spoke with him, she was now somewhat cool and distant. All he got from the Irlandais was a nod. He surmised they were probably embarrassed by their mistreatment of his mother.

Ah, but he did miss the food. His diet since those days consisted of watery vegetable soups, moldy potatoes, hard black bread and an occasional bit of meat. Most of all he missed those hard chunks of brown sugar that he would filch from the kitchen. He remembered with embarrassment the day he met Madame Deschaines while going out of the back kitchen door with a huge lump of sugar bulging out his cheek. Although she did not ask about his facial disfigurement, Maurice recalled blushing hotly at her obvious mirth.

Madame Deschaines moved Fleury in another way. She was an attractive, middle-aged woman, slim, with warm brown eyes and cropped dark brown hair. Somehow she reminded him of chocolate. There was a sort of *gaminerie*, a certain boyishness, about her. She was given to the wearing of trousers, had an occasional smoke and was avidly interested in dogs and horses. Her riding of her racing bicycle through the streets of Couderouge had an earnestness about it. A witticism from the local postman said that Helene Deschaines would probably be the first woman to enter the Tour de France but, because of her boyish physique, no one would notice. Maurice assumed that his mother was right in her discernment of Helene Deschaines' fondness for women. For him, that made her all the more interesting. What was it that she did with other women? In his fantasies he saw her locked in naked embrace with Madeleine. They probably fondled and kissed each other's breasts. What was the name of that thing that women like her used on themselves? It was something like dodo or dolo. Maurice often thought of Helene Deschaines when he masturbated.

The Irlandais was abreast of the self-absorbed young man before Maurice noticed him. He pedaled by without a nod of recognition. Fleury watched him as he continued up the street and turned left onto Ormeau road. "Well Monsieur l'*Etranger*", he mused, "your days are now numbered".

Raking the gravel in front of his little church, St. Gregoire Le Thaumaturge, Père Paul Bassard glanced up to see his friend, Marcus McQuillan, just turning onto Ormeau Road from the main street of the village. He lifted his rake high above him in greeting. Catching sight of Bassard, Marcus performed a theatrical tipping of his cap. Watching Marcus riding away toward his adopted home, Bassard considered the warm affection he had for the Irlandais. He enjoyed nothing better than the frequent evening visits to the Deschaines, when after the dinner to which Marcus was always invited, he would sit with Auguste and Marcus and converse late into the night. They drank table wine and talked of whatever captured their mutual interest with no inhibitions on their discussion because of Bassard's calling. Although the priest considered himself a competent theologian, he had to admit that he had learned quite a bit concerning religious truth from Auguste Deschaines. Deschaines had studied in depth.

Auguste and Marcus were Catholic but their faith was not predicated on a simple devotional attitude. With both men belief arose from an application of reason to ontological meaning. Auguste was quite familiar with the works of Aquinas and adamantly maintained that no thinker had surpassed his theological achievement. He was of the opinion that the modern thinkers simply didn't have the cognitive competence to scale those heights. Over the years Marcus had borrowed liberally from Deschaines' private library and had read many of the modern philosophers. He was inclined to agree with Auguste's criticism of their work. "It is not in their lack of logical thought where they fail, Marcus" Deschaines had said, "it is rather in their mistaken assumptions concerning reality where they are deficient."

Marcus and Auguste attended Mass somewhat regularly and always at Christmas and Easter. Marcus and the Deschaines would pull up in the old Peugeot Berline as close to the church as possible. Marcus then helped Auguste into the high, wicker-backed wheelchair and he and Helene, often with help from a villager, lifted Auguste up the granite steps. Auguste insisted on sitting in the back of the church during Mass and was wheeled up to the altar by Helene for Communion. Neither Auguste nor Marcus chose Bassard as their confessor. That had something to do with their friendship with the priest. Bassard was grateful.

Père Bassard recalled a cold night some winters ago when the profundity of Auguste's erudition became plainly evident. Following a late dinner Helene had excused herself and Madeleine had cleared the table. The men sat drinking *vin ordinaire* as Bassard smoked the rare cigarette he allowed himself. Their discussion concerned the paradoxical nature of the soul and the priest had quoted Eduoard Schure, *"L'ame est la clef de l'univers,* the soul is the key to the universe."

"Why is it, Auguste, that there's so damned little sense concerning the nature of the soul in modern philosophy?" Marcus had asked.

Auguste smiled mischievously toward Bassard. "Ironically it is the result of inadequate theology," he answered gaily.

The priest sat up, widened his eyes in mild surprise and sought an explanation for Auguste's friendly jibe. "Inadequate theology? How is it the result of inadequate theology, *mon ami?*"

Almost expecting some sort of humorous aphorism often employed by Deschaines, Bassard was further surprised by his apparently serious response. "There is a conspicuous contradiction in contemporary theological thinking concerning the essential nature of man."

Because of their regard for Auguste's intellect both Paul and Marcus were genuinely interested in his expansion of his statement. "What contradiction is that, Auguste?" Bassard queried.

"Have you not noticed, Paul, that contemporary religious thinkers addressing the problem of the true nature of man commonly make two contradictory propositions. On the one hand they maintain that man is a soul and body, on the other, they say man has a soul and body."

Bassard, drawing on his own extensive study, pondered a short time then turned toward Marcus. "You know I believe he has something. Both of those propositions can't be true simultaneously."

Marcus smiled roguishly, took a swallow of wine and said, "Well, can either of you fine scholars explain to me the ultimate importance of it all."

"Auguste, you have the floor," Bassard quipped.

Deschaines explained. "Marcus, the importance is this. Since the traditional view of man as a spiritual being endowed with a soul has been eclipsed, modern thinkers, particularly secular thinkers, have defined man as almost anything that suits their fancy. This fellow Freud defined him as a being driven by sexual instincts. Marx insisted he was inevitably driven by economic concerns and class antagonisms. And the scientists, well you know, to them man is merely a walking bag of chemical processes at the mercy of his environment. In this respect, they insist, man is no different than an animal."

"The definition of man as a rational animal is commonly held these days, wouldn't you agree, Auguste?" Bassard offered.

"Indeed, Paul, spiritual considerations are generally ignored by the contemporary intelligentsia. That is, of course a function of their limited education. What is not noticed is the modern tendency to strip man of his true humanity."

"What do you mean, Auguste?" Marcus asked.

A certain somberness crossed Auguste's features. "In modern times civilization has become increasingly political and ideological. Ideologues delight in their ignorant heated assertions about the nature of man. Man is increasingly reduced to an abstract being molded and shaped by natural and technological forces. Moral and spiritual considerations no longer have the weight they had in earlier times. Europe is rife with contending ideologies and is wracked again by warfare. Notions of a common spiritual origin do not hold sway in people's minds. The brotherhood of man is considered by many to be a religious illusion."

Auguste paused, looked out into the darkness and commented, "So you see, my dear friends, flawed theology does indeed have serious practical consequences."

Bassard was a man of simple virtue. He felt no need to go to the defense of the Church's theological positions on the matter. This was not necessary with Auguste anyway. He saw the problem and was inclined to agree with his friend's assessment. He asked gently, "Are you pessimistic about the future then, Auguste?"

"No, I'm not pessimistic, Paul," Auguste replied quietly, "two very real things work against pessimism. One is the fact that we have each other and the other is the absolute reality of our experience of love."

Marcus and Bassard said nothing. Paul resolved to give himself to a more extensive study of Auguste's thesis. Marcus' mind went back to his teaching days in Dublin when he reluctantly involved himself with Irish nationalism.

There was a side to the Irishman that Bassard had seen on only one occasion that he guessed few knew about. He knew for certain that the local Marxist was aware of it. Marcus had accompanied him one afternoon to the vintner's shop just off the main street in Couderouge. The priest wanted to replenish his small stock of wine that he kept with him in the rectory. The proprietor was a Communist and of course felt himself obliged to be an enemy of organized religion. Anton Fedou was a large, homely man with thin lips, unruly black hair and small dark eyes magnified behind thick dirty eyeglasses. He was bitter about his not doing a better business and attributed his sad financial state to vague, sinister economic forces arising from free market capitalism. The truth was that most of the villagers did not choose to listen to Fedou's giving forth if they had an option. Since wine was not a scarce commodity in the Rhone-Saone Valley, they did business elsewhere.

Fedou had a few cronies that lingered about his establishment throughout the day. Listening to his diatribes was a small price to pay for the none too frequent free glass of *vin ordinaire*. He was adorning his nonsense with the ornaments of Party jargon the afternoon Bassard and Marcus visited for the last time.

"The priest," Fedou sniggered to his chums at the back of the dusty untidy shop as they entered. "Well priest, what can I take your money for?" Fedou smirked, "perhaps some good wine that I changed from water this very morning."

"Yes, Monsieur Fedou," Bassard countered, "some good wine. Evidently you forgot the transformation on the last batch I purchased here."

Fedou did not like someone getting the better of him and, although desirous of a sale, searched for something to say in retaliation. "You know priest" he intoned, "Marx said the very best wine is the blood of the struggling proletariat." Fedou had no trouble inventing history if it suited his purpose.

"Martyrdom is a singular act," Bassard replied. The subtlety was lost on Fedou.

"No priest, the common people will rise en masse at every opportunity they are afforded" the large man blared.

In the small stillness that followed Fedou's stridence Marcus quietly remarked, "You know, that surely didn't happen in Dublin in 1916."

"What's that, Irlandais?" Fedou said turning his attention to Marcus, "Dublin? What about Dublin?"

"When that small group of men went after the British Army at Easter in 1916, the people of Dublin didn't rise in support. Most of them were opposed to it. And when the British brought in a large number of troops to put those boys down, most of us ducked for cover."

Fedou was completely ignorant of the Irish people's history but obscurely felt some dislike toward them because of the association he had made with their being Catholic. "I don't believe you," he said in response.

"I was there," Marcus said softly.

"I don't believe you," Fedou willfully repeated.

Bassard was looking at Marcus as the shopkeeper spoke. He saw the abrupt change in his countenance and posture at the man's words. There was the smallest pulling back of the hairline and squinting of the eyes as the skin of his forehead tightened. There was the barely discernible movement forward as his jaw muscles tensed and his hands closed upon themselves.

"Account for what I just said," Marcus said ominously.

The large man did not understand Marcus' words but was unsettled by something in his tone. "What?" he said, as he frowned and made small shaking movements of negation with his head. "What are you saying?"

"You said you didn't believe me. Now account for my saying what I said," Marcus insisted.

"What?" Fedou repeated while raising his hands palms up to just outside his shoulders, "What are you talking about, Irlandais?"

Marcus' left arm shot out across the counter. He grabbed Fedou's shirt just below his chin and jerked the startled man across the counter so their faces were inches apart. He cocked his arm at his waist and clenched his fist into a hard ball. "Well, you might say I was lying," Marcus suggested as he whispered with a menacing grin, "you might say anything. You know the priest won't smack you. But then, I'm no priest, big man."

Fedou said nothing in return but looked to his friends behind Marcus. There was the uneasy shuffling of feet but no one came forward. Marcus suddenly released the shopkeeper by shoving him violently into the high wine racks behind the counter. Amid the rattle of the glass bottles Fedou struggled to remain standing.

"Let's be going now, Marcus," Bassard said, putting his hand on the Irlandais' shoulder. As they left, the priest turned back to the shaken Fedou grinning impishly, "*Au revoir, camarade,*" he chirped.

As Marcus biked toward the Deschaines' home in the softening light of the late afternoon, he looked up at the trees forming a partial canopy above Ormeau Road. It was a puzzlement to him as to why the road had been named after young elm trees. There wasn't an elm in sight. The heavy woods coming up to the roadway, on both sides, were primarily white oak. He had asked Auguste about it and his friend had speculated that the elms had been harvested years ago by local farmers. Elm wood, he said, had certain urine resistant properties and might have been used in barn flooring.

The oaks reminded Marcus of Ireland. East of Sligo near his home in County Leitrim, a few remnant oak stands grew near along the Bonet River. He remembered, as a boy, eating their acorns after repeated boilings to remove the bitterness. The occasional oak groves were all that remained of the lush primeval forests that once covered the island. The forests were reduced in the unsettled times of the sixteenth and seventeenth centuries when landowners sold their timber on a large scale and made no attempt at replanting. It was said the forests of Ireland at one time floated upon the world's oceans as planking for the British Navy.

When a boy, Marcus lived with his parents, three brothers and two sisters on a tiny farm outside of Cloonaquin at the foot of Benbo. Because the rocky soil could not sustain his family, Thomas McQuillan, saw to the holdings of a local landowner with extensive property on Lough Gill. The squire, an Anglo-Irish Protestant, was a generous man and therefore the McQuillans received an ample sustenance. Since the McQuillan children were not required to put in long hours of laborious farm work, as was the case with most poor Irish families, they were afforded the opportunity of going to school. Early each weekday morning they hiked barefooted the two miles to the basement of St. Brendan's church in Dundaragh. They were barefooted most of the year except in the coldest weather when they wore woolen socks and rough-cut leather sandals. The youngest boy, Wee Sean, was required to lug their lunches of buttered hard bread and boiled eggs in a large cloth sack. The children did well at school because Tom and Maggie McQuillan wanted their children to be properly educated and made sure they paid strict attention to the schoolmaster at St. Brendan's.

This was not really necessary with Marcus. He loved learning about everything and hung on every word spoken by Master Raye. Never was the strap applied to his young bottom, save in the one case when he forgot himself and used the expression, "Jesus Christ" in exasperation over the taunting of his sister, Oona.

Marcus had the facility of learning by rote. He easily took in content, forgetting little and later reworking in his mind what he had heard from Master Raye and saw chalked on the slateboard. He enjoyed no schoolwork more than his schoolmaster's dramatic recitation of the myths of ancient Ireland. As Master Raye recounted from the ancient chronicles, Marcus created a rich imaginative world peopled by gods, warriors, beautiful faeries and demons. The McQuillans were an *Ultach* people and had come down into the area from Northwest Ulster following the O'Neil adventures with Elizabeth I in the early seventeenth century. The boy thrilled to hear of the exploits of his ancestors contained in the *Lebor Gabala* that told of when in antiquity the human Milesians wrested control of Ireland from the magical *Tuatha de Danann*. His youthful heart fairly thumped with excitement as he saw, in his mind's eye, the Red Branch Knight, Cuchulainn, spitting fire in battle and slaughtering his enemies. Marcus was to become familiar with the stark ugly nature of slaughter one soft night in the early autumn of his twelfth year.

The McQuillans kept a small flock of sheep that they pastured on southern flanks of Benbo above their farmstead. The animals found sufficient grazing upon the wild grasses that grew below the peaty higher ground on the abundantly heathered and gravelly slopes. The McQuillan boys took turns looking after the little flock, the chickens, geese and their cow and ass. It had happened that during the past summer local natives brought large numbers of dogs to the annual Sligo Fair in the mistaken belief that the British Army was in need of them. Someone had concocted a story about the use of canines by the military in British colonial holdings in Africa and Asia. The most common speculation said that they would be used for tracking insurgents and in providing security at British installations. When no British Army purchasing agents appeared, the hoax became apparent. The majority of the dogs were simply let go into the countryside to fend for themselves. Soon enough, feral packs formed that began preying on local livestock. Although their numbers became reduced rather quickly by rifle shot, enough of them remained at large to cause continued apprehension among farmers, particularly sheep and fowl owners.

Tom McQuillan had told the boys to tend the sheep in twos when possible and keep a cache of good-sized stones handy. The boys were scrupulous in their following of their father's bidding, but after a few weeks without incident they reverted to their former casual shepherding.

One warm evening in late September, his mother had told Marcus to go up on Benbo and help Wee Sean bring the sheep down to the cote before nightfall. Marcus had snatched up his old, stone-battered hurling stick and set out up the rock-strewn slope of the mountain. He picked up crabapple-sized stones as he went and practiced bouncing them up and down on his stick before picking them out of the air with a full swing and cracking them a distance. As Marcus approached, Sean sat on a large boulder playing with a bit of string, the scattered sheep grazing about him. On the ridge high to the right the movement of two low skulking figures, black against the light sky, caught Marcus' attention. Suddenly, the dispersed flock fled down slope to the left breaking into a cacophony of bleating. A bewildered Wee Sean jumped to his feet, looking about frantically. Upon seeing the plunging attack of the dogs from the ridge toward their prey, the young boy bolted in raw terror straight down the slope toward Marcus. Marcus began sprinting up toward his brother and felt a quick electric surge of fear as he saw the larger dog, a dull yellow greyhound, veer from its pursuit of the flock and head for the small figure scrambling down the slope. Understanding that the hunter was obeying its predatory instinct to make after a fleeing quarry, Marcus shouted out, "Don't run, Seanie, don't run!"

The terrified little boy continued his flight when the hound hit him in the back of the legs putting him into a tumbling fall down the shingly incline. As Wee Sean skidded on his belly to a stop, the dog set upon him, biting savagely at his buttocks and bare legs. It did not notice Marcus as he came upon it. Lifting the curved hard-bladed hurling stick high above him, he struck sharply downward at the top of its skull. With a dull craunching sound of breaking bone, the heavy pointed end of the club buried itself in the hound's brainpan. The greyhound shivered violently in spasm and fell to its side. Again Marcus hoisted the weapon high above and hammered at the dog's face just behind the ear. It went still. He knelt to his whimpering brother examining the small cuts on the upper rear of his legs, "Are you all right, then, Seanie?" Marcus panted.

"Marcus, Marcus," Wee Sean sobbed.

Marcus looked back up the mountain and saw that the smaller second dog, a dark gray whippet, had locked its jaws high on the side of the neck of a struggling ewe. "Wait here, Seanie," he said through his labored breathing.

Wee Sean rose to his hands and knees and watched as his older brother charged obliquely up and across the slope toward the struggling animals, waving his bloody stick and screaming. The whippet was wildly wagging its head from side to side trying to pull the larger, stiff-legged ewe to the ground. It yelped in pain and released its grip as Marcus' first blow struck its spine just above the tail. Growling, the confused animal turned toward Marcus, lifting its slender snout and baring its yellowed teeth. Swinging his weapon in a wide upward arc, Marcus struck solidly the soft middle of the lower jaw. The dog's head snapped back as it began tumbling down the slope. After a few yards its fall was arrested by one of the many large limestone boulders that dotted the incline. The unconscious dog's slim body lay twitching on its side, its scrawny ribcage heaving.

Marcus felt no hot battle frenzy. A pang of pity for the broken animal came upon him. He looked back at his frail little brother trembling on skinny white legs over the body of the first dog. An existential sadness swept over him. He lifted his gaze to the pastel sky in the west. Marcus would never again feel an excited youthful enthusiasm for Master Raye's heroic tales of slaughter. There was an uncomfortable heavy sensation in the pit of his stomach when he reluctantly walked down to the whippet and finished the kill.

Later that evening Marcus sat solemnly in the dark corner of the kitchen as his father spoke quietly with Wee Sean. Maggie McQuillan had told her husband of the ugliness on Benbo upon his return from the Squire's estate. Framed as a dark silhouette against the orange glow of hearth fire, the man bent down to the small boy. His soft words were below Marcus' hearing. He then came to Marcus. "Are you all right, then?" his father asked solicitously.

"I am Da," Marcus replied

After a short silence, his father asked, "Was it a hard thing to do, Marcus?"

Marcus' lower lip extended slightly and his eyes misted as he looked down at the earthen floor. "No Da," he weakly replied, "only after."

His father's strong, calloused hand gently patted the top of his head. He then held it there in a light grip and as if giving the benediction of a priest, he said, "You're a good little man, Marcus."

The children near about Sligo Town looked forward to the annual fair with anticipation and dread. It was the time of the fearful visitation of the itinerant blacksmith. With small tongs in hand, the smith made rounds of the farms offering a cheap dentistry for the poor families. The children were made to stand, mouths agape, for inspection as their fathers sought likely candidates for extraction. If they had the misfortune of possessing a badly decayed tooth, they were held tightly while the blacksmith energetically and adroitly plucked it from their mouths. The bloody gap was plugged with cotton and they were given a stick of hard candy to suck and assuage their misery. They were later to be seen, here and there at the fair, darting up and down the rows of tents with swollen sticky cheeks.

At fair time in his sixteenth year, Marcus again escaped the painful indignity. Wee Sean and his older sister, Aileen, had not. The McQuillan children had no money but spent their one day at the fair amid the dusty aromatic haze gawking at the common merchandise and exotic gadgetry on display in the stalls. Marcus would, sooner or later, gravitate to the stand of his elder acquaintance, Avram Goldner, a Jewish jewelry merchant from Dublin.

During the summer months, Goldner followed the fair trade around the coastal towns of Ireland. He belonged to a small conservative community north of the River Liffey and owned a modest shop just off Grafton Street with his brother. Marcus was enamored of Avram's daughter, Sarah, a girl two years his senior, whom he had met and befriended several years back when she began traveling with her father on his summer itinerary.

On a previous August day, when at dusk the fair crowd had thinned to a few, Sarah closed the stall and walked out with Marcus in the thickets by Cummeen Strand on the enclosed inlet of nearby Sligo Bay. They sat secluded together, talking, teasing and watching the rose and orange clouds above the Atlantic Ocean to the west. The older experienced city girl had initiated the lovemaking by pulling Marcus down on top of her, kissing him firmly and wetly, and embracing him with her arms and legs. The energetic spooning went on for a while, when suddenly Marcus felt a rush of pleasure as Sarah plunged both hands brazenly down his trousers and began fondling him. Almost involuntarily, he began copulatory movements against her. After a very short time of kissing, gasping and tumultuous pelvic movement, he ejaculated with a loud sigh and went limp upon her. Neither spoke as he lay there atop her, his face buried in the softness of her neck. Sarah stroked Marcus' hair and murmured something he didn't quite make out, except for the expression, "country boy".

The Goldner extended family had left Salzberg in the middle of the eighteenth century following the War of the Spanish Succession. They had emigrated to London, not because of ethnic antagonisms, but at the urging of their English relatives who saw great economic promise within the expanding British Empire. Avram's father had moved his family and gemstone business from London across the Irish Sea to Dublin in 1851 when Avram was a little boy. The family had not become wealthy but earned a comfortable livelihood from their jewelry store in the heart of the Irish capital.

Avram liked Ireland and the Irish people. There was no anti-Semitism to speak of among the educated British and Anglo-Irish who composed his clientele. It was a rarity for a member of the Catholic majority to enter his shop with the means to make an expensive purchase. He kept, however, an ample stock of rhinestone and paste for their benefit.

It was not out of necessity that he did his annual following of the fairs. Rather, he enjoyed getting out of the busy city as if on vacation, traveling about the countryside and mingling with the Irish people. His tolerant older brother, David, was left to mind the shop. He found that the rural Irishman had a certain cultural simplicity about them and tended to treat Avram, when learning of his Judaism, with open friendly curiosity. Sarah's young friend, Marcus, epitomized this cultural naiveté. One Sligo Fair day years ago, as Sarah and the boy sat on the grass outside the stall chatting, perhaps having to do with their respective religions, Marcus looked up to Goldner and out of the blue asked, "Mr. Goldner, why was it the Jews killed Christ?"

Goldner could hardly contain his amusement over the boy's innocent bluntness and laughed as he sought an appropriate answer. "Well, Marcus, I think it was Jewish business," he had finally said, "it had something to do with the rabbis and the law."

Avram was further entertained with the boy's immediate open-eyed uncomprehending acceptance of the pronouncement coming as it did from Sarah's sophisticated cityman of a father. The world beyond his little corner of northwest Ireland was a great waiting mystery for the boy and he thought often enough about someday venturing out there and learning about its marvels and enticements.

Goldner, sitting in a high stool in his stall, looked up from his reading and saw the approach of Sarah's maturing, sixteen year old boyfriend. Marcus smiled in greeting at the tall, spare, bearded man grinning widely below his black derby. Avram knew, however, he must disappoint the lad with the news of Sarah's marriage earlier in the spring. "And good day to you, my fine, young friend," he said, clasping and shaking Marcus' hand while also grasping his shoulder.

"And good day to you, Mr. Goldner," Marcus brightly replied, "would Sarah be about?"

"I'm afraid I've got some disappointing news for you, Marcus. Sarah was married to a young man from our community back in Dublin this past April and she won't be doing the fair circuit anymore."

Marcus was acutely disappointed he wouldn't be seeing the girl again, but he wasn't heartbroken. "She's married, is she? Well I'm happy for her, sir."

"She is, Marcus, she is, and she's already with child."

"Well, that's a grand thing. I'm happy for her, sir, and happy for you as well."

The two exchanged pleasantries for a while before Goldner asked with a more serious tone, "Marcus, have you given serious thought to your future, particularly your education?"

"Well, I have sir, but I've no definite plans."

"Marcus my young friend, I can't stress the importance of education enough. A formally educated man has so many more opportunities than one who isn't. I've wished many times that I had become a university student when I had the chance as a younger man. Here in Ireland, if a young fellow, like yourself, doesn't go to the university, he'll probably end up at hard labor working for somebody else."

Goldner was making the implicit suggestion that Marcus' Catholic people had no real economic future in their own country. "You're no doubt right, sir," Marcus said, "I've thought about going on to university but I don't have the money."

"Have you done well in your schooling?" Goldner inquired.

"Yes, I've done well. I've done better than others because I've always loved the learning and because it was important to my Ma and Da."

"Now listen closely Marcus," Goldner began, "I belong to a philanthropic group of Jewish businessmen in Dublin. We often provide scholarships and stipends to needy young people wishing to attend university. They must provide proof of academic promise by doing well on entrance exams. Now, the money is primarily for young persons of our own community but it is not rare for a promising gentile to be awarded a substantial grant. Are you interested, Marcus?"

"Oh, I am sir, I am indeed," Marcus answered excitedly.

Goldner continued, "I'll give you my address in Dublin. Send me the pertinent information about your schooling and the names of your schoolmasters. You've probably attended one of the local schools run by your church, is that right?"

"That's right, sir, St. Brendan's up in Dundaragh. God in heaven, do you think I've a decent chance of getting a scholarship, Mr. Goldner?"

Avram smiled at the boy's enthusiasm, "I'll do what I can for you, Marcus, say a prayer to whatever saint your people have who's in charge of education."

Marcus did not go directly home when he left the fair. Instead he hiked along the Bonet up toward Dundaragh. In the single narrow street of the town he found the cramped, small-roomed stone house of Master Raye and knocked on the green-painted, oaken door. Raye was a married man with four children. The Raye family lived in the tiny house in near poverty as a result of the pitifully small salary paid the schoolmaster. He did private tutoring for the children of families with means to add to his income. He had difficulty taking the few pennies from the impoverished illiterate rural people who sought his services as scribe.

Raye was surprised to see Marcus standing at his door after nightfall when he had come from the kitchen table to answer the knocking. "Marcus McQuillan, what is it lad?"

"Master Raye," Marcus exclaimed, "I've important news concerning something that's been offered me, sir. I must tell you about it and get your advice."

"Well then, come in, come in" Raye said, noting the boy's excitement. "Mary, we've company, put the kettle on for tea."

Marcus told the schoolmaster about Goldner's offer and when Raye was convinced, through sufficient questioning, that there was substance for the boy's optimism, he began sharing with him considerations Marcus must take into account. They sat over their teacups at the lantern-lit, scarred kitchen table. Mrs. Raye had ordered her children away from the immediate area to provide something suggesting privacy for her husband and now sat sewing by the edge of the lantern light.

"Are you at all interested in becoming a priest, Marcus?" Raye asked.

Marcus, slightly surprised by the question, smiled broadly and answered, "No sir, I never thought of that for myself. No, I never thought of that."

"Well then, that being the case, the best choices for you to go after are either Catholic University of Ireland, founded just a few decades ago, or Trinity College, which goes back to the late sixteenth century, I think. Both are in Dublin. The great churchman, John Henry Newman, was the first rector of the Catholic University, but without doubt, Trinity College is the more prestigious."

"Trinity College is the better school, then?"

"No Marcus, I'm not saying that. It's better known outside of Ireland and quite a few famous men have graduated from it," then Raye added mischievously, "none of whom I can bring to mind at the moment."

"Would it be the better place for me?"

"No, I'd say it wouldn't be, Marcus. It's the school for the young Protestant gentlemen of Ireland. There's quite a few of the British upper crust as well. There's but a handful of us at the place and I suspect they play the quota game."

"Quota game, sir?"

"I've no doubt we do as well on the entrance exams, but can you bring to mind a wealthy Catholic family hereabouts? The school counts on endowments and such from the wealthy families of the students and their alumni. Over time, it doesn't behoove them financially to have a great number of young Catholics going there. Besides Marcus, what would you do at the social affairs in your rough boots and patched trousers?"

"Ah, there's a truth in that, sir."

"Well lad, your best bet is the Catholic University. Your man, Goldner, wouldn't have a problem with that now, would he?"

"I don't think so, sir, I don't think so."

"Let it be Catholic University then. You'll need preparation for the entrance exams, Marcus. I'll be doing that for you."

"Master Raye, I've no money for tutoring."

"Well, we'll work something out, lad. It must be done and you must put your whole heart into it."

"I will, sir, I will indeed."

Mary Raye looked at her tired husband, sitting in the light of the lantern in his threadbare, brown tweed suit and scuffed shoes. She said a small prayer for him as she felt that quiet pride that is often the only solace for the wives of decent men. "God bless that man," she said within herself.

Marcus and Wee Sean sat on the grassy embankment of the stream that flowed a half mile below their farm. Earlier in the day, they had worked with their father at turf-cutting on the hill bogs above Lough Gill. Wee Sean was still a bit too small to be adept in the use of the long-handled *slean* but Marcus was able, for a while, to keep up with his father. Their Da had released them after half a day of cutting and stacking and they had decided to go after trout in one of the streams that flowed down from Benbo to the Bonet.

Their method was the building of a weir of stones and sod damming the stream and then the quick teeming of water out of the holes lower down before their frantic efforts to empty them were defeated by the rush of muddy water overflowing the weir. Tired after two unsuccessful attempts with no trout to show for their efforts, they sat in the gathering dusk. Marcus aimlessly plaited rushes while Wee Sean succeeded in making occasional squeaky notes from a rough flute cut from a corn stalk. With a quick nodding of his head toward their home, Marcus indicated to his brother that it was time for them to go home for supper. As the boys neared the front door, recessed beneath the overhanging thick thatching of the farmhouse, they heard a familiar hoarse, throaty voice in song.

"Oh how green are the fields
That are washed boy the fen
And how foin are the homes
That the squoires lev in
How green are the crops in the valley ta see
But the heat' is the home of the woild rapparee"

Their Da's old friend and drinking companion, Ould Sean Mulcahy, sat at the fire of the kitchen and was well in his cups from the drinking of the McQuillan's home-brewed poteen. That would mean, thought Marcus, it was Saturday night and there was a celebration over the fact there was no work to be done by Ould Sean the following day. The modifiers had been added to the Christian names of Old Mulcahy and the youngest McQuillan by Marcus' mother to differentiate between the two.

As he entered the kitchen, Marcus psychologically braced himself awaiting the greeting of Ould Sean which inevitably consisted in his calling out the nickname he had put on the boy following the dog-killings on Benbo.

"Ah, the *cu buailtear*, the coo boolter himself, and Wee Sean," he said mirthfully, using the Irish expression for "hound-thrasher".

"Good evening, Ould Sean," Marcus replied looking over to his father and wagging his head slightly in resignation.

Ould Sean's ruddy craggy face seemed to bear a perpetual grin below his slouched hat, bushy eyebrows and pointed hirsute ears. With an almost theatrical leprechaunish aspect, Ould Sean displayed his emotions readily in the quick quirky twisting of his facial features.

"You're goin' ta univarsity, is it?" the old man said.

"I'm going to try to, sir," Marcus replied.

"That's a foin thing, lad," Ould Sean continued, "that's a far better thing than dart work or the bloody army." The old man was segueing into an animated recitation of his military adventures as a young man in the American army. He knew full well the McQuillan children delighted in listening to his repeated yarn-spinning. Ould Sean Mulcahy was known as perhaps the best raconteur in all Leitrim. After banging his old charred pipe against the palm of his thin hand, he dug it deeply into the mixture of a few strands of tobacco and local herbs he kept in his trousers' pocket. Packing the pipe firmly with his thumb, he lifted a glowing ember from the kitchen hearth and lit it, clouds of smoke billowing about his head.

"Oi moind it well," he began in the attentive silence, "shippin' outa Galway in one of them tall ships. There was only a few steamers back then. Oi was off to Amerikay for a new loife. We couldn't get dacent wark here about and we'd been told there was scads of wark across the ocean. So off Oi go, begod, Oi was that sick the whole way with the constant risin' and fallin' of it. Oi was either loyin' like a dead man below or retchin' at the rails. Oi was weak as a babby when we landed in New Yark. Me and some lads got jobs roight off and was shipped up the Houdson River to a camp in the Cattyskill Mountains. We ended up diggin' in the shale on a mountainsoide. Oi can't even remember what the hell we were diggin' fer."

"Sean, now," Maggie McQuillan quietly interjected.

"What Maggie?" Ould Sean answered, "Ah yes, the children. Oi'm sorry, Maggie. Well, Oi forgot a lot of it, but Oi left there and went out ta Buffalo warkin' to make their bloody canal bigger. It was backbreakin' toil and Oi was desperate with the thinkin' that Oi'd be doin' this kind of dart work the rest of me loife.

Then it happened that a fancy-dressed soldier showed up in our camp and he makes a foin speech sayin' the United States was soon goin' ta war with Mexico and any man that jined up would get pay, dacent rations and a bit o' land when it was over. Oi jined up to get out o' the mud hole and wear one of them foin fancy uniforms. Oi was a roight stupid lad in them days.

Well, then Oi end up in a trainin' camp after a railroad roide. That's when the trouble began. We were beaten into soldierin' and Oi mean exactly that. We were beaten and tied up and beaten again. They called it buckin'. They tied ye up ta a pole after twistin' your legs up and kept you there the length of the day. This was done for the smallest of things and they said it had to do with discipline. Discipline, me arse. After gettin' down to Texas later on we figured out what the truth of it was.

After the constant drillin' and shootin' and beatin' they packed us on steamboats and down the great Mississippi we go. Then off across the Gulf o' Mexico and out of the boats then marchin' inland to a place called Carpus Christy. Carpus Christy, Body of Chroist, would ye believe?"

"Next, we're marchin' down to a camp just across the Rio Grandy from the Mexican town of Mattymarris. And it's there in that camp most of us figure out what all the beatin' and buckin' is about."

"And what was it about, Sean?" Maggie McQuillan asked, not having heard this part of Ould Sean's narrative before."

"Well, ye see, John Bull's little bruther, Uncle Sam, had his heart set on stealin' great bits of Mexico, Texas, Calyfornee and the rest of it from the Mexicans. Now the Mexicans are a poor Catholic people like us and the Yankee government knew their little ragtag army wouldn't be able to stop the theft of the land.

We noticed we got bucked and beaten if we had a bit of a drink or if we attended Mass. The same dart would be handed out to some of the Geerman boys, but only the Catholics, not the others. A lot of the officers were Freemasons and they put us and the Mexicans in the same boat. The worst of them were them young squints from West Pint.

Well, some of the lads and some Geermans as well, startin' goin' over to the Mexicans, swimmin' the river at night, a whole bunch of them over time. There was churches, drink and foin lookin' women over there. Oi don't know how bad things would've got for us who stayed put but, looky enough, the war breaks out and over the river we go. The Mexicans fought hard but we bate the hell out o them toime and again.

Now an odd thing happened in the foightin'. Those lads who went over were formed up by the Mexicans into a cannon outfit. They called it the St. Patrick's Battalion and it was headed up by John Riley, a Galway man. We felt queer enough chargin' against that green silk flag they had with a harp and the image of St. Patrick, himself, on it. Ah, but we did our soldier's job anyway, God help us. We were wearin' loight blue and Riley and his gun crews could pick out the dark blue uniforms of the officers at a distance. That's where their fire went, so if a man stayed away from them squints you had a great chance of comin' out of it.

Riley's lads fought like woildcats, they did, but most of them were killed or captured. Oi was on guard duty the time that blackguard, Colonel Haney, hanged some of them. Oi should have shot the man. He put about thirty of them up on wagons with ropes around their necks at the last big battle. Now with the raisin' of the Yankee flag over the Mexican fart as a signal, he had the mules whipped, leaving those poor lads danglin' and kickin' in the air. A bit before the raisin' of the flag, one o' them lads on the wagons said somethin' of a joke to him. Well, the bahstard got down off his harse, cloimbed up on the wagon and punched the lad roight in the gob. Can ye imagine? And the man with his hands toyed behind him. Argh, begod, Oi shoulda put a ball in him roight there." Ould Sean stopped his storytelling and spat into the fire, lost for a moment in the bitter memory.

In the quiet, Maggie spoke gently from her chair in a dark corner of the kitchen, "Why did you stay in the army, Sean?"

"Oi don't roightly know, Maggie, Oi don't roightly know," the old man whispered, staring vacantly into the hearth while fingering the stubble on his chin. Then sitting up and squinting into the darkness as if trying to summon a sensible answer, he continued. "Oi guess Oi didn't want to go back to the diggin' or such. Maybe Oi was thinkin' Oi'd be able to do better out west. Gineral Zachary Taylor, not a bad sart, give us a grand speech after the last battle at Cherryboosko about stayin' in and providin' sarvice against the red Injuns in the west. So, Oi soigned on again. Oi spent the next years goin' from one dusty, little post to the next on the great, grassy American prairie. It was nothin' but dust and heat and floies. The fightin' of the red Injuns was best done by the cavalry, since foot soldierin' was, boy and large, useless against them. We made many long marches across the prairie to no purpose. Begod, you'd think them grassy rollin' hills went on forever. Yet lucky enough, none of us got killed.

Somewhere along the way they made me a carporal. Oi drank a lot and damn near married a red Injun woman. Cheyenne she was."

Ould Sean paused, smiled to himself, and laughingly commented, "Ah, but that's another story."

"Well, the great Civil War broke out back east. When Oi heard that one of our own, Colonel Francis Thomas Meagher, was farmin' up the Irish Brigade in New Yark, I got meself transferred to the 88th New Yark Volunteer Infantry Regiment. They were mostly immigrant lads just loike Oi once was and the 88th was happy to get a few veterans. Roight off, Oi was made a sergeant to look after the young lads.

After a short bit of trainin', we were put into action. Mostly in the beginnin' it was just skirmishin', but soon enough in the fall of sixty-two, we're in the thick of it at Antietam. Many a good lad went down at a place called Bloody Lane. That was bloody enough, but nothin' can compare to what happened to us at Fredericksburg.

In December, a week or so before Christmas, they sent us marchin' down along the Rappyhanick. We crossed over in barges and got into the big town of Fredericksburg. The rebels were waitin' for us on the ridges to the west of the town. We spent a cold noight in the muddy streets of the place, not gettin' much sleep. Early in the marnin' we farmed up and marched out into the fields to the west of town. Some of the lads put sprigs of boxwood on their caps. We were a foin brave bunch standin' ready in the liftin' fog. The rebels just waited, a quarter moil away up on Marye's Hoights, four deep, behind stonewalls, their batteries loaded and ready. Then off we go at them, company boy company. They started blastin' at us roight off and whole bunches of lads went down together. It was loike the air around us was filled with shot. It was nothin' but slaughter. Not a man of us got anywheres near the wall. Young Danny McGinty was blown to pieces roight there besoide me. And roight after, Oi went down with a bit o' me torn out above the hip. The lads fell back and after a time, came on again, then again, then again. Oi lay there watchin' it all. Battered as we were, they kept sendin' us against those hoights. After awhoile, the whole field was littered with our dead and doyin'. And them bahstards kept sendin' us.

Many o' them young buggers from the Mexican War were now field grade, colonels and generals and all. They knew damned well who we were. They knew damned well who to send into them rebel guns. There wasn't a man on our soide or the rebel soide who didn't know that goin' out into that field meant you were goin' to be cut down. And the bahstards kept sendin' us."

Ould Sean's voice had risen in anger and his eyes were moist as he spoke in the firelight. "Easy now, Sean, easy now," Tom McQuillan whispered, trying to calm the old man.

Ould Sean took a deep breath, nodded his head and continued in a steady voice, "Oi lay there the noight, shiverin' in the cold, listening to the pitiful croies and moanin' of the doyin'. The bit of ball wasn't stuck in me and the bleedin' had stopped. In the marnin', Oi stumbled back to the town and got meself bandaged up. Someone told me we had two hundred and some standin' from the twelve hundred that went in, argh, the bloody harshness of it. Oi decoided roight then Oi was done with it.

As soon as Oi was strong enough for it, Oi took what pay Oi had comin' and made out for New Yark. Oi walked by noight and hid out durin' the day in the woods and fields. Oi managed to foind some of our people in New Yark and Oi suppose Oi was the farst to tell them of what happened at Fredericksburg. Later on, them lads put on one hell of a royot over the ongoin' slaughter. Well, they helped me to get passage out of New Yark ta back home. Oi shoveled coal on a steamer to Cark. Oi jumped ship in Cark harbor and made me way back up here to Leitrim. The marchin' Oi'd done made the long walks easy. And that was the end of it."

Ould Sean took a wet suck on his pipe and turned to gaze down into the dying fire. "Will you have another drink, Sean?" Tom McQuillan asked, holding out the porcelain jug on a curled finger.

"Oi will," the old man replied.

Years later, when an older Marcus McQuillan left Ireland, he had no thought of ever going to America. The stories of Ould Sean Mulcahy lay quietly in the recesses of his memory. Despite his liberal education, the faintest vestige of a childhood antipathy toward the hard Yankee republic remained with him.

Marcus passed between the large cobblestone pillars and the permanently opened iron gates that stood at the foot of the Deschaines' gray, quartzite gravel driveway. He passed over onto the grass that lined the drive between the two rows of tall, droop-branched Norway spruce and dismounted, walking the bicycle toward the dark gray modest manse.

The old peasant, Philibert Savard, one of several employed by the Deschaines in the upkeep of their property, walked down the gravel toward Marcus. He carried a large scythe over his shoulder. Happy to be done with his work and on his way home, he smiled widely in a toothless grin and pointed with a bony forefinger at the crescent moon low in the western sky. "The moon lies, Irlandais," he grinned.

"It does, Philibert, it does," Marcus replied.

It was a private sharing between the two as a result of Savard's telling a piece of local folklore to Marcus some time ago. As with most agricultural people, and as had their forebears, the French farmers of the Rhone Valley still observed natural phenomena with an eye to its correlation with the seasons of growth, fruition and decay. The moon, it was said, was a liar for in its waxing phase its crescent formed a "D" as in the word *decroitre*, meaning to decrease and in its waning phase it formed a "C", as in *croitre*, meaning to increase. Savard, having the misfortune of being married many long years to somewhat of a harpy, added that the moon, in this respect, was like some women.

Marcus went around to the back of the house and put the bicycle against the wall of the small, attached, two-car garage that housed the Deschaines' old Peugeot and an assortment of tools and agricultural devices for maintenance of the property. He entered the house through the glass-paned backdoor and stepped into the large kitchen. Madeleine stood slicing vegetables at the large butcher block table that occupied the middle of the room. Madeleine, who kept her light brown hair unfashionably short, wore an unnecessary dark blue kerchief tied at the nape of her neck, a rough-textured gray work dress and the heavy short-heeled shoes of the French working women. She smiled happily upon Marcus' entry. "Did you get the trap, Marcooz?"

"I did, Maddy."

The bicycle trip to Privas was the result of Madeleine's asking Marcus to repair the leaking, rusted galvanized trap below the large kitchen sink. Since gasoline was strictly rationed in wartime France, trips by automobile were rare for the Deschaines and their employees. Marcus had left midmorning and had leisurely biked south from Couderouge enjoying the open countryside. After first purchasing the new trap in a plumber's shop, he had strolled the narrow cobblestone streets of Privas engaging townspeople in light conversation now and again. He had started back in the late afternoon and was approaching Couderouge when stopped by Sergeant Poissy.

"Did you enjoy the trip?" Madeleine asked as she repeatedly pushed down the large kitchen knife into several sizeable peppers.

"I did," Marcus responded as he thought momentarily about mentioning the encounter with Poissy. "I always enjoy a bit of a ride in the open."

Madeleine continued smiling at Marcus as he went over to the sink and knelt to open the cabinet doors below. Picking up the heavy adjustable wrench he had left by the trap in the morning, he lay on his back inside the cabinet below the trap. His body, from the waist down, protruded out onto the kitchen floor. He was just at the moment of removing the rusted trap when he involuntarily stiffened and dropped the heavy tool and trap into the middle of his face. Madeleine, feigning a task at the sink, had stood quietly over Marcus and then had lightly tapped the toe of her heavy shoe into his crotch. Upon hearing the sudden gasp and disordered clanking of metal, she giggled and said, "What is the matter, Marcooz, are you having trouble down there?"

Marcus, wiping the greasy trap water from his face said after a pause, "No Maddy, there's no trouble at all. I never have any trouble down there."

Madeleine grinned and began a sustained, light toe tapping between Marcus' legs. "That's true. And I am so happy that it is that way."

"Are you, Maddy?" Marcus asked rhetorically as he began to install the new trap.

"Oh yes," Madeleine answered, "but one can never be too sure about such things. I think this evening I will perform a close inspection down there to make sure that everything is still in working order."

As Madeleine remained over him, Marcus fitted the new trap and tightened it into place. "It looks grand up there now," he said, then sliding out from under the sink, as he lay on his back between Madeleine's legs peering up her skirt into the darkness above her white thighs, he added, "and it looks grand up there as well."

Madeleine put her hands on her backside and energetically gyrated her hips for the Irishman. "You're a fine trollop of a woman, you are," he said in English.

Madeleine Paquette was a middle-aged, married woman and mother of three grown children. Her husband had returned to stay only briefly with her in their apartment on the outskirts of Marseille following his release from internment in the fall of 1940. Madeleine concluded from his abrupt disappearance with a few friends that he had become involved with the Resistance and was now probably somewhere toward the north in the mountains. When the youngest of her children married shortly after he left, she found herself alone in the apartment and without self-supporting work. A cousin, living in the Rhone Valley, mentioned a possible job opportunity as a cook at a small estate near the small village of Couderouge. Madeleine liked the idea of a return to the rural life she had enjoyed as a child. She made the journey to Couderouge, was interviewed by the Deschaines and employed on the same day. She considered that when the war ended it would only be proper for her husband to find her. If France, friendship, and adventure were his first loves then she would seriously have to think about resuming their living together. Madeleine was Catholic. There would be no question of divorce.

Marcus had taken an immediate liking to the bold Frenchwoman the very evening of the day she was hired to replace the light-fingered Madame Fleury. Marcus was having dinner with the Deschaines and as Madeleine was setting out the dinner before them, Auguste had jested, "I hope you've prepared boiled potatoes, Madeleine, my friend here is from Ireland and cannot survive without that particular staple."

"Oh yes, there are potatoes, Monsieur Deschaines, but they are baked not boiled," she had responded.

"Ah well," Auguste continued, "I hope he can eat them prepared in that way."

"There will be no problem, Monsieur," Madeleine had happily countered, "he will either eat them or wear them."

Madeleine detested covert men. While she allowed that women were sometimes required by circumstances to practice a certain subterfuge, still she did not like it in them either. She would have much preferred from her husband a simple declaration that he was leaving her prior to his post-internment disappearance. Even as a young woman she did not care for the kind of young suitors who approached her with indirectness and innuendo. She always assumed there was the weakness of fear behind it. Perhaps it might be a fear of being rejected, of being accused of lewd intent, of feeling unworthy, but for her it remained weakness nonetheless. The appearance of confidence notwithstanding, if a man was insincere with Madeleine, she had no further dealings with him. Yes, well Henri was her husband, but now he was entitled to nothing from her.

During the initial weeks of her employment in the Deschaines' kitchen she had observed Marcus in his comings and goings. He was Auguste's factotum and his friend, something quite more than a mere employee. He appeared to her as easy-going and pleasant without the need to remind the working people at the small estate that he was someone above them. It was not uncommon for Marcus to ask her if she needed help in the kitchen or in her personal affairs. On one occasion after Marcus had asked her if there was something that she might need from him, she had thought to herself, "Well there is something you can do for me, Irlandais, but I'm wondering if you'll ever get around to it."

Marcus had not flirted with Madeleine or if he had, she had not noticed it. One evening when Marcus came into her kitchen from the garage she decided to explore the issue. He had washed his hands and face at the sink and sat at her worktable reaching within his coat for a cigarette.

"Do you like melons, Marcooz?" she asked, smiling wryly.

"Melons? Did you say melons? Sure, I like melons," he nodded, dragging on the cigarette.

"Do you like these?" she smiled, holding two large yellow melons at breast height for his inspection.

"Those are four lovely fruits you have there, Madeleine," Marcus said, laughing easily.

"Well, two can be eaten, Marcooz, what would you like to do with the others?"

"They'd make lovely pillows for my head, on them I'd rest contented."

Madeleine said nothing more. She returned to her peeling of potatoes. She began humming a tune that was popular when she was an adolescent. Marcus finished his cigarette and bade her goodnight.

"Sweet dreams, Marcooz," she cooed as he left.

"And for you as well, Maddy," he said softly.

A week later, one evening after dark, when Marcus came to the kitchen to heat a large pot of water for his twice-weekly sponge bath, Madeleine asked, what was to her an obvious question. "Marcooz, why is it that you do not come to visit me?"

"What are you saying, Maddy? I come to see you almost every day."

"I don't mean this kind of a visit. I mean, why is it you don't come to see me upstairs? You know where my room is, yes?"

"Well actually, Maddy, I don't know where your bedroom is, but it doesn't make a difference if I did or not. I'm not going to be slinking around the sleeping quarters in Monsieur and Madame Deschaines's home in any event. I wouldn't feel right about it." Then after a short pause, he added, "Now though, I'm surely going to be tempted about it."

Madeleine smiled, enjoying Marcus' small problem concerning social etiquette. "Do you think you'll succumb to temptation?"

"Probably not, even if I've had the drink. But you are certainly a woman who a man might easily make a fool of himself over."

Madeleine sensing that she had the upper hand in the exchange, asked coyly, "Perhaps Marcooz, it is not that at all. Perhaps you are a little bit afraid of me."

Marcus laughed easily at Madeleine's remark and sat for a moment sticking his finger into the pot of water to test its temperature. He rose and walked over to the worktable before her and lightly placed his hands on her breasts. Kneading them gently and looking directly into her eyes, he smiled, "Maybe you're right, Maddy, maybe I'm afraid of you."

Madeleine did something she had not done for a long time. She blushed and broke eye contact.

The following Saturday night, knowing that Marcus was in Couderouge and would be returning soon to his quarters in the small stone cottage not far from the main house, Madeleine hastily finished her kitchen chores. She went upstairs for her bath and preparation. While standing naked in her bedroom, she splashed vanilla extract on her body and donned her best bra and only pair of silk panties. She applied lipstick and vigorously brushed her short brown hair, humming a popular tune. She put on her Sunday dress and high-heeled shoes and went quickly down the back stairway hoping to avoid meeting anyone, especially Helene Deschaines. Once out of the house, she walked through the tall spruce trees to Marcus' cottage. She entered the darkness of the small house and fumbled in the small alcove that served as a general purpose room before finding candles and matches on a shelf above the sink. Carrying a candlestand, she went into a much larger room that contained a bed, a tall bookcase, and two bureaus. Marcus' clothes hung neatly on a pipe between the bureaus with his shoes and work boots aligned below. Madeleine saw that Marcus was a neat fellow and that his quarters had a monkish aspect to them. She went to the bookcase and chose a book that had something to do with the French Revolution. She sat on the bed to pass the time reading.

Madeleine was dozing off when she heard the footsteps approaching the cottage. She blew out the candle and thought about the various poses she might take to pleasantly surprise Marcus. She considered the idea of stripping to the nude and lying out on the bed invitingly with her arms behind her head but there was not time for that. She heard the door opening and then soft breathy singing. The song was in English and she understood not a word of it.

"Alive he has boasted, they'll never take me
No redcoat will capture the wild Rapparee."

Marcus lit a lantern in the alcove and walked unsteadily into the large room. When he saw Madeleine lying on the bed, her head propped up with one arm, smiling suggestively at him, Marcus gawked in wide-eyed surprise.

"Maddy darlin'," he stammered.

Madeleine knew immediately from his slight swaying, bleary eyes and the tinge of slurring in his speech that Marcus was drunk.

"Are you happy to see me?" she grinned.

Marcus nodded his head repeatedly and answered with a confused sounding, "Yes."

Thinking that this was a man who needed immediate attention, Madeleine arose from the bed and took the lantern from Marcus, placing it on a bureau. She returned to him and placed her hands behind his neck, moving her body into his. She was amused by his apparent inability to focus his eyes as he alternated between a wide-eyed stare and a furrowed squinting. "I will help you undress?" she asked.

Marcus shakily nodded several times and simply responded, "Yes."

Madeleine's face was just inches from his and she smelled the sweet scent of whisky on his breath as he spoke. She took him to the bed, sitting him on the edge of it. She pushed his dark-gray tweed jacket over his shoulders and unbuttoned and removed his shirt. She pushed him down on his back, removed his shoes and socks then unbuckled his belt and removed his trousers. Marcus lay in his shorts looking up at her with a silly smile on his face. Standing above him, she hoisted her dress above her head, tossing it over onto the bureau. She unhooked her bra and let her ample breasts swing free. She cupped them in her hands and said teasingly, "Would you like some melons, Monsieur Makeeyon?"

Marcus still smiling foolishly, nodded his assent. Madeleine looked down on the prone man appreciative of his still trim body. She climbed onto the bed, straddling him with her legs and planted a wet kiss on his whiskey-tasting mouth. Wrapping her legs around him and hugging him at the waist, she rolled him over on top of her. She pulled his face to her breasts and began making vigorous thrusting movements with her pelvis. His rough stubbled chin caused a delightful tingle in her nipples as she tightly gripped his tousled black hair in her fingers. Madeleine had the sudden urge to tear off her panties and his shorts but checked herself, thinking that she would allow him to initiate lovemaking.

Despite her enthusiastic encouragement, after a short time, Madeleine began to notice that Marcus was not becoming more animated. She stopped her wiggling to ascertain his state of arousal and slid her hand down into the front of his shorts. Marcus, while not completely flaccid, was not hard and erect but somewhere in a stuporous middle state. She smiled to herself and shook her head. It was plainly evident that this was a man who needed sleep more than pleasure. Tugging and rolling him about, she got them both under the covers. She curled up, thrusting her buttocks into the warm concavity of his body and pulled his arm over her. "These Irish," she thought, wondering if what she had once heard about them were true, "perhaps they are a people who are really only interested in war, religion and whiskey."

In the early morning as Madeleine looked over at the sleeping man, it occurred to her that his hangover would probably hamper any attempt at amorous activity. She arose, dressed and, carrying her shoes, stole quietly out of the cottage. She hoped no one would see her entering the main house. No one saw her but Helene Deschaines, sitting in her twin bed reading, heard her light footfalls in the upstairs hallway and the closing of her bedroom door.

"I've a few things to do Madeleine, will I be able to get a bite to eat a bit later?" Marcus asked, as he washed his face and hands standing at the sink.

"Yes, there will be some veal and potatoes from dinner," Madeleine answered.

"That will be fine," Marcus nodded, wiping his face with a damp kitchen towel. He went outside and discarded the old trap and returned the wrench to its place in the garage. He thought he would stop in to visit Auguste and mention his encounter with the Milice. He walked back through the kitchen then up a short stairway into a dark wood-paneled hallway that led to the foyer. He turned right passed the curving staircase and down another short dim hallway to the door that led to Deschaines' study. The door was half open and Marcus saw Auguste sitting in his wheelchair facing outward toward the large window, reading in the failing light of the day.

"Auguste," Marcus spoke out, seeking permission to enter, "do you have a moment?"

"Ah, Marcooz," Deschaines responded, as he wheeled himself about, "come in, come in. Did you find what you needed in Privas?"

"I did," Marcus answered, stepping into the study and dropping into a heavy leather armchair before Deschaines' desk. He reached into his jacket for a cigarette, lit it and took a long drag. "I was stopped on the way back just below Couderouge by the Milice."

"Oh yes?" Auguste asked with concern, "and was it problematic?"

"No, no trouble. At first the man tried a bit of the old dragooning but when he got the Irish business straight in his mind, he slacked off and actually tried to be friendly."

"Did he ascertain that you lived here?"

"No, he never asked about my particulars. I thought that odd. He was asking me questions and then kind of relaxed and tried to be conversational.

He was a strange bird, sort of reminded me of a bantam rooster. He wasn't at all like the scum you usually meet up with in the Milice." Marcus laughed softly to himself thinking back to Poissy. "Maybe it's dawned on the poor bastard that Vichy has no future."

"Perhaps," Auguste nodded in agreement, "but I hope his stopping you is not an indication of an increased systematic inquisition in this area by the Milice and their masters."

There was a tacit understanding between Auguste and Marcus that they would not share information regarding the unhappy state of affairs in this part of occupied France with other members of the household. They saw no point in alarming others with bad news or threat if there were no immediate consequences for them. Auguste would tell others of events in their environs as he saw fit. If it were possible, Auguste would bear the heaviest anxiety himself and discuss the grimmer aspects of Nazi occupation only with Marcus and, of course, Paul Bassard.

"If that were the case, I think Bassard would know of it," Marcus commented, "he hasn't said as much, has he?"

"No, he hasn't. Let's hope this is a random thing."

After a short pause, Marcus said, "I haven't seen Zalman about lately although I see Ruth almost every day helping out in the kitchen. He was in the habit of coming to me asking if he could help out with the work around the place up until a few weeks ago. But I don't see him much anymore."

"I'm afraid Zalman is becoming somewhat of a recluse. I think perhaps the sustained anxiety of their situation is beginning to tell on him. He was coming in to chat with me every few days or so, but that is becoming more rare. Without being foolishly optimistic, I would speak with him about an eventual return to normalcy. I pointed out that the Germans have been driven from North Africa, have been stopped in Russia and are being driven out of Sicily. It is but a matter of time before the Allies invade France. Perhaps their thrust will be from the Mediterranean northward, perhaps up the Rhone Valley. Living here, their chances of escaping detection are excellent. But, after all Marcooz, you and I are not the hunted. No one is seeking to deport Messieurs Makeeyon and Deschaines. We do not suffer the anxiety that our loved ones will be victimized by that pack of curs who call themselves soldiers."

"Well, that's true enough, Auguste," Marcus reflected, "there was that time years ago when I thought there were those who might take my life from me. But it was my life they were after, not those of my family. Besides, I had the option of escape to another place well beyond their reach. It's not the same for Zalman and Ruth, I'm afraid."

"To be sure, Marcooz. And, ah, you were speaking of that business of yours in Dublin?"

"I was."

Zalman and Ruth did not flee their home in Munich when Hitler became chancellor of Germany in 1933. Zalman was a loan officer at a savings bank at the time and earned a substanial salary for the support of his wife and two children, Asher and Leah. In 1935, when Zalman lost his job and German Jews lost all their rights as citizens, Ruth began urging her husband to seriously consider escaping Germany. A kind of malaise of indecision had fallen upon Zalman. He had vague hopes that living conditions would not worsen for them and that moderate political elements would eventually return to power. The horror of *Kristallnacht* in the fall of 1938 gave Ruth the power to demand their immediate flight. The woman saw that the murders, arrests and destruction were no spontaneous retaliation for the shooting of a German embassy official by a Polish Jew. It had clearly been well planned out in advance and she knew instinctively that a methodical comprehensive horror was at hand.

The Meyers sold what personal property they could and with their modest savings they purchased small gemstones. The small jewels were sewn into the linings of their coats to serve as items of barter in the future. They fled to the south of France to the home of Ruth's second cousin, hoping that the geographical distance would provide an adequate buffer from the cold bestiality in their homeland.

They lived in Marseille in the cousin's cramped apartment not far from the dockyards. For an exorbitant price they obtained high-quality, forged identification papers for themselves. The Meyers became the Mineurs; Marcel, Renate, Andre and Lisette. They kept their Jewish identity. When France fell in the spring of 1940 and the armistice provided for a German occupied zone in the north and east and a puppet French regime in southern France, the Meyers were alarmed but not to the point of panic.

Their false papers gave their place of birth as Strasbourg, a city in the Rhine Valley close to the German border. It was their hope that this would provide an explanation for their accent in speaking French. The children had no difficulty in soon acquiring the Marseille patois and were generally able to move about the city confidently, less so their parents. Ruth would venture out to shop with fair regularity, but Zalman, with his heavily accented fractured French stayed in the apartment by day. He took short strolls at night and pretended drunkenness if approached by a Frenchman.

The Meyers' fragile sense of security was shattered by news of the roundups in Paris in July of 1942. Thousands of Jews were collected by the Gestapo with the help of elements of the French police. Many of those arrested were French citizens. The obvious conclusion was that this policy would soon spread throughout greater France starting in the urban areas.

By a stroke of good fortune, a French woman living in the apartment below approached Ruth with the opportunity to contact a clandestine organization called the *Oeuvre de Secours aux Enfants*. The O.S.E. was committed to helping Jewish children, many of whom were without parents. One of their agents arranged for Asher and Leah to be provided a safe haven in a Catholic convent and school in the Alps, beyond Grenoble, near the Swiss border. On a cold, rainy Sunday morning in October, the grieving parents packed their weeping children off to what they hoped would be safety.

As the arrests of foreign Jews became ever more frequent in Marseille during the fall, the Meyers became convinced that it was but a matter of time before they too were taken. There would someday surely come the heavy stomping of boots in the hallway outside and then the harsh rapping at the door demanding entrance. Ruth did not want to simply sit and wait for it but could think of nothing to be done as she watched her husband slide into deep depression. One evening as they lay huddled in their tiny bed beneath a thin coverlet, she made a suggestion. "Zalman, I don't want to simply do nothing but wait for them to come for us."

"What can we do, Ruth, what can we do?"

"I don't know. Let's just leave. Let's just start going somewhere."

"Where will we go? Who will take us in?"

"Zalman, we must try to survive for the children's sake. We owe that to them."

"I don't know, I don't know."

"I was thinking of the story of Abram and Sarai in the Bible. They did not know where they were going. They just packed up and left their home without knowing what was to become of them."

"But God has not spoken to me, Ruth, I have prayed at length but God has not spoken to me."

"I have prayed too. Perhaps God has spoken to me by giving me this recurring thought. We must go, Zalman."

Zalman sighed deeply. "When should we go? When?"

There was a long silence between the two. In the stillness, Ruth spoke, "Now."

They arose from the bed and by the light of a kerosene lamp, dressed and packed their few belongings. Ruth scribbled a note of thanks and goodbye to her cousin asleep in the next room. Quietly they left the apartment, went down the creaking wooden steps and out into the dark wet street. They held hands as they walked toward the northern end of the city.

Old Giles Michaud did not give a wharf rat's ass for the Boches, police or Vichy. He burped loudly at the wheel of his lorry tasting the sausage he had wolfed down for breakfast. He was making his weekly run from the Marseilles docks, up the Rhone Valley to Lyon, a distance of some 250 kilometers. The small trucking firm for which Giles worked was allotted an adequate gas ration for their business because they often hauled goods and material utilized by the German army. When he loaded the truck Giles made it his habit to discreetly urinate on specific items in the freight, particularly the edibles.

Michaud would have liked to join his two sons in the Resistance and it was not his age that prevented it. In his sons' absence he had several grandchildren to support and it was necessary that he remain in Marseille and have employment. Still, he would have much preferred life on the run doing something practical against the occupiers.

As he left the northern limits of the city and swung east toward the Rhone River crossing at Arles, the deep pink light of dawn was appearing on the horizon. In his headlamps' light he picked out two figures with suitcases walking, hand in hand, along the side of the road. He slowed the truck until he came abreast of them and braked to a stop, reaching across to roll down the side window. He recognized a forlorn middle-aged couple looking at him nervously. He surmised that they were refugees trying to get out of Marseille because of the current roundups. The poor fools are probably Jews, he thought, and are more at risk out here on the open highways then tucked away in a corner of the city.

Neither of them spoke but only gazed at Michaud morosely. "North," he said, "up along the Rhone Valley, Lyon."

They did not move. He abruptly jabbed his thumb to the rear, "In the back, get behind crates and drums."

With this, the couple moved to the rear of the truck. When he no longer heard the shifting of heavy items on the truck bed, he put the vehicle in gear and moved out.

Michaud's trip permit was displayed prominently on the inside of the windshield. He knew he would be stopped at the Arles river crossing and perhaps here and there along the route north. He counted on the inspection at Arles as being as cursory as usual. It was routinely a stop, a glance at his papers, a quick look after lifting the canvas flap at the rear and a wave through. Should a German soldier or policeman pass him on with a friendly wave, Giles would return the wave amiably and then, when not seen, flip his palm up and give the well-known two fingered, obscene gesture. If by mischance the couple were discovered, he would claim that they had probably stowed away while the truck was still at the Marseille waterfront. He was not concerned about that.

It was full light when Michaud reached the Rhone crossing and luckily the inspection was a haphazard one performed by a young, bored *Wermacht* private. He drove north through the morning and was just above Privas when he thought of what to do with his human contraband. He would stop close to a church in the very next village.

Giles saw the cross-topped steeple in the distance above the trees that encircled the village. A small sign by the roadside indicated that the name of the place was Couderouge. He downshifted in the main street and proceeded slowly, then made the left turn that brought him in front of the church. He got out of the cab and went to the rear of the truck, untied the flap and climbed up into the darkness. He spoke out, "Monsieur, Madame."

The pale-faced woman rose from behind the steel drums and responded timidly, "Yes Monsieur?"

"We are in a small village called Couderouge," he began, "maybe 100 kilometers below Lyon. You cannot go there. The place is filthy with Gestapo. You must take your chances among the rural people. I am not a religious man but I know that the priests will generally help if they can. We are right outside a church. Go in and sit. Wait until the priest comes upon you and ask for help. If you do not want to do that then make for the woods and try to make contact with someone else. Move only at night and remain hidden during the day. On no account should you be on the highways."

"Zalman?" Ruth whispered, looking down on her husband, "what should we do?"

Zalman got to his feet and looked from his wife to Michaud. "What do you think we should do, Monsieur?"

"What does the word 'thaumaturgist' mean?"

"What, Monsieur?"

"What does the word 'thaumaturgist' mean? This church is called Saint Gregory Thaumaturgist. Do you know what a thaumaturgist is?"

"I think it means something like miracle maker or wonder worker," Ruth said hesitantly.

"Well then, I think you should try the priest first," Giles said.

"We will do that, Ruth," Zalman said softly.

Looking cautiously about from under the flap, Giles helped the couple to the ground with their suitcases. After they had thanked him for his kindness, he watched them as they walked uncertainly and slowly toward the stone steps that led to vestibule. "May your God bless you," he called after them.

Ruth turned toward him and smiled weakly, "And may He also bless you as a righteous man."

The Meyers stood at the top of the main aisle listening to Michaud's truck pull away. They were grateful that the church was empty but nonetheless felt strange as they looked at the statues and the ornate paraphernalia around the altar. Will these people who are so different from us, actually help us? Ruth thought. They helped our children. We must trust that they will do the same for us.

The Meyers sat in a back pew throughout the day with their suitcases down out of sight. A few villagers came in and went up toward the altar where they knelt in prayer. Ruth studied their behavior in case there would be a time when they must feign the practice of Catholicism.

She made no eye contact with them as they left the church. Late in the day, a tall man with aquiline features, wearing the black cassock of a priest, entered the church and walked directly to them. "*Bon soir*, I am Father Paul Bassard, the rector here. Are you in need of help?"

Ruth was frightened and almost unwilling to tell this austere, almost alien, black-clad figure of their circumstances. She began to weep and stammered, "We are from Marseilles, we are now...," she sobbed and struggled to continue.

"You are Jews?" the priest asked bluntly.

Ruth shivered in fear. She looked down at the floor and whispered, "Yes, we are Jews."

A terrible dread overwhelmed her and she began to shake and weep uncontrollably. She felt the priest brush against her as he sat down in the pew. Then suddenly she felt his arm across her shoulders as he pulled her to his breast. "Cry for those of your people who are alone out there this day, Madame. But do not cry for yourself or your husband. You are now among friends."

At that moment with her face pressed against the damp breast of the priest, a glimmer of hope arose within Ruth Meyer, a hope that she and Zalman would survive and that they would again see their children. She also felt the first small measure of peace she had had since the terror of *Kristallnacht* in Munich years ago.

Bassard took the couple to his rectory, prepared a meal and gave them the use of his spare bedroom. He noticed they hungrily consumed their dinner of potatoes, beets and bread without touching the meat. In serving pork, he had forgotten the Jewish dietary laws and the Meyers were far too courteous to mention it. He excused himself after dinner mentioning that he had business to attend to. When he returned well after midnight, the Meyers had been asleep for hours.

In the morning a woman from the area drove up to the rectory in an old Peugeot. The pert, friendly woman introduced herself as Helene Deschaines, a friend of Père Bassard and a local homeowner. She asked if the Meyers would like to come to her home and determine if it might be the kind of living situation they were looking for. She indicated that they could earn their keep by helping out with the estate maintenance. Seeing that they were well-educated, middle-class people, Helene made it a point to mention that most of their work would be of a menial nature. The Meyers readily assented with appropriate expressions of gratitude.

Helene drove them to her home and put them in the two storage rooms that were above the garage. Throughout the day Zalman helped Marcus move heavy objects about while the women cleaned and made the rooms livable with the addition of borrowed furnishings. After dark, the Meyers sat by candlelight and gave a special prayer of thanksgiving for the events of the past two days.

"We've met some very good people since leaving the apartment, Ruth. Have we simply been very fortunate or are most people like this?" Zalman mused.

"I don't know," Ruth replied, "I would like to think that most people are like this."

"Well, I don't know either, but I know that many people have been good to this dirty old Jew."

Startled, Ruth asked, "Zalman, what in God's name are you saying?"

Meyer laughed softly holding out his begrimed hands and comically pointing to the dirty smears on his face and forearms, "And this important banker has always been so concerned about his personal appearance."

Ruth smiled and thought about how good it was to make jokes again, "*Tu es fou*, Zalman, you are really crazy."

Marcus rose from the leather armchair, brushing away cigarette ash that clung to his lapel, "I'll be going now, Auguste. I've a few things to do."

"Bassard is coming for dinner, you'll join us?"

"I will," Marcus indicated as he strode to the door.

Auguste watched Marcus as he left and thought of his good fortune in having such a man for his friend. They had met in 1933 when Marcus answered the advertisement placed in the Lyon newspapers by the Deschaines. This had been necessary because the doctors had indicated that Auguste was suffering from a progressive degeneration of the lower spinal cord and nerve roots. Deschaines had been severely wounded in 1916 in the mud and blood of Verdun. As a Captain of Infantry, he had been one of the half million casualties in the French lunatic counterattack to the German assault on the fortress city. He had walked with the aid of a cane in the years afterward before the staggering gait and postural instability from increasing leg ataxia made the use of a wheelchair necessary. The attendant loss of physical sensation in his lower body had made him impotent. He had not been intimate with Helene for several years.

The Deschaines needed an attendant for Auguste but because of his general vitality, self-reliance and sense of pride, they wished more than an ever present physical custodian. They wanted a person with the willingness and ability to take on whatever additional tasks that might be required in the management of their estate. Auguste and Marcus immediately took to each other and the employment interview ended in their sharing a drink and the laughter of repartee. Helene was not so impressed but was willing to defer to her husband's wishes. She found the Irlandais somewhat insouciant. She had asked him if he drank and he had replied, "Only when I can get it, Madame."

She had been further irritated when she admonished, "There can be no question of drinking at those times when you are required to help my husband in his physical movements."

"Well, I can understand that, all right, Madame Deschaines," Marcus quipped, "but if he's drunk as well, he'll never notice if I drop him."

Auguste decided at that moment that Marcus was his man. Helene went into a reserved glacial state. The fact that she would eventually fall in love with this Gaelic quipster was the furthest thing from her mind.

Auguste Deschaines had what would have been considered in classical times a noble countenance. Despite his use of a wheelchair, he had a natural bearing that encouraged a certain deference from those in his presence. He had an almost martial posture in his chair and he held his head in such a way as to suggest a full attention to that which he brought under his consideration. His thick white hair brushed back away from his face gave him a leonine aspect. His face was tanned and slightly ruddy from his propensity to remain outdoors in the sunlight. Warm brown eyes that peered occasionally over reading spectacles, bespoke a lively friendly intelligence. Auguste was a man whose humanity had not been diminished by personal misfortune.

As a young man he had entertained the notion of becoming a priest but had finally decided on the life of a scholar. He planned to obtain a doctoral degree in philosophy and history and then, perhaps, secure a teaching position at a university.

The Deschaines family was one of moderate wealth and Auguste decided to intersperse his studies with periods of extended travel. His intermittent sojourns included Algeria, India and French Indo-China. While abroad he dabbled in archaeology and anthropology.

In May of 1914 while on an informal anthropological junket to the ancient Vietnamese city of Hue, Deschaines was notified by the colonial authorities in Saigon of the requirement for his immediate return to France. Auguste held a reserve commission in the French army and a recent remark by the German ambassador in Paris to the effect that European peace remained at the mercy of an accident had sent silent perturbations throughout French officialdom. In June, he was at home in Couderouge when far away in Sarajevo, shots fired from the running board of an Austrian archduke's limousine provided the goad that sent poised European armies into the meat grinder.

At the outbreak of war Deschaines was assigned as a lieutenant to an infantry regiment from the Lyon area. The unit was immediately railroaded to the city of Douai in the northwest. Dressed in their absurd Napoleonic red trousers, red caps and long blue overcoats, the regiment was deployed before the German advance on Paris from Belgium. The naïve French military policy of a reliance on patriotic élan among its soldiery quickly proved no match for German machine guns. Auguste's unit joined the general retreat to the south, below the Marne, where they emulated the German decision to entrench their armies.

For a while Deschaines lived in relative safety because the Lyon regiment was not assigned to assault duty in the French probes of German lines. They remained crouched in the trenches that stretched from the North Sea to the Swiss border. This changed when the unit was reassigned to the defense of Verdun in February of 1916. Auguste's hopes, as well as those of millions of other soldiers, that the ongoing stalemate would lead to an armistice were crushed when the German general staff, with almost predictable Teutonic bravado, decided to break the deadlock dramatically.

The Lyon regiment was well entrenched in one of the outer rings of defense of the city and suffered few casualties as they hunkered down during the initial twenty-four hour German bombardment. Over the succeeding months as the Germans lost thousands of men but advanced no farther than 6 kilometers, Auguste lived in a subterranean world of anxiety, mud and excrement. Finally, when the Germans broke off the assault, a pale Lieutenant Deschaines and his men gratefully crawled above ground and began to spend extended periods beneath the blue summer sky.

Their relief was short lived. The French general staff, ignoring the constraints of common sense, conceived of the moronic idea that the Germans were exhausted and that a heroic bold French counterstrike might break them and bring an end to the war. The Lyon regiment, with the newly promoted Captain of Infantry Auguste Charles Deschaines leading one of its companies, spearheaded the insanity.

Whenever the whistles blew, following heavy French artillery assaults, Auguste led his men over the parapet into a crater-pocked moonscape. He ran in front and as soon as the German machine guns opened up, he immediately demonstrated the proper tactical maneuvering for his men by diving headfirst into the nearest water-filled shell hole. Despite his best efforts, Deschaines lost half his men in the first week of the French offensive.

For the French infantryman there were but two ways to escape the madness. One was death and the other was a serious wounding. Auguste survived the maelstrom outside of Verdun because fortunately, in the predawn darkness on a moonless night in August, a German shell fragment put him into the latter category.

Deschaines had been roused from a fitful sleep in the scrap wood framed cubicle cut into the earthen wall of the battalion headquarters by Major Marchand's firm shaking and the dreaded word, patrol. He drowsily swung down onto the floor planking, donned his mud-encrusted boots, field jacket, pistol belt and dented steel helmet. Winding his way wearily through the dark passages, he found Sergeant Saurin sleeping beneath a sheet of oil-stained canvas. He tapped lightly on the man's helmet with his pistol. Auguste waited for Saurin to come to his senses before simply saying, "Patrol, just seven men, Sergeant."

The noncom rose slowly, stretched grumpily then turned and disappeared into the darkness down the trench. Auguste sloshed through the ankle-deep, liquid clay to the point at which two trenches joined to form an angle jutting out into no man's land. He leaned back against the revetment and waited for his men. The seven reporting *poilus* chosen by Saurin were, of course, recent replacements and wore relatively clean uniforms. It was quite natural for new men to be chosen first for hazardous duties by the sergeants until such time as they had had experienced sufficient ugliness and were deemed combat veterans.

"Does everyone understand what we are going to do?" Auguste asked, assuming that even the new men understood the well-known survival techniques employed by front line soldiers. All accoutrements that could make noise were left behind. There was to be no talking and no one, under any circumstances, was to try anything heroic. The men were to follow Deschaines out to any protective depression, preferably a shell hole, about half way to the German lines, some 400 meters distance. They would remain there for perhaps an hour in absolute silence and then quietly steal back to the French lines. There was to be no probing of German barbed wire and absolutely no reconnaissance. Everyone at the front held the general assumption that the German engineering corps contained no fools.

The junior officers in the French regiments facing the Germans at Verdun had developed these insubordinate techniques in their determination to save their own lives and the lives of the men under their command. Those that did not had relatively short military careers. It was commonly surmised that some general staff officer with a great deal of time on his hands, had pored over a map with multi-colored symbols on it and come up with the brilliant notion of nightly reconnaissance to sniff out weaknesses in the enemy's lines. No doubt, it was further thought, he was at the time smoking a cigarette held in an appropriately long, expensive, ornate cigarette holder and had suffered the outrageous indignity of scuffing his well-polished boots when he ran eagerly to write out the shrewd order.

"Follow me, stay close," Deschaines whispered as he hoisted himself clear of the trench. He hunched over and began picking his way from one section of high ground, between himself and the Germans, to another. He stopped frequently to listen for the labored breathing behind him and soon found a large enough shell crater for the patrol to squat in that was roughly equidistant between the two great entrenchments.

They sat in silence for perhaps thirty minutes when the young soldier directly across from Deschaines began a series of short, explosive, though muffled coughs. The hair on the nape of Auguste's neck stood on end as the poor *poilu* struggled to suppress the spasmodic coughing with a grimy hand clapped across his mouth. The low murmurings and metallic sounds of the sliding of bolts on weapons in the darkness toward the German lines reached Auguste's ears. The Germans were now aware that somebody was out there close to them and Deschaines knew exactly what was going to happen. He heard the single crack, the airy whooshing noise and the pop as the flare detonated high above them. Suddenly the men and the gray broken terrain around them were bathed in a fierce bright light. The soldiers looked to Auguste in wide-eyed panic awaiting his order for them to make a run for it. But he knew they could not be seen down in the mire of the depression and indicated, with a repeated palms down motion of his hands, that they were to remain still. As the flare expended itself they were again enclosed in silence and protective darkness. The shock of sudden fear had stopped the young soldier's coughing fit and Deschaines assumed that they could now move out quietly toward the French positions. He started up the slope of the shell hole then suddenly froze as he heard the all too familiar short thump that came from just behind the front German trenches. He heard the rhythmic whistling sound as an object passed over them and then saw the bright flash and heard the loud crump of an exploding shell between them and the French barbed wire. Again, he heard the single thump from behind the Germans. This time the shell did not carry beyond them but fell short between their position and the enemy. The patrol had been bracketed by German mortars. The coming barrage would fall between the first two rounds and squarely on top of them. "Run for it, we're bracketed," Auguste hoarsely shouted, dispensing with any consideration of delay.

The men bolted from the hole. They ran, stumbling in the dark uneven landscape, desperately hoping they would not be cut down by overly nervous French sentries set on edge by the barrage. Deschaines waited until the last man disappeared over the rim of the depression before sprinting after them. He had not gotten half way back before the shrieking of mortar rounds and the blasts of impact began right behind him. Twice he was knocked to the muck by concussion before scrambling to his feet and again slogging toward safety. The flash of the explosions enabled him to see the oblique lane through the barbed wire leading to the forward trenches. He was in that space and almost to the trenches when a detonation blew him forward. Simultaneously, he felt what seemed like the blow of a sledgehammer to his lower back. He soared, his body twisting in the air, before plunging down into the trench headfirst. He was aware, momentarily, of being face down in the cold liquefaction of mud before losing consciousness.

Deschaines lay unconscious for a considerable time before medical help arrived. One of the two middle-aged corpsmen noticed the dark bloodstain on the lower rear of Deschaines' field jacket and grunted, "Wait, don't move him," to his companion.

He knelt and placed his face close to Auguste's while he scraped the mud from around the inert Captain's mouth with his fingers. The veteran medic had developed over time a strange, delicate aural ability to determine if a man was dying by simply listening to his breath. "Face down," he directed.

With well-practiced movements minimizing the risk of further injury, the corpsmen slid Auguste onto the thick cushion of mud that lay upon the canvass stretcher. They lifted him and began the long winding trek through the maze of trenches toward the rear area.

Amid the rubble of Verdun, as his stretcher was placed on one of the rough wooden racks in a roofless grocery store serving as the receiving area for the field hospital, Deschaines began to regain consciousness. Because of the medical policy of triage, the military surgeon on duty spent little time with the dying soldier who had come in just before Auguste. Seeing the prominent bloodstain, he quickly cut through Deschaines uniform from buttocks to collar with a razor-sharp bayonet and pulled the material apart. A small pool of blood had collected in the hollow of Auguste's lower back and a dark ring of coagulum was forming at its edges. He observed the entry wound above, just to the right of the spinal sacral nerves and dismissed an immediate inclination to probe the wound with his finger. He turned to a nearby orderly, "Get this man to a table at once. Etherize him."

Within the space of a few minutes, the surgeon had located the walnut-sized shard of shrapnel. He made an incision to the right of it and, drawing away from the spine, deftly removed it. He had no idea as to the extent of neurological damage.

Deschaines spent the next three days in a tent next to the field hospital lying face down on a filthy, blood-encrusted mattress. He slept most of the time and was oblivious to the state of his rags of clothes and the mud still caked in his hair. The pain in his lower back was bearable and its mere presence, he was told by an orderly, was a good sign. He was then transported south by lorry to a recuperative hospital in Dijon.

In a month's time Auguste was able to rest comfortably on his back but his civilian attending physician, a Dr. Jonas Benjamin, had kept him abed. One day while on his morning rounds in the crowded officer's ward, Dr. Benjamin sat down at the foot of Auguste's bed and quickly reviewed his notes from a clipboard. "Captain Deschaines, I know you must be anxious to learn something of your condition," he began, "but the nature of your wound does not really permit a prognosis with a great deal of exactitude. I can tell you that the man who removed the piece of shrapnel from your spinal area did an excellent job of it by minimizing further damage to surrounding tissue which, by the way, is the inevitable result of invasive surgery. There is no proper way for me to determine the extent of injury without my reopening the wound and in that case the probability of additional tissue damage is high. You understand, eh?"

Auguste nodded and asked, "Doctor, is there anything that you can tell me at all?"

"Well Captain, I think I can make at least two substantive medical judgments from the informal tests I've conducted since you've been with us. Your ataxia, the loss of coordinate movement in your legs is at the moment, I would say, moderate to severe. You will, I think, walk again but not without an impaired gait. I would guess that because you are a man of excellent physique you will be able to walk using a cane. The second judgment is somewhat more troubling. You have reported periodic numbness and tingling in your lower body. That would indicate to me that there has been damage to the dorsal roots that carry sensory fibers and connect to the spinal cord. The condition is known as paresthesia. I'm afraid, Captain, that it is not uncommon for this to become, over time, paresis, that is, partial paralysis. And paresis, unfortunately, can lead to complete paralysis.

The doctor paused, waiting for Auguste to digest the information. "But understand Captain, I am not saying that you are to become a paralytic in the near future. You strike me as a man of character and determination. My medical opinion, culled from my experience of similar situations, is that you will be walking with the help of a cane in several months and the physical deterioration, of which I spoke, will not affect you noticeably perhaps for a decade, maybe two. Do you have questions, Captain?"

It was clear to Deschaines that the doctor could provide no definite information about the future and he saw no point in pressing the man in that direction. "Pain, Doctor? Will I be feeling a great deal of pain?"

"No, I would not say so. There will be discomfort, perhaps chronic, but I would not say extreme pain."

Deschaines said no more. He knew he could make no plans for his future until he experienced the extent of his rehabilitation. He was emotionally neutral regarding his wound and the impact of it on his life. He would wait and see. However, Deschaines knew one thing for certain. He was grateful. He was grateful that he was now in a world that made sense, a world where one could think about normal affairs among people doing ordinary natural things. He appreciated clean sheets, glass paned windows, sunlight, even the steel bedpan. The sounds of human activity here at the hospital remained well below the constant, painful thunderclaps of explosions. The smell of the clean, fresh autumn air through open windows delighted him. He was finally done with the stink of cordite and rotting human flesh in the purgatory of trench warfare.

In the winter, Auguste returned to his home in Couderouge and under the care of his widowed mother he gradually regained his physical vitality. He maintained a bucolic existence reading philosophy and history while attending to the affairs of the estate. He required of himself a daily extended walk through the woods or along the roadsides outside of the village. Despite his pronounced limp and weather-dependent lumbar discomfort, Deschaines did not consider himself disabled.

With the coming of the Armistice, Auguste decided to resume his doctoral studies at the *Université de Paris-Sorbonne*. Upon reading the works of several modern Thomistic thinkers, Deschaines, for the most part, rejected the tendency of modern philosophy to lose itself in quagmiry epistemological concerns. He saw that the traditional reasoned search for essential truth had been sidetracked into a self-indulgent, mindless blizzard of opaque terminologies. This view was to cause him immediate difficulties with the resumption of his studies.

His faculty advisor, Professor Jean Ragueneau, a man two years his junior, was threatened by Deschaines' general erudition and independence of mind. His professional hackles were raised each time Auguste pointed out flaws in the professor's thinking concerning the views of renowned modern philosophers. At one particular advisory session Ragueneau had alluded, thoughtlessly, to Descartes' famous dictum, "*Je pense donc je suis*".

"Well Professor, I must say that particular philosophic insight has always caused me a bit of difficulty".

"What do you mean, Monsieur Deschaines?"

"On the face of it, Descartes seems to be saying he has two ideas in his mind simultaneously."

"Pardon?"

" 'I am thinking' and 'I have being' are two distinct thoughts that cannot be held simultaneously in consciousness."

The professor furrowed his brow, trying to understand what he had just heard. There seemed to be some sense to it but that would mean that there just might be a flaw in Descartes' thesis. He decided, as a function of will rather than thought, that the latter could not possibly be true. He filled in the conversational gap by mindlessly remarking, "That's absurd."

"How so?" Auguste responded.

At a loss to explain how one could hold two thoughts simultaneously, he recommended that Deschaines reread Descartes' *Discourses*.

Auguste, realizing that further discussion would go nowhere, did not push the point. He smiled to himself, looked out at the blue sky through the professor's office window and said quietly, "I remember that I just had a thought. That memory requires that someone exists to have it. That someone must be me. On the other hand, when I think about objective or subjective phenomena, I am completely without self-consciousness, that is, without awareness of self. I think, therefore I am not."

He looked back to the professor who averted the laughing brown eyes by looking at the floor with tight-lipped irritation.

Deschaines' doctoral dissertation did not, in the normal academic fashion, have a designation several lines long. It was entitled simply, *Cognition*. He coined no neologisms. It was a short work that arose out of pure thinking and required a meditative reading. This was a problem for several of his oral examiners who generally liked to display their sophistry during such collective scrutiny since they were irksomely aware that nobody read their books.

Quite unable to comprehend Deschaines' thesis from his own reading, the advisor had bided his time before questioning Auguste in what he thought was an adroit scholarly pouncing. "And what do you think of Kant's transcendental apperception, Monsieur Deschaines?"

Auguste, fully aware along with most of the examiners that he was confronted with a non sequitur in the discussion, was now faced with a small moral dilemma. He knew with certainty that if he engaged in scholarly debate with Ragueneau, his advisor's intellectual limitations would soon become manifest. He considered the small man sitting smugly across the table from him and briefly struggled with the temptation to administer a scholarly chastening. However, with an inaudible sigh he opted for compassion and geniality. "Perhaps you would like to expound on its importance for us, Professor Ragueneau," he said amiably.

Ragueneau smiled condescendingly and happily launched himself into a small self-indulgent lecture. Several of the older more seasoned professors, aware of Auguste's gentlemanly gesture, sought eye contact with him during his advisor's rambling discourse.

Because of intradepartmental rivalries and an instinctive wariness that this Deschaines fellow might prove a more than competent adversary in disputation, the examiners confined their remaining questions to the banal.

At some financial cost to himself, Auguste had a few copies of his dissertation printed and made hardbound. The slim volumes found their way into several French and Swiss university libraries quite lost among the large tomes bearing grandiose titles. His name and work appeared in the bibliographies of papers written by various scholars in succeeding years. All but a few of them put down the book when, after a few pages, the effort to follow his thinking became too arduous. Not one of them discovered that Auguste Deschaines had, more or less, demolished the underpinnings of modern philosophy. Indeed, if Kant was the father of modern philosophy, Deschaines had committed philosophic patricide.

In the fall of 1921, Deschaines secured a teaching position giving undergraduate courses in philosophy and history at the University of Montpellier in Southern France not far from the Mediterranean Coast. He was attracted to Montpellier because of the warm climate and relative closeness to the Rhone Valley.

Notwithstanding his rigorous academic requirements, Auguste was generally popular with his students because of his constant geniality and tendency toward self-effacing humor. There was, of course, curiosity among some of them as to the cause of the professor's pronounced limp. For those who did not make the obvious assumption that it was a war wound and had the temerity to inquire, Auguste entertained himself by concocting a new story on each occasion. Two young men, part of a larger group who, when discussing the infirmity discovered his good-natured deceptions, decided to exact a certain revenge. They fabricated and spread a story, which they insisted was the truth about the limp, while invoking the authority of a fictitious Montpellier newspaper article of some years before. Professor Deschaines, it seemed, could really not share the truth concerning his infirmity without soiling the good name of a married woman who lived quite close to the campus. Her husband, a police detective, had caught the pair *en flagrant délit* in the doorway of the couple's kitchen and had intended to shoot Deschaines in the behind. The spinal wound was the result of the man's poor aim in the midst of understandable outrage and upset. Nonetheless, a formal apology was required at the subsequent closed hearing. There was no filing of charges. The University and the local government conspired to suppress the public airing of the incident to protect reputations and that is why Professor Deschaines, a man of fine character, resorts to this wiliness. The duo's story was accepted as the truth by many of Deschaines' students and consequently their esteem for the good-natured, old roué increased immeasurably. Auguste never discovered the young men's rumor-mongering coup and often had occasion to wonder why his students no longer asked him about his limp.

Auguste observed, over time, that his best students were the veterans. They seemed the most serious and conscientious. They did not involve themselves in the frivolities of campus life and held rather moderate political and sociological views. The younger students, primarily from the upper middle-class, were more apt to indulge themselves in collective goings-on. They were particularly active when a political issue, whether of a right-wing or left-wing bias, could be the vehicle for the expression of their immature exuberance.

The French national political scene provided periodic inducements for the activist students at the University of Montpellier to organize small rallies and sponsor heated speech-making by those of Deschaines' professional colleagues who, of course, possessed academic credentials but, unfortunately, little in the way of common sense. Just after the French and Belgian occupation of the Ruhr, Auguste had the honor of being denounced at a small gathering of would-be Communists as a militarist. The accuser, a Marxist professor of Economics was, in truth, simply envious of Auguste's war record and popularity among the student body. On the other hand, at another rally his patriotism was questioned by an undergraduate member of the *Action Français* because of classroom remarks indicating his opposition to reparation payments by the Germans.

Auguste was inclined toward a benign tolerance for students who involved themselves in political ferment. He attributed their partisan inanities to youth and inexperience in the world of necessity. He noted that below the doctrinaire cant and animation, oftentimes for many students, a sincere desire for social justice and improvement in general living conditions for working people were paramount. The grim-faced resolve and intransigent demands of noisy students practicing the "dismal science" had the tendency, he observed, to dissolve at rally's end into smiles and the shared laughter of *amitié*. Did you then ask a man his politics when he offered to buy you a drink, or a young women hers before the attempt to steal a kiss? Life, he observed, for the young, at least, would inevitably outweigh abstractions.

Deschaines, however, was much less inclined to abide the ideological machinations of his colleagues. The adoption and advocacy of a partisan view that tended to set one group of human beings against another was, in Auguste's estimation, a kind of betrayal of the teacher's vocation. It was, for him, an unpardonable sin for which there could be no excuse. It did not matter to Deschaines whether the ideological garbage took the form of an international Communism that pitted classes against each other or a French jingoism that advanced notions of pure patriotism and social acceptability. An ideologue was, for Auguste, an egotistical moral midget. He deemed him a man who was crystallized in his psychological deformations and was quite willing to wound others to protect the integrity of that ugliness. The professional zealots could generally count on Deschaines' social affability but learned to be quite wary of him when voicing their political prejudices within the University's community.

France, in the years following the Great War, was plagued by the outbreak of a series of workers' general strikes, inflation and an instability of the *franc*. An influx of foreign workers because of the war-related manpower shortages coupled with a nameless anxiety over the mysterious upheaval of the Bolshevik revolution in Russia, set the Gallic political kettle bubbling. The University, as many other educational institutions were apt to do, attributed to itself a national importance quite beyond reason and scheduled a number of symposiums to discuss the various political issues. Auguste had avoided participation in what he considered academic palavering but consented, against his better judgment, to be a last minute substitute for a conservative don who had opted out the day before one of the scheduled conferences.

In a crowded auditorium, filled mostly by youthful adherents of popular political movements, Auguste found himself seated to the right, naturally, of the moderator with a priest and two old-school professors. Beyond the moderator sat a Communist, Socialist, biologist and social scientist. In his preliminary remarks, he spoke briefly of the war and its aftermath from a strictly phenomenological point of view without moral evaluation. He was then prepared to sit quietly through the remainder of the symposium without comment.

The Communist, in responding to a comment by the priest, used the opportunity to inveigh vehemently again the social sins of the Church. He closed his remarks with the famous Marxist dictum about religion being an opiate of the masses while smiling icily at the cleric. At this point, Auguste decided to contribute and indicated his willingness with the slight raising of a forefinger. Deliberately omitting the honorific of "Professor", he said to the chairman, "I would like to ask Monsieur Leygues to expand a bit on his last remark."

"I would be glad to, Professor Deschaines, and I am certainly glad you have chosen to break your stolid silence at this point."

Auguste grinned broadly and raised an eyebrow, responding, "Your personal emotional reactions to my participation in this foolishness are of no moment. I am simply curious to know if you understand what Marx was talking about."

"Of course I do."

"Well, what is it that he was saying about religion?"

"He was saying, my metaphysical friend, that religion is something that beclouds the mind, something that interferes with the proper grasping of the reality of the material dialectic. It has the same effect as drunkenness."

"You've read Marx?"

"Of course, I have."

"Can you tell us, Monsieur, the medical use of an opiate?"

"Why yes, it's used for....," Leygues looked to his colleagues beside him, whispering, while seeking an appropriate answer, "I believe it's used to induce unconsciousness," he responded brightly.

There was a scattering of laughter in the audience and Deschaines waited until it abated. Turning to the biologist, he asked, "Professor Millerand, can you tell us what the primary medical use of opiates is?"

"Well yes, it is commonly used to alleviate pain."

"So it is," said Deschaines, "Monsieur Leygues, in that passage Marx is saying that the common working man has no relief from the pain of his day-to-day existence except that provided by the practice of religion. Reread the section, you will see that this is true. You have apparently fallen victim to the platitudes of your party which is in the habit of pulling historical facts out of their context."

The moderator, sensing Leygues' embarrassment, shifted attention from the issue by quickly asking the Socialist his thoughts on the government's latest economic proposals.

As the symposium drew to an end, Auguste's concluding remarks consisted in the pointing out of the obvious contradictions and anomalies inherent in a materialistic worldview. A few in the audience followed his reasoning. As he stepped down from the stage and was engaged in a polite conversation with an admiring student, he felt a light touch on his forearm. Turning to his right, he found himself looking into the earnest brown eyes of a pert, well-dressed woman, perhaps six or seven years his junior. "Professor Deschaines, I am Helene Brun, a doctoral candidate here at the University," she began, "some of us were just discussing your participation at this symposium. We are at a loss with regard to determining your political views. Do you have a *politiques*, Professor?"

Auguste smiled, appreciating the woman's directness, "Hmm, well, I suppose some would call me a Roman Catholic."

"Catholic? I did not ask about your religion, Professor, I would like a brief indication of your political views."

"Mademoiselle? Madame?" Auguste replied, "I believe that people should try to live morally with each other."

"It is Mademoiselle, Professor. Under what kind of a government should they try to live morally together?"

"The Emperor, Mademoiselle," Auguste grinned.

"Professor Deschaines, we would really like to know your views on government and policy. Perhaps you are playing with me because I am a woman and you will not trouble yourself to take my questions seriously."

"Mademoiselle Brun, if it were true that I was playing with you, it would not be simply because you are a woman, but rather because you are an attractive person."

"If you think that is so, it is of no consequence. I would really appreciate your giving me an indication of the form of government and policies you favor."

"Are you a student of history?"

"Yes, to some degree."

"Are you familiar with Charlemagne; his character, his policies?"

"Only vaguely, Professor."

"What of Joan of Arc? Are you familiar with her character?"

"Yes, as a matter of fact, I am. I've read quite a bit about her."

"Do you admire her?"

"Yes, I do."

"Then I'll say I am for government with Joan of Arc as its head."

"As Premier?"

"As Empress."

Auguste and Helene continued their conversation oblivious to the others that clustered about them. Deschaines, quite taken by this serious interrogatrix, asked if she would like to accompany him to a nearby café for coffee. Helene, looking about but seeing no sign of her friends, assented.

Marcus left Auguste's study and when in the foyer turned to look up as he heard his name called out from the upstairs hallway. He felt that same small rush of pleasure he did whenever he laid eyes on Helene Deschaines. She stood with both hands on the banister, smiling down on him. "Did Auguste mention that Père Bassard will be here for dinner?"

"He did, Helene."

"Will you be there?"

"I will," he said, as he shifted his weight preparing to go toward the kitchen. He paused and looked up to Helene again as she spoke.

"Did you find a trap in Privas for Madeleine?"

"I did," he nodded and stepped to go when Helene said nothing more.

He froze and looked upward to the ceiling, pressing his lips together as he heard her brightly ask, "Did you have difficulty with the installation?"

He turned, looked up to Helene again, smiling slightly. He knew she was in one of her playful moods. She was toying with him again and he expected that she would soon indirectly allude to the relationship he had with Madeleine. Marcus guessed that Helene would be amused if she could elicit from him some measure of uneasiness over the fact that she was aware of it. What Helene did not know was that her approval or disapproval of his coupling with the cook meant very little to him. Marcus had had considerable experience with psychologically manipulative women in his life. His two older sisters, Sarah Goldner, several young women at university and Kate Jamieson had, at one time or other, attempted to impose their will on him through delicate subterfuge. It was the very absence of this artfulness that contributed greatly to his attraction to Madeleine.

"No, Madeleine is satisfied," he beamed, pushing beyond Helene in their *plaisanterie*.

Helene said nothing in response. She stood in amusement simply waiting for Marcus to begin to leave. She allowed him two steps before saying, "I'm glad Madeleine is so easy to please."

He stopped and turned, saying, "Yes, I'm glad she's that way too. She isn't one of those sort who beat around the bush expecting you to figure out what's on her mind. If she has a problem with something, she says so right off."

"Well, aren't you the fortunate one, Marcooz?"

"I am that, Helene." He stood looking up at her, determined to remain in place until Helene indicated in someway that their exchange was over.

Helene gave Marcus what she hoped was an inscrutable smile and turned to go down the upstairs hall. There were two important things, one about herself and one about Marcus, to which she was oblivious. The first was that she was somewhat jealous of Madeleine. This particular lack of self-awareness was excusable because she had never before been covetous of another person's romantic relationship. The second was that Marcus would have preferred, at any time, bantering with her than even copulating with any other woman in the world. Helene was like many women. She possessed an instinctive maternal insight that was quite capable of discerning the motivation of boys but was generally wanting in her understanding of mature men.

Sergeant Poissy had his driver drop him in front of Milice headquarters before their truck was returned to the motor pool. He climbed the narrow wooden stairway and entered one of the dingy cramped offices on the second floor. After scrawling his name in the dog-eared logbook atop a rusted, metal filing cabinet, he sat behind the overly large cluttered desk. He tossed his black beret on the desk, lit a cigarette, flicked the match on the floor and pulled a report form from the lower, right-hand drawer.

Accounting for his time in the area north of Privas during the day, Poissy filled out the form, embellishing here and there to give an impression of conscientiousness. He made informal notes at the bottom of the form: *Dechene, Route Aurmeau, Couderouge, les estrangers? Informateur-Michel Fleur.* He went to the filing cabinet, dropped and heeled the cigarette butt into the unswept floor and filed his report in a folder labeled *Ardeche, Nord.*

Claude walked from the office with no more on his mind than his evening meal. He could not know of the grim events that were soon to happen as a result of his additional notes to what was, after all, a routine report.

At the conclusion of dinner at the Deschaines, the animated table discussion concerned aspects and issues of French higher education then soon evolved into shared reminiscences and anecdotes from student days. "Ah yes," Auguste was saying, "it was very difficult for me to wean Helene away from her *jeunesse dorée.* Her young friends were so wealthy, so stylish, so sophisticated. I was drab in comparison."

Helene smiled and peered into her wine glass that she held in her two hands with arms extended out upon the table. "That is so true, Père Bassard, for I felt so sorry for him."

"She was the compleat social critic," Auguste continued, "and championed a cornucopia of causes. I suppose, in my case, she found the rehabilitation of a bumpkin apolitical philosopher irresistible."

There was general laughter around the table as Helene commented, "Actually my love, it was your Platonic sex appeal."

Bassard turned to Marcus, "Were you politically active as a young man, Marcooz?"

"No, hardly at all when I went to university. Later when I was teaching in Dublin I became embroiled in it but that was due to circumstances rather than strong political beliefs."

"What was your major area of study? I've forgotten," Bassard asked.

"Well, initially it was just the liberal arts. I wanted to learn about everything. When I had to choose a concentration, I chose history."

"Why history? If you don't mind my asking."

"I suppose it was the lingering influence of my boyhood teacher, Master Raye. There were more learned men than Master Raye at the University, but no one with greater character."

"Do you suppose character is the most important thing in a teacher?"

"I believe so, Père Bassard, the area of expertise is nowhere near as important."

"Do you agree, Auguste?" Bassard asked.

"Without doubt, without doubt," Auguste replied, "there is a Sufi saying, 'to become who you are, you must see yourself in another, who is better able to manifest yourself than you are.' It means that if you see, say nobility, in another person, that is so because nobility exists in you. You know what it is and can recognize it manifested in another. Another example might be indicated in the Legend of the Holy Grail. Parsifal, the hero, was utterly confused by dishonesty in others. He was unfamiliar with it because it didn't exist in him. Similarly, I know something of the humanity of an Irishman named Raye who taught children years ago in that country because I see it in Marcooz."

Helene, somewhat squiffy from three glasses of wine, quipped, "*Je suis Heathcliff.*"

Puzzled by the remark, Bassard asked, "You are what, Helene?"

Auguste, smiling resignedly and shaking his head slowly from side to side, explained, "It is a line from *Wuthering Heights*. She is making fun of me."

But Auguste was wrong. The remark was directed, in a vague way, toward Marcus and somehow he sensed it. He looked across the table at Helene and although her eyes gazed down at the table, he knew she was mindful of him. Marcus had begun to notice this sea change in Helene's attitude toward him since about the time he had taken up with Madeleine. He was puzzled by it.

For years there had been an amiable understanding between them. He had felt love for Helene from the very day he had come down to Couderouge for the employment interview when he had seen her for the first time as she popped into the hallway from Auguste's study. There had been no falling in love, no gradual growth of affection, no progressive quickening of romantic feeling. It was there from the beginning in its completeness. In a nonlinear way, where cause and effect were one, in that moment just outside the study, he remembered her. And his memory of her was made up of living elements from his past and his future.

Marcus had never been given to extended self-analysis and deep introspection. What he experienced in his subjectivity he tended to treat rather phenomenologically. He did not feel an egocentricity or uniqueness and assumed that his interior life was much the same as another man's. It was a kind of mystery for Marcus why any man would not love Helene.

But with regard to women generally, he was not so sure. Their general tendency toward lack of candor was something he really did not like and did not understand. He was not, however, a misogynist. He had been treated far too well by women over the course of his life to come to that conclusion. Marcus attributed their want of frankness to an indistinct fragility that mistrusted consequences and resolution but was not, necessarily, blatant deceit for purposes of advantage. He was aware that his periodic difficulty with women was the result of his impatience and unwillingness to live with nuance.

Helene's remark had created for him one of those points of obscurity now. Were they alone he would ask her what the hell she meant and why her change in attitude toward him. Yet, he guessed that she probably would not respond simply and directly but rather set for him another conundrum. So he did what he had generally done when in the company of a woman who he suspected was indulging herself. He left. "Well friends, I'm off," he said rising from his chair.

"Ah Marcooz, is there something you must attend to?" Père Bassard inquired.

Marcus, who had never mastered the technique of the small social lie, responded, "No, I'm just going to stretch my legs for a bit." He nodded a goodbye to Auguste and left the dining room. Helene did not look up from her wine glass.

Auguste, noting her behavior, asked bluntly, "Helene, are you upset with Marcooz?"

The question took her completely by surprise. She looked at her husband without the faintest idea of what to say. If she indicated that she was irritated, Auguste might ask her the reason and then what could she possibly say? If she said she wasn't upset, she would be lying and that would strike against the pride she felt in her always being honest with her husband. She opted for the truth knowing that she could speak of anything with Auguste and rely on his understanding and tact. At the same time she hoped there would be no social awkwardness for Père Bassard. She responded with a pregnant, "I don't know, Auguste," finishing the last of the wine in her glass.

Marcus crunched down the gravel driveway in the semi-darkness of twilight. He had never before regretted telling Helene those years ago that he loved her. He was thinking now that perhaps he should have said nothing. They had been sitting together in her *chambrette* just beyond Auguste's study one afternoon about a year after his employment. She was discussing the social appropriateness of their being together on a planned trip north to Lyon. "Well, if someone has a problem," Marcus had offered, "just tell them the truth of it."

"The truth of it?"

"Well, if someone asks about this Marcus fellow you're with, just say, 'he loves me'."

"Oh Marcooz," Helene laughed, "are you never serious?"

"Helene Deschaines, that is the truth of it."

She looked at him in perplexity. Marcus realized she had no idea of what he was saying. "Helene, look at me."

"Look at you? I am looking at you."

"No, no you're not. Look at me."

Helene peered into Marcus' eyes wondering what he was saying. At first she saw nothing but his blue eyes and then, suddenly, she saw something unnameable. She blushed and looked away.

Afterward, they remained matter of fact with each other for there was really nothing of pressing necessity to say. Both of them were mature people and knew each other well enough to realize that there would be no expectations, no demands, no practical consequences, but above all, no intimacy. The latter limitation was something they both accepted quite willingly. What they never discovered was that this rather unnatural celibacy, although self-imposed because of a mutual regard for Auguste, was ironically something that would never have been denied them by the man who loved them.

After his brief walk along Ormeau Road, Marcus leaned back against the cobblestone gate pillars, smoking while looking into the night sky. He heard footsteps scrunching toward him from the direction of the house. It was Bassard.

"Ah Marcooz, there you are. You are needed at the house. I believe Auguste will be sleeping upstairs tonight."

"Right," Marcus answered, flicking the cigarette into the road, "are you off home then?"

"Yes, perhaps I'll be seeing you in the middle of next week, eh?"

Marcus said nothing in reply but raised his hand to his friend's shoulder with a light grip. He turned and started for the house.

Finding Auguste in the study, Marcus leaned into the doorway, "Will you be needing me, Auguste?"

"Yes, I will be upstairs tonight."

"When?"

"Now is fine," Auguste said, dropping his eyeglasses and book into his lap.

He wheeled himself from behind the desk and out and down the hallway to the base of the stairway. He pushed his body upward from the wheelchair and gripping the banister in a practiced maneuver, he swung himself over to sit on the second stair step. Marcus picked the chair up by the arm rests and carrying it before him, mounted the stairs. He returned and stood before Auguste. He bent low at the knees while Auguste threw his arm behind Marcus' head and across the shoulders. With Auguste's chest pressing across his back, Marcus stood, still bent at the waist and put a hand lock on the wrist of Auguste's extended arm. He placed his own extended arm between the legs of the now standing Auguste, and hoisted him across his shoulders in the fireman's carry. With deliberate steps, he carried Auguste upstairs. In the upstairs hallway, he again bent deeply at the knees and deposited Auguste neatly into the wheelchair. This particular task was the most strenuous of Marcus' physical exertions for Deschaines was not a small man. But whether sober or mellow with drink, he concentrated in its execution and had never come near to mishap.

Breathing through an opened mouth, Marcus asked, "Is there anything else, Auguste?"

"No, my friend, I'm good for the evening. You can come anytime in the morning to bring me downstairs."

"Good night then," Marcus said as he started down toward the foyer.

Auguste watched Marcus' descent and thought about Helene's response to his question earlier at dinner. He had been aware of Helene's ambivalence toward Marcus for years. Without availing himself of what he considered a useless psychoanalytic delving, Auguste had become familiar with most of his wife's personality quirks simply through observation and intelligent insight. He remembered an instance when they had first begun discussing marriage back in Montpellier. She had solemnly admitted to him that she was not a virgin. He had not asked about the particulars because he was not terribly interested, at that time, in her sexual experiences. He assumed that if she wanted to talk about it, she would, and he would listen politely and without comment. After the admission, Helene had gazed at him, perhaps expecting a reaction. There was none.

"Auguste," she continued gravely, "I lived with a woman, who was Algerian for awhile."

Auguste pressed his lips together in order to contain his genuinely amused reaction to Helene's syntactical error. His anxiety in wanting to avoid giving offense to Helene's sincere attempt to be honest with him, only added to his self-consciousness.

Fearing that he would soon snort in laughter through his tense facial musculature and unable to contain his utter amusement, he finally blurted, "Well, how long was she Algerian?"

The ridiculousness of his question and the levity of its tone put Helene immediately at ease. She knew he was not mocking her but only indicating, albeit in a stumbling way, that he was accepting her and all of her personal history, whatever it might be. She remembered the words of a Dominican sister, who had been her teacher, to the effect that there was no moral judgment in love. She knew then, without doubt, that Auguste really loved her.

A solitary, kithless Poissy sat alone at his evening meal of roast chicken and turnips at *La Belle Dame Sans La Tête Café* just down the street from Milice headquarters. Now and then, when he thought circumstances warranted it, the sergeant treated himself to a proper meal and he considered his rather brave foray to the north this day such an occasion. The café was run by an obsequious little man who had absolutely no problem catering to the officers of the 48th Panzergrenadier Regiment stationed in and around Privas, as well as minor Vichy officials and the Milice. The canny proprietor calculated that what he lost in trade from the local citizenry he more than made up for in business from the Wermacht and collaborators. Should the war go against the Germans, forcing them out of France, he was prepared to claim he had no choice in the matter and his friendliness to the occupiers was merely a ploy to protect his family. The local Maquis did not bomb or burn the establishment mainly because of the physical fact that the building itself was connected to other innocent businesses. They chose rather to plant agents as employees in order to gain information by eavesdropping. It occurred, therefore, that the owner became well pleased with the attendance records of one of his waiters and one of his cooks and the Wermacht personnel continuously displayed a decided inability to detect the taste of urine and phlegm in their meals.

Poissy took a swallow of wine and peered at the Waffen-SS recruitment poster on the wall across the small dining room. A Nordic-looking young man, clad in the black SS uniform with the conspicuous lightening bolts on the collar, gazed heroically upward into the future. In large blood-red letters the name, *Charlemagne*, was emblazoned across the top and a small French tricolor was affixed to the young demigod's shoulder.

In July of 1943 at the behest of his subjugators, Vichy Propaganda Minister Paul Marion had begun sponsorship of the creation of a special Nazi military unit to be drawn from among the French. The Vichy government was assured that the French SS division would never serve on Gallic soil but would be posted to the east against the Soviets. Initially the legion drew its recruits from collaborators, colonials, university students and the

Milice. It had no appeal for Poissy. Although he liked the uniform, brutal combat against hordes of Eurasians in the bitter cold was not something for which he would readily choose to volunteer. He remembered that earlier in the summer a young Milicien had approached him breathlessly announcing his enrollment in the division. Poissy detested the brazen little jackass who had adopted the grim habit of securing sexual favors from refugee women with threats of arrest. The twerp often snickered that after obtaining his favorite pleasure, *l'amour américain*, he would take them into custody anyway. Poissy feigned interest and fraternity, "Ah Pierre, you will do well. I'm told that Slavic women are especially fond of Frenchmen. And don't forget your long underwear."

Pierre nodded happily in mindless agreement, missing Poissy's jest about cold weather by assuming his reference to underwear had something to do with the bizarre sexual habits of Russian women.

It was through the accumulation of small incidents like this that Poissy had begun to feel a vague unease concerning his decision to join the Milice Française. Still, if it were required, he could mouth the words of fervent patriotism to another but he increasingly noticed he was having difficulty always convincing himself. He also began to notice that he felt no real animosity toward refugees for the mere fact that they were Jewish. He was at the point where, although still willing to do his job, his main concern was his future. If the Allies gained the upper hand in the war, what future was there for Vichy? In a post-war France, what would fellow Frenchmen think about the Milice Francaise? Most detested them now. What would happen to him if the Germans withdrew and Vichy collapsed?

He thought again about the Irlandais he had met near Couderouge. Maybe he was mistaken but the man seemed to like him and was apparently unconcerned about his uniform. How could he ask about Makeeyon's whereabouts when he returned to Couderouge without giving the impression of official police business? Yes, he would visit the residence the informer spoke of and start from there. Perhaps things would work out. Claude Poissy did not know he was soon to face a crisis in his manhood that would require something he had always hoped, *in extremis,* he would possess naturally. Like most little boys and those men who have not quite surrendered to the worldly concern for self-preservation, he secretly hoped he possessed valor.

Marcus stepped down the short stairway into the kitchen on his way out of the house. Madeleine and Helene stood at the sink rinsing and drying the tableware from dinner. As he exited the back door with a quick upward movement of his head in their direction, he piped, *"Bon nuit, Mesdames."*

"Bon nuit, Marcooz," Madeleine replied, passing a wet plate to Helene for drying.

The two women continued for a time without speaking, then Madeleine sensing the slight discomfort between them went directly to its source, *"Cet homme a du chien."*

"He has some dog?" Helene asked, furrowing her brow.

"Oui, he is sexy, *n'est-ce pas?"*

Helene paused for a moment, trying to give the impression of thinking about something that was completely new to her. "Oh, I suppose so."

Madeleine was not taken in by the conversational ploy and smiled knowingly while running faucet water over a plate.

Helene waited for Madeleine to say something more. When the cook did not, she regretted her disingenuousness. "Do you like him, Madeleine?" she continued, hoping to ascertain something more from the very tone of Madeleine's answer.

"If I did not, I wouldn't sleep with him."

The matter-of-fact manner of Madeleine's response told Helene nothing. It was the simple indication that she knew of Helene's awareness of her intimacy with the Irlandais but said nothing of her own feelings concerning him.

"But you are a married woman." The words were out before Helene considered their impact.

Madeleine looked at Helene making her feel as if she were a complete idiot. Helene was quite unprepared for the riposte, "Yes, Madame Deschaines, we are married women."

Helene inwardly stiffened at the implication of the cook's remark. Suddenly, she regretted her inept probing. She had a genuine affection for Madeleine Paquette and realized that the remark about marriage was truly offensive. She wished now only to apologize and establish some form of trust between them. "Oh God, Madeleine, I am sorry for saying that. It was thoughtless. Your private life is none of my business. Please forgive me, please."

Helene's contrite tone and demeanor convinced Madeleine of her sincerity. She, in turn, reached out. "Yes, we are married women, Madame, but circumstances have denied us the full benefits of matrimony, eh? I have chosen to do something about that."

Helene Deschaines was a person who had no difficulty in discussing human sexuality as long as it was in an objective detached manner. She had never shared her disappointment with her husband concerning his impotence for fear of causing him a measure of psychological pain. Whenever he had broached the subject she would invariably put on a brave face maintaining that it was not of great importance to her. Over time, Helene had almost persuaded herself that her celibacy was of no moment. She did not know that she had never convinced Auguste. Her attitude toward her intermittent self-pleasuring was like that of a woman who occasionally allowed herself some chocolates. She did not fantasize with erotic mental images but only relaxed into sensual tension and release. What she would have noticed, were she more cognizant of her psyche, was that she tended to pleasure herself at those times when she had been with Marcus during the day, especially if there had been one of their many minor clashes of will.

Out of curiosity she broached the subject following confession with Père Bassard years ago. He had shrugged saying, "Well Helene, the church teaches that it is a disordered act, but no more grave or disordered than any number of acts of concupiscence. You are in an unfortunate situation and it would be rather stupid of you to perseverate in some form of guilt. Contrary to what many non-Catholics and overly zealous Catholics assume, the Church has never placed sins of the flesh very high on the list of human immoralities. I think Aquinas pointed that out in his disputations with the Manichees. Your intimacies with women when you were single are, like most carnal indiscretions, in the same category. They all simply fall short of the ideal of conjugal union, considerably closer to the picking of the nose than the commission of murder."

Helene was unsatisfied with Madeleine's casual imparting of her reason for intimacy with Marcus. It was commonsensical yet spoke of nothing beyond biological need. She really wished for something of the subtle, the romantic, even the erotic. "Do you think, Madeleine, that Marcus is, in a way, taking advantage of the fact that your husband is away?"

"Taking advantage? No, no, Marcus isn't that kind of man."

"Did he make obvious advances?"

Madeleine laughed, "Are you asking me if he came sniffing around me because of my earlier reference to his 'having some of the dog'? That is something else entirely. Oh, but I must admit, I put out plenty of signals before I got the proper response from him."

"Well, if you don't mind my asking, how did it first happen?"

Madeleine laughed again, rattling tableware in the water in the sink, "I asked him to come to my bedroom but he would not intrude into the upstairs sleeping quarters. So I went to his cottage and seduced him."

It was now Helene who giggled, "Well, how did you do that?"

"If a man does not respond to the sight of a naked woman, there is something wrong with him."

"Oh Madeleine," Helene said almost enviously, "you are such a character."

"But, Madame, that is only half the story."

"What? Tell me, please. What happened?"

"Well, you know these Irish, eh?"

"What? What about them?"

"He was drunk when he came in and went to sleep before we could make love, as a matter of fact, right in the middle of it."

An image of Marcus came into Helene's mind. She saw his face clearly in one of those moments when he was inebriated and puzzled about something. His head tilted awkwardly upward, his brow knitted, eyes squinting, lips set in befuddled concentration, the consummate buffoon. She felt a delicious wave of endearment for him and began to chuckle heartily. With the picture in her mind, her merriment changed to wide-eyed mirth then tears began rolling down her cheeks as her full throaty laughter cascaded into utter hilarity.

As Helene regained her composure, she asked, "Uh, well did you leave then?"

"Oh no, I stayed the night with him."

"And uh, in the morning?"

"I awoke before him and left."

"But uh, why did you just leave, if, uh, you were intent on being intimate?"

"Well Madame, I guessed that he would have a hangover and not be in the proper mood."

"Hmm, yes, I suppose that would be the case."

"Yes, and it is a good thing for old Philibert that I did not meet him on the way back to the house, eh?"

Helene laughed, "Oh Madeleine, you are something."

A short silence ensued where Helene hoped Madeleine would continue. The cook, however, only began humming a popular tune while she went on her with work at the sink. With some trepidation Helene hesitantly asked, "So, uh, when did you, uh, finally...," and made forward circular motions with her hand.

Madeleine stopped her rinsing and smiled benignly at Helene, "That very evening."

"Oh yes? And uh, and uh, where?"

"Madeleine laughed heartily, "About where you're standing."

Irlandais

Helene's jaw dropped and her eyes opened widely in wonderment. If she had been asked at that moment to describe her feelings she would not have been able to respond. Suddenly she became almost fearful of hearing the particulars of the scene. "Is there any wine about, Madeleine?"

In the semidarkness of the cottage Marcus lit the lantern and placed it on the small nightstand next to his bed. He undressed to his shorts and undershirt and hung his clothes on the pipe rack placing his boots beneath them. He propped a pillow against the headboard and swung under the light cotton blanket. He sat up and reached for a worn book of Irish poetry atop the nightstand. Marcus read Yeats for a time but noticed that his mind kept returning to the conversation at dinner and his exchange with Helene earlier in the evening. He recollected the trip to Lyon those years ago when Auguste had asked him to share the driving with her. She had wanted to visit an old man who was a friend of hers and had been recently placed in a sanitarium by his family. Marcus remembered his mild irritation as he sat in the visitors' lobby where Helene had told him to wait while she ran errands. He also recalled the tenderness with which she had treated the old farmer and the man's natural curiosity concerning Marcus' identity. Helene was briefly annoyed with his quip, "I'm the boyfriend."

On the drive home they had stopped at a small café for a light meal. While sipping her wine Helene had wistfully reminisced about the old man and Marcus observed a soft sadness that came over her features as she alluded to the rapid deterioration of his health. He surmised that Helene was having a moment of angst, that existential unease that sensitive people seem to suffer when they consider human mortality. Rather suddenly, Marcus felt a desire to comfort her and dispel her melancholy. Impulsively, he leaned toward her and kissed her lightly. She stiffened immediately, "I gave you no permission to do that."

Marcus made no response. He sat studying Helene's features. They gave what he thought was an inappropriate prudish impression. He felt absolutely no impropriety. There had been no intrigue in his gesture. To his mind, her reaction had something of the archaic about it. It suggested a lack of social experience at best and, at worst, a pronounced sense of self-importance. He had the fleeting thought that there would be a Presbyterian Pope before he ever did something similar again. Yet, from a practical side, he also noticed that his harmless gesture had had its effect. Her melancholy had passed.

It followed that a certain contention grew between Marcus and Helene. They were, of course, cordial and cooperative in the practical matters at the Deschaines residence. Both invariably put Auguste's wants and intentions ahead of any of their respective inclinations and desires. In this consideration they were bonded and there was never a need to allude to it. However, in other matters, the small as well as the significant, there was an obscure clashing of wills. One cold winter day as the three were birding on a wooded section of the property and the *Mistral* blew down the Rhone Valley with particular zest, Helene became concerned regarding Auguste's physical comfort. She asked Marcus to return to the house and fetch a muffler. In such an instance, Marcus would generally do nothing without an indication from Auguste. He did not respond to Helene's wishes.

"Marcooz," she said after a time.

"Yes?"

"Are you going to get the muffler?"

"Are you cold, Helene?"

"No, no, it's for Auguste."

"He hasn't said anything about the cold," Marcus replied, then he called out to Auguste, some distance away, "Auguste, did you want me to get you a muffler?"

"Are you cold, Irlandais?" Auguste responded mockingly.

"No, I'm fine. It's your bloody woman again."

Auguste raised one hand palm up and hunched his shoulders, indicating more or less, that Marcus should deal with it.

Helene tensed inwardly. She knew Marcus intended no slight to her by his jest yet she felt that same resentment when she thought he was not taking her seriously enough. She marched purposely back toward the house and returned in a few minutes with a heavy, red woolen muffler. She stepped directly up to Marcus and extended the muffler, "Here, put this on Auguste," she directed, and added sarcastically, "he'll feel better about it if you do it."

Marcus responded angrily, "Helene, if you were concerned about his feelings you wouldn't have gone off and gotten the muffler. It's your own feelings you're concerned with here. You put the goddamned thing on him."

Helene suppressed an urge to curse. She turned from Marcus, strode earnestly to Auguste and wrapped the muffler about his neck in quick, circular flourishes. She wheeled away from the two men and tramped away.

Sauntering over to his friend, Marcus reached into his overcoat for a cigarette, "Are you cozy now, Monsieur Deschaines? It's your color alright," he quipped snidely.

Auguste sighed deeply and slowly unwound the muffler from his neck. He dropped it into his lap and raised his field glasses to his eyes, "Women," he whispered philosophically.

Commonly, after such an occasion, Helene would be distant with Marcus for a day or two and keep her conversation with him to a bare minimum. At these times she would notice in him an equal reserve as well as a certain vacant, inattentive aspect in his eyes when they spoke. She assumed, as a matter of course, that he was reacting emotionally as she did, that is, that the muffler incident elicited a similar emotionally reflunce from him. She was sure it would pass in a short time.

She admitted to herself that she had suffered her fair share of personal snits in her life and noticed, only afterward of course, how they suddenly captured the emotional life, soured the feelings briefly and then dissipated. Helene observed also that her husband did not seem to possess this particular human frailty. His emotional makeup gave no evidence of even the slightest instability. Marcus, however, was quite capable of anger and an offhand remark by Père Bassard, regarding his temperament, had lingered in the back of her mind.

In Marcus' absence at dinner one evening, Bassard had related the incident that occurred in the shop of Anton Fedou, the village vinter. "Yes it was something to see," he had said, "poor Fedou had no idea that his disregarding Marcooz's word would get him into a precarious situation quite quickly."

"The Irish temper, eh?" Auguste offered.

"Yes, that's certainly been said of them. Yet, they are also known as a cheerful hospitable people. Marcooz, I suppose, embodies these very qualities."

Auguste thought for a moment and said, "We've known Marcooz these many years now. I can't recall ever seeing him in an enraged state."

"Nor have I, Auguste, since I wouldn't characterize his behavior in the wine shop as raging or furious. As a matter of fact he spoke quietly. There was a cool decisiveness about him."

"But wasn't it quite inappropriate for the situation?" Helene chimed in.

"As a priest, I guess I'm supposed to say yes, it was inappropriate. But as a man I must confess I enjoyed it immensely."

"I don't understand you men," Helene remarked, "the whole affair sounds stupid to me."

"Would you say as much if Marcooz were here, Helene?" Auguste asked.

"Of course I would."

"Ah, but what of his feelings, my dear?" Auguste teased.

Helene sipped her wine and smiled, "It would be for his own good."

Bassard chuckled, "Yes? Then perhaps, similarly, it was also true that heaven was using Marcooz as a corrective for Fedou's arrogance."

"Probably not," Helene answered, "let us just say our friend, Monsieur Makeeyon, can be a very touchy fellow."

"There might be some truth in what you say, Helene," Bassard responded, "but you must bear in mind that the fellow Fedou was insulting to me beforehand. I think it was this that caused Marcus to seek a means of confrontation with him."

"How can you be sure of that? How do you know it wasn't simply that he was just defending his own sense of pride or honor?" She continued.

"Because I don't think that such things concern the man," Bassard explained, "I think that at the time the most important thing to him was our friendship. He simply went to the defense of his friend. That is all."

"Really?" Helene commented, still harboring other notions concerning Marcus' behavior.

"Helene," Auguste said, "there is the possibility that you are attributing certain qualities to Marcooz that he does not possess. I'm inclined to agree with Paul's assessment of Marcus' motivation in the wine shop. You and I have often discussed what I have referred to as your abstract assumption of psychological equality between the sexes."

"And you are probably wrong again, my love," Helene grinned.

Auguste smiled and shook his head, "Suppose it were you who was with Paul in the wine shop and it were you who went to his defense as a result of Fedou's insults. I quite imagine you would have been your formidable self. But Marcooz was not simply formidable. He was downright dangerous. Therein is the difference."

"But, Auguste," Helene smilingly countered, "you are only pointing out that he is physically more able to threaten than I am by virtue of his greater size."

"Not at all, my love. Had you a weapon in that situation, would you have been ready to use it simply to intimidate Monsieur Fedou? Of course you wouldn't. You would have been scathing in your speech but nothing else. You would have said something to try to effect some psychological change in the man. Perhaps you might have been successful, but I rather think not. Marcooz, on the other hand, did not rely on speech. He did something. Fedou, in his wisdom, acquiesced. Had he not, Marcooz most certainly would have done something more. It is not really a question of physical strength, my dear, but rather one of will and intent."

"I have no idea what you're talking about, Auguste," Helene remarked.

"No, I don't suppose you do. You might now be annoyed with me should I say it is not in your nature, as a woman, to understand what I am saying. I am not saying that you cannot be as willful or intentional as a man. I am saying that as a result of your nature, whether inherited or acquired, you are not suited to attempt to impose your will or intentions in certain human situations. In other circumstances, of course, Marcooz, Paul and I are equally unsuited."

"What circumstances, Auguste?" Helene asked rhetorically.

Auguste grinned broadly, "We would be utter failures as wives and mothers."

"Speak for yourself, Deschaines," Bassard laughed, "there are priests who are quite adept at nurturing."

Auguste responded laughingly, "Indeed that is so, but did I say that a man could not be sensitive and giving? Tell me, Paul, at the seminary, did you do well in your course work on breast-feeding and the proper cleaning of dirty bottoms?"

Helene giggled, "I think that Paul would be an excellent wife and mother."

"I don't think I'll ever feel comfortable in a cassock again," Bassard commented drolly.

"Actually, Paul, I think you look rather sexy in your cassock," Helene quipped.

"Sexy? And what is sexy? Oh yes, it's the adjectival form of the word 'sex'. I'm afraid I don't know what that word means. We didn't cover it in seminary."

Helene giggled and was tempted to remark that she didn't know what it was either. But fearing that she might cause discomfiture in Auguste, she let the remark pass.

"I used to know what it meant," Auguste said with a feigned wistfulness, "but I seem to have forgotten. Maybe it means the ability to run very rapidly when someone is trying to blow you into bits."

There was a brief silence at the table. However, it was not one of discomfort or awkwardness. Helene, mildly tipsy, gazed at the refracted light scheme in the chandelier above the table. She commented pensively, "So here we three are, in continuing convivial continence," then added after a pause, "where is that damned Irlandais?"

Auguste, in the middle of a quaff of wine, burst noisily into a spasm of laughter. He was not quick enough to stop the dribble of red liquid from running down his chin.

Marcus heard the light tapping at his door. He put down the book of poetry, swung out of bed and retrieved his trousers from the rack. Upon opening the door, he saw Zalman standing in the darkness.

"Good evening, Marcus," Zalman began, "I saw the light. I hope I'm not disturbing you."

"No Zalman, you're not. I was just reading. Come in, come in."

As he stepped into the cottage, Zalman explained, "While in Marseille I got into the habit of walking about at night. I've trouble sleeping and pass the night walking on the property or reading."

"You might mention the sleeplessness to Madeleine. I think she might have some kind of tea or something for it."

"Oh yes? I'll do that."

Zalman stood before the small bookcase examining the titles, which were in English and French. "What are you reading?"

"Poetry," Marcus said, "you're welcome to anything there."

"I'm afraid I can't read English and my French vocabulary isn't very large. Auguste has a few books in German, mostly philosophy."

"Have you asked Bassard?"

"No, I hadn't thought of that."

Marcus uncorked a half-filled bottle of wine next to the sink. "Will you have a drink?"

"No thank you, I'm not much of a drinker."

Marcus poured some wine into a mug and lit a cigarette before sitting at a small table in the alcove. "Have a seat, Zalman."

The two men sat together in silence for a short time. Marcus peered into the smoke above the table. Zalman sat hunched over, hands clasped between his thighs, staring at the floor.

Reading Zalman's demeanor, Marcus asked, "Does time weigh heavily on you?"

"Yes, it does. I feel totally useless here."

"Well, I guess you would. You're been uprooted from your life and work. A man needs some kind of meaningful work."

"Helene Deschaines keeps trying to get me involved in something, but I'm afraid I've no enthusiasm anymore. My life seems to have ended since leaving Munich. It's rather like an extended nightmare from which I can't awaken."

"It's a nightmare alright, but it's not something that simply exists in your mind. It's real enough."

Zalman simply nodded, staring at the floor. Marcus thought for a moment, "Do you ever think about trying to make a trip to see your children?"

"Yes, I've thought about that and discussed it with Ruth. We seem to agree that it would be too dangerous."

"How about leaving her here and going yourself."

"I don't know," Zalman said softly.

"Well, it would probably put an edge on you. I mean, living by your wits and dealing with the danger of it."

Zalman said nothing as he considered the suggestion.

"Or you could join the Resistance. I think Bassard could put you in touch with them."

"The Resistance?"

"Sure enough, and the nice thing about it is that maybe you could get in a few licks at the Germans."

"I don't know," Zalman replied, as he considered Marcus' suggestions.

"Then, of course, there is the distinct possibility you could get your head blown off. A man could be quite enthusiastic about trying to avoid that."

Zalman smiled weakly, "I suppose that's true."

"Not being a family man, I really can't imagine what it's like to have a wife and children. I suppose you can't make decisions for yourself without taking them into account. Maybe mere survival is what should concern a family man. I don't know. It's easy for me to make these kinds of suggestions without being in your situation."

"Yes, I understand what you mean. But Marcus, sometimes I'm not sure whether I'm interested in survival for their sake, or simply for my own sake, or whether I'm interested in survival at all."

"Well, the idea of self-preservation is common to all of us and a man doesn't always know the full truth about himself in that regard."

Zalman nodded in agreement. They sat for some time lost in their own memories and imaginings. Zalman considered his sojourn since Munich, Marcus, his life in Dublin.

The steam locomotive puffed and hissed to a stop at Westland Row Station. Stepping down off the train in his slightly snug, secondhand tweed suit donated by the Squire, Marcus surveyed the bustle about him. Except at the Sligo Fair he had never seen so large a group of people in the ferment of movement. It occurred to him that there would probably be a wait before his small trunk would be offloaded from the baggage car.

He decided to try to get some information from a Dubliner concerning his bearings and the location of his lodgings. He approached an older workingman leaning against a handcart who appeared to have an open cheerful aspect about him.

"Excuse me, sir," Marcus spoke out, "will you tell me how I get to the college and Camden Row?"

The man smiled in a friendly manner, "Sure enough, lad. Are ye a student then?"

"I am, sir."

"Well farst let me tell ye, the college isn't on Camden Row."

"I know, sir, that's where my lodgings are."

"Oh yis, yis, Oi understand. Well, the college is within spittin' distance but Camden Row is a small stretch of the legs. About a moil, Oi'd say."

"A mile, is it? Well I've got to tote a trunk with me." Marcus had observed that the well-dressed travelers had been entering waiting hansoms and had guessed that the price of a fare would be beyond his liking.

"How big is yer trunk, lad?"

"Easy enough for two, but a job for one."

The man lifted his cap and scratched at his scalp. "Well, let me see now. Oi'm a baggage man and oi've got ta be helpin' with yer train that's joost come in. But, if ye wait around for an hour or so, Oi'll hunt up a cart and take ye there meself. How'd that be?"

"Ah, that would be grand, sir, I'd be grateful to you."

"Roight then, Oi'll be back to ye," the man said, pushing off with his handcart toward the rear of the train.

Marcus took the incident as an omen. Dublin would be good to him and it was here that he belonged. He walked out of the station to discover that the stately buildings of Trinity College stood before him. He strolled leisurely through the campus impressed by the dark gray, stone architectural splendor. He paused for a time below tall massive pillars wondering if the ornate capital atop them were Doric, Ionic or Corinthian. He smiled to himself thinking of Master Rayes' thoroughness. Would he be the academic equal of these serious-looking, young people trudging past him? Upon returning to the station, he found the baggage man hitching a heavy-legged horse to a cart. "Get on up lad, ye can have a good look at yer school on yer way to yer digs."

"You mean Trinity? Oh no, sir, I'm enrolled at the University near a place called St. Stephen's Green."

"Argh well, woy didn't ye say? Yer goin' to our school, is it?" The man laughed, "Now that Oi look at ye, ye don't look the Trinity man."

"Oh yes?" Marcus grinned, "and how can you tell?"

The baggage man snapped the reins putting the horse into motion, "Well, Oi know by yer country accent yer from the West, mebbe Donegal, Oi'm guessin'."

"Close enough, Leitrim."

"And yer wearin' somebody else's suit as a hand-me-down. Then, acourse, Trinity people have more than one trunk."

"Right you are," Marcus laughed.

"Not ta be impahrtinent, lad, but d'ye moind me askin' how ye can affard the schoolin'?"

"I won a scholarship from a group of people right here in Dublin. They're paying for almost all of it and my Da's employer gave me decent clothes and a nice lump of spending money."

"Well, isn't that grand for ye? Who were the Dublin people, lad?"

"Some Jewish businessmen who do such things. I got the scholarship with the help of a friend of mine who has a jewelry business somewhere near here."

"Well, Oi'll be jiggered. Jews, ye say?"

"Sure enough, they did."

"Can ye joost bate that?" The man laughed.

Marcus hungrily took in the exotic sights of the city as the cart bobbled over the cobblestone streets. The lush greenery of St. Stephen's Green passed to his left as the horse and cart swung around a corner. The baggage man pointed ahead to the right at two large Georgian buildings, "That, lad, is yer school, the Cathlic Univarsity of Oireland."

Though not as imposing as the Trinity Campus, the two granite-faced, four-story buildings were nonetheless, in Marcus' eyes, eloquent enough. He remembered the larger building was called Newman House in honor of the College's founder. He sensed he would feel right at home within its classrooms.

Passing on for a few blocks, he found himself on Camden Row before a modest two-story brick building owned by a Mrs. Mary Quinn. The baggage man helped Marcus carry his trunk to the simply furnished, second-story room. He emphatically refused Marcus' offer of recompense, "Oi've a lad about yer age, young Master McQuillan, and it's a pleasure to be helpin' ye. Good look now, and be a credit to yer people."

He shook Marcus' hand firmly and strode away down the narrow staircase. Since Mrs. Quinn had indicated that dinner was in half an hour, Marcus immediately set to unpacking while periodically peering out of his window at the vibrant city life below.

At the front of the classroom Father Charles Feeney S.J., paused briefly in his lecturing to finger through his notes arranged neatly on the lectern. Marcus used the break to lean back in his chair and stretch out his legs below the pitted, oak writing table before him. He looked upward at the delicate flowing figures in the white rococo plasterwork above. His eyes scanned the familiar frozen leaves, intertwined vegetation and feral animals but lingered on the bland cherubic faces of what were, Marcus assumed, angels. The latter evoked a mild ennui in him not unlike that caused by an extended repetitious homily at Mass. He looked down at the green and white, tiled marble floor at his feet, then out of the large paned windows to his right. The electric blue sky to the north bespoke an uncommon clarity and cold crispness in the January day.

As Father Feeney began again, Marcus had the thought that perhaps he should ink some notes as most of his classmates seemed to be doing. But it was only occasionally that the Jesuit alluded to a bit of Irish mythology with which he was unfamiliar and therefore he continued to rely on his auditory retentive skills acquired with Master Raye. Marcus was conscientious and enthusiastic with most of his first year academic coursework but this requirement in Gaelic Studies had proven an unexpected disappointment.

Father Feeney periodically paused after proffering a bit of a thesis as if hoping for a response from any of the young men before him. Finding none, he returned somberly to his well-annotated didactics. "And so, indeed, we must consider the saga of Cuchulain and Ferdiad at the Ford, although of archetypical socio-psychological moment, no more than the mere fervid imaginings of our forebears."

Marcus, on sudden youthful impulse well beyond his comprehension, was moved to speak out. His hand shot up. The Jesuit, surprised by a student response, pointed a curved finger in Marcus' direction, nodded his head toward his shoulder and said dryly, "Yes, Mr. McQuillan?"

"Are you saying, Father, that it didn't happen?"

"You mean the combat at the ford?"

"I do, Father."

"Well, isn't it obvious?"

Marcus squinted upward at the plasterwork. "Why is it obvious?"

Father Feeney's eyes fell to the lectern, "The overwhelming majority of learned men in Ireland, as well as abroad, hold that opinion. When you finish your education here, Mr. McQuillan, presumably you'll hold that opinion as well."

"That may be, Father, but right now I know it to be a fact that there's a place north of here, above Drogheda I think, that's called Ferdiad's Ford and there's a good many Irish people thinking that the combat actually took place.

"Would they be educated people, McQuillan?"

"Yes, Father, some are."

"And who might that be?"

"My schoolmaster, Master Raye of County Leitrim."

The priest smiled condescendingly. "Your schoolmaster? Yes, your country schoolmaster. I would suppose he would be somewhat educated."

Marcus felt the hot rush of anger at the slight to his mentor. "Oh, he's educated alright, Father, and without meaning any disrespect to you, I'm of the opinion that he'd know more of Irish history than you do."

At the bold remark, heads shot up around the classroom. Without betraying the slightest emotion, the old Jesuit peered intently at Marcus, "You think so, do you?"

"Yes sir, that is my considered opinion having been exposed to some education here at this University."

Father Feeney gave a tight-lipped smile, "And it is your somewhat educated opinion that the combat actually took place, eh?"

"Yes, Father."

"Why? Pray tell."

"Well, Father Feeney, after reading the many history books in our library by all those men who are generally of the opinion that those early events reported never really happened, it occurred to me that the facts they presented generally contradicted one another. So, as a group, they couldn't possibly know very much about whether those things happened or not. Now, I know by experience that Master Raye is a man of fine character who is not given to lazy sentimental thoughts. He is rigorous and demanding. Therefore, at this point, I'm inclined to take his word for it. That the combat actually happened."

"You realize, of course, you put yourself in disagreement with the faculty at this institution, some of whom are very learned men. Are you not thinking a little too highly of yourself, young Mr. McQuillan?" The priest spoke quietly with a slight trace of sarcasm.

The attention of the other students turned directly toward Marcus. "What are you going to say now, country boy?" came the unsaid challenge.

Undaunted, Marcus offered, "Well, I've no doubt there's learned men here, Father. But they've a problem. They say the accounts of prehistory by various peoples are not to be taken literally, but rather arose from their imaginative sense. But with regard to one particular people, namely the

Hebrews, they maintain that their account of prehistory is, in fact, fact. We are to accept the proposition that the Irish accounts of times long ago are not true, while the Hebrew's accounts are true. Why would a learned reasoning person have that opinion, especially when the archeological findings don't really give us an answer one way or another."

There was a scattering of suppressed chuckles throughout the classroom. A few students looked at the lad from out of the West as if through new eyes.

"Interesting question, Mr. McQuillan," the priest answered and then solemnly invoking a certain gravity and authority, intoned, "the answer to which cannot be given in a few words, especially to a young individual without the proper academic and theological preparation. I will, however, reference a few tomes you might try to grapple with in order to gain some understanding. You did not, I understand, have the benefit of a fine private school preparation as did many of our students."

It was quite apparent to most of the young men that Father Feeney had not answered Marcus' question and his suggestion of additional reading was simply an expediency to deal with his own problem. Similarly, they saw that his allusion to Marcus' schooling had the hint of pettiness about it and their glances toward one another acknowledged a measured loss of respect for the Jesuit. Father Feeney, oblivious to the sea change, flipped a page of notes and droned on.

"There are no fat Jesuits," young Liam McNamara laughed, "they're all lean and bright and hard as the stones in the street."

"Well, their order was founded by a soldier, wasn't it?" Mickey Blake chimed in. "They needed men like that when Europe was going Protestant."

"Sure and they've been thrown out of almost every country for meddling in internal affairs, haven't they?" Cherry Ross commented.

Marcus and his three friends sat on the steps outside Newman House on an unseasonably warm April day, enjoying the sun on their faces and the warmth of the granite steppingstones.

"Who's got a cigarette?" Cherry asked, looking about at his friends.

"I'm out," Marcus replied, "isn't it your turn to buy them anyway?"

"Ah, I guess it is. I think my landlord's been filching mine."

"He has?" McNamara piped, "the bugger, why don't you retaliate by doing his wife, Cherry?"

"Oh, I wish that I could. But I don't think I'm the man for it. If I had my druthers I'd like to be lying with your landlady, that fine Quinn woman."

"Argh, you dirty pig, the woman's like a mother to us. Isn't she, Marcus?"

"Yes, she is that. We're probably the best fed students at the University and our underwear is always sparkling."

Marcus' quip was not altogether an exaggeration. Mrs. Quinn took pride in being the surrogate mother for her four student lodgers. Much of her workday was spent seeing to the immediate physical needs of her boys. This could include the most menial of self-appointed tasks. The boots of her charges were, at all times, to be clean and shining. If they didn't do that task as a result of her nagging, she would, and then accuse them of sheer indolence and the unchristian laying of burdens on others. The boys' secret nickname for her was the Whiffer. Mary Quinn habitually sat up late waiting for her boys to return from a night on the town. Upon their entry into the foyer she would pounce upon them, grabbing each in turn by the lapels and pulling her determined face up to theirs. She would then demand that they exhale as she sniffed for the scent of alcohol then nosed around their necks and shoulders for the aroma of cheap perfume. They would be scolded and threatened if found to be under the influence and none of them dared to imagine their fate if the good woman discovered that they had fallen prey to a woman of the night. It was common knowledge that the corps of painted Dublin damsels stalked the university students finding them obliging and generous marks owing to their youthful randiness. Marcus was no exception to that rule. He had only escaped indulging himself on a number of occasions because of the roisterous intervention by his housemate, McNamara. "Jesus man," Liam snapped at the tipsy Marcus during the last street encounter, "will you come to your senses? The woman's old enough to be your mother and smelling like the Gardens of Versailles. The Whiffer will know for sure, you idiot. She'll throw the two of us out into the street, she will."

Notwithstanding his befuddlement, Marcus allowed that what Liam said might, after all, be true and reluctantly restrained himself. "Well, thank you for your kind offer, Ma'am, but I must be off to my bed," he said, bowing graciously, "may you be forever successful in your professional endeavors and may all your sons be Jesuits."

Upon returning to Camden Row, Marcus scored a major coup in the eyes of his fellow lodgers. He took Mrs. Quinn's olfactory inspection and subsequent berating with true upright stoicism. Then, as she finished her harangue, he lazily placed both hands to the sides of her head and planted a wet kiss on her mouth. The widow recoiled in shock. She had not been bussed like that in many years. "What in God's name was that, young man?" She demanded.

"That was a kiss, Mrs. Quinn," Marcus slurred.

"Have you no decency at all?"

"What else would one do to such a fine looking woman as yourself who makes a point of coming within kissing range?

"Marcus McQuillan, I've a good mind to write your people at home."

"Well, you do what you think you have to do, Ma'am. I couldn't help myself."

"Go to bed, Marcus, and say a prayer asking forgiveness."

"Yes, Mrs. Quinn, I'm off now but my prayer will be one of gratitude for such a grand experience."

"You too, Liam, get up the stair, the two of you," she commanded, turning away down the hall to her back bedroom.

"The young squint," she thought, "imagine that, taking those liberties with me."

Was it alcohol she tasted on her lips? She smiled wryly. "He'll make some lass happy, that boyo will. I hope to God she's able for him."

She spoke to her long departed husband, as she often did. "He's as bad as you, Jimmy, a handsome devil of a man, a natural heart breaker and hell raiser. Ah, but I was able for you always, wasn't I Jimmy boy, me, Mary Docherty, James Quinn's one true love."

She considered treating herself to a short one before bed and thought of the rapscallion upstairs. She blessed herself quickly and began to undress.

At the end of the term, Marcus returned home to Leitrim after paying his proper respects to his benefactor, Avram Goldner. Goldner was genuinely pleased with Marcus' first year academic achievements and offered him summer work in the Dublin jewelry shop. Marcus, however, was anxious to see his family again and help his father on the Squire's holdings. The Squire had substantially increased his kennel of greyhounds and the high-spirited racers needed feeding, grooming and training in the fields above and north of Lough Gill. Marcus carried home with him an additional canvas satchel filled with a variety of books on loan from the University library. He intended to share these with Master Raye.

The summer passed quickly and in September Marcus returned by rail to Camden Row and a full schedule of academics. Liam, Cherry and Marcus resumed their fellowship. The fourth of the musketeers, Mickey

Blake, sent word that he hadn't the means to continue schooling and had joined the British Army.

Marcus' reputation as the casual scholar went before him. He had the respect of his classmates owing to his easygoing nature, lack of pedantry and ready willingness to help other students with the thornier aspects of required course work. When asked by Cherry on one occasion how he was able to retain the voluminous material given in lectures without the benefit of extensive note taking, Marcus explained it as an ingrained technique learned from Master Raye. "The man taught me to make vivid imaginative pictures in my mind as I listened to him. That's visual, of course, but you can do it with single words and expressions, as well. The important trick is not to let your mind be distracted by other things, otherwise you just have a jumble of images or no images at all. If Father Keane speaks about St. Thomas, keep your mind in the Middle Ages. Don't let it wander into the streets of Dublin or to your sweetheart back home."

"That's not so easy to do, Marcus," young Cherry replied.

"Well, it's a function of the will, isn't it?"

"Will? You mean the strength of sheer will power?"

"Well, if you have to fight for it, doesn't that mean you're not all that happy with the learning to begin with? If you really want to learn something then paying attention shouldn't be too hard, should it?"

"I guess that makes sense."

"I kind of think that the lads who are having trouble here at the University are those who would rather be doing something else. That was true of Mickey, wasn't it?"

"I think you're right about that alright," Cherry agreed.

"Aah, poor Mickey, he'll be paying attention now, I'm thinking. Some British sergeant will see to that."

"I hope to God the poor bugger doesn't end up dodging Boer bullets in the Transvaal. That's where the troops are going these days."

"If he's sent there, our Mickey better damned well mind what's going on about him."

The boys continued their converse as they strolled north on Grafton Street toward the Liffey. A short time ago, they had been well fed on the mutton and potatoes of Mrs. Quinn's Saturday evening dinner. "Shall we do one or two pints and maybe search out some of the lads?" Marcus suggested.

"Ah, we might then, but I'm a bit short, Marcus,"
Cherry answered.

"It's alright, I've a few coins."

"Well, it's my lucky day, it is. I'm invited to the table of your grand landlady for a fine Saturday dinner and now I'm to be treated to a pint. My stars must be set in proper place."

"We can't be too long. I've got to get back and stick my nose in a French text. I promised Liam we'd knock it down together."

"Where will we go?"

"How about Hogan's up by Custom's House Quay."

"Hogan's it is."

The boys proceeded on past the Trinity campus for a few blocks, then just over the Liffey they entered a small public house which catered primarily to workingmen and students. The dark smoky alehouse was crowded and it took a few minutes for Marcus and Cherry to position themselves against the counter and get the attention of the balding, red-faced bartender. "Two pints please," Marcus sang out, dropping the proper coins on the bar top.

The bartender nodded, poured out the pints, scraped the excess tan foam away and then let them sit for a bit in order to attain gaseous equilibrium. With their glasses filled to the brim with dark brown porter and clasped close to their chests, the two maneuvered their way through the knots of drinkers toward the dim posterior of the pub. Marcus made eye contact with a somewhat familiar face. The tall, thin, bespectacled young fellow nodded toward the empty seats beside him at the table. As Marcus sat beside him, the bleary-eyed fellow inquired, "You're McQuillan aren't you?"

"I am, and my friend here is Cherry Ross. You're an upperclassman at the University, aren't you?"

"Aye, the name's Joyce, Jim Joyce. Now, wasn't it you who gave old Feeney a hard time last year in the Gaelic studies?" Joyce asked, grinning slightly.

"A hard time? No, I don't think so. I just asked some obvious questions after he told me that I was missing the obvious."

"Didn't you tell him that your country schoolmaster knew more Irish history than he did?"

"Well, I did that, I guess."

"Really? Remarkable, that is. That's really remarkable."

The three students drank their porter and discussed aspects of their specific studies and University life in general, salting the conversation with hyperbole, jesting and the inevitable criticism of their Jesuit instructors.

"Aah, but in the final analysis these birds are driven by an iron will," Cherry was saying.

"That's part and parcel of their initial training," Joyce indicated, "they're not like Franciscans or Dominicans. Their special spiritual exercises develop the will, not the intellect."

"Is that true, Joyce?" Marcus asked.

"I was told that by an old Franciscan friar before I attended the University. He said that the Jesuit's reputation for academic excellence is a bit of a myth. They've never produced an Aquinas or Bonaventure, have they? Those that can, do. Those that can't, teach. That's why I was interested when I heard that you made that remark about your schoolmaster to Feeney."

"But I think they do well enough in teaching the basics," Marcus commented.

"I suppose they're good enough for this insular place," Joyce continued.

"You mean Ireland?" Cherry queried.

"I do. Ireland's a backward country without the innate capacity to develop a civilization of its own, rather like a piglet at the teat of the old sow Britannia. We can't even throw off the yoke of our Anglo-Saxon keepers. Do we even use a language of our own, for Christ's sake? No, if a man wants a good education from life and intends to make an impact, he's got to go to England or over to the continent. Dublin's obviously not London and it sure as hell isn't Paris."

"Hmm, you think that, do you?" Marcus commented, rubbing his chin and squinting toward the ceiling. "You might be right there, Joyce, you might be right there."

"Then, is there nothing of true worth in Ireland?" Cherry asked.

Joyce suddenly beamed. "Actually, there is, Cherry, there is indeed. Somehow or other, and I'm not saying I understand the reasons for it, but somehow or other, we're better at the English language than the English are. That's the one thing we have, gentlemen, our literature. Notwithstanding Shakespeare, Irish literature is second to none."

Joyce continued giving forth over the following hour. Marcus and Cherry listened attentively to his erudite musings on the state of affairs in Ireland given with a certain eloquence of expression. "The fellow's living proof of his thesis," Marcus thought to himself.

At the end of the second pint, Marcus and Cherry made ready to leave. Rising, Marcus remarked, "It's been a pleasure, Mr. Joyce, we'll blather again, will we not?"

Joyce looked up and grinning through slightly drooping eyelids, he assented, "We will, lads, we will."

Marcus saw Joyce now and again as they passed each other with friendly nods in the green marble hallways of Newman House. Joyce, Marcus noted, tended to be a loner, the kind of person who seems to be contentedly absorbed by his own perceptions and mental processes. One late May afternoon after mathematics class, as Marcus was leaving Newman, he saw Joyce sitting alone on a bench across the street in St. Stephen's Green. He crossed over and approached along the gravel path that led into the park. "Jim Joyce, deep in his cogitations, how are you?"

"Ah, McQuillan," Joyce responded, removing his glasses and rubbing his eyes, "are you done for the day?"

"I am. Are you reading something?" Marcus asked, noting the book at Joyce's side.

"No, not at the moment, anyway. I'm just at ease and eyeing the skirts now and again."

"That's best done on Sunday afternoon. There's a regular parade out here."

"I'll keep that in mind. Do you come down here on Sundays, then?"

"Aye, Liam and I generally come here after Mass and enjoy the comeliness passing through."

"Mass? Don't tell me you still do that?"

"Oh yes indeed," Marcus laughed, "our landlady, a woman not to be crossed, sees to it."

"Under the gun, is it?"

"Sure enough."

"I've the same requirement from my people at home. I take care of it by absenting myself for a few hours Sunday morning. They probably suspect, but they don't ask about it. Tell me, if it weren't for the landlady, would you be going?"

"I don't know. Maybe it would be a now and again thing. I'd probably keep my hand in though."

"You strike me as too intelligent to be a practicing Catholic, McQuillan."

"Really? Well, to date I haven't discovered anything more comprehensive or deeper that the Church's dogmatics. But that doesn't mean I won't."

"Well, it's nice to know you've an open mind. A man must have freedom of thought before all else."

"Well, human freedom is another thing altogether, isn't it? Tell me, Joyce, are you free not to look at the skirts?"

Joyce laughed easily, "An interesting point there, do I have thoughts or do the thoughts have me?"

The likelihood of an extended discussion on religion and its trappings was squelched as Joyce's eye fell on the sunlit shapely rump of a woman across the spacious green lawn. "Am I free not to look upon that delightful derriere over there?" Joyce said as he nodded toward the woman.

"You're probably free only after you reflect on it. Before that it's instinctive, isn't it?"

"Yes, it appears so," Joyce grinned, "the women have this terrible power over us, don't they? Concupiscence is quicker than cognizance."

Marcus laughed, "Joyce, are you making a case for celibacy? Must desire be sacrificed on the altar of reason?"

"My God, I hope not. Might it not be, McQuillan, that our unmediated desire is integral to creation?"

"Well, it certainly appears to be the *sine qua non* for procreation, alright."

An ironic grin crossed Joyce's features. "We're stuck in our nature that consists of desire, ambition, dissatisfaction and the rest of it."

With a wicked chuckle he continued, "It's a terrible thought to have that the priests might, after all, be the happiest of men."

"The secret of life then," Marcus gaily offered, "is to give women their due and then have no more to do with them."

"Ah, but they'd insist on defining their due, wouldn't they?"

"Right enough, and they do seem to do just that, don't they? My God, if my mother heard me now she'd be giving me a clout on the head."

"Mine too, but my Da would give me secret sympathy I'm thinking. I remember his telling me once, after he'd had a few, that he'd discovered the secret of women. He said it's a strange thing but the more you get to know them, the less you like them and trust them. With men, he said, you can have true friendship. With women, the best you'll get is a comfortable arrangement."

Marcus laughed, "Is your Da a, what is the word, woman hater?"

"Misogynist. No, my Da isn't that sort. He hates no one. He's been a good husband and father over the years, but he's remained his own man, I'd guess."

"You know, while my schoolmaster was advising me about going to college, he asked me from out of the blue if I ever considered becoming a priest. I never quite understood what he was driving at. Now, I'm thinking he meant that I should consider the implications of marriage and the family on my career. He's married, has many children and must struggle continually to put bread on the table. I think Master Raye might have been trying to tell me something at the time. I don't know."

"He probably was. I think you've got the makings of a scholar, McQuillan, and I'm not sure at all that scholarship and changing nappies can be a good mix."

Joyce and Marcus sat in silence for a short time. "So what do you expect will be happening to us, Joyce?" Marcus asked.

"I don't know rightly. I'll not be married in the foreseeable future. In the meantime, it'd be grand to be able to indulge myself whenever the opportunity arises."

"If you don't mind my asking, are you very experienced along those lines?"

"Experienced? Some, I'd say, a few times with girls on a roof or down an alleyway and a few times with the professionals. And you?"

"Not much to speak of, an incident or two of pawing and rolling around."

"*Frottage.*"

"What's that you said?"

"*Frottage,* a French word meaning friction or rubbing, it does quite nicely sometimes."

"I've been drunk and come near to it with a few prostitutes, but Mrs. Quinn watches for that like a hawk."

"Look now, I've a friend, McQuillan, a young lady and a very decent person. Would you like me to introduce you? I'll bring her to the park this Sunday, if you like. Bring Cherry along and that other mate of yours."

"Sounds grand. I'll be looking forward to it."

Frequently, during the class lectures throughout the week, Marcus found himself drifting from attentiveness into imagined scenarios of the much anticipated Sabbath sensuality. He allowed himself the indulgence. Liam and Cherry were enthusiastically animated upon hearing of the opportunity and carried on much like children on the eve of a visit by Father Christmas.

Hard fate struck on Saturday afternoon. Marcus came down with a fever quickly diagnosed by Mrs. Quinn as a touch of the influenza. He was abed on Sunday morning, damp with sweat, sipping hot tea and reading Newman's *Idea of a University.* He often found himself staring out of his window at the cloud patterns above the Dublin rooftops. Liam, without the support of his confrère, suffered an acute case of the puckers and begged off. He suspected divine intervention.

Cherry Francis Ross strode manfully into the park on Sunday afternoon carrying the heavy mantle of male honor. The buxom Maisie Driscoll was immediately pleased with the fresh-faced university lad as she spied his approach while sitting demurely on the appointed bench beneath the oak tree. The factory girl fairly beamed as she walked out with her well-mannered ersatz suitor, a fully qualified part of the Dublin Sunday promenade. As Joyce had promised, Maisie was a decent sort. That evening, amid the boxes and crates of a small backroom in Maisie's place of employment, Cherry suffered the delights of gratitude.

Poissy motored down the main street of Couderouge looking to his left for the turnoff onto Ormeau Road. He had asked a farmer standing by the roadside before entering the village for directions to the Deschaines residence. The old man had obliged him while correcting his mispronunciation of the family name and the address. When he saw the road leading past the church, Poissy made a left knowing that the stone pillars of the estate were but a few kilometers straight ahead.

From the waist up Poissy was in mufti. He did not want to chance the trip north along the highway in his uniform while also driving a vehicle bearing the conspicuous Milice insignia. In the morning he had secured an old, battered blue Citroën from the motor pool. Just after driving out of Privas he had pulled to the side of the highway and removed his beret, jacket, shirt and tie. He stuffed them into a canvas bag. Claude quickly donned a white shirt and gray, flannel sports coat. If stopped by a German patrol he planned to produce his Milice identity papers with the assertion that he was involved in undercover investigative work. Should the Resistance stop him, he intended to claim that he was in the process of deserting the Milice and on his way to joining the Free French. He knew the latter possibility could be an inherently dicey proposition for him.

At the stone pillars Poissy again pulled to the side of the road and changed back into his full uniform. He drove boldly up the gravel driveway and parked before the main entrance. He closed the car door and stood for a moment looking about casually with his hands behind his back. He wished to give the impression of confident nonchalance to anyone watching from the house.

He knocked firmly at the front door then stepped back. Again, putting his hands behind his back, he turned and looked back down the driveway. He heard the door opening and a woman's voice. "Yes?"

He did not turn immediately but pretended he was observing something toward the road. He slowly came about and saw an attractive, full-bosomed middle-aged woman wearing a gray work dress standing in the doorway.

"You are the proprietor?" Poissy asked curtly.

"Do I look like I'm the proprietor here?" came the sarcastic response.

Poissy, slightly flustered, continued, "No, of course not Madame, er, I mean, well ah, is the owner at home?"

"What is your business with him?"

"Um, uh, security business."

"That is obvious from that uniform," Madeleine commented with obvious contempt.

"Is the proprietor available, Madame?" Poissy asked thinly.

"I'll see," she said, and abruptly closed the door.

Poissy stood uneasily at the door for several minutes quite unsure as to what posture he should try to affect. He tensed slightly as Madeleine opened the door and stood to one side indicating that he should enter. "Wipe your boots and take your cap off, Monsieur Milicien. You may see Monsieur Deschaines for a very brief time," she said harshly.

Thoroughly intimidated, Claude did as he was told and was escorted down the hallway to Deschaines's study. He was immediately impressed and somewhat cowed when he saw the commanding figure sitting behind the large desk. He hesitated before entering the room.

"Yes?" Auguste said sternly.

The unnerved Milicien tightly gripped his beret in his hands, "Pardon me, Monsieur Deschaines, I am Sergeant Claude Poissy of the Milice Francaise. I am required, as part of my duties you understand, to conduct a survey of the residents in this area."

"For what purpose?" Auguste asked coldly.

"You see, Monsieur, I am seeking the most general of information in order to facilitate the protection of the local populace. In these sad times it is necessary for the authorities to have sufficient information, the demographic facts as it were."

"What is your name again?"

"Sergeant Claude Poissy"

"Sergeant Poissy, the unfortunate demographic facts are these. These are indeed sad times for there are invaders in our country. They are all about. If you and your authorities were so concerned about protecting the local populace you would do something about these foreign aggressors, would you not? You would not help them subjugate France, would you?"

Poissy reddened with shame. He could not find words to answer Deschaines' barbed question. In an odd way he was grateful that he was alone before this impressive man. The presence of fellow Miliciens would have required the maintenance of that shallow assertiveness of which he had become so adept. "I do what I am ordered to do, Monsieur, I agreed to that when I put on this uniform."

"Do you really think that uniform represents the interests of France, Sergeant?"

"I thought so at one time, Monsieur Deschaines."

"And now, Claude Poissy?"

"I don't know," Poissy replied, looking down at his hands.

Auguste said nothing. He studied the nervous man before him and was moved by his own natural softheartedness, "Ask your questions, Sergeant," he said softly.

A sudden melancholy came upon Poissy. He felt himself a clumsy intruder into the lives of decent people, a charlatan playing at respectability, an imposter in a clownish uniform. His masquerade weighed on him as he gazed out the windows of the study. He began to feel the mild sting of tears forming in his eyes. He said quietly, "I really have no questions, Monsieur Deschaines. No one sent me here. I came of my own accord and I came only with the hope of securing my own future. But I can see that I have no future to speak of. I have no future among decent Frenchmen. I've made a terrible mistake and I made that mistake because of my foolish notions of self-importance."

Poissy looked down at the carpet to hide his tears. "I'm sorry, Monsieur, I'll leave now."

He turned to leave the study. "Poissy," Auguste directed, "sit down. We are not finished."

Taken by surprise, the sergeant did as he was told. He sat before Deschaines in the leather easy chair.

"For the record," Auguste indicated, "there are none on the premises who are not French citizens. The one exception is an Irishman who's been living in France for many years."

"An Irlandais, Monsieur?" Poissy asked in sudden surprise, "is his name Makeeyon?"

"You know Marcooz?"

Poissy was tempted to claim a friendly relationship with Marcus in order to ingratiate himself with Auguste. He avoided the small dishonesty and said simply, "Well, we met one time."

"Ah yes, I remember his telling me a short time ago that he was stopped on the road by the Milice. You were the officer?"

"Yes, yes I was. He is quite a character, that Irlandais."

"Marcooz is an exceptional man, Poissy. He is my dearest friend."

Poissy nodded, "Is Monsieur Makeeyon about?"

"I believe he is. I'll call him in and we'll continue our chat, eh?"

"Yes, yes, do that, Monsieur Deschaines."

Auguste picked up the large brass bell on his desk and shook it vigorously. Poissy winced, imagining that even a person at a kilometer's distance would hear its clanging.

They waited. Noticing the cigarette butts in a nearby ashtray, Poissy fished his pack from his jacket and offered one to Auguste. "No thank you, Sergeant, but you have one."

As Poissy lit up, he heard footsteps coming down the hallway toward the study. He quietly hoped it was not that harridan of a servant. It was Marcus who came striding through doorway. "Officer Sticky, what the hell are you doing here?"

Poissy corrected him, "Claude Poissy, Monsieur Makeeyon, it is Poissy."

Marcus had used the French word, *poisseux,* meaning "sticky" in making a small joke at the sergeant's expense. Poissy had not been called Claude Sticky since his days in the schoolyard.

Auguste smiled and interjected, "Monsieur Poissy is on a, ah, social call and he inquired after you, Marcooz."

"He did, did he? Well now, back where I come from that calls for a drink. We'll have a drink, won't we?"

Marcus pulled down three glasses from the shelf above Auguste and set them on the desk. Auguste withdrew a bottle of expensive cognac from a lower drawer and gave each glass a good measure of the dark brandy.

The three men immediately entered into a male palaver concerning the present state of affairs in wartime France. Auguste and Marcus saw no point in concealing what was, after all, a ubiquitous contempt for the Vichy government and the Milice Française.

"You've got yourself in a hell of a fix, Poissy. The Allies are sure to prevail over the Nazis. What in God's name will you do when Vichy collapses?" Marcus asked.

"I have no idea at the moment," Claude responded feeling the effect of the cognac, "perhaps you people will hide me, eh?"

"Well, perhaps we can shoot you and bury you out back," Auguste offered, "we'll say you died gallantly in a firefight with a German patrol after undergoing a sudden patriotic conversion."

"I do not aspire to that kind of sacrifice, Monsieur Deschaines," Poissy countered in mock protest, "I would prefer to die of old age if you don't mind."

The three men laughed at the irony of Poissy's predicament. The sergeant suddenly remembered the young informant. "I must tell you something, my friends. I found your residence through information given to me by a certain unpleasant young fellow in your village. He said that several foreigners were living here. I think he said there were foreign Jews here."

"His name?" Auguste asked.

"I really don't remember. I believe I have a note on it back at the office."

"Was it Fleury, Maurice Fleury?" Marcus queried.

"Yes, Makeeyon, I think that's it. He has a bad complexion, yes?"

"That little bastard," Marcus said through clenched teeth.

"Marcooz," Auguste intoned gravely, "that will have to be dealt with. That must be taken care of."

Poissy noticed the serious exchange between the two, "My God, Monsieur Deschaines, you do not have Jews here, do you?" He blurted out in surprise.

Marcus and Auguste looked grimly at each other then turned to Poissy. He knew he was being closely scrutinized now and the wrong remark on his part might prove costly, perhaps fatal. These men were not the shallow frightened men with whom he was accustomed to dealing. These men, it seemed, could be the very best of friends but also the fiercest and deadliest of enemies. He wondered if Auguste kept a revolver in his desk. He guessed that he did. Could the Irlandais use the bottle of brandy as a weapon? Probably.

"Gentlemen, may I ask a question?" Poissy smiled, taking a quaff of cognac.

"Yes?" Auguste answered.

"What will happen if I decide to leave now?"

Marcus grinned and laughed soundlessly, "You'll not make the door."

"I thought as much. May I have another cognac, *s'il vous plaît?*"

Helene Deschaines noticed the old Citroën in the driveway as she returned on her bicycle from marketing in Couderouge. Madeleine immediately informed her of the presence of the Militiaman. "Where are Zalman and Ruth?" Helene asked anxiously.

"I told Ruth to go back to the apartment and remain out of sight, Madame."

"Yes, that's good. Is the Milicien in the study with Auguste?"

"Yes, he is. Marcooz went in some time ago."

Helene hoped that the Milicien had come on a purely routine matter. She was aware that roundups were usually conducted by squads of soldiers and Milice in trucks. She walked briskly through the house and stopped to listen in the hallway just past the stairs. Was that laughter she heard? She continued warily down the hallway and into Auguste's study.

"Ah Helene, my love, are you done with your marketing?" Auguste sang out as she entered.

She looked at Auguste, Marcus and the uniformed stranger who stood and smiled insipidly at her. They were drunk.

"You've been drinking, drinking at this time of day? What is going on?" she scolded.

Auguste gaily explained, "Helene, love of my life, we are celebrating Monsieur Claude Poissy's resignation from the Milice Francaise. Claude, my friend, may I introduce my lovely wife, Madame Helene-Marie Deschaines?"

In a flat business-like tone Helene remarked, "Congratulations, Monsieur, I'm glad you've come to your senses."

"Well Helene," Marcus slurred, "it was that or we were going to finish him, right here, right now. But it seems he's a good old bird and it would have been a terrible misuse of a bullet. Besides, we knew you'd have a great snit for yourself about the blood on the carpet. Isn't that right, Auguste?"

"Correct," Auguste agreed.

Helene sighed and looked upward. "Will you two be sober enough for dinner? Your friend should eat something too. He's in no condition to drive."

"A wonderful idea. You'll stay for dinner, Claude?" Auguste asked.

"Yes, my friend, I'd enjoy that," Poissy responded. He was confident that no one would come out from headquarters to look for him. His superiors would assume he had broken down or run into the worst kind of trouble. In the case of the latter, they would find neither his body nor the vehicle. To cover himself upon return he would concoct a story about a breakdown in an isolated rural area, his reluctance to seek help among the citizenry and his spending an uncomfortable night in the Citroën.

When Helene returned to the kitchen, she indicated the plans for dinner to Madeleine and alluded to the men's tipsiness.

The cook laughed. "Madame Deschaines, those men will be in no fit condition for a formal meal. Let's you and I eat here after I bring up a portion of stew for them. It will be ready soon."

An hour later Helene and her cook carried the stew, bread, plates and silverware up to the study. They placed them on a large maple side table below the window. Auguste nodded his thanks and resumed talking to Claude. He was speaking of Verdun as Poissy sat before him, leaning forward in attentiveness. Marcus had dozed off, his arms folded across his chest, his crossed legs stretched out from his chair and his cap covering the top half of his face.

"Men. They can be so stupid. How is it that we can love them, Madame?" Madeleine asked soon after they returned to the kitchen.

"I don't know. My Auguste is perhaps the most mature and urbane man I've ever known but there are those times when he is no more than a boy."

"You have been very fortunate in your marriage, Madame, my husband was a boy most of the time."

The women sat at the kitchen table, eating their stew and moving the bits of vegetables and meat about with their large spoons."Ah, but I had my children, so he was good for something, eh?" Madeleine continued.

Helene smiled weakly, "That is a wonderful thing for you. Are you looking forward to having grandchildren?"

"Yes, of course I am." Madeleine knew of Helene's regret in not having children of her own. She would not broach the subject without Helene's initiative.

"Until you see your family again, you have Marcooz, eh?"

"Yes, that's true. I have Marcooz." Madeleine hesitated wondering whether or not to maintain the direction of the conversation. She was quite aware of Helene's curiosity about their relationship and she knew it involved something much deeper than sexuality. She regarded Helene, as the latter looked downward playing with the floating viands in the stew, her head leaning lazily against a supporting hand. "Madame is quite a pretty woman," she thought, "it is so terribly sad that she is denied lovemaking."

Madeleine felt compassion for the gentle wistful woman. She wanted to show affection for her. She wanted to express her fondness for her. What could she give her? True to her nature, she chose to be open and direct. "Madame, it is not me who Marcooz loves."

Helene lifted her head and gazed at Madeleine with apprehension anticipating what she was about to say. "Oh yes, it is you and no other, Madame Deschaines. That Irlandais loves you. He has a warm affection for me and he is my friend, but without doubt, he is in love with you."

"Oh Madeleine, what can I say?"

"There is no need to say anything. I know you are apprehensive about it. You are concerned for everyone who lives here at your home. But you shouldn't really concern yourself with that. It is a problem for no one, including your husband."

"What?" Helene's eyes widened in anxiety, "you are saying Auguste knows?"

"Don't be a foolish little girl, Madame, of course your husband knows. Père Bassard knows. Everyone here knows. And everyone here knows that it's none of their business. Marcooz is a decent man and he would do nothing to offend you or Auguste."

There was silence for a moment as Helene stared ahead and considered what Madeleine had just said. She relaxed somewhat with the realization of Madeleine's common sense observations.

Madeleine smiled knowingly and continued, "So there is no danger or unhappy implications for anyone, is there? No, there will be no trouble. Everything will remain as it is."

Helene nodded her agreement with Madeleine's assessment. "No, no trouble. Everything is fine," and then, after a pregnant pause, Madeleine added, "but that is exactly the problem, *n'est-ce pas,* Madame?"

Again Helene sat erect in alarm. "Problem? What problem? What do you mean?"

"Everything is fine for everyone. But not for you, your problem remains."

"Madeleine, I have no problem."

Madeleine did not smile but looked challengingly and directly into Helene's eyes. "Madame, either we are going to converse honestly or not. If you do not want to discuss it with me, that is all right. We can close the subject. But understand, Madame Deschaines, I will not speak of it again. And I will specifically avoid talking to you about the Irlandais."

Helene considered the very real implications of the cook's remarks. Did she wish to talk about her private feelings? Did she want to admit that she was not happy in her cool contained chastity? Her eyes misted. "Yes, you are right again, Madeleine. I have my values. I live with them from day to day. But it is not easy. I envy you your strength, your freedom, your lack of inhibition. I have physical desires but I can do nothing about them. There is no one for me."

Seeing Helene's unhappiness, Madeleine sought relief for her in humor. "There is old Philibert."

Helene smiled weakly. "Père Bassard?" Madeleine asked inanely.

Helene's gazed down at the floor, her shoulders slumping imperceptibly. "Helene Deschaines," Madeleine said sharply, "you must go for that Irlandais. Go for him."

Helene perked up with sudden interest, "Oh, I couldn't. I wouldn't know what to do. I don't have enough experience with men. I'd feel so terribly awkward about it. I'd feel guilty afterward."

"No, no, Madame. Your problem is much worse than that."

"Worse? How can it be worse than that? Do you mean that you would be jealous of us? Is that it?"

Madeleine howled in glee. "Jealous? Oh no, *ma cherie*, I would not be jealous at all. I would be happy for you. You must believe me."

"Then what?"

"Well you see, unfortunately the object of our mutual desire happens to be the closest of friends with your husband. It is almost sure that he would see intimacy with you as a betrayal of his friendship with the Monsieur. The Irlandais is sometimes a fool but he is never a small man seeking for himself. That is your ultimate problem, Madame, and I don't think there is a solution to it. *Quel dommage.*"

"Oh, I didn't consider that. I've been thinking of my honor only. It's true. Marcus would not assent to intimacy with me no matter what I did. There again it is an indication of my ignorance with regard to men. In the past, when I was younger, I was able to relate so much better to women."

"Yes, I know," Madeleine smiled.

"You know? How could you know?"

"Madame, I've had some experience along those lines. I've always assumed you have as well. Let us call it women's intuition."

Helene was truly startled and intrigued by the cook's admission. "You've had experience with women?"

"Yes, when I was a young woman I was involved with an older couple. They were both wonderful people and it was a beautiful experience for me. Then, of course, you'll remember that my husband was absent from me for quite some time."

"You've been involved in a ménage à trois?"

"Oh yes, I have indeed. I have never spoken to anyone about it except to my girlfriend back in Marseille. I was young and employed by a wealthy family in my hometown. Despite the difference in our ages, the woman and I became close friends. Our affection for one another grew and one day she simply asked me if I wished to be part of the lovemaking between her and her husband. I did."

"In retrospect, do you think you were seduced?" "

Madeleine giggled and played with the hair at the side of her head. "Seduced? Oh no, I had had considerable experience before them. The Monsieur, after all, was quite attractive. He was a gentleman. They both treated me with respect and kindness over the years."

"Over the years?"

"Oh yes, of course. We were friends, you see? Even after I was married they continued to be my friends. I stopped seeing them only because my husband and I moved to Marseille."

"And your husband, did he know?"

"No, he never did."

"You couldn't tell him?"

With a wry cool smile, Madeleine asked, "Madame Deschaines, are you going to discuss your desire for Marcus with your husband? He would certainly understand, *n'est-ce pas*?"

Helene also grinned coyly, "No, I suppose not. I had some difficulty in telling him of my previous relationships with women but I distinctly remember that his acceptance of that put me immediately at ease. But this, well, I don't think I will mention it."

The two women laughed in mutual recognition of their covertness. Madeleine said, "Perhaps if we spoke of it we would lose some of the excitement of it, the intrigue of it, the delicious forbiddance of it."

"Delicious? Yes, oh yes, that's exactly the word, delicious."

Madeleine's hand slid across the table and sought Helene's. Their fingers intertwined. Their eyes met and went moist and soft in tender understanding. They smiled ever so delicately in sweet sharing.

"Helene, tu es belle."

Madame Annette-Yvonne Brun was a vain woman. She was also religious. In her own mind she could have been the most devout and effective *religieuse*. Instead of the deserted wife, Annette felt that as Mother Superior Marie Magdalene she would have, no doubt, found her true calling. She would have run an elite private school for girls or a hospital renowned for its tender care and periodic cures suggesting the miraculous. But alas, because of her natural beauty and flair, God had seen fit to make her the object of desire for one Louis Brun, a would-be artist working as a ticket seller in the *Gare de Vincennes.*

One warm June evening in 1895, Louis had taken the plain mawkish Annette boating on one of the small lakes in the *Bois de Boulogne*. With his dark hair and lively brown eyes, Louis was able to arrange discreet assignations for himself from time to time outside the knowledge of his fiancée in Montmartre. Convinced he hung on her every word, Mlle. Didier had talked almost incessantly as Louis lazily pulled at the oars moving slowly away from the other rowboats toward a sheltered cove. It was not quite dark enough to suit him as he watched the reddening western sky over the Paris rooftops. A few times he had leaned forward and bussed her lightly on the lips gladly noticing her appreciative demure smile in response. He had two aims in these apparently harmless gestures. The first was the softening of her defenses, the second, and of equal importance to him, was the stemming of the flow of her maudlin chatter. With his patience wearing thin and because he was quite ready to apologize profusely and row directly for the pier, he decided to risk outraged rejection. "Annette, Annette," he sighed, "I cannot help myself, I must have you."

He embraced her and kissed her firmly. She did not resist. Annette, cocksure of the truth of his plea, acquiesced as he lowered her gently to the bottom of the boat and happily allowed the subsequent fumbling with her underclothes. In this way was Helene-Marie Brun conceived.

The trysting continued for several weeks before Annette realized she was with child. Louis immediately received a visit at the train station from Annette, her father and two brothers. Within two weeks the couple was married in a simple ceremony in a side chapel in the *Basilique du Sacre Coeur*. Annette's mother was cousin to one of the deacons.

Annette moved in with Louis in his tiny apartment three blocks from the train station and at once began reordering the elements of his life. The baby was born in February and was considered by the hospital nurses as quite comely owing to the fact that she favored Louis. They were none too happy with the incessant complaints of the child's mother but delighted by the flirtatious attention of her father.

The arrangement lasted for just over seven years. Louis left Annette and Helene and moved in with his old sweetheart in Montmartre. He would have liked to share himself between the two domiciles but the women would not have it.

Naturally, Annette was bitter and in an insidious way began to retaliate against Louis by the subtle demeaning of his pretty, brown-eyed daughter. The little girl, unaware that she was not loved, was persuaded over time that she was inelegant, uncomely and clearly without her mother's artistic sensitivities. Her inborn ability to run and gambol with the neighborhood street urchins was severely curtailed. The sweet, unassuming little girl's religious education consisted of a directed devotion to the fair-haired, blue-eyed, vanilla Virgin.

There were, of course, the frequent suggestions that men and boys were, in some indistinct way, dangerous and dirty as well as, most importantly, untrustworthy. Helene was ten years old when she heard, by chance, about the one and only thing that boys were interested in getting from girls. It had something to do with the "downthere" area, the unmentionable part of the human anatomy. Consequently, a nameless obscure anxiety engendered a constant scrupulosity in her personal hygiene and tended to dampen her desire to play with other children in anything that had the element of risk. Helene became, for the little boys along *Rue Adelard*, the girl who inevitably tried to change the rules once the game was underway. Almost predictably, her first love was a delicate, flaxen-haired *fillette* who sat across from her in class and had eyes the color of sapphire.

The men had spent the night in Auguste's study. There evolved a mutual agreement that Claude should return to his duties in Privas to serve as mole within the Milice Française. In this way valuable intelligence could be passed through Auguste and Marcus to Père Bassard and thence to agents of the Maquis. Poissy was not informed of Bassard's role as link in the chain of information.

At first light, Marcus accompanied Claude to the Citroën where the Milicien changed back into mufti. Poissy had performed his morning toiletries with a quick rinsing of his mouth with wine. As he sat behind the steering wheel, he lit a cigarette and looked up, grinning at his new friend. "Are you sober enough to make the drive, Claude?" Marcus asked.

"Oh, I think so, my friend. I hope if I run into the Maquis, they'll get me with the first burst."

"Ah lad," Marcus laughed, "that's the spirit."

"And you people will be taking care of that Fleury fellow?"

"He's sure to be dealt with."

The men remained silent for a time as if Poissy were reluctant to leave. He started the engine, "*Au revoir,* Irlandais."

Marcus lifted his right hand in a thumbs-up gesture and watched as Poissy backed down the driveway onto Ormeau Road. As Poissy shifted into first gear and rolled forward, Marcus felt a pang of compassion for the vulnerable man. He knew Claude was putting on a brave face as he returned to Privas. Poissy would now be at risk and Marcus hoped he would be equal to it. Marcus reflected on the ironies of life. Here he was, standing in the driveway feeling a kind of pity for a man who, just last night, he was ready to brain with a bottle.

He returned to the study and found Auguste asleep in his wheelchair. He took a small blanket from the cabinet and draped it across his friend's torso. He collected the plates, glasses and silverware and dropped them in the kitchen sink on his way out of the main house. In a few minutes he lay abed in his clothes drifting off to sleep, listening to the morning chirpings of the birds.

Helene was awake, curled under the covers of her bed. She had heard the Citroën in the driveway and the subsequent footfalls downstairs. The men had finished with their business to which she was not privy. She knew that no matter how she approached Auguste in her questioning he would not divulge the entire truth to her regarding the evening's conclave. In as much as she and Auguste did not share physical intimacy she wondered, for a time, in what way was she closer to him than was Marcus. She could think of nothing. It was not uncommon, she thought, that when she and Auguste were alone in the process of decision making, her husband would reference the Irlandais and tend to put off bringing things to closure until he had the man's input. It was almost as if Auguste did not trust her judgment or sense of practicality, at least not as much as Marcus'.

She rolled over on her back and gazed at the bedroom ceiling, pulling the bedspread to her chin. Last night had proven quite a disappointment. She had assumed that she and Madeleine had mutually reached out to each other in affection and commitment. Her heart had fairly leaped when Madeleine had grasped her hand and told her she was beautiful. They had continued for some time thereafter sharing vignettes from their pasts. Helene had spoken at length of her Algerian lover, a woman with whom she had lived several years in Paris. Didn't she detect a coquettish manner in Madeleine several times during the telling?

At bedtime the two women left the kitchen together. She had anticipated that perhaps Madeleine would invite her to her bedroom. Perhaps they would kiss, perhaps something more.

She had looked briefly into the study before going upstairs. The men had eaten and were hunched around Auguste's desk speaking almost in whispers. She and Madeleine mounted the stairs together. Madeleine's room lay beyond her own. There was a moment of awkwardness as she came to her bedroom door. Should she stop or continue down the hall with Madeleine? She continued on, though just behind.

Madeleine turned the knob and opened her door and as she stepped into her room, Helene spoke, "Madeleine."

The woman turned and finding Helene just behind her seemed genuinely surprised, "Madame?"

Helene noticed the absence of the use of her first name and flushed slightly in embarrassment. "Ah, I, ah, just wanted to say goodnight."

"Oh yes, of course, *bon nuit,* Madame," and as she spoke, Madeleine reached out and gently squeezed Helene's hand.

"*Bon nuit,* Madeleine." Helene hurriedly turned toward her own room.

The echo of embarrassment lingered with her now as she lay in her bed in morning reverie. Would she ask Madeleine how things stood between them? Would that be too bold? She knew well enough that any indirectness on her part would be immediately detected by the cook. Had she simply misconstrued Madeleine's demeanor? What was it that might stand between her and a relationship with Madeleine? The answer was not long in coming. It was not a question of "what". It was a question of "who". It was the same person who stood between her and Auguste.

One of her dogs barked from the back property. It sounded like the bitch, *Yaourt*. With no small amount of irritation, she thought of how even her dogs gravitated toward Marcus as if seeking his approval. Wasn't it true that if they were sitting by him and she called them, they would not immediately come to her? And only by repeated commands would they come, walking hesitantly, looking back in his direction.

It was almost as if Marcus were her rival. She wanted the things he had, things that had come to him without an apparent effort on his part. But was he as sensitive as she? Did he have her intuitive sense for the nuances and vagaries of human relationships, her commitment to the welfare of others? Deep down, she surmised, he probably realized his inadequacies. That would, of course, explain the excessive drinking and violent outbursts such as the one he had perpetrated on the wine merchant Fedou. Had Marcus, over time, insinuated himself into life at the Deschaines residence, disarming her, the mistress, with a false profession of love? Perhaps he had. Perhaps, despite appearances, Marcooz Mayeeyon was a charlatan. Perhaps, she thought, he had always been. The dogs knew better.

At midmorning, after Auguste had his sponge bath with the assistance of Marcus and a change into clean clothes, he asked his man to bring Zalman and Ruth to his study. In a few minutes they entered with Marcus trailing behind them. Both were haggard with sleeplessness and had the look of those prepared to receive bad tidings. "Ah, my friends," Auguste began, "I am so very sorry I did not speak with you last night regarding the visit of the militiaman. It would have spared you considerable anxiety. I beg your forgiveness for my oversight."

"Oh no, Monsieur Deschaines, you owe us no apology. You must always do as you deem fit," replied Ruth.

"Well, as it happens, I have good news for you this morning."

"Good news, Monsieur?"

"It seems that the Milicien considers himself a friend of Marcooz. He and I talked through the evening and I am convinced he will not betray your situation with us to the authorities. As a matter of fact, he is willing to provide valuable information to us."

Zalman spoke. "Monsieur Deschaines please forgive my asking, but how can you be certain that he can be trusted? How did he know that we were here?"

"Well Zalman, Sergeant Poissy is, after all, an experienced investigator. He was tipped off by an informant and surmised the rest as a result of his visit here."

"Oh my God," Ruth interjected, "an informer knows about us?"

"On that score, Ruth, we have the upper hand. Poissy gave us the person's identity. Shortly, that situation will be taken care of. Poissy is the only person with the authorities who had the information."

"Is the informer a local person?"

"It is not necessary for you to know anything about the person. For your own piece of mind, however, I will inform you as soon as the problem is taken care of."

Zalman nodded slowly and put his arm around Ruth's shoulders, "We are so grateful, Monsieur Deschaines, perhaps someday we will be able to show our gratitude in a tangible way."

"Show your gratitude, Herr Meyer, by living well and surviving. The war cannot last forever and when it is done there will be much work to do for all of us. Be optimistic. I am."

Zalman smiled and nodded in agreement, "Yes, and there is much work to be done now. I think I will be joining Philibert in the orchard to help out with the pruning."

As was his habit, Zalman shook Auguste's hand and escorted Ruth out of the study with his arm around her protectively.

"I'll be off to Père Bassard then, Auguste," Marcus said as he moved to the door, "will you be needing anything in town?"

"See Madeleine on the way out, perhaps there is something for the house."

"I'd like to strangle the little bastard, myself."

Auguste grinned broadly and chuckled, "Marcooz Makeeyon, I do not think I'd like to get on your wrong side."

As he pedaled the rutted *chemin de terre* west of the village, Maurice Fleury thought of the priest. Bassard had approached Maurice in the street outside of Fedou's shop just a few days ago. Maurice had found a new leaning post recently as a result of his becoming an associate member of the Communist's entourage of wine-mooching fellow travelers. He was somewhat surprised, therefore, when Père Bassard had greeted him and engaged him in conversation.

After asking after the Fleury family, Bassard had inquired regarding Maurice's current practice of the Faith. Maurice had been irritated and dispensed with politeness by telling the priest it was, more or less, none of his business. Bassard had persisted, however, contending that in these dangerous times it was of crucial importance for Catholics to maintain their practice including, most significantly, the sacraments of Penance and Holy Communion.

"I have nothing to confess," Maurice had responded, deliberately omitting the honorific due the clergyman.

"Maurice, my son, we all have something to confess."

"Well, I am not going to Confession. I am no longer the foolish little boy I once was. You can go bother someone else, priest."

The priest neither became angry nor took another line of reasoning with Maurice but said something that caused the faintest of chills to run through the young man. "Maurice Henri Fleury, for the good of your immortal soul you will come to me for Confession this very evening."

Having spoken and after peering unflinchingly into Maurice's eyes implying an unsaid gravity, Bassard turned abruptly and walked away toward the church.

Despite his mild anxiety over his meeting with the priest, Fleury had not gone to see him that evening. He was encouraged in that decision by the anti-religious remarks of Fedou and his cronies when Maurice broached the subject with them.

The incident only came to his mind now as he pumped strenuously over the rutted track toward the Souvay farmstead several kilometers to the west.

Fleury looked up to see two men emerge from a thicket at the side of the lane some fifty meters in front of him. By their dress he knew they were not farmers. Their boots indicated they might be hikers or perhaps black marketeers. It did not occur to Maurice that they might be Maquis.

The men stood in the middle of the lane as if to block his path. Fleury felt no apprehension when he stopped before them assuming that perhaps they were going to ask for directions. The older man, wearing a dark beret and badly in need of a shave, spoke first. "You are making some kind of a delivery out here?"

"Yes, I am," Maurice replied with a smile, assuming the man had observed the baked goods in his pannier.

"For the baker in Couderouge?"

"Why yes," Maurice said still grinning, not fully aware that the younger man with a heavy cloth wrapping around his right hand had maneuvered to his rear.

"Then you are Maurice Fleury, eh?" the older man asked with the trace of a smile.

"Yes, yes I am," Maurice responded, mindlessly pleased that the stranger knew his name.

Fleury did not hear the muffled cough of the pistol shot directed behind his left ear that ended his life. His executioners dragged his body several hundred yards into the thicket and made off with his bicycle over the countryside to the north. Over the next few weeks the feeding activity of a pack of feral dogs prevented his remains from ever being found.

Several days later the women at the Deschaines residence, Helene, Madeleine and Ruth sat together in the kitchen chatting during the late afternoon. They were enjoying Madeleine's homemade *gâteau* with tea, although a recent reserve had developed between the two French women. "These are quite tasty, Madeleine," Ruth commented, "they are better than the ones from the bakery."

"That reminds me, Madeleine," Helene interjected, "this morning Monsieur Goulet told me it might be some time before he could deliver baked goods to us. It seems his delivery boy has been missing for almost a week. You'll bear that in mind and make extra bread?"

"Yes, Madame."

"The delivery boy is missing, Helene?" Ruth asked with a troubled frown, "the one that comes on his bicycle?"

"Yes, so I am told."

"Oh my God," Ruth gasped, "I hope he was not the one Zalman spoke of."

"The one Zalman spoke of?"

"Yes, he told me this morning that Marcus had indicated to him that the problem with the informer had been taken care of."

There was a tense silence. Ruth looked nervously from one woman to the other in perplexity suddenly thinking she should not have mentioned Zalman's information. "Informer? What informer? What are you talking about, Ruth?" Helene questioned pointedly.

"Perhaps I should not have spoken of it. I thought everyone knew. I should say no more."

"Are you saying Maurice Fleury was an informer and that something has happened to him? Madeleine, do you know anything of this?"

Madeleine shrugged, sipping from her cup, "I know nothing of it."

"Ruth," Helene persisted, "tell me what you know. Tell me all that Zalman said. I demand to know."

Ruth replied weakly, "I was there in the study when your husband made mention of it and said we would be informed when the problem was taken care of. I know nothing else except what Zalman told me this morning. I know nothing of the delivery boy."

A hot resentment took hold of Helene. She rose from her chair and strode out of the kitchen. "I will get to the bottom of this business," she angrily asserted.

She entered the study directly and confronted Auguste who was writing at his desk. "What is going on here, Auguste?" She demanded hotly. "What is this business about an informer and the Meyers? And about the problem being taken care of? You will tell me everything. Do you understand? Everything."

Auguste took his glasses from the bridge of his nose and looked calmly out of the window. "Who were you talking to, Helene?"

"Never mind that. What has happened to Maurice Fleury?"

Auguste held the glasses to the light of the window inspecting the lenses for cleanliness. He looked directly up at his wife, laid the glasses on the desk and rubbed his eyes with a thumb and forefinger as if preparing to lecture a child. "Maurice Fleury is dead," he said simply.

Helene waited for him to say more. When he did not it occurred to her that her demanding posture was not having its desired effect. She realized she would not get all the information she wanted. She wouldn't get the respect she felt was due her and the acknowledgment as an equal with her husband that she demanded. "I am to be left out again. Is that it, Auguste?"

Auguste took a moment before responding. "Yes Helene, you are to be left out of the ugliness."

Helene did not expect that answer and sought an appropriate retort. "I am too weak. Is that it? I am too emotional. I am just a woman. I am too unreliable to be involved in murder. Is that it?"

"Murder? Is that what you would call it?"

"What else would you call it, Auguste?"

"Helene, today the Meyers are more secure here than they were last week. There was no other way."

Helene was adamant, "Nothing justifies murder. Nothing."

Because of his sense of responsibility for the entire household, Auguste had no intention of indulging his wife. He knew whatever he said would be taken as condescension. He said nothing.

Helene waited briefly for her husband to speak then turned abruptly and strode toward the door. She was almost out of the room when the dark inspiration came to her. She turned and solemnly pronounced, "I will not be patronized. Either the Irlandais leaves or I do."

As he sat with the stem of his glasses in his teeth looking out of the window at the gray cumulus clouds to the east, Auguste felt no surprise. He found it interesting that he was not surprised. His wife was simply using her native intelligence to finally have her own way. There was, of course, no outrage on her part over the death of Fleury. She was cannily using the incident to arrange circumstances at the Deschaines residence to her liking. Marcus' influence with Auguste and the others had been a constant thorn in her side. Her husband knew he had no insight into the depths of her psyche and could only speculate as to what it really was about Marcus that rankled her. He suspected the answer lay somewhere in the realm of psychological archetypes and the primordial gulf between men and women. Helene was blind to her chief feature, the axis about which her personality revolved. Marcus was a rival simply because he was Marcus. Auguste had always seen that his wife had no problem with weaker men. Were his physical infirmity and passivity in the face of her complaints and insistencies over the years the basis of their marriage? He didn't know.

In a way she had trapped him in his own values. There were the sacramental vows in addition to his acceptance of her peccadilloes when they courted. She had trapped him in his religious beliefs and his love for her. Helene had claimed the rights of a wife and Auguste would certainly accede to them.

He thought now of Marcus and his eyes misted over. Where would he go? What would happen to him? Marcus was entering old age and was being put out of his home. Perhaps Bassard could arrange something. A deep melancholy swept over Auguste. He would be able to manage with the help of others of course, but that remarkable presence that had helped sustain and nurture his own manhood would be gone. He was about to lose the person he felt closest to, Marcooz Makeeyon, his *bon camarade*.

After thinking for a time about the pointlessness of deliberations, Auguste steeled himself and lifted the brass bell. He had in his mind vague visions of a ship sinking into a dark turbulent sea with its bell tolling in alarm and anguish. Marcus entered the study shortly, stood before the desk, rubbed the stubble on his chin and said, "Yes, Auguste?"

"Sit down Marcus," Auguste indicated and as the Irlandais sank into the easy chair, he added, "we've come to the end of it."

Marcus said nothing but reached into his jacket for a cigarette and lit it. He took a long drag and waited for Auguste to continue. "You are required to leave our employ," Auguste said morosely, "no, that's not true at all. You are being required to leave your home."

"You mean leave permanently?"

Auguste dropped his eyes to the desktop, "Yes, permanently."

Marcus pursed his lips, "The Fleury thing? I've just talked to Maddy."

"No, not really, Marcooz, you must leave because you are you."

Marcus looked out of the window, "Helene?"

"Yes. You will leave or she will leave."

Marcus chewed on the inside of his lip, "Ah well, that's it then. I'll be gone shortly."

"Marcooz, my friend, do you want me to talk about it? You are entitled to know the truth of it and I will withhold nothing. I think you are owed that."

Marcus looked directly at Auguste pursing his lips and knitting his brow indicating not puzzlement but a grim acceptance of circumstances. "No, no explanation is needed. I have my own understanding," then after a short pause he added, "how will you make out getting about and whatnot?"

"I don't know, I haven't thought about it," Auguste said quietly and with a wistful grin, he added, "I suppose the deep woods and the upstairs will become memories."

"Zalman's a good man, Auguste, he'll look after you as well as he can."

Auguste nodded but said nothing. The men sat together in quiet sadness, each with his thoughts and recollections. Marcus finally rose, "I'll get my things, say my goodbyes and go now. There's no sense in lingering. Maybe I can put in with Bassard until I get my bearings."

"That isn't necessary Marcus. Take what time is necessary to arrange your affairs."

Marcus smiled, "You rang the bell and got on with this, didn't you, Auguste?"

Auguste returned the smile, "Yes, I did, didn't I?"

"You must have been one hell of a soldier," Marcus commented quietly as he came around the desk.

He tenderly cradled Auguste's head in his arm and hugged it to him. Auguste placed both arms around Marcus' waist and patted his lower back. Tears welled in both men's eyes.

"*Adieu,* my friend," Auguste whispered.

"To God it is," Marcus replied hoarsely as he released his friend and walked from the study.

Madeleine seethed with anger as she washed the dishes from dinner. She had been shocked with disbelief when Marcus told her of his imminent leaving on his way out of the house to pack his belongings. Despite his protests, she told him emphatically she would be leaving shortly as well. Perhaps, she suggested, they could go to Marseille or Lyon together and find immediate work. In any event, she promised, this was not the last he would see of her.

When serving dinner she had avoided eye contact and conversation with the Deschaines. She had placed the bowls of food and bottle of wine upon the table with such force so as to cause the couple to wince imperceptibly in their seats. What a disappointment the Monsieur had turned out to be. Could he not tell his wife to go to the devil? The brave war hero from the fine aristocratic family, so free with his advice and sage pronouncements, had turned out to be no more than a mouse. The scheming lowborn *gamine* from the back streets of Paris had cowed him.

Madeleine's gaze fell upon the dainty glass figurines above the sink that Madame so cherished. She took the swan with its spread wings into her hand and squeezed it with all her strength. The years of wringing clothes dry by hand had its effect. The swan shattered and the glass shards sliced into Madeleine's palm. Madeleine wept and made two promises to herself. The first was that she would leave suddenly and without notice. The second would be the mentioning to Madame that she really had no idea what a little snake she was.

In the study, the Deschaines picked at their meal in silence. Auguste finally spoke, "Madeleine will be leaving."

"You think so?" Helene replied and after a pause added, "well my love, we'll still have our Jews."

Auguste's head snapped up. "Our Jews?"

He looked intently at Helene whose gaze remained down at her plate. Auguste Deschaines was not a man capable of contempt and he was curiously unsettled with this sudden surge of repugnance.

In the darkness on Ormeau Road a lone forlorn figure trudged wearily toward Couderouge. A duffel bag hastily crammed with his few belongings was slung across his shoulder. He had but a few francs. He looked up at the starry sky through the oak canopy and his mind went back to Ireland. He saw the oak stands along the Bonet and then a solitary one at the eastern edge of St. Stephen's Green on Easter Monday, 1916.

Marcus and Kate Jamieson had taken a rest from their holiday stroll south of the Liffey beneath a massive oak in St. Stephan's Green. They sat on the very bench where Joyce's young lady friend had met Cherry Ross those many years ago. Marcus and Kate were schoolteachers and were thoroughly enjoying the Easter recess from the drudgery of the classroom.

Marcus sat lost in thought when he heard the crunching footsteps approaching them along the graveled walkway. A pair of ragged boots with conspicuous holes in the toes and topped with loosely bound puttees came into his field of vision. Looking up, he saw a slightly embarrassed, pale-faced youth smiling weakly at him. The boy had an old, sawed-off Martini rifle over his shoulder and bandoliers of ammunition crisscrossing his chest. An oversized cap held up only by his ears gave the impression of a street urchin playing at soldier.

"Excuse me, sar," the boy began, "will ye please take the lady from the park. Soon enough now it's goin' to be no place for women."

"Take her from the park? Why, lad? What's going on?"

"Oi have me arders, sar. The park is to be cleared of civilians for their own safety. There's goin' to be gunplay shortly."

"Gunplay? What the hell is going on?"

"We're takin' the city, sar, us Volunteers are takin' Dublin and the rest of the country."

"You mean rebellion, lad? You people are going to take on the British Army?"

"That we are, sar. We're goin' to droive them out and have our own country."

The trio's heads turned in unison as cracks of rifle shots came from the direction of the Shelbourne Hotel just north of the park. The boy's eyes widened in fear and he grasped the rifle with both hands. "Oh Jasus, get the lady out o' here, sar. I'm away now."

He spun and sprinted across the grass toward the hotel.

"Marcus," Kate exclaimed nervously as she gripped his arm. "What is happening? What should we do?"

"We're leaving the park, Kate, but not that way," Marcus said as he nodded toward the Shelbourne Hotel.

They hurried from the park along Harcourt Street and saw bands of men with rifles stopping vehicles and ordering the occupants out into the streets. The leaders wore dark green uniforms and directed the confused pedestrians away to the south. As they passed one officer speaking to an irate citizen they heard him say, "We need the vehicle for transport or barricades. The Republic will reimburse your loss."

"What goddamned Republic? You bastards are nothing but thieves," the indignant, well-dressed man retorted.

The officer calmly took his revolver from its holster and pointed it into the man's face. He gravely warned, "Move out now, sir. There's nothing you can do about it and I'll shoot you if I must."

The man uttered a curse and strode off.

Marcus and Kate continued hurrying south as the crackle of rifle fire became more frequent from the direction of the city center behind them. After a few blocks they paused to catch their breath on a low stonewall. "Merciful God, Marcus, this is madness," Kate gasped. "What do these fools hope to accomplish? They'll bring ruin to us all. Have they no decency?"

Marcus could only shrug in response. Over the last few years he had paid little attention to politics, particularly national and local politics. Like most educated Irishmen, Marcus' attention and interest had been on the war raging on the continent between the superpowers. There were hundreds of thousands of Irishmen serving in the British armed forces. Notions of home rule and self-determination for the Irish had been put on the back burner by the governments in London and their agents in Dublin.

Marcus put Kate on a bus for Blackrock and started walking South Circular Road stopping and speaking to people in order to get information concerning the insurrection. He noticed immediately that individual men he spoke with were careful not to indicate their sympathies with respect to the situation. The men were wary of each other. The women, on the other hand, especially the mothers and wives of men in uniform were almost universally outspoken in their condemnation of the rebels. "The feckin' bahstards," he heard one exclaim, "Oi hope ta God all of thim are shot to death and killed as well."

The wildest rumors were circulating. The Germans had landed in Galway. The British fleet was on the way to shell Dublin. The rebels were killing priests wholesale and robbing the churches. By nightfall Marcus had gleaned the barest of reliable information regarding the events of the day. The rebels had posted a proclamation of a provisional government throughout Ireland. They had commandeered strategic points in the city including the General Post Office, Four Courts, Shelbourne Hotel and the North and South Dublin Unions. They were evidently well armed, well trained and determined to make a fight of it. The Crown Forces had been caught with their jodhpurs around their ankles. Most of the British officer corps was at the Fairyhouse Races and military security had been lax. After all, who but a bunch of bungling amateurs would start an insurrection against perhaps the most formidable military adversary in the world on a quiet holiday afternoon.

In the fading light of evening Marcus sat on the curbside and read the proclamation. Despite himself, he was moved by it. He was familiar with none of the signatories but he knew one of them could write well. He reread the opening lines. "Irishmen and Irishwomen: In the name of God and the dead generations from which she receives her old tradition of nationhood, Ireland, through us, summons her children to her flag and strikes for her freedom..."

He thought of his father and his mother, Master Raye, Ould Sean Mulcahy, and the faces of loved ones from his past. Then he thought of Ould Sean again, the wizened old man at the hearth with his pipe, his songs, his laughter, his dark anger, and his passion. An exultation somewhere between laughter and tears swept over him. Something had come alive this day in Dublin, something sweetly nostalgic and unspeakably beautiful. Marcus' heart pounded in time to its silent music.

The days of the week passed like deep, sonorous single gongs of a massive cathedral bell. Most educated Dubliners expected the absurd insurrection to collapse immediately with the quick tactical infusion of British infantry units. But it didn't. Throughout the days and into the nights the brooding atmosphere over the old city was perturbed by the continual pops of rifle fire, the harsh cackling of machine guns and the dull thudding of heavy weapons.

On several evenings Marcus found himself with other Dubliners on the heights of Howth Head observing the dim orange fire-glow from the General Post Office and the white flashes from the guns of the *Helga* shelling the city center from the Liffey. He had, like most men, that natural dark fascination with the violence in a contest of arms. Each morning, one man asked another, "Are they still holding out?"

Toward week's end the "they" had become "the lads". The conscious self-sacrifice of Pearse, Connally, MacDonagh and the others was having its inevitable effect. The Fenian spirit was coming alive in Irishmen throughout the Island. The war pipes in the ether began their ancient plaintive drone. Cuchulainn stirred, rose from his grave and unsheathed his sword.

Padraig Pearse, the poet-warrior, called a halt to the carnage from the epicenter of the holocaust on Saturday afternoon. The indiscriminate British shelling had killed and wounded enough of the Dublin citizenry and had destroyed the greater part of the city's heart. The next day as some of the rebels were marched off at bayonet point to Richmond Barracks in the western part of the city, Marcus stood in the crowd along their route of march.

"Goddamn ye all ta hell," screamed a soldier's wife as they passed, spitting emphatically into their ranks.

"Yer finished now, ye lousy bahstards," echoed another.

One old man in a slouch hat and of a quite different persuasion climbed atop a bus and called out to the bedraggled rebels, "Ye did well, lads. Ye done us proud. God bless ye."

Marcus smiled quietly and then as he looked down the line of rebels between the soldiers he saw a grimy tired, familiar face. It was the boy he and Kate had met in the park. The boy walked slowly forward, his head down, his shoulders slightly hunched as if to protect himself. As he drew abreast, Marcus spoke out sharply, "lad."

The boy looked up and about and then directly at Marcus. Marcus grinned warmly and raised his fist with a thumbs-up gesture. The boy smiled in recognition and returned the gesture. He continued on, his head now up, his step sprightlier.

The boy was not to die. His leaders were. In the ensuing week by use of the firing squad and quicklime grave, the British sealed their fate in Ireland and consequently the rest of the Empire.

Marcus watched the lace curtains by the open window in Kate's groundfloor flat billowing in the May breeze. He heard the shouts of children somewhere up the street. "Marcus, are you listening to me?" he heard the woman say then turned to look at her.

"I'm sorry Kate, what is it you're saying?"

"Are you not listening to me?"

"I'm sorry, what is it then?"

"What is it you're telling your boys when they ask about the Troubles?"

"At the end of the day when they're done with their lessons, I spend some time going over the recent events and I add the history of it."

"Well, what is it you're really telling them, Marcus?"

"The truth, Kate, the truth as near as I understand it."

"And what might that be?"

"About the same as I say to you."

"Merciful God, you don't do that do you?"

"I do. Why wouldn't I?"

"Because you're their teacher, Marcus, and you can't be filling their young minds with that nonsense about the glory of Old Ireland and the Fenians and whatnot."

Marcus smiled to himself and scratched the back of his neck while he thought of Master Raye before the chalkboard. "Maybe you're right, Miss Jamieson. Maybe I should leave those nice, little Catholic boys as they are, those nice little boys with absolutely no future at all in their own country. Someday they will be nice, well-behaved young men doing menial work for their masters, not their betters, mind you, just their masters."

"Well, you did well enough, didn't you?"

"I did, I suppose. But that happened because I was given the opportunity by other people. I can't imagine the same will happen to the majority of my boys. No, if most of them have a decent future, it'll be because they leave Ireland for America or Australia or even England."

"Well, you and I have done well here, as well as most of our friends. Isn't that true?"

"Our friends, Kate? Most of them are your friends and most of them were born into privilege. How many working people do you know, Kate Jamieson? How many people with calloused hands from off the land and into Dublin looking for work, do you hobnob with socially? You know their children all right, the ones that come to you each day. You must be a kind of goddess for them, all clean, smelling lovely and dressed in grand clothes. But when was the last time you had tea with their parents? Your father had money and position, Kate, and you got yourself a good education as a result. How many of those little girls in your classroom with their grimy faces, bad teeth and scabby knees are going to get the same education? How many?"

Kate flushed slightly in irritation. She really didn't want to discuss the state of affairs in Ireland or its future. She wanted to discuss her own future with Marcus McQuillan. "Will you have more tea?" She said, putting her hand to the teapot.

"No, thank you."

"Marcus, there's nothing you and I can do about general social conditions in Ireland. I think we should be concerned about our own future, our own immediate future.

"You mean marriage."

"I do."

"Well, before the Rising I suppose we might have made definite plans. But now, after that and what's been done to Pearse, Connally and the others, I think all of us are in for evil times. I think things are now going to get much worse. The average person's attitude is different because of the things that have been done to their own kind. There's a great deal of bitterness over the murdering done by the Crown. It was cold and ugly and there's no way decent people can let it go at that. I don't think we can really make definite plans now, Kate. No, now's not the time."

"Could we not go away together, Marcus? Leave Dublin, perhaps even Ireland?"

Marcus smiled grimly. "Do you think you'd be happy away from that huge family of yours, Kate? You'd miss those sisters of yours something fierce. What would your nieces and nephews do without their Auntie Kate?"

Kate said nothing in reply as she stirred her tea but thought about the truth of what Marcus had just said. "You're right, we'll wait," she finally said, "but not too long, Mr. McQuillan."

Following the insurrection and subsequent executions of the rebel leaders, a period of quiet foreboding settled over the Irish capital and throughout the countryside. Inevitably, however, under the nose of British security forces a quiet, clandestine, highly organized resistance to British hegemony began to form among Irish men and women determined to take their country out of the Empire.

For centuries a shrewd, pragmatic colonial policy had enabled the Crown Forces to disrupt and arrest the ever recurrent blossoming of Gaelic nationalism. Capitalizing on an innate Irish naivete and tendency to revert to anachronistic means of warfare, the British genius for maintaining an imperial presence had survived since the sixteenth century. The pike had been no match for the musket, the musket for the rifle and the rifle for the machine gun. Easter week 1916 changed all of that.

An adaptive canny Corkman named Michael Collins, a survivor of the Rising, saw clearly what was necessary and set out to decisively beat the Anglo-Saxons at their own game. In the increasingly complex world of the twentieth century, information and intelligence gathering had been lifted into almost an art form by British security forces. The Royal Irish Constabulary, the Dublin Metropolitan Police with its infamous G division and the brilliant secretive administration in the bowels of Dublin Castle were the machinery with which the Crown fully expected to maintain its grip on Ireland. It was exactly these that Collins infiltrated with men and women loyal to the cause of Irish independence. The delicate web of spies, informers and intriguers on whom the British intelligence agencies depended came under fierce and sudden attack. The revolver and trench coat replaced the pike and woolen tunic. The terrorists became the terrorized.

Generally oblivious to momentous events taking place in back offices, side streets and hidden glens, the majority of Dubliners went about their daily mundane affairs. Their experience of Collins' successful war on the Empire consisted in the occasional distant crackling of a gun duel, running footfalls down a dark alley in the middle of the night and the ever present patrolling by police-laden armored cars. The rebels succeeded because they moved in that sea of common people sympathetic to their enterprise. Men in the brutal war of attrition were taken in and given succor, substance and, most importantly, information. Predictably, British reprisals served only to stiffen rebel resistance and antagonize people on the farms and in the mills.

Marcus continued to teach school and study while choosing to socialize with those of like mind during these morbid days. He saw no point, as some did, in concealing his sympathies during conversation with strangers or distant acquaintances. He felt rather proud when he was secretively informed of his brother Sean's active participation in a Flying Column operating in the Sligo area. Still, like most reasonable men, he would have preferred an end to the killing and the establishment of an equitable peace between the belligerents.

He did not bear hatred toward the British Crown or loyalist factions among the Irish population. He disagreed adamantly with Kate's father, an importer of agricultural machinery, but bore the man no ill will because of his anti-rebel sentiments.

Kate, because of an ugly incident one day while out walking with Marcus, began to have private rebel sympathies but could not speak of them for fear of castigation by her middle-class friends.

One cold late afternoon in January the couple strolled along the Liffey on Victoria Quay not far from Phoenix Park. They were looking forward to getting out of the wind at a little teashop just up the street when they heard the purring of a lorry approaching from behind. The lorry pulled alongside and braked to a halt. Without turning about Marcus heard the claps of boot heels on the cobblestones as Black and Tan paramilitaries jumped down from the back of the vehicle. "Arrh, youse two, 'alt where yew are."

"Marcus," Kate whispered softly, clutching at his coat sleeve.

Two of the Tans circled to the front of them. One had drawn a revolver and held it loosely at his side, barrel down toward the pavement. "Identify yerselfs," he commanded.

"Marcus McQuillan, I've a flat in Ranelagh just south of the Canal. I'm a schoolteacher. She's Miss Kathleen Jamieson, lives out toward Blackrock. She teaches school as well."

"Let the bit o' skirt speak for 'erself, Paddy," the Tan roughly retorted.

Marcus noticed the paramilitary's tam was askew and his eyes were red and moist. He surmised that he'd been drinking. "Give us yer coats," the Tan ordered.

"What's that?"

"D'ye 'ave shit in yer ears, Paddy? Give us yer fuckin' coats."

Marcus turned to the wide-eyed Kate, "Easy Kate, just let them have your coat. They're looking for weapons."

"Not just guns, Paddy. We're lookin' for little notes and such. That's 'ow yew bahstards pass informaishun."

The ersatz policeman rummaged through the coat pockets and felt the linings before dropping them to the pavement. Kate shivered and clasped her arms to her chest while hunching herself again the biting wind. Smiling slightly, the drunken Tan came up and stood face to face with Marcus, the reek of cheap whiskey on his breath. He lifted his revolver and put it just under Marcus' chin. "So, Paddy's a schooltaicher. I 'ated me fuckin' taichers when I wuz et school. They didn't taich me nuthin'."

"Evidently," Marcus commented quietly.

"Wot? Wot's 'at?" The Tan snarled not quite understanding the insult.

Marcus said nothing. The Tan leered toward Kate, "Are yew doin'it wiff 'er, Paddy?"

Marcus stiffened but remained silent. Kate reddened hotly and against her better judgment spoke out angrily, "My father, sir, is John C. Jamieson Esquire, of Jamieson's Imports Limited. I'll have you know that he's the personal friend of Lord Shillington as well as other members of the Dublin Council. He is the closest of friends with members of the Metropolitan Police at the Castle as well. Let me assure you that they'll certainly hear of this indignity. What is your name, sergeant or corporal or whatever you are?"

The side door of the lorry suddenly swung open and out stepped a tall, black-uniformed officer of the Auxiliaries, a glengarry bonnet worn rakishly on the side of his head. "That's enough, corporal," he said curtly, "I'll take over from here."

The Auxiliary collected both coats from the pavement and handed them politely to the couple. Kate refused his offer of assistance in donning her coat. "Please excuse the man's impertinence. Let me apologize on behalf of His Majesty's Forces to both of you," the Officer said uneasily.

"That will be all, Officer," Kate said huffily, "come Marcus," she added as she took Marcus by the arm and led him away from the chastened group.

A few yards up the street the lorry roared past them. Marcus turned to Kate, "Who's Lord Shillington, Kate?"

"I don't know," she replied, "the teashop's just ahead."

"Will you have more of the mutton, Marcus?" Kate asked.

"No, that was grand," Marcus replied, loosening his tie with his finger against the warmth of the late August day.

"You know, they said the funeral cortège was three miles long on the way out to Glasnevin. I never thought I would be, but I was moved by the tragedy of the whole affair. Imagine me, John Jamieson, a dyed in the wool loyalist, bereaving a man like Michael Collins." Kate's father spoke softly, looking down at his half eaten supper.

"The man seemed indestructible, Jack. He'd the respect of friend and foe alike. The British sought his end for years but ironically, it was a bullet fired by an Irish rebel that did the job."

"Marcus, you know well what my opinions have been. It seemed lunacy from its inception. Imagine a full rebellion against the Crown being launched by Commander-in-Chief Pearse from the seat of a Raleigh bicycle. And it all ends with those bloody fools in a treaty with the strongest military power on earth and civil war here in Ireland. The tragic comedy of it is staggering."

Marcus smiled. "What was it Disraeli said about us? The Gael's irascible and pugnacious mind invariably threatens world sanity, something like that."

"You men," Kate interjected, "if it's not this issue, it's that, the posturing, the crowing, the foolishness."

Jamieson's and Marcus' eyes met in silent understanding that transcended their respective politics. Marcus jibed, "I understand that Countess Markievicz had no problem using a revolver, Kate. Do you think those ruffians that day outside of Phoenix Park would have listened to sweet reason?"

"No, I suppose not, Mr. McQuillan, but they were men, weren't they?"

"And what about that Auxiliary officer that got us out of there? What of him?"

"Well, I suppose he was one of those rare gentlemen."

"Because he went for your lying, Kate? Is that what made him a gentleman?"

"Marcus, my love, would you care to wear the mutton?"

"You'll never have the last word with that one, laddy," Jamieson chortled.

"I suppose not. You know, sometimes I think we should have sent the women over to negotiate that treaty. They'd have been a match for Churchill and Lloyd-George."

"I'll agree with you there, Marcus. Dressing that poor crowd up in monkey suits and sending them over to deal with British sophisticates was the height of comic opera. By God, some of them still had the grass growing out of their ears."

Marcus laughed heartily, "Well, they got the British out, didn't they?"

"Oh really? You don't think the British still control things, eh? Who do you think still controls economic affairs? Who dictates Ireland's international situation? Who arranged it so that the dirty work of breaking Irish Republicanism is done by the Irish themselves? You must give the Anglo-Saxons their credit, Marcus. The Irish were no more successful against them at the bargaining table than the Zulus or Chinamen. We've a Free State, is it? Free State, my arse."

"Marcus grinned broadly, "Well, it's good for business. Isn't that right, Jack?"

Jamieson, always a man to appreciate a good comeback, laughed, "Yes, my fine academic friend, it's good for business, sure enough, and if you worked for me, you'd have a good piece of it."

The conversation was interrupted with the demure entry of the head maid into the dining room. "Mr. Jamieson, sar, Father Beasley has joost arrooived. Will Oi show him in?"

Jamieson nodded, "Oh yes, do that Clare," then after a pause added, "the man is nosing about for a meal. He's got his arrivals down to a science."

"Da," Kate frowned, "I'm sure he's here for a friendly social visit."

Jamieson turned to Marcus grinning impishly, "What do you think, Marcus?"

Marcus smiled slightly and shook his head, "I'm sure you don't want to hear what I think."

Marcus had never liked the priest. He found his manner deliberately effete, his conversation a curious blend of the opinionated and the obsequious and his hair overly pomaded. Father Beasley entered gaily, took the offered chair confidently and readily agreed to his portion of the mutton stew. He gave Marcus but a cursory nod and immediately engaged himself in a gossip-laden exchange with Mrs. Jamieson and Kate.

For a while, Marcus' thoughts went to the preparations necessary for the new school term at the end of the summer. He didn't notice the shift in discussion to the day's events and the death of Collins.

"I think the provisional government will take a more civilized and reasonable posture without the presence of Collins," the cleric was saying.

"Probably," Jamieson responded, "what do you think Marcus?"

"I don't know, perhaps."

In an attempt to be playful, Beasley remarked, "Mr. McQuillan, I'd surmise, is one of the more action- oriented Irish citizens. I'd further guess he has definite sympathies for the republican movement, perhaps owing to his rural origins."

"Maybe so," Marcus agreed amiably.

"Maybe?" Beasley continued with a mock frown, "well, wouldn't you just like to be out in the West in a Flying Column with your brother these days?"

Marcus reacted as if he had just been pelted by a stone. "My brother? What do you know of my brother?" he said angrily.

Beasley, thoroughly discomposed, looked inquiringly about the table, "Well, isn't it common knowledge your brother Sean is a rebel leader with the irregulars out in the Sligo area?"

Marcus' face went white in anger. "How the hell do you know that? Where did you get that information about my brother?"

Beasley reddened and continued to look about the table for support, "Jack? Mrs. Jamieson? Kate? Don't all of us know that's the case? I was told that very thing by one of the family."

"One of the family?" Marcus snapped, "which one of the family?"

No one at the table spoke. "Which one of the family? God damn it," Marcus demanded.

The priest, completely non-plussed, blurted, "Margaret, I'm sure it was Margaret."

"Jesus Christ," Marcus snarled and glared at Kate. "What the hell have you done? You sat at tea with your sisters and lost yourself in female blather, didn't you? No one in the Jamieson family knew about Sean but you, did they Kate? But you ran your tongue to your sisters and they, in turn, shared the juicy morsel over tea with this idiot of a priest."

Marcus, struggling to control his rage, rose to his feet. Gripping the back of his chair, he repeated his accusing question to Kate, "What the hell have you done? You bloody, little ………," and stopped suddenly, completely at a loss to end his accusation with a definitive word.

Marcus suddenly relaxed with a long exhalation and looked upward with a pained expression. He closed his eyes, pursed his lips and slowly shook his head in negation.

"Marcus," Jamieson began.

"No, Jack, no," Marcus interrupted, as he raised his hand as if to push away the man's attempts at amelioration, "there's nothing to be said."

Marcus walked abruptly and definitively to the head of the table and offered Jamieson his hand for the shaking. Jamieson took it, knowing full well what was happening. He was the sole member of the dinner party who understood what Marcus was doing and could think of nothing to say appropriate for the moment.

Kate sat in abject terror. Her initial existential shame was now lost in the flood of panic that gripped her. She sensed the gravity and finality in Marcus's gesture toward her father and sat helplessly as he strode from the dining room, through the foyer to the front door.

With a sick feeling in the pit of his stomach Jamieson jumped quickly from his chair to intercept his daughter's sudden bolt toward the front door. He hugged her tightly as she struggled to free herself and follow Marcus into the street.

"No, Katie, no," he whispered into her ear, "Marcus is gone. You can do nothing. Let it go, Katie, merciful God, let it go."

Kate shuddered in agony, the hot tears coursing down her cheeks. She buried her face in her father's chest and clawed at his coat sleeves. "No," she whimpered, "no, it can't be like this. Marcus loves me. He does, Da. He does love me."

Jamieson waited, his arms enveloping his distraught child. He listened grimly to her sobs, knowing there was no comfort to be given her. He knew Marcus McQuillan well and he knew the man was gone. Jamieson refused to lie to give his daughter false hope. He gently stroked the side of her head and looked over her shoulder to his wife indicating the woman should see to her wounded daughter.

Mrs. Jamieson came quietly, put her arm around Kate's waist and led her from her father's embrace and out of the dining room. Jamieson sighed and stood behind his tall-backed chair at the head of the table. He looked vacantly at the dinnerware and lacey tablecloth, oblivious to Beasley. His gaze then fell on the priest's long, delicate bony fingers.

"That man has absolutely no regard for the feelings of others," Beasley offered.

"What's that?" Jamieson said, trying to pay attention.

"I said that man has no regard for the feelings of others."

Jamieson looked into the smug, self-righteous countenance below the slicked-down black hair. "That man. Aye, that man who was to marry my daughter, that man and that woman. And what the hell would a girlish little squint like you know about that kind of thing?"

He paused and looked to the ceiling. He was aware that above in one of the bedrooms his wife was doing her motherly best to accomplish the impossible. "I'm going to have my pipe now," he asserted calmly, "you finish your meal if you'd like. Then get your nancyboy arse out of here."

That night, politely eschewing the company of fellow drinkers, Marcus sat alone at a table in the rear of McGivney's Pub with a bottle of single malt scotch. He tried, without success, to drink himself into insensibility. In a light drizzle he walked the wet empty streets the mile south to his flat in Ranelagh. He lay abed for a long time waiting for the oblivion of sleep while buoyed on successive waves of anger and sadness. Then he slept and heard the barking of hounds and bleating of sheep. He saw one of the little boys he taught, naked and bleeding at the knees, scrambling down Benbo. Someone in distress called his name. It was a woman. He looked for her among the deep rushes but only came upon a flock of clucking hens and a black undersized rooster.

In succeeding months, Kate was not the Jamieson whom Marcus missed most. Her father, Marcus began to observe, was quite correct in what first appeared as a flippant analysis of the Irish civil turmoil. Michael Collins had died because the rebels in the West Cork area decided to "joost have a go at thim uppity Treaty boyos comin' down from Dublin." They were as shocked as anyone when a bullet shattered the back of the Big Fellow's skull.

Without Collin's strong principled leadership, the jackals soon moved in. The Pro-Treaty Free State forces became infected by solicitors, would-be careerists, ex-British Army personnel, and inevitably the clergy. The Crown happily continued to send over thousands of Lee-Enfield rifles, armored cars, artillery, and, of course, pounds sterling.

The republican opposition held large sections of rural Ireland owing to the common people's natural reversion to a vague atavistic clannishness in the absence of their hereditary enemy. Sides were chosen not because of political ideology but because of an ingrained loyalty to family and friends. "Begod, didn't some of thim damned Kiernans sarve with the Royal Constabulary and now aren't they runnin' with the Provisonals out o' Dublin?"

Marcus' brother, Sean McQuillan, like most of the Irish, was not viscerally opposed to the Treaty. But hadn't he spent those years dodging British patrols with Captain Clooney in the mountains and glens of the northwest? Because Clooney was for holding out, so would he. Wasn't DeValera, himself, against the Treaty? Without the faintest desire to put bullets into Irishmen, Sean soldiered on.

He was thinking of these very things while having a pint at Dillon's in Rathcormack when half a dozen, green-uniformed Provisionals walked in the front door and directly to him. The officer spoke right up, "Yer Sean McQuillan and in the name of the Constitutional Government, Oi'm placing you under arrest."

Sean looked about at the other men in the pub, two of whom belonged to his column. He knew that if he bolted for it, he'd get their help but that there was also a good chance of bloodshed.

Sean said nothing. The arresting lieutenant, an older, gray haired man with apparent social awareness said, "Finish yer drink McQuillan and don't be thinkin' of makin' for the back door. We've men outside."

Sean nodded amiably and quaffed the porter down. "Am I to be manacled, then?"

"Manacled? Oh, handcooffed ye mean? No, Oi don't have thim things. You joost come quoietly and sit noicely up front with me and the droiver."

"I will," Sean replied quietly.

Dillon, the owner, approached from the other side of the bar, "Will ye have a drink with me and the farmidable Sean McQuillan, Officer? You'd niver have taken him if he was out on the hills, boyo. He'd have dropped ye all with his Enfield before ye got within shoutin' distance."

"Thanks for yer offer, pubman, but Oi can't be drinkin' on the job. What ye say is probably truth. But, ye see, he's not on the hills. He's here and so are we."

The officer smiled wryly and put his hand on Sean's shoulder, "We'll be off now, eh, McQuillan?"

"Aye, we will," Sean answered gently.

The genial elderly lieutenant expected that Sean would be put with the other detainees and would eventually be released when the Irish civil strife was over. He was unaware of the change in attitude and policy of the provisional government concerning rebel leaders.

The little boy approached Marcus timidly as he sat at his classroom desk in the late afternoon correcting English grammar papers. "Mashter McQuillan, sar, thar's a man outsoide ta see ye."

"There is, lad? And what is it the man wants?"

"Oi don't know, sar, but he give me a pinny ta tell ye."

"A penny, is it? And what is it you'll do with that penny, lad?"

"Boy sweets, sar."

"Sweets? You mean you'll not put it in the collection at Sunday Mass?"

The boy put his head down and shuffled his feet, "Oi will, sar, if ye want me to."

Marcus laughed and patted the boy's head, "Ah no, Declan, Master McQuillan is just jesting with you. You take that bright penny and buy yourself a grand treat. You do that. Now, go tell that man that I'll see him."

Marcus could immediately tell from the mud-caked boots and sunburnt face that he was dealing with a countryman. "Come in," he said to the hesitant figure in the doorway.

The man strode purposefully before the desk and looked intently down on Marcus. "You're Marcus McQuillan, the brother of Sean McQuillan?"

"I am," Marcus nodded.

"I've bad news for you, McQuillan."

"And what would that news be?"

"Your brother Sean's been taken into custody by the Treaty crowd."

"I see," Marcus answered, mildly surprised by his reaction of relief over the fact that Sean was now out of the fighting. "Where is it they have him?"

"They've got him at a barracks out by Aughris Head. He's all right now, but soon he won't be."

"Won't be? What do you mean?"

"They're going to shoot him."

"Shoot him? What are you saying, man?"

"Your brother was one of Dermott Clooney's lieutenants and ran one of his columns out of the Ox Mountains. Cosgrave and the Dublin crowd have decided on reprisal executions because we've taken out some of their best. It stands to reason they'd finally get around to this sort of thing."

"Oh Jesus, Sean," Marcus groaned, running his fingers through his hair. Then, collecting himself, he asked grimly, "Are there plans to do something? Are you people going to try to get him out?"

"Aye, we are, McQuillan, and that's why I've come up to Dublin to see you. Clooney's had the barracks and land about scouted out. We've a plan to break in and get him and we'll need someone who can get into him beforehand. You're his family. They'll let you in to see him before he's shot. Are you willing to help us"?

Without hesitation, Marcus responded, "I will. Can you tell me of the plan now?"

"No, McQuillan. You go home to Leitrim. You'll be contacted there. You'll be given the particulars."

"When do you want me there?"

The man looked gravely at Marcus, "Do you understand, McQuillan, your life here in Dublin is now over. You're done with living here and teaching here as well. Once you're involved the government will have your identity and they'll be looking for you. You'll be on the run like the rest of us. And there's no telling when there's an end of it. When you throw in with us and leave tonight, or latest tomorrow morning, you can't be coming back here. If there's goodbying to be done, get it done and be off to Leitrim. D'ye understand?"

Marcus slowly nodded his head in assent. He rose and solemnly shook the countryman's calloused hand. "I'll do what has to be done here tonight and be off on the first train in the morning."

"When next we meet, we'll be out in the West. God help us all, McQuillan." The man turned and went from the classroom leaving Marcus staring off toward the rear wall. He soon roused himself from his sober thoughts and began preparing the classroom for his successor.

Marcus got to the bank just before closing and withdrew what savings he had. He went to his flat, packed some belongings and placed a note for his landlady on the mantel. The only person he visited that night was his longtime friend and benefactor, Avram Goldner. He informed the old man that he was leaving Dublin and would not be back. Goldner shrewdly surmised it had something to do with the Troubles. He suggested to Marcus that should he find himself without options, he would be wise to make his way back to the little shop off Grafton Street. "I have resources, Marcus my boy, and contact with people abroad. You might need me. Don't you forget Father Avram, eh?"

"I won't, I won't indeed," Marcus said quietly as he stepped forward and embraced Avram. He placed his hands on Goldner's shoulders and looked into the soft brown eyes above the pince-nez perched on the old man's nose before turning to leave the shop. He walked slowly back to Ranelagh along empty dark streets brooding on the unexpected turn of events. He could not bring himself to be concerned about his immediate future. He thought only of boyhood days below Benbo and his tagalong, skinny-legged brother.

It was a soft evening with the orange sun low in the sky out toward Sligo Bay as Marcus sauntered along the trout stream flowing down to the Bonet. He periodically plunked stones into the water since it was far too narrow for skimming. He looked back up to the cottage and saw his older sister speaking with two men at the front door. The spinster, Oona, now kept house for his aged father despite the persistent matrimonial interest of several widowers in the area.

Marcus guessed who they were as they warily watched him approach them across the deep grasses of the front pasture. "Oi'll be makin' the tay for ye," Oona said as she entered the dimly lit kitchen.

"Marcus McQuillan?" The tough-looking, older man asked.

"I am," Marcus replied, as he nodded in recognition to the other man who had been the messenger sent to Dublin.

"I'm Dermott Clooney and this is Matt Davies. We've come to speak of the plan to spring Sean. You've said you'd help us."

"I have."

"Well, we've been talking about the job at length, the doing of it and such, but all of us think there's something damned queer about it all."

"Queer? What do you mean?"

Clooney sat down on an oaken barrel at the side of the flat stones of the entranceway and rubbed his chin. "Well, we've scouted it out, the barrack's layout, the size of the guard force and whatnot and it looks just too damned easy. It looks like we can just bang in, shoot the hell out of them and be off with Sean in no time at all."

"So what is it you think might be the problem?"

"You see, McQuillan, we think it might be that those Treaty bastards are arranging things so that when we hit them they can shoot Sean without the bother of a court-martial. Davies here thinks different. Isn't that right, Matt?"

"Aye," Davies responded, "I was there in the pub at Rathcormack the night they took Sean. The Free State Officer who led the bunch was old

Tam McGivern. McGivern is known thereabouts to be a decent man and surely wouldn't put his hand to murder. Now, he's also the Chief Warder at the barracks and I'm thinking he's recoiled at the order that's come down from Dublin to execute Sean. I'm thinking he's keeping thing lax so we can get in and take Sean. That's what I'm thinking."

"God Almighty, I hope that's the case," Marcus said, yet added to Clooney, "but you don't think it is."

"Well now, I can't say for certain it's not true. But if we decide it is and we're wrong and go in light, it might mean your brother's life," Clooney answered looking out over the fields.

The three men sat silently. An idea suddenly occurred to Marcus. "Look, how about this? You people set up to go in. I'll go into the barracks compound just beforehand and speak with McGivern. I'll tell him we've come for Sean and there's nothing his little garrison can do except maybe die over it. Let's assume Davies is right about his being a decent man. He'd then be willing to participate in a show that covers himself and his people with regard to the Dublin crowd. If he's a lunatic hard head and you see me being taken into custody then come in hard and shoot to kill. Never mind about Sean and me in the shooting and killing. You see, if you don't come in blazing, Sean's a dead man anyway."

Clooney studied Marcus as he thought about what he had just said. He smiled broadly and shook his head in amusement, "Be God, McQuillan, if we'd a few more like you and your brother those Treaty boyos would never think about venturing outside of Dublin. What do you think, Davies, will we do as the man says?"

"Aye, Captain, I like his notion. Let's have a go at it like he says then."

Oona appeared at the kitchen door. "Yer tay's ready, gintlemen. Mind ye wipe yer feet," she said emphatically while standing elegantly erect for the benefit of Sean's dangerous and good-looking friends.

In the dying light of day, the McQuillans sat with the two rebels at the kitchen table and spoke of the weather, the crops and the recent hurling match in Sligo. An important thought came to Clooney. "Marcus, it occurs to me that as a result of our going along with your plan, it's no longer necessary for you to be involved in the affair. Anyone of us can go in and speak with McGivern. You're free to stay out of it, if you'd like."

"Yes, that's occurred to me as well. I'm not under oath like you fellows but it's my brother who's locked up, you know. I want to be there. I'll get the point across to McGivern all right."

"Oi'll want to be there as well. It's moy youngest involved," Tom McQuillan broke in.

Clooney laughed and shook his head in resignation, "I suppose you'll want to have a hand in it too, Oona."

"Oi'll be there if needed," Oona replied, looking up from tending the fire at the hearth.

"It's all right, Tom, you can be involved," Clooney continued, "you can go out there with Marcus. But once there, you'll do exactly as you're told. You and some others not part of the column can be involved. You might say you can be part of the general impression we'll want to make. But you'll follow orders like the rest. D'ye understand?"

"I do and I will," the old man responded, jutting out his chin in determination.

The police barracks near Aughris Head had not been built by the British at the end of the nineteenth century with an eye to strategic defense. It lay on open undulating terrain below a sharply rising, boulder-strewn ridge to the south. Its one large room served as barracks and mess, the small adjoining rooms as offices, detention cells and storage. The tiny Free State garrison saw patrol duty through the outlying villages as welcomed relief from its windswept isolation.

Clooney had chosen a Sunday morning for the raid that was to free Sean McQuillan. In the predawn darkness some of his men pulled hay from over an armored car that had been hidden on the back property of a crofter below Knockalongy. The Lancia armored personnel carrier, armed with two Lewis machine guns, had been commandeered months before from inexperienced government troops who had used it to attend a dance in Sligo.

In a small glen, some two miles from the barracks, a sizeable group of men, volunteer and impressed, gathered in the darkness. Clooney's Irregulars carried their rifles and shotguns while the others carried farm implements and good-sized sticks. The latter items were to be taken as firearms when seen from a sufficient distance. Old Tom McQuillan bore his *slean*.

One part of the phantom brigade would proceed behind the armored car directly along the mud track toward the barracks. The other part would take positions within rifle shot behind boulders on the ridge overlooking the camp. Those bearing tools and sticks would be positioned higher up among the outcrops of limestone.

At mid morning the armored car came to a stop a quarter of a mile from the main gate, steam hissing from beneath the engine hood. As the men fanned out behind the vehicle, no movement could be discerned in the barracks compound. Clooney decided to get their attention with a short burst from one of the Lewis guns.

Marcus saw a head peek out furtively from the front door and pop back in again as he stepped out of the armored car. He had a large British service revolver struck in at his waist below his jacket. He had no idea whether or not he could bring himself to use it to kill a man on behalf of his brother.

He began walking purposefully up the track toward the unmanned front gate. Just as he arrived at the chain-locked barricade, he saw a green-uniformed figure emerge from the building. The older man, with a bit of shaving cream on his cheek, confronted him through the crossbeams and wire. "Can Oi help ye in some way?" the officer said with a trace of a sardonic smile.

"We've come for Sean McQuillan. You'll be giving him to us."

"Oi will, will Oi?" came the reply.

Marcus turned toward the ridge and flapped both arms upward as a signal. With this, the host on the heights stood up from behind their concealment waving a modest number of Enfields among the props.

"Howly Good Chroist," whistled McGivern through his teeth, "you've got a bloody regiment up there."

Emboldened, Marcus pulled the revolver from his belt and held it barrel-down at his side. With his other hand he pointed ominously at McGivern's chest, "You'll give us Sean now, sir, or you'll all die, starting with you, right here, right now."

"Aisy now, aisy," McGivern responded calmly, "how will we do it?"

"Tell your men to come out without their weapons and stand against the wall by the door."

"What do ye mean aginst the wall?" McGivern responded grimly.

Marcus understood the implication, "All right then, have them stand over to the left there, well away from the barracks and the front gate. You'll come to no harm. I promise you."

"Oi'll bring out McQuillan with them," McGivern nodded, "will that suit ye?"

"It will. Get on with it."

McGivern went to the front door, opened it and called in instructions to his men. The thoroughly intimidated, half-dressed group of nine soldiers filed out, looking anxiously up at the ridge and down the mud track. Sean was among them. McGivern returned to the front gate. "Now what?" he queried.

"Stand clear Officer," Marcus indicated as he stood to the side of the track and waved the armored car forward, "we'll put on a bit of a show for the benefit of your report to Dublin."

The Lancia roared forward flinging heavy clumps of mud behind. The motley entourage with it broke into a sudden exuberant charge, Gaelic battle cries erupting here and there from the oldest men. McGivern scrambled to join his men as the wooden beams of the front gate splintered with a loud crack under the impact of the Lancia.

The Lancia skidded to a halt as it came about amid billowing clouds of steam. Clooney leaped out from the passenger side brandishing a parabellum. "Sean!" he called out as he gestured with this thumb, "in the back now."

He strode over to the thoroughly cowed cluster of Free Staters. "McGivern, I'm Captain Dermott Clooney. You've saved many a life this day, I can tell you."

"Oi have, have Oi?" McGivern responded laconically, "Oim a hero, is it?"

Clooney grinned amiably and shouted to his men who had begun to gather around the armored car. "You men, into the barracks for the weapons. Quick now, load them into the back."

The suddenly amused McGivern observed the teenagers and old men with their farm implements. "Oi'd guess ye'll be goin' after Dublin Castle soon with yer republican army, Clooney," he commented dryly.

"Look now, McGivern, most of these locals were impressed into service, you might say. There should be no reprisals. It's not that we can't come back in the night, you understand."

"Oi understand that all roight. No reproisals it is."

The camp yard was now filled with the untried, yet game infantrymen. They milled about, shared cigarettes and indulged themselves in individual palavers that included, of course, the Free Staters.

Clooney began ordering the members of his column into the vehicle. "Have you got a smoke?" he asked McGivern.

"Here, have the pack," Tam answered, "boy the way, Clooney, who was yer man at the gate?"

"That would be General Rory O'Hara, head of the 3rd Ulster Republican Division. He's to lead the new republican army unit being formed from the arrival of thousands of Yanks and Colonials flooding into the country to help us."

"He seemed more ta me loike a priest or schoolteacher."

"You're a perceptive man, McGivern. Why aren't you in the hills with us?"

"Argh, Oi'm too old to be trampin' about in the cold and wet. Besoides, Oi'm thinkin' about moy pension and a hot cup o' tay boy the foire."

"Good luck to you then, and I hope you're not put to going after us, " Clooney said, bidding the old officer goodbye with a firm handshake as he got into the Lancia.

Marcus climbed in right after him. As he sat by the open side window, a gapped-toothed, hoary codger limped past with a digging spade over his shoulder. "And what was it you were planning to do with that, old man?" Marcus asked with a friendly smile.

"This ye mean?" answered the old warrior gripping the spade with both hands and grinning devilishly. "Oi've foiled the one soide of it til it's razor sharp. Ef ye get close enough to a man, ye can behead him wit' it."

Just then, the *Morrigu,* ancient Irish goddess of battle and slaughter called out Marcus' name through the prophetic cawing of crows high above the ridge to the south.

A few hundred yards out from the barracks Clooney had the Lancia halted. He fired a few bursts with the Lewis guns well over the heads of those still lingering in the yard for purposes of posterity. Now, he said, the boyos would be able to speak in the future about their participation in the Battle of Aughris Head.

Two items of sociocultural significance occurred as a result of the morning's events. One was the immediate dispatch from Dublin of additional Free State troops to cope with the hostile presence of a well-armed brigade of Irregulars now boldly operating in the northwest beyond Sligo. The other was the composition of a local ditty entitled "Colonel Cooney's Raid", wherein the rebel, Sean McGilligan, was rescued by direct assault on a fortress dungeon and the bullets, naturally, were as "tick as floies".

After a few miles The Lancia could take no more mechanical abuse and gave out outside of Owenbeg. The small group loaded down with confiscated Enfields and ammunition, doused it with gasoline, set it afire and set out across the heath south toward Bunnyconnellan's safe houses. Marcus and Sean hiked together. "It was surprised I was to see that mug of yours when I came out of the barracks, Marcus," Sean said casually.

"And me holding a revolver, eh?"

"Ah, the McQuillan brothers in action, Ould Mulcahey would fairly dance in delight, wouldn't he?"

"Yes, he would, but he'd insist it was child's play compared to Fredericksburg."

"God, how I miss the old bugger."

They trudged in silence for a while, breathing heavily with their burdens. "Will we have a break, Clooney?" Sean called out.

"Aye, we will then, just up by those rocks ahead," came the answer.

Marcus and Sean squatted on low rocks and began smoking. Marcus gazed back across the heather in the direction from which they had come at a small flock of crows, circling and cawing in the distance. Now and again it seemed to him that they were following and crying out some inscrutable message.

"What will you do now, Marcus?" Sean said, interrupting Marcus' reverie.

"Do now? I just don't know."

"Well, after this you'll be on the run, won't you? Will you be joining us?"

"No, I don't think so. I don't have any strong beliefs about the Troubles one way or another, at least, not since the Treaty. What about you? How long will you go on with Clooney?"

"I don't know about that either, Marcus. It's been turning ugly of late. The hard heads are taking over on both sides with assassinations, burnings, reprisals and whatnot. It's not like the days when we were up against the British. We had the people's full support then, now, well, I think most people want an end to the fighting. We don't get the support we used to."

"So, you're thinking you can't win, is it?"

Sean laughed philosophically, "Win? Is it ever about winning with our kind? The calculators think about winning and the profit of it. The British built their empire by thinking that way. You must give them the respect due them. But us, the Irish, well, we don't seem to think beyond the contention itself and the going home and blathering about it over a pint. I think we are a gloriously stupid people with a natural gift for populating the military graveyards around the world. Who but the bloody British would have had the genius to discern that racial trait and put it to their service? Now, they've got us killing one another under their terms and conditions. Remarkable, isn't it Marcus, remarkable and somehow terribly tragic?"

"I know an older man in Dublin with essentially the same insight," replied Marcus, as he thought of Jack Jamieson, "but he's figured out how to profit from it."

"Yes, well there it is then. He's probably an up-to-date, adaptable, intelligent gentleman, not at all like our sort."

Marcus laughed. "What was it that Master Raye taught about the old legend that explains the Irish way of being in the world? He said, didn't he, that certain spiritual elements of paradise had to be separated out before Lucifer could enter in and tempt mankind? Those separated elements manifested in the physical world as Ireland. Lucifer, he said, was subsequently prevented from having an effect on the human beings that lived in this particular region of the earth. Here, there would be no development of the abstract calculating intelligence that enables one man to profit at the expense of another."

"Yes, I remember his saying that and not quite understanding the meaning of it then. He was always saying there was more truth in myth and legend than the scientific analysis of things and events. Old Master Raye, ah, we were lucky little lads, weren't we Marcus?"

The brothers sat in the silence of nostalgia, lost in memories of their childhood on the hills of Leitrim. They were both startled suddenly by a loud raucous squall directly above them. Looking up, they saw a huge black bird against the sun that shone glaringly through a break in the gray cumulus clouds.

"Jesus, Marcus, will you look at the size of that crow," Sean exclaimed, getting to his feet.

Cathal O'Neil, the oldest member of Clooney's column, sitting quietly away from the group, interjected, "That's no crow, McQuillan, that's a raven. She's brought a message from Herself. She's givin' us a ward, and that ward moight be that we should git ta hell outa here."

Avram Goldner squinted through the thick lenses of his workbench magnifier at the broken hasp of an expensive gold necklace. He had just pinched the separated ends of the filament together with his jeweler's pliers when the bells above the front door jangled loudly. As he saw the familiar figure enter his shop, his heart leaped with gladness. "Marcus, Marcus, my boy," he exclaimed.

"Father Avram," Marcus happily responded.

Avram studied Marcus' appearance. He now had the healthy ruddy face of the rural Irish. His once fine suit was now frayed at the cuffs and darned at the knees. It had a dull, brownish gray color with ground-in dirt. Avram grasped Marcus' hands with affection and felt the hard calloused palms and fingers. "What happened to my fine scholar? With some coal dust on you, they'd say you've just returned from long labor in the Welsh mines."

"Well, I've been out in the West on the land these past months. You know, a man must do the work at hand for his upkeep. I've used every farm tool imaginable, Avram, and been outside in the weather from dawn until dusk. I liked it though. I surely did. I'd just as soon do that kind of manual labor as get stuck in a classroom again."

Avram considered Marcus's remarks and said "I've been afraid for you, Marcus, since the time you told me you were leaving Dublin. It was so abrupt. I assumed you were somehow involved in the Troubles."

"Well, I was for a short bit but it had to do with family, not politics."

"Are you clear of it now?"

"No, I don't think so. I'm guessing the Treaty Government's people are on the lookout for me."

"I think they are, Marcus," Avram commented with a look of concern.

"Why do you say that, Avram?"

"Soon after you left a woman came to me asking for your whereabouts. Then a few days later, two members of the Civic Guard came asking for information about you. Somehow, it seemed the two visits were connected. I have no idea who told them of our friendship."

"Was the woman's name Kate Jamieson? She'd have had light hair, green eyes."

"No, the woman was a dark brunette and the name she gave me wasn't Jamieson."

"Aah, it might have been one of Kate's sisters come to put a knife into me," Marcus said drolly. "What did the police ask about?"

"Just your whereabouts. They seemed to know you'd left your job and lodgings. They asked if I knew your brother, Sean."

"Ah by God, they've made the connection. I'm for it now," Marcus sighed.

"Look now Marcus, you put in with me upstairs for now. I'll see to you and tell the rest of my family you're to be treated as one of them. I'm the Patriarch and they'll do as bidden. There's no need to discuss your situation with any of them."

Avram put his hand on Marcus' back. "I'll lock up and we'll go upstairs for tea and a bite to eat. My widowed daughter, Esther, looks after me now. You keep your papish paws off of her, eh?" Avram quipped with a wink.

Marcus held up his hands and stared open-eyed at them. "Oh, I will, Father Avram, I will. These rough paws would take the very skin off her."

"One last thing, my boy, you'll earn your keep here too. I just hope you're as good in the fine work with delicate instruments as you are at the cutting of peat."

Later that night, Marcus went to bed between clean sheets and with a full stomach. He had earlier soaked in the hot soapy water of the first full bath he had had in several weeks.

Avram took a certain pride in being seen with his gentile protégé. He had Marcus accompany him about Dublin on his visits to relations, business associates and members of the Jewish community. Marcus wore the old man's secondhand dark clothes including a black derby worn at a slightly rakish angle. To his own amusement, he also began sporting a full beard. Socially, he adopted a posture of reticence and deference to Avram and in a short time impressed the paterfamilias' people as the epitome of a righteous man.

Marcus was permitted to sit wearing a yarmulke at Avram's side during study at the orthodox shul within Grenville Hall Synagogue. Occasionally, he was able to ask questions of the rabbi that would cause the learned man to go silent in meditative thought for a short while before answering. The members of the congregation were duly impressed. One evening after class one of Avram's nephews, Jacob, politely asked Marcus about his education and knowledge of the Pentateuch. "Oh, I learned that at school when I was a lad," came the reply.

"At school? You attended a shul as a boy, Marcus?"

"Oh no, no, Jacob, I attended a little school in Dundaragh out in Leitrim."

"Who was your teacher?"

"Master Raye, he was a very learned man."

"Oh yes? This Master Raye, was he Jewish?"

Marcus began to laugh and shook his head in merriment, "Oh no, Master Raye was as Catholic as the Pope. The man was one great scholar. I learned more from him about the things discussed here than from my Jesuit teachers at the University."

Jacob, his curiosity piqued, thought for a moment and then asked quietly, "And what, Marcus, would be Master Raye's final pronouncement on the continued existence of Judaism within Christendom?"

Marcus looked down and fingered his beard while searching his memory for an adequate answer. "Well," he finally said, "I think Master Raye would say that the western world is no longer to be considered Christendom. Life has changed radically in modern times, hasn't it?

Judaism, in a sense, is different from other religions. I remember his saying it wasn't just a religious creed. It was part of a divine and human truth embodied in the very flesh of a living people. There was no earthly reason, he said, explaining why Judaism survives throughout history. A true Christian, therefore, would never feel enmity toward Jews."

Jacob nodded. Marcus' head perked up as another memory came to him. He gestured with a forefinger, "Oh yes, I remember another thing he said about it. He said the Jews were our elder spiritual brothers and were to be treated as such."

The nephew continued nodding, "This Master Raye, he sounds like a remarkable man, Marcus. I'll remember him in my prayers."

Now Marcus nodded and was filled with a warm nostalgia as he looked into the indigo evening sky above the Dublin rooftops. "Master Raye," he intoned quietly.

"Do you know Robert Briscoe, Marcus?" Jacob continued.

"Briscoe? No, I can't say that I do."

"He's one of our people who's been involved in the Troubles."

"Is he?"

"Yes, he fought against the British and was sent at that time over to America to raise funds for the rebels."

"He did, did he?"

Jacob, driven by simple human curiosity concerning Marcus' circumstances but ever mindful of Uncle Avram's admonition about propriety, continued, "I understand that he's with the anti-Treaty forces now. I think he's Eamon DeValera's adjutant."

"He is, is he?"

Marcus, amused by the expectant look in the young man's eyes, decided to satisfy his inquisitiveness. "Are you wondering, Jacob, if I'm an active republican on the run and going to ground among your people?"

"Well ah, I ah, we were wondering about that, Marcus."

"No Jacob, I'm no republican. I think I'm like most Irishmen and would like to see an end to the killing. I can't say I agree with the Treaty but it's what we have. I can live with it. It's because of a personal relationship that I was involved in a bit of trouble out in the West. I suppose I'm a wanted man, but understand now, I've been involved in no killing."

Jacob nodded, "I'm glad for that, Marcus, and I hope you'll forgive my intrusiveness."

Marcus smiled, "Not at all."

After initial misgivings concerning the gentile stranger in her home, Esther began to feel the beginnings of affection toward Marcus. His easy casual manner coupled with his filial devotion toward her father dissipated her natural wariness. He laughed easily at her occasional satirical comments regarding men. He was appreciative of her cooking and did not take the performance of her household duties for granted. It did not hurt the situation that Esther found the blue-eyed Gael easy to look at.

There was an aspect to Esther, known to her father and inner members of the congregation, to which Marcus was not privy. She was periodically clairvoyant. The spinster had lucid dreams concerning certain individuals that had a prophetic sibylline character well beyond that which could be attributed to coincidence. Some months before Marcus' arrival, Esther had told her father that his friend, Chaim, the taxi fleet owner, would be involved in a life-threatening accident but would not die. Later that week, it happened that Chaim was struck by a coal lorry while exiting one of his taxis. He was hospitalized with severe injuries but survived. It was therefore with sudden stark interest that Avram's head came up from his soup bowl while sitting with Esther in their kitchen one evening when Marcus was away on an errand. "I dreamed," she said, simply.

"Oh yes? About whom, Esther?"

"Marcus", she replied solemnly.

Avram felt a small qualm of trepidation. "You dreamed about someone who is not a member of the community?"

"Yes, Abba," Esther answered, using the term of respect and endearment.

Almost afraid to hear the contents of the dream, Avram asked, "Do you fully understand the meaning of it Esther?"

"No, I've thought about it but I can't understand all of it, Abba."

"Hmm", Avram uttered to himself. "Tell me of it, then"

Esther began. "There were sheep being kept by a seated shepherd. The sheep were our people. I don't know who the shepherd was but I know he was protecting our people. A pack of wolves came for the sheep and took them and the shepherd could do nothing because he was a cripple. One of those huge shaggy dogs came on the scene. What do you call those huge dogs, Abba?"

"Wolfhounds, Esther, I used to see them at the country fairs when I was traveling."

"Yes, one those huge dogs came on the scene. He went after the pack of wolves. He was hunting the largest wolf," Esther paused, looking off into space trying to remember her vision.

She continued. "Then there were many images. An old man with hairy pointed ears was singing and dancing and enjoying the mayhem. A golem took the sheep from the wolves. The largest wolf was cowering and yelping like a frightened puppy."

"A golem?"

"Yes, a disfigured golem took the sheep. He was not a danger to them. There was a raging fire, a woman crying out and there were gunshots. The sheep were not there."

"What happened to the wolfhound, Esther?"

"I don't know, Abba. I only know that the sheep remained in safety and the large wolf was slaughtered instead.

"Why do you think the dream was about Marcus?"

"I'm not sure why except that I saw that the wolfhound had Marcus' blue eyes and somehow I know that the old man who was egging him on was an old friend of his from the past."

"Do you think that the dream is connected to his present situation?"

"No, I don't think so. Somehow it seems to me that Marcus will be taking a journey soon and he won't be coming back."

"Journey? Do you know where?"

"No, I don't."

"Is his going away connected to your dream, Esther?"

"No, I don't think so. What I saw will come to pass many years from now in a faraway place. I can't tell you of the exact circumstances. There will be a terrible danger to our people somewhere and Marcus will be there. What I saw will come to pass."

Avram was now somewhat relieved of his anxiety for Marcus. He was a deeply religious man and considered that Marcus' fate, like that of any man, rested finally in the hands of the living God. He knew for certain, however, that sometime in the future, in some place, Marcus McQuillan, his spiritual son, would be again connected to his people. Marcus would act decisively on their behalf. He would give a good account of himself and Avram would somehow, perhaps preternaturally, be there.

"Well, Marcus," the fashionably-dressed woman beneath the black cloche began, "the beard hardly becomes you. Are you a Jew now?"

Marcus looked up from the magnifying glass as he sat repairing a silver bracelet in the rear of Avram's shop. He looked into the hard dark eyes of Margaret, Kate Jamieson's married sister.

Marcus nodded. "Hello, Margaret."

"Well?" Margaret continued.

"What, Margaret?"

"Are you a Jew now? Or are you attempting to disguise yourself for some reason?"

Marcus was neither put off by Margaret's hostility nor was he terribly surprised to see her. He had considered that, at almost anytime after his return to Dublin, he might run into someone who knew him. "No Margaret, I'm not in disguise and I'm not trying to stay out of sight."

"Really? One would think you were."

"Oh yes? And why would that be the case?"

Margaret glowered with sullen dislike. She paused before she spoke. "Considering what you did to my sister and your covert republican activities as well, one might expect you to attempt to fade out of sight for awhile. Whether motivated by shame or the desire for self-preservation, I must admit, I can't make a judgment about."

Marcus ruminated before he spoke. He knew that no matter what he said, Margaret was not to be conciliated. He also knew that whatever he said now would surely reach the ears of Kate and her father. He let his fondness for them guide his words. "Margaret, this is the truth of it. Your sister Kate and your father are fine decent people. I think of them often and I sorely regret that I can't see them anymore. I will always have the fondest feelings for Kate and I wish her every success and happiness in her life."

Marcus paused, looking down at the cluttered worktable before him. A soft sadness came upon him. "She'll do better than me."

From above, the harsh unforgiving words came down upon him, "Every man she meets is better than you, farm boy. You were never deserving of her."

Marcus accepted the chastisement without rancor. He looked back up at Margaret waiting for whatever further calumny she wished to pour on him. He commented, all too casually for Margaret's liking, "There's probably truth in that."

Margaret studied Marcus's features looking in vain for that psychological discomfort she saw so often in her husband and children after one of her accusatory diatribes. She found none and in a small spasm of anger, she adjusted her gray velvet gloves and turned to leave the shop. As she walked purposefully toward the front door, she heard Marcus's quiet voice behind her. "Say hello to Father Beastly."

Her ears reddened as she clenched her jaw. Had she a revolver, she would have wheeled about and shot him. A few minutes out of the shop as she turned onto the bustle of Grafton Street, Margaret determined that she would visit the Civil Guard headquarters the first thing in the morning. It was, she convinced herself, her civic duty and had nothing to do with her personal feelings toward her family.

Actually, it had everything to do with her personal feelings. If Margaret had been the least bit conscious of her motivation, she would have become aware of the primary reason she sought Marcus out. She simply had always found her sister's former fiancé attractive and had really come to the shop on her own behalf. She didn't know that about herself and would have found the suggestion of it preposterous. Yet, there was a far more important thing concerning Marcus she didn't know at the time. Her sister, Kate, was with child.

"She'll go to the police, Marcus," Avram suggested after hearing the details of Margaret's conversation with his ward, "I'm sure she was the woman who was looking for you some time ago. The Civil Guard came soon after that."

"I think you might be right."

"You must leave immediately, you are most probably a wanted man and we can waste no time. The provisional government is now executing rebels."

"I can go to the West again."

"Marcus, I have many contacts abroad, in England, Belgium and France. Can you speak French?"

"I can, as a matter of fact. I studied French for four years at the University and occasionally I've read in French."

"I can send you for now to my cousin in Bordeaux. It's on the Atlantic Coast toward the south of France. You can act as courier and deliver a few, small expensive items for me. I can write a letter of introduction as well. What do you say to that, Marcus?"

"France? Yes, that has some appeal. I've never been out of Ireland and have always intended to spend some time abroad. France, yes, I think I'd like to do that."

"Go upstairs and have Esther prepare a good meal for you. Pack your belongings. I'll make the necessary travel arrangements. Don't worry about money, I'll take care of that."

Marcus simply nodded in assent. To his mind, he was simply traveling abroad for the first time in his life. He had no idea of the melancholy that gripped Avram as the old man thought of Esther's pronouncements.

Just before dawn on the following day, Marcus, Avram and Esther stood on the wet pier at Dun Laoghaire below a rusted old freighter that was to take Marcus from Ireland. Marcus was chipper as he bade the

Goldner's goodbye and fairly bounced up the gangway. He stayed at the railing looking down into the darkness at his friends as the ship pulled its hawsers and made for the Irish Sea. The sun had just cleared the horizon to the east as Marcus looked back to the two tiny figures bathed in orange light on the green barnacled pier. They waved. He waved in return. He could not know of the tears that coursed down their cheeks and the silent prayers that were being said for him.

Marcus was not a wanted man. The detectives who appeared in Avram's shop two days later made only perfunctory inquiries about him. They were interested in finding Sean McQuillan, not his older brother. Marcus had not been connected with the raid at Aughris Head. Lieutenant McGivern's official report to Dublin made no mention of the identity of the rescuers. McGivern, being the kind of man he was, wouldn't have supplied the name of the amiable republican he met at the front gate even if he had known it.

In the dim early morning light of the upstairs hallway Madeleine carried her suitcase toward the stairwell. She made no effort to be quiet with her footfalls. She guessed Helene would probably be awake but she did not care whether the woman was aware of her going or not.

Madeline had not slept. She still felt the hotness of anger because of what Helene had done to Marcus and had lay in the darkness going through in her mind the events that had led to his leaving. Did that woman really think that her life would be improved in some way with Marcus gone? Did she really think that the people at the Deschaines residence would believe her action came as the result of her outrage over young Fleury's death? "She must think we are idiots," Madeleine conjectured to herself.

Helene heard the footsteps in the hall. She hadn't slept either. She quickly arose from her bed, put on her gray flannel robe and walked barefooted to the top of the stairwell. She heard the front door opening and slamming shut. She knew, of course, it was Madeleine and that if she did not now move quickly to catch up with her in the driveway, she would probably never see her again. What, in any event, could she say to the cook that would change things? Helene felt a small pang of surprise and anxiety over the realization that she had not at all anticipated Madeleine's reaction to her decision. Not for one moment would that canny woman believe that Helene had acted out of moral considerations. No, Madeleine would not see it that way.

Helene descended the stairs and went toward the kitchen to see to some kind of breakfast for herself and Auguste. She was surprised to see Ruth and Zalman sitting quietly at the butcher-block table. "Oh, *bon matin*, I didn't know you were here," she said pleasantly.

Both rose from their seats immediately, "*Bon matin*, Madame Deschaines," they replied almost in unison.

There was an awkwardness as the couple stood in silence looking at the floor waiting for Helene to say something further. Helene said quietly, "Madeleine has gone. I really don't know what we'll do for now. We'll just have to manage."

"We are staying then, Madame Deschaines?" Ruth asked timorously.

"What? What are you asking?"

"Will we be staying on, Madame Deschaines?" Zalman asked again pointedly.

"Will you be staying on? I don't understand why you are asking such a question."

Again there was an awkward silence before Ruth spoke, "We were thinking that perhaps because of the incident regarding the delivery boy you might ask us to leave."

Helene was momentarily at a loss for words. She could not think of an immediate appropriate reply, "Oh no, no, I would not ask you to leave because of that. Oh no, no, I would not do that."

A heavy silence ensued. Helene was well aware now that for the Meyers nothing she had said had put them at their ease. They could, after all, have no understanding as to why she would demand that Marcus leave because of the Fleury incident yet there would be no apparent implications for them. Because of her own discomfort, Helene sought a reason for leaving the kitchen. "I'm going to the study to see if Auguste is awake yet. Ruth, will you please light the stove?"

"Yes, Madame."

In an effort to relax the situation, Helene smiled, "Please use my Christian name, Ruth, you are guests here, not servants."

Ruth simply looked at Helene without the softening Helene had hoped for, "If you wish, Madame Deschaines."

Helene padded quietly toward the study. She poked her head in and seeing Auguste sitting at his desk looking pensively out of the window, she greeted him, "*Bon matin*, my love."

Auguste turned his head slowly toward her and simply nodded. He turned again to the window as she approached his desk. "Madeleine is gone, Auguste, she left earlier," she offered, attempting to engage her husband in conversation.

Still looking out of the window, Auguste said coolly, "Yes, she stopped in to see me last night before retiring."

"I wonder why she didn't speak to me about her leaving."

A look of disdain crossed Auguste's features. The fingers of his left hand lightly caressed his forehead as he shut his eyes. He set his lips tightly together and shook his head in negation.

"Don't you think it was unseemly of her, Auguste?"

Auguste stared at Helene, the rigidity of his jaw suggesting something close to anger. "Helene," he said curtly.

"What Auguste? What are you upset about?"

Auguste said nothing but continued to glower at his wife. He began to feel the sting of tears in his eyes with his feelings lost somewhere between sorrow and vexation. "Never before, in all the time we've been married have I had the thought of hurting you," he began, "never before. But now, with this pretense of yours about not knowing what other people around you are upset about. With your intent to pretend that you are outraged over the death of young Fleury and befuddled by people's reaction to the events of yesterday, well, that is something I will not indulge you in. No, Helene, you will not have it that way."

"But Auguste, if..."

"Be still!" Auguste ejaculated angrily, "goddamn it, be still! Say nothing. I will not listen to you. You've said and done quite enough. Have the decency to say nothing."

Auguste placed both hands on his desk and looked down into his lap as if to terminate the conversation with Helene. In a tight trembling voice Helene attempted again to begin what she would call, in another situation, dialogue. "Auguste, we must talk."

"Get out!" He snarled, as his head snapped up. "Get out now, before you try to say another word and I lunge from this wheelchair and throttle you."

Poissy sat absentmindedly at the routine briefing in Captain of Milice Vendeur's smoked-filled office. He inspected his fingernails as Vendeur repeated his inevitable demand for correct paperwork as documentation for Milice activities. "I'll be reviewing the files, men, I'll expect to see accuracy and timeliness from everyone. Am I making myself clear?"

Poissy was torn away from his contemplation of the half-moon at the base of his thumbnail with the Captain's next remark. "We've been alerted that the Gestapo will be coming down from Lyon shortly to audit our records with respect to the detection and apprehension of undesirables in our area."

"The Gestapo, Captain? When are they due?" inquired the militiaman to Poissy's immediate right.

"I would not be surprised if they are here by next week, Germaine. It is the kind of thing these people do periodically. You know, Teutonic efficiency and whatnot. I have every confidence they'll find our work in order. We French can be efficient as well, eh?"

There was a low murmuring throughout the cramped office as the men conferred with one another. "That will be all for now, men," Vendeur announced, "if I find problems while going through the files and logs, you'll be hearing from me directly. Any questions? No? Then to your duties."

Poissy remained seated as the briefing broke up. He thought of his friends on Ormeau Road and quickly determined that he would go to Couderouge at the first opportunity and inform Auguste and Marcus of the impending arrival of the Gestapo in the vicinity. Had he been more mindful at the moment, he would have performed a simple clerical adjustment on behalf of his friends. He would have remembered the initial notes he had made and filed on his return to his office the day he met Marcus on the road outside of Couderouge. That day he had also spoken with young Fleury and become familiar with the situation at the Deschaines residence. He would have destroyed those notes.

But his scribbled addendum to the report he made that day, several weeks ago, lay forgotten in the dog-eared folder labeled *Ardeche Nord,* filed in the metal cabinet in his office. It lay buried and forgotten rather like one of the corroded, unexploded artillery shells beneath the topsoil of Verdun.

Oberst Friedrich von Rugen, commander of the 48th Panzergrenadiers stationed in Privas, sat in his immaculate office in the commandeered town council house listening to his adjutant read military communiqués. The Prussian Colonel did not read because he chose not to. He refused to use an eyeglass for his one good eye and had determined quite for himself that anything he heard and did not retain was simply not worth remembering.

The Colonel had lost his eye and major fragments of the right side of his face, as well as full use of his right arm and leg, near the western bank of the Volga River in October of the previous year. He had been serving in von Paulus' sixth army and was assigned to a spearhead battalion in the advance on Stalingrad.

Colonel von Rugen had always been an excellent, if somewhat eccentric, officer. His family was part of the Junker aristocracy, distantly related to the Hohenzollern royal family. His life had been one of soldiering and somewhere in the course of it he had completely lost the human emotion of fear. The naked apprehension he observed in others in a combat situation was a mystery to him.

On that frosty morning on the Volga Major von Rugen's battalion had been given a *himmelfahrts kommando,* that is, a journey-to-heaven-mission. It had been ordered to impede the counterassault of a Soviet tank division while the German army consolidated its firepower. Without hesitation and without his helmet, von Rugen had leaped into his staff car at the head of a column of armor and went straight away for the attacking Russians. He remembered the white morning sky to the east and below it the bright flashes of the Russian gunners as the serial detonations of shell bursts began approaching his bouncing vehicle. In the blast that killed his driver, von Rugen was thrown from the shattered staff car into the long brown grasses at the side of the road. He remembered struggling to get to his feet and being perplexed and angered because he could not see and his legs continually buckled beneath him. Finally, he knelt and shouted incoherent orders at the tanks rumbling past him on the way to engage the Russians.

The German rashness initiated by von Rugen had its effect as the Soviet onslaught was halted. His battalion lost most of its men and vehicles. Major von Rugen was promoted to colonel and shipped to a hospital near Breslau. After an incomplete recuperation he was given a week's leave to see his family and reassigned to Privas in occupied France.

As *Oberst* von Rugen was without fear so also was he frequently without the ability to maintain social conventions. He remained in command in Privas simply because he was well connected to the Prussian in-group in the German High Command. For extended periods the Colonel would talk to no one but simply limp imperiously among his men scrutinizing their activity with his glaring eye. His commands took the form of either a loud crack of his riding crop against his knee-high, shiny black boots or a mere nod of approval. His staff meetings, arranged by his adjutant, Captain Shinse, were punctuated by long periods of silence before von Rugen would point at an officer with his riding crop with the obvious meaning that the man should report. Often enough, these reports were cut short by the single bang of his riding crop on his desk.

It was obvious to those about him that the war hero held the Nazis in contempt. He never returned the salute of a soldier who used the extended arm gesture and several times it was observed that when a subordinate used the expression, *"Heil Hitler"*, von Rugen would simply grunt, "Be still, idiot".

Captain Shinse had come to the last of the communiqués from higher headquarters. "So, *Oberst,* we are expected to become exceedingly familiar with the topography between here and the Mediterranean Coast in preparation for a possible invasion from that direction."

He waited for a response from von Rugen. There was none. "Shall I begin organizing map exercises with the staff, sir?"

After a prolonged silence, von Rugen spoke, "No".

"No? No, sir?"

"The invasion will come from across the Channel in the late spring or summer of next year."

Shinse nodded indicating he understood and waited for von Rugen to say more. He didn't. Shinse remained standing and waited to be excused. Minutes passed.

Von Rugen spoke suddenly, "That little swine in Berlin has managed to destroy our army in the east. He will now go about doing the same in the west. Eisenhower will see to its destruction by use of that gigantic aircraft carrier moored off the northwest coast of France, namely Great Britain."

Despite himself, Shinse smiled. As he looked at his commander the adjutant found the electric blue, Cyclopean eye upon him, "You are amused, Captain?"

Shinse went rigid, "Oh no, *Oberst!"*

Hating dishonesty even of the smallest kind, von Rugen slapped his riding crop on his desk, "What else?"

The chastised adjutant shuffled the papers nervously in his hands, "*Oberst,* we are informed that Gestapo personnel will be with us shortly."

"With us? What do you mean 'with us'?" von Rugen snapped.

"Ah, er, ah, they'll be in Privas perhaps by next week, sir."

The Prussian was not in the least interested as to why the Gestapo would be in Privas. He sourly commented, "Are there not enough vermin in the back alleys of this town?"

Shinse could think of no response to von Rugen's remark. He felt relieved when the Colonel continued, "Dismissed, Captain," then added as the adjutant strode gratefully to the door, "keep those pieces of excrement out of my sight."

Oberst Friedrich von Rugen alone at his desk now, sat erectly, his crippled, claw-like right hand in his lap. He stared unseeingly at the highly polished, empty desktop. He was lost in the vagaries of his mind as now and again memories of his earlier life condensed amid the clutter. He saw the old woman and his features softened perceptively. "Trudi".

Helene felt isolated and vulnerable. It seemed that her delicate crystalline constellation of old habits and interpersonal poses that she had constructed for herself over the years were now shattered. In the days that followed Auguste's outburst, she moved about her residence as if in the throes of a bad dream where the attempt at contact with anyone might prove hurtful to her. "What have you done?" She asked herself. "Why didn't you know it would be like this?"

She tried to see beyond her morose state. She had the insight that while one's emotions might be useful in discerning elements of reality outside oneself, they were useless with regard to introspection. As Auguste had said, for that enterprise the clear light of critical reason was the *sine qua non*. And if that were true then perhaps she really didn't know herself. Had she been blind all these years to her own peccadilloes, her own pettinesses dressed up as they were in a benign, lifeless social theory. No, she was not outraged over Fleury's death at all. Why did she expect anyone to believe that she was? She felt her own charlatanism. Marcus, as she had stupidly suspected, was not the *Tartuffe*. She was.

She acknowledged the very plain reason for her palpable quarantine. She had hurt someone for whom these people cared very much. She had done that and then mouthed sentimental garbage to justify herself. She remembered quite clearly that she had carried off her self-serving speech to Auguste that day in the study demanding Marcus' leaving without the least anxiety. It was almost as if she had been intoxicated with her own righteousness. She had been so very sure of herself, so confident in her own correctness. God in heaven, where did that self-righteousness come from?

Yes, yet now she was willing to make things right. Ah, but how? Could she go to the rectory to see Marcus, ask his forgiveness and implore him to return? Could she tell him that he was absolutely essential at the Deschaines residence? Could she ask him to let bygones be bygones? Could she do that? Inwardly, Helene balked. There was something deeper in her being that she could not see.

Helene, in her soul searching, was approaching something with which most people never come to grips, a kind of threshold having to do with the unmentionable dark side of one's humanity. The psychological deformations in Helene were not truly of an inorganic crystalline nature but rather something else. They were her own creations and as biologically one can participate in creation, so psychologically, one can spawn living entities.

That entity loved no one, neither Auguste, nor the mother, nor the Algerian woman, nor Helene herself. It recognized Marcus McQuillan as its mortal enemy and had cunningly moved against him. It had, after all, a conscious intelligence well beyond that of the ordinary person. In terms of its survival it had but one flaw and that flaw was its ignorance of the fact of human love. For although it did not love, Helene-Marie Deschaines did. And Helene Deschaines loved Marcus McQuillan.

It was, therefore, late in the third day of her purgatory that Helene came across the dragon and despite reeling in the ferment of her existential agony, she slew it.

That evening she had eaten alone in the kitchen and then spared Ruth the task of the after dinner wash up. She had walked out on the wooded back property until the soft light of dusk descended and on her return found herself near the spruce-enclosed, stone cottage. Her retrievers, *Yaourt* and *Biscuit*, sat before the green-enameled door as if on sentry duty. Both dogs rose at her approach but hardly reacted to her soft petting of their heads. With a sudden urge to enter the stillness within, she opened the door and stepped into the semidarkness. She stood for several minutes at the base of the neatly made bed staring vacantly down on the coarse, gray woolen coverlet. Hanging at the head of the bed from the brass bedpost a draping fragment of heavy cloth caught her eye. She moved to the side of the bed, sat and lifted what appeared to be a sweater into her lap. She recognized it as the dark gray cardigan that she had given Auguste several Christmases ago. She remembered that he had never worn it and the pang of pique she had felt when she saw it on Marcus and realized that her husband must have given it to him. "Imagine that," she thought to herself, "I was irritated because of my husband's generosity."

She recalled making some remark to Marcus about it and then afterward, never seeing it on him again. She shuddered within herself surmising that he had left it because he probably never thought that it was truly his. Tears welled in her eyes as she lifted the cardigan to her face. She smelled traces of Marcus on it, the nicotine, his earthiness, his physical exudations, yes, his sweet strong manliness. Helene began to sob softly and spasm lightly throughout her body. She curled into a fetal position on the bed clutching the cardigan to her face. She began to convulse, first moderately, then violently as her face contorted into an open-mouthed, silent screaming. She frantically pressed the sweater to her mouth as if to protect herself from the horror of self-hating that was engulfing her. She mercifully slipped into unconsciousness and as she did she was faintly aware of an electric discharge from deep within her.

    Helene was briefly disoriented as she came to consciousness in the darkness of the cottage. She was tempted to remain within the tranquility of her mind and enjoy the delectable, almost sensual, relaxation of her body. She rose to a sitting position and her mind went to the distance between her home and the rectory and the night walk that lay before her. She stood and smiled ever so slightly as she donned the cardigan against the night chill and felt the dampness of her tears on her arm.

    The dogs rose excitedly to their feet as she exited the cottage and she grinned knowingly as they nosed busily at the front of the sweater that hung well below her hips. *Yaourt* and *Biscuit* fell in just behind her as escort as she walked purposefully across the property and onto Ormeau Road. She had no idea of the time as she walked in the star-speckled night but saw the sky lightening to the east as she approached St. Gregoire's.

    At the rectory door the dogs complied with her command to sit. She opened the heavy door quietly so as not to disturb Paul Bassard's sleep and proceeded soundlessly down the short, white-walled corridor to the guestroom. The oaken door was slightly ajar as Helene pushed it open and entered. Marcus was asleep on his side facing away from her with his right arm crooked beneath his head. She went around the bed and stood over him. She experienced a small unexplainable delight in the observation that, as usual, he was in need of a shave. She was also amused that although bare-chested, he was sleeping in his trousers, his dark suspenders draped over his white shoulders. A picture from childhood came to her. Her father was singing and shaving before the mirror in the family's tiny washroom. He was barefooted and shirtless with a thumb tucked under one of his braces as he turned and winked at her.

    She put her hand lightly to Marcus' bare shoulder. "Marcooz," She whispered softly.

    When he did not respond she shook him gently and repeated. "Marcooz."

    His eyes opened and for a moment he stared straight ahead. He rolled over to a half-sitting position propped on his elbows and looked up at her with his customary bewildered squint and pursed lips. She supressed an amused laugh and collected herself. She gazed into his eyes unabashedly and expressed herself in the only way she could at the moment. She placed her hand gently in the middle of his chest and murmured, "Come home."

Marcus responded as a man does following benediction from a woman. He placed his hand upon the hand that was warming his heart. "I will," he whispered.

Von Rugen's notions of proper military engagement were considerably older than old school. As his father, a decorated field grade officer of the Great War, had detested trench warfare so Von Rugen maintained a cool contempt for the technologies employed by modern armies. For him, the elegant encounter occurred between individuals, skill against skill, preferably with sabers. He had no dueling scars because as a young cadet he had been too good a swordsman, and besides, he was not given to ostentation.

Following his injuries he forced himself with daily practice to become adroit with the cavalry saber using his left hand. This he did with facility owing to the fact that he had been born left-handed and when still a little boy had been changed to right-handed in keeping with the accepted practice of his antedeluvian mentors. Once a week he arranged for personal exercise against selected men in his unit known for their ability with the bayonet. He specifically warned each man that he expected his full effort against him and promised he would skewer any man he thought fainthearted.

No one knew of the Colonel's dark sardonic sense of humor. Once, when nervously exuberant young *Unteroffizer* Trager gashed him in the thigh of his good leg, he lurched back and passively grunted, *"Gut."*

Von Rugen, ignoring the wound, walked purposefully to the chair by the sidewall on the back of which hung his tunic and leather holster. He slowly withdrew his old Luger from the holster, chambered a round with the slide mechanism and placed it back into the holster. He casually stepped back to his ready position, took a few singing decapitating slashes with his saber and pointed it at the soldier's navel. He surpressed a self-amused smile as he observed the rather large areas of white in the young man's eyes.

Captain Wilhelm Shinse tried to ignore the knot of constriction he felt in his bowels as the *Kubelwagen* he was driving jounced along a country road east of Privas. He had the grim thought that the nickname for the light utility vehicle given it by the men of the *Wehrmacht* was, in this present situation, quite appropriate. He deemed it entirely possible, perhaps probable, that if fired upon from the leafy thickets along the lane he would soil himself. In that case he would indeed be in need of the bathtub suggested by the shape of the boxy vehicle.

Shinse and the Colonel were on one of the latter's weekly hunting forays into the French countryside seeking an encounter with the *Maquis*. He had once made the mistake of indicating to the Colonel his unhappiness with garrison duty. The remark was made more from the desire to impress rather than conviction. Von Rugen had smiled or grimaced, the Captain knew not which because of the older man's facial disfigurement, and suggested the foraying enterprise. Despite himself, with a sudden rapid rise in heartbeat, Shinse quickly assented.

A German army Gewehr 41 rifle with telescopic sight and MP40 machine pistol lay across the back seat. Captain Shinse would have much preferred their being in front where, after screeching to a halt at the sound of gunfire, he could grab the automatic weapon and dive into the nearest roadside ditch. He knew von Rugen would do no such thing. He was, after all, sitting impassively beside the Captain as if presenting himself as a target.

To diminish his anxiety, Shinse attempted to engage the silent stern figure next to him in conversation. "You said, *Oberst,* the Allies would be invading from Great Britain, yes?"

"Ja," von Rugen replied curtly.

When von Rugen said nothing further, the Captain continued. "We would be deployed in that direction?"

"Ja."

"And not remain here facing a possible southern front?"

"No, not that."

"If I may ask, *Oberst,* have you been assured by the general staff of our deployment to the northwest coast?"

"Shinse," von Rugen hissed, obliterating the Captain's anxiety regarding ambush and replacing it with the dread he invariably felt when confronted by this demigod of a commander.

"*Oberst?*" he fawned.

"The war is lost," von Rugen said emphatically, "we are soldiers and can do nothing but wage war until surrender or death or severe injury. Your question is appropriate for a politician or diplomat or one of those monkeys in uniform currently hiding behind the *Wehrmacht*."

"Monkeys in uniform, *Oberst?*"

"The government, you young idiot. This Corporal Shicklgruber is not Bismarck but unfortunately the army has gone along with his lunacy. He destroyed our forces in the east thinking he could personally master the Russian winter and the infinity of the steppes. He will do likewise in the west. Atlantic Wall? Fortress Europa? These are not strategic concepts, Shinse, they are the fervid imaginings of a self-absorbed fool."

The Captain glumly considered what he had just heard. "And us, Oberst, what of the 48th?"

"We will do as you and I are doing now. We will seek engagement with the enemy and if we are fortunate we will find ourselves pitted against the American, Patton."

"Patton, Oberst?"

"Yes. That man has a genius for tactical warfare. The British are perhaps the greatest static fighters in the world but the Americans are the most resourceful. You would wish such an eventuality, would you not, Shinse?"

"Why yes, of course, *mein Oberst,*" the Captain responded rather lamely knowing now that the particular facial configuration he saw below his commander's shiny black visor was indeed a cynical smile.

The Colonel ordered Shinse to bring the *Kubelwagen* about and start back toward Privas. The officers drove in silence for several kilometers when von Rugen did something he had never done before with his adjutant. He asked him about his personal affairs. "You are married, correct Shinse?"

"Yes, *Oberst.*"

"Children?"

"Yes, *Oberst,* a boy and a girl."

"Ages?"

"The boy is five, *mein Oberst,* the little girl is two."

"They are well?"

"Yes, sir, the last letter from my wife indicates all is well at home and there is enough to eat."

Von Rugen nodded and went silent. Curious about his commanding officer and sensing something of an opportunity, Shinse asked respectfully. "And your family, my Colonel?"

"My wife writes that she is well," von Rugen replied and after a short pause, added, "we are childless."

Shinse simply nodded. "She writes," von Rugen continued to Shinse's surprise, "that my old governess has been eliminated."

Shinse felt a quick twinge of anxiety and was absolutely at a loss to find an appropriate response to the Colonel's remark. He had never discussed politics with von Rugen and assiduously practiced what most men in the armed forces thought wise. He avoided the subject. Then, to Shinse's dismay, the Colonel continued, "You are not a member of the Party, eh Shinse?"

"No *Oberst,* I'm not."

"And why is that, Captain?"

"Well, *Oberst,*" Shinse stammered nervously, "I, ah, I have no political aspirations."

"Yes, you are a soldier, eh?" von Rugen sarcastically suggested, "but do you find yourself sympathetic to the Party's aims?"

Shinse felt his breath constricted. He imagined that he would have been able to mealymouth his way out of being definitive with almost anyone else. But this disfigured ogre before him was not just anyone. Like a frightened little boy before a demanding father, Shinse took a deep breath and without qualification answered, "No."

Von Rugen said nothing as the vehicle continued bouncing along the lane. Shinse was hopeful the conversation was at an end. It wasn't. "*Ja,* Fraulein Gertrude Lichtenberg has been eliminated. Old Jewess Trudi Lichtenberg, governess and lady's companion to the von Rugen's of Greifswald, was collected and designated for deportation to the east. The swine could finally do this because old General von Rugen passed away in the spring and his son was far away on garrison duty in the south of France. It has been reported to Frau von Rugen that in keeping with the policy toward the aged and infirm, the kind old woman was murdered en route."

Shinse maintained a deferential silence. When the Colonel added nothing further, Shinse politely offered his condolences, "I am sorry for you and your family, *Oberst,* I am truly sorry."

Captain Shinse's gaze went to a dense copse atop a small knoll to his left, noting its favorable position above the roadway. They motored past it and his eyes scanned ahead for other possible places of concealment. He gasped almost audibly and the hairs at the back of his neck stood as he heard the words suddenly said from the seat to his right, "My wife is reliably informed that she was bludgeoned to death in an organized mass killing."

Inspektor Rochus Finckh could never be accused of schadenfreude. Like all psychopaths he simply had no cognizance of the affective life of others. When he was fourteen years old his mother died suddenly of a stroke. After his surprise upon hearing of it, his very next thought was of food. He wondered who would be preparing the evening meal. It had been on a late September afternoon as he helped his father and brother stacking hay and he was just beginning to feel the pangs of hunger. His father and brother wept at the news. Rochus curiously examined the crusty brown callouses on his hands suddenly rather happy that the long workday had been shortened.

Rochus enjoyed working under Chief of Gestapo Barbie in Lyon. He routinely took part in the interrogations and torture conducted on the upper floors of Gestapo headquarters in the elegant Terminus Hotel. He was good at what he did and did not find it necessary to adopt the sullen demeanor of his fellow policemen. He, of course, believed in the aryanization of Europe and considered himself an essential cog in the machinery of its implementation.

Sitting in the office that he shared with two of his colleagues on the ground floor of the hotel, Rochus scrutinized the woman standing across the desk from him. She was perhaps in her late thirties, rather plain but full bosomed. Rochus knew he could not conduct a full interrogation. He was scheduled to leave later in the day with a truck convoy for Privas. Although it generally was a truism that women did not last as long as men when subject to the protocol, something in the Mlle. Loiselle's demeanor suggested to Finckh that she might be time consuming.

His gaze lingered on the swelling of her hips beneath the flowered print dress. Quite spontaneously, he decided to indulge himself. "You will be detained," he said matter-of-factly, "follow me."

Rochus rose from his desk, pointed at the office door and directed, "Out, to the right."

He followed the woman, giving directions, his eyes repeatedly going to her buttocks. They went down the hallway to the narrow stairwell leading to the detention cells. Stopping at a storage room that contained nothing but a long table and chair, Rochus indicated with a nod of the head that the woman should enter. He smirked knowingly at the young guard seated at the end of the corridor before following her within.

The woman stood facing the table with her back to Finckh. "Turn around," he ordered.

She turned, keeping her eyes on the concrete floor. "Open your dress," he commanded.

The woman raised her eyes to him. He saw fear but not submission. Rochus curled his fingers into the fabric of her bodice and tore downward violently. Mlle. Loiselle twisted sideways, crossing her arms to cover her exposed breasts. Looking over her forward shoulder with hot angry eyes, she hissed, "You bald pig."

Rochus felt no anger. He simply did what was necessary to insure the woman's compliance. With practiced savagery he punched the woman just below the ribcage. She gasped in pain and doubled over. He seized the back of her neck and forced her over the table, stepped back and lifted the bottom of her dress over her hips.

Rochus did not feel anything faintly resembling eroticism. There was no person before him. The bloomers he pulled down to the woman's thighs were merely a white cloth covering over the cleaved white mounds of flesh beneath them. Unhurriedly he unbuckled his belt and unbuttoned his trousers, letting them fall to the knees of his bent legs.

The woman made no sound as he entered her in repeated emphatic thrustings. He finished quickly with a barely audible grunt, stepped back and used the hem of the woman's dress to dry himself. He arranged his trousers, walked to the door, opened it and barked out, "Guard."

As the soldier came to him, Rochus said casually "Put her in a cell" and strode nonchalantly back to his office.

Mlle. Loiselle remained bent over the table in her grotesque state of dishevelment. The guard, a young Catholic conscript from Bavaria, went to her, arranged her clothing and helped her to stand. He knew he could do nothing for her. As he helped her shuffle awkwardly to the cells, he thought about how much he hated his recent support posting with the Gestapo.

The camouflaged open staff car braked to a halt in front of the 48th Panzergrenadier's headquarters in Privas. *Inspektor* Finckh stepped from the vehicle, adjusted his black, wide-brimmed fedora and knocked road dust from his gabardine overcoat. He directed his driver to wait then walked confidently into the beige brick building. He flashed his identity badge at the young sentry who challenged his entry and continued past him. "Halt," the soldier commanded from behind.

Finckh turned to the soldier. "Did you not see my credentials? I am Gestapo."

The boy hesitated briefly then called out, "Sergeant Traub."

A stocky, blonde veteran soldier rose from his desk in the anteroom and approached Finckh. "Your business?" he questioned curtly.

"Inspektor Finckh, *Geheimes Staatpolizei,* from area headquarters in Lyon. I'm here to present my credentials to your commanding officer, *Oberst* von Rugen."

Traub thought for a moment, "Sit, I'll inform captain Shinse, the adjutant."

"Be quick about it," Rochus snapped, "I must see to my lodgings before dinner."

The sergeant left the anteroom, knocked on a door to the left of a long corridor and entered an office. In what seemed to Finckh an unnecessarily long time he returned. "Captain Shinse will see you shortly."

"Shortly?"

"Shortly."

"I must wait?"

"*Ja.*"

"A veteran member of the *Geheimes Staatpolizie* must sit and wait to be seen by a mere captain of infantry?"

"You can stand if you like," Traub remarked unemotionally and left Finckh to return to his desk.

Rochus began pacing back and forth across the reception room. "This Shinse had better show the proper respect," he thought to himself.

In a quarter of an hour the door to the adjutant's office opened and a tall, good-looking *Wehrmacht* captain beckoned Sergeant Traub to him. The two spoke briefly then Traub turned toward Rochus and nodded toward the interior of the office. As Finckh walked to the open doorway, Traub stepped in front of him. "Your weapon."

"My weapon?"

"*Ja*, no one but authorized personnel carries weapons in this building."

"Do you understand who I am?"

"You're not wearing a uniform of the 48th, so it doesn't matter who you are. The weapon."

"What is your name?" Finckh growled in irritation.

"Traub, T,R,A,U,B, Traub. Your weapon."

Rochus made a mental note. There would be repercussions for this insult. He reached indignantly into his shoulder holster and withdrew his Walther PPK, the short pistol preferred by many German policemen. He thought to have some satisfaction at the expense of the sergeant and offered it to him by extending his arm and pointing at the man's face. With a swiftness that startled Rochus, the pistol was torn from his hand with an adroit snatching motion by the noncom. "Go in. Pick this toy up on the way out," Traub said matter-of-factly.

Somewhat ruffled, Finckh entered the office. He stood before the desk of the adjutant waiting to be acknowledged and asked to sit down. Without looking up from his writing the Captain said, "What?"

"*Inspektor* Finckh, *Geheimes Staatpolizei,* Lyon Headquarters," Rochus attempted to intone authoritatively.

The Captain neither stopped writing nor looked up. Rochus continued, "I'm here to present my credentials to your commanding officer and advise him of my activities in his jurisdiction."

"Consider it done," the Captain said, continuing his writing."

"Captain," Rochus snapped, "I wish to speak to your commanding officer."

Shinse lifted his gaze to the policeman. He casually rubbed his eyes with thumb and forefinger. "That is not possible."

"Not possible?" Rochus blurted, "What is this nonsense? I am here on the Reich's business."

"Standing orders," came the reply, "the Colonel is also on the Reich's business and, pursuant to that, no one who is not above him in the chain of command determines what he does or does not do."

"I see," Finckh said, as he craftily changed his demeanor. He was well aware of the rivalries and subtle power struggles in the upper echelons of the Reich. The *Wehrmacht*, it was said among Party men, was in need of a good housecleaning. The entrenched officer corps was not always cooperative with regard to the activities of the political elements of the government. "Perhaps," he thought, "I should have worn my uniform to remind these people of my status and to whom I am connected."

Rochus probed a bit. While smiling, he asked good-naturedly, "If Heinrich Himmler, himself, were standing here, would your Colonel see him?"

"He would not."

"He would not see Heinrich Himmler, eh? That's interesting, Captain, very interesting," Rochus responded beaming broadly.

Shinse leaned back in his chair. "*Inspektor* Finckh, there is nothing terribly interesting in standing orders that are predicated on traditional military procedure. Is there anything else?"

Rochus continued to smile, "Am I being dismissed?"

Shinse ruminated briefly about this little cat and mouse game, "I am not your commanding officer, *Inspektor*. I am indicating that our business is at an end."

"Well, Captain perhaps it is, but then again, perhaps it isn't," Finckh said coyly.

"Good day, *Inspektor*," Shinse said and returned to the papers at his desk.

Finckh stood before the desk. He raised his right arm in stiff salute. "*Heil Hitler*," he voiced emphatically and cannily waited for the adjutant's reaction.

A faint tremor of trepidation passed through the Captain. What should he do now? He knew full well that he was being tested by a dedicated Party man. Shinse was about to succumb to his fear and return the salute when suddenly he saw in his imagination a scrutinizing, steel- blue eye beneath a black visor. In some odd way he felt protected. *"Auf Wiedersehen,"* he said without looking up.

Later in the evening Finckh sat at a small wall table in *La Belle Dame Sans La Tête* restaurant slurping vichyssoise. He had earlier secured a room at *Le Cygne Noir*, a hotel down the street. Part of that establishment had been requisitioned for the billeting of German Officers. He surmised that it was secure enough and registered by presenting a Gestapo chit to the manager. The recoupment voucher would find its way back to Lyon Headquarters where it would be promptly deposited in a wastebasket. He later indicated at the restaurant that he would be running up a tab for his meals. The obliging restauranteur was accustomed to dealing with the German Army. He was uninformed regarding the Gestapo reimbursement policy.

Rochus had forgotten his earlier irritation. He knew he would find Party men in the 48th who would help him in his assignment. The names of specific individuals he suspected of disloyalty to the Reich would be included in his report. He wondered if it would be wise to mention von Rugen. The Prussian Colonel might, after all, have a personal relationship with Field Marshall von Runestedt.

Tomorrow he would visit Milice headquarters. There would be no problem with those clowns. He would find inefficiency and he would correct it.

As he spooned the soup into his mouth he kept getting what he thought was a faint scent of ammonia. He attributed it to the use of bleach in the cleaning of the dining room.

In the early morning light, Auguste peered through his binoculars at the tree line bordering his overgrown fallow field. He spoke more to himself than to Marcus, "Nuthatch, prefers deciduous trees to coniferous."

He held the glasses out to Marcus, "A look?"

"No, it's all right."

Auguste studied his friend. Marcus had been back a week now and something in his general bearing suggested that he was not himself. There was a certain lack of spontaneity and uncharacteristic disinclination to converse at length. "Are you missing Madeleine, my friend?"

"I do," Marcus nodded as he looked vacantly over the field, "I do miss her."

"Is that what's troubling you, Marcooz?"

"Troubling me?"

"Yes, you haven't been yourself since you returned to us."

Marcus nodded to acknowledge Auguste's observation but said nothing. From his squatting position next to the wheelchair, he looked down to the ground, mused to himself and shrugged.

"Is it Helene, my friend?"

Marcus looked suddenly up to Auguste as if roused from a fitful sleep, "Helene?"

"Yes Helene, Marcooz, your love for Helene. Is that what's troubling you?"

This was not something that Marcus wanted to talk about. He rather assumed that for some of the questions posed by life there could be no answers. "What does it matter, Auguste?"

"But it does matter, my dense Irish friend. Your happiness matters to Helene and it matters to me. Is it not possible that you have been victimized by your own values?"

"Victimized? What do you mean?"

"I know you, Irlandais. You will not seek your own happiness because, in your judgment, that would be done at the expense of others who are dear to you. No, you could not possibly take advantage of a friend despite your deep feelings for his wife. You would shoot yourself before you would cuckold your impotent friend."

Marcus smiled sardonically, "Is that so? Well, you degenerate Frenchy bastard, there's been the many times I've thought of taking you out here to the woods and doing you in."

Auguste laughed heartily. "Oh yes? Well, that would certainly make things easier, eh?"

The men enjoyed the moment of levity and lapsed into silence. Auguste put the glasses to his eyes and scanned further along the wood line. "Take her," he said abruptly.

"What's that?"

"You heard me, Irlandais, take her."

"Jesus Christ, Auguste, your paralysis is up your spine into your brain."

Auguste chortled agreeably. He was happy that the issue was out and that he had found a way to talk with his friend about it. He paused and with a feigned seriousness offered a sham apology. "Oh, I'm sorry, Irlandais, I assumed you would be up to it. I didn't consider that such a thing might be too daunting for you. Yes, I begin to understand now. A quick coupling with the hired help is one thing but mature intimacy with a cultured woman, well, that is something else again."

Marcus knew what Auguste was up to. In a way, he was being challenged. He had no immediate comeback. Auguste peered through the binoculars and continued, "Yes that makes perfect sense. It is much easier for the Irish farm boy to nobly love the aristocratic French woman from afar rather than risk the ignominy of her rejection."

Marcus' mind went back to Kate Jamieson's sister's insult in Avram's shop those many years ago. His response to Auguste's playful taunting was the same he gave that day to Margaret. "Well, there's probably some truth in that."

Auguste, satisfied that he had made his point, went back to his birding. Marcus, musing on the ridiculousness of the situation at the Deschaines residence, took the cigarette from behind his ear and lit it.

It was dark and a light rain was falling as Helene went to the cottage to tell Marcus that Auguste wished to retire upstairs for the evening. Marcus went to his task. He was surprised when he returned to find Helene sitting at the table in the small alcove. "Do you have wine?" she asked quietly.

"I always do. Would you like something a bit stronger?"

"No, wine will do."

"I've just the mugs to drink out of, is that all right?"

She smiled, shook her head slowly and sighed. "I'll be back, Marcooz," she said, rising from the table and going to the door.

In a few minutes she returned with two wine glasses and an expensive Rhone. "*Vin ordinaire* in a mug, good God Marcooz, your taste is in your mouth," she teased.

She poured the wine. "Put out the lantern, we'll drink by candlelight, yes?"

They sat in silence for a time. Helene peered through her wine at the candlelight in the middle of the table. She looked at Marcus with soft eyes and the barest trace of a smile, "Marcooz Makeeyon," she murmured.

"Madame Helene-Marie Deschaines."

Helene broke into a full smile. "Do you miss Madeleine?"

"Not right now."

"Oh no? And why is that?"

Marcus said nothing. He smiled and looked down at the table while rubbing the stubble on his chin.

Helene went on with her mischief. "There is a gentle rain outside. Your cottage is dark and warm and quiet. There is the soft light of the candles. Are you saying that you do not wish that Madeleine were here with you right now?"

Marcus looked off into the darkness with a hint of a grin. "Well, my body might want that, but my soul, well, that's something else."

"Your soul? Well, aren't we the poet?"

Marcus thought of a response. "Of the two of us, Helene Deschaines, which is the more delicate one?"

"I suppose you'd say I am."

"I would."

Before Marcus' sojourn at the rectory Helene would have been tempted to take issue with him. She was no longer so inclined. "Was Madeleine that way sometimes? Was she ever, uh, fragile?"

"Not so much. But now and again she was what you might call wistful."

"About what?"

"Well, she'd get that way when she thought of her family or perhaps when she thought of getting older."

"Ah yes, women can be that way."

There was a silence as they sipped at their wine. Helene listened to the rain pattering above them. "Marcooz I must say something."

"What's that, Helene?"

"In an odd way, although what I did to you was selfish and inexcusable, still, there was a good side to it."

"Helene, you don't have to explain things to me. This is your home, you can do as you see fit."

"No, no, Marcooz, let me say what I have to say. What I did was reprehensible and, in my own way, I paid for it. First I lied to myself about you. I invented a justification for what I did and the horror of it was that I think I could have gone on with it despite the disapproval of those who cared for you. But in there, lying on the bed where you sleep, it suddenly came to me. I care deeply for you, Marcooz. You mean so much to me that I can't imagine a life without your being part of it. I'm telling you, Marcooz, that I ... ."

Marcus' fingers were suddenly there on her lips, "Hush now, say no more."

He reached across the table and took her hand in both of his. She looked into his eyes and saw a great sadness. She saw a vulnerable melancholy, a resignation, a humanity.

Instinctively she knew that Marcus' pain came from his inability to resolve the implications of his deep feelings for her and his love for Auguste. Madeline had, in a sense, been a buffer. Certainly she was not just a simple diversion, she was more of a comfort and, of course, a natural release for tension. Marcus no longer had that.

In the same way that some men will not take recompense for services given to others in obvious need, so Marcus could not seek self-aggrandizement as a result of the misfortune of others. The man and the woman holding hands across the table knew her husband was no impediment to their physical union. Yet, for Marcus, that possibility only existed because of a brutal blow of fate to his friend. Auguste Deschaines had been denied a full measure of life. If he were not infirm would he then be open to a physical relationship between his wife and his dearest friend? That was an imponderable.

Marcus had sometimes considered the archetypal myths of history and literature with regard to his situation at Ormeau Road. In all of them, particularly the Celtic, the affair had come to grief. Naoise, Diarmuid and Lancelot all had succumbed to temptation with the king's wife and, inevitably, sorrow had ensued. Always, after these kinds of musings, Marcus chastised himself for his stupid pretentious analogies between these young heroes and an old bugger like himself.

And Marcus had no gift for intrigue. He did nothing surreptitiously. A secret trysting with anyone was quite beyond his competence. The simple declaration of love that he had made to Helene those years ago was not wise in a worldly sense. It was the honest statement of a naïve man.

Helene was moved to dispel Marcus' despondency. "Marcooz you are a good man, a good friend and a man with a conscience. It is, perhaps, too bad that you do not possess, what do I say, the accommodating sophistication of we, French."

Marcus perked up. "What's that? Accommodating sophistication? French?"

"Yes, Marcooz, you were an older man when you came to France, eh? You came out of, let us say, a less worldly-wise, less urbane culture. Sometimes Irlandais, you are conspicuously without savoir-faire."

Marcus laughed easily, "Others have said as much. I guess that's why that name has been put on me from the beginning."

Helene refilled the glasses. "And you really don't know what to do now, do you?"

"Well Helene, I know what I'm not going to do."

The remark was not emphatic. It had about it a dispirited tone connoting an almost grim resoluteness. Helene thought back over the years since Marcus had come to the Deschaines. She thought of the respectful distance that the two of them had kept from one another. She saw that for her part there had always been an element of mistrust. Although Marcus had said plainly that he loved her, he had never really done anything that would indicate to her that, without doubt, it was true. She remembered a remark from her Algerian lover during her student days in Paris. "Anyone can say anything."

If he really loved her why hadn't he, at least once or twice, been the fool. Perhaps his relationship with Madeleine had prevented that. Yet, hadn't even that sensible woman said that it was she who Marcus loved.

At this point, the Helene of several weeks ago would have quaffed down the wine and bade Marcus good night. But she was different now. The elements within her that had caused doubt and misgiving had been dissipated by her psychological epiphany. She would, here and now, seek clarity with the man who had said he loved her.

She probed. "You do not want me as a woman?"

A pained expression came to Marcus' face. "Jesus, Helene, of course I want you."

"And you know that Auguste is no bar to that."

"I know that."

"Then?"

"Helene, it would come to no good."

"And what we have now, this is good?"

"No, it's not good, God help me, it's not good."

"Then?"

"Then nothing. I was thinking while at the rectory that I shouldn't come back. I knew it would be like this for me."

"Why then Marcooz, did you come back?"

"Because you asked it of me and I said I would."

"You came back for me, not for Auguste, not for yourself."

Marcus paused, "Yes, I came back for you."

"You came back for me because you love me."

"Yes."

"You knew you would be unhappy yet you came back for me."

"Yes."

Helene was confident now. In her frankness she had elicited from Marcus a certain purity and distinctness concerning matters that had been left unsaid for many years. "Should we not just leave it alone, Helene?" Marcus offered.

"No. As you said, it is not good. Perhaps you were speaking only for yourself but know that it is not good for me either. I know you, Irlandais. I know that if it goes on as it is, you will leave us. You will leave me."

Marcus nodded unhappily. His eventual leaving was more than just a possibility. "God, I need a drink."

Helene was amused that Marcus did not consider her wine a drink in the real sense. "Have one then," and after a pause, "if you think you need one."

He rose from the table, tossed the splash of wine remaining in his glass into the sink and brought down a bottle of whiskey from the cluttered shelf above. He poured a copious amount into one of his mugs and drank. Marcus exhaled audibly and lightly smacked his lips in pleasure. He leaned back against the sink crossing his legs and folding his arms while his chin sunk to his chest. He appeared to Helene the personification of troubled befuddled cogitation. She had difficulty supressing a giggle. "I don't know, Helene."

"You don't know what, Marcooz?"

Marcus looked off into space shaking his head in negation. "I only know I love you."

"Is that not enough?"

"It should be, shouldn't it?"

A peculiar yet delightful thought occurred to Helene. In the past, as a result of her inclination toward self-assertion, Marcus had maintained what might fairly be called a psychological edge in their subtle contentions. Almost always his would be the definitive act or timely delivery of the bon mot. Now, following what could aptly be called her inward self-sacrifice, Helene found herself the affectively weightier of the two. There had been a tidal change in the ambiance at the Deschaines residence.

She sat relaxed, self-possessed, savoring the wine on her tongue. She knew her man. A quiet warm inspiration had come to her. She would wait until, after enough whiskey, she would see that particular look come over Marcus' countenance. She had remembered Madeleine's sharing with her concerning the latter's initial maneuvering with the Irlandais. In this present situation, she reflected, she was not manipulating Marcus. She was more the shepherdess guiding events toward an elegant outcome.

Marcus reached into his shirt pocket and withdrew a cigarette. "Don't do that," Helene said quietly.

He looked toward her with a puzzled expression. She stood and walked slowly around the table until she was before him looking up into his face. She took the cigarette from his fingers and slipped it back into the pack in his chest pocket then brushed her fingertips lightly across his heart area. Her hand came up and she delicately ran her fingers through his hair at the side of his head. From his leaning posture, Marcus stood erect. Helene took his hands and placed them on her hips. She took his face in her hands, and with a fey smile looked with utter intention into his eyes. "Marcooz loves and wants Helene?"

Like a guilt-ridden man admitting some unpardonable sin before his confessor, Marcus swallowed uneasily and nodded. Helene softly murmured, "But she is not rightfully his. It is sinful. And he is afraid."

"Afraid?" Marcus asked as if of himself, "Helene, are you mocking me?"

"Well Irlandais, are you afraid?"

"In a way I am, I guess. I don't like to think of myself walking about here in the future assuming things that I don't have a right to."

Helene grew pensive. She stepped back. "Your self-respect, that is more important to you than anything else?"

"Helene, what would you think of a man who came sniffing around like a dog seeing to his own gratification?"

"I can't imagine that you would be that way."

"Oh, I could all right. And I wouldn't need the drink."

Helene felt Marcus' distancing. She knew instinctively that it had been triggered by her whispered teasing concerning sinfulness. She had committed that archaic and habitual female error with respect to a sensitive man. She simply did not know the depth of feeling he had for her, for Auguste, and his impotence to resolve that with his own desire, a desire which arose from what he considered his own weakness.

Marcus sighed deeply. Helene saw what might be tears in his eyes. He walked from the alcove into the darkness of the bedroom. He returned shortly into the candlelight wearing his cap and pulling on a black oilskin raincoat. "I'm going out for a walk, Helene," Marcus indicated, snapping the collar up at the back of his neck.

He smiled tristfully and walked out into the darkness and the rain. Helene felt no disappointment or sense of rejection. She could not say if what had just transpired between them was for the good or not. She knew only that there was, as yet, no clarity.

She went into the bedroom and in the stillness sat for a time on the edge of the bed. She would wait for him to return however long that would take. Helene kicked off her shoes, pulled back the coverlet and curled beneath it. She laughed to herself thinking that perhaps she should adopt Madeleine's technique and strip herself naked below the bedspread. What would the befuddled Irlandais do in that case?

She heard, in the distance, the muffled sound of thunder. Her mind went to vignettes from the past concerning Marcus and her. She remembered the trip they had made to visit the old friend of hers who was dying. In the little restaurant, Marcus had leaned across the table and kissed her. She had protested. He then remarked, characteristically, that he would probably never do that again. God, what an idiot she was.

Helene awoke to rustling and the clinking of tableware in the alcove. By the light it was just dawn. She sat up and rubbed her eyes trying to clear her head of sleep. She arose, took her shoes under her arm and padded out into the tiny kitchen.

Marcus sat at the table before the almost finished bottle of whiskey. His rain-sodden cap lay on the table and he still wore his shiny wet oilskin. He looked worn and haggard. Wisps of dark wet hair clung to his forehead.

"Marcooz, where did you go? Did you just come back?"

In a quiet voice that was not that of a drunken man, he replied, "I walked the woods well beyond the pond and then some."

He looked at her with tired, red-rimmed eyes. "You'll tell him?"

"Auguste?"

"Yes."

"Tell him?"

"That we didn't sleep together. You'll tell him, won't you?"

Helene heard in the tone of his request a certain plaintiveness, a certain vulnerability. "Yes Marcooz, I'll tell him."

Marcus breathed out and stubbed his cigarette into the pile of butts in the small porcelain candy dish that served as an ashtray. "I'll come up in a bit and bring him downstairs."

"Shall I make you some breakfast?"

"No thank you, Helene, I'll attend to Auguste and come back here. I'm tired. I'd like to sleep."

Helene saw his weariness. *"Bon matin,* Marcooz."

Helene stepped out into a light rain and walked toward the house. She began to weep but her tears were not for herself. Something Paul Bassard confided about Marcus had come to her mind. Bassard had said that Marcus candidly admitted to him once that had it not been for his life at the Deschaines he would have ended up a broken alcoholic, going from place to place aimlessly. Through Auguste's misfortune he had been given a life with some purpose. Paul had further asserted that it was a certainty that Marcus would lay down his life for Auguste in a heartbeat. The word *miséricorde*, heart sorrow, came to her mind. Objectively, without the faintest trace of romantic self-indulgence, Helene realized that Marcus had been suffering because of his love for her. Through the years he had borne that wounding silently. She knew only now that his love for her had been obvious to everyone alhough she, with her past penchant for form and surface honesty, had never been convinced of it. But, without doubt, she had seen it this morning in a man exhausted within himself.

Helene stopped at the kitchen entrance to compose herself. With her hand she wiped the tears from her cheeks and looked back through the rain at the little cottage sheltered by the spruce trees. Last night she had unwittingly put Marcus through a kind of purgatory. She imagined his forlorn figure stumbling through the dark woods in the rain. His act, of course, was a stupidity required of him by no one. It was unnecessary, asinine, in a way, comedic. And yet, she thought, how very much the Irlandais. Marcooz Makeeyon, Auguste's man. Bassard was right about him. The Irlandais had attained to an enigmatic level quite beyond that of conventional human wisdom. Indeed, he had the courage to be a fool for love.

When he reported to headquarters, Poissy was notified that Captain of Milice Vendeur wanted to see him immediately. He knocked at the Captain's office door and entered. Poissy felt a small rush of anxiety as he saw the stout balding man in civilian clothes sitting at the Captain's desk. He saluted the Captain who stood just behind the man, "You wanted me, Captain?"

"Yes Poissy. This is Inspector Finckh who is currently auditing our unit. He has been inspecting the files. We need some clarification regarding one of your reports. Sit down."

Poissy took the chair in front of the desk. He made immediate eye contact with the Gestapo man attempting to give an impression of relaxed confidence. The cold inert eyes scanned him.

The Nazi looked down on a paper before him. "This is a report of a patrol you made in August to the town of Couderouge. Do you remember it?"

"The patrol? Yes, I do."

"Was there anything noteworthy about it?"

Poissy's heart missed a beat as he suddenly remembered Maurice Fleury and the notes he had added to his report. Struggling to maintain an air of disinterested calm, he looked off into space as if trying to remember something of little consequence. "Noteworthy? No, nothing of importance."

"You made notes at the bottom."

"Oh yes?" Poissy commented casually.

"Who is Fleur?"

Claude could feel his pulse in his ears. "Fleur," he said maintaining his pretense of mild perplexity. "Fleur. I have no recollection."

"Who lives at the Dechene residence?"

"Dechene residence? Inspector, may I have a look at my notes?"
"No." Finckh said coldly.
"Perhaps if I saw them it would refresh my memory."
Finckh said nothing to Poissy. He turned to Vendeur, "That's all I need."
Vendeur looked uneasily at Claude, "You're dismissed, Sergeant."
When Poissy closed the door behind him, Finckh lifted the paper from the desk. "The man is lying."
"Lying? I assure you, Inspector, Sergeant Poissy is one of my best men. There would be no reason for his lying. He has been loyal and conscientious in his work."
"The quality of the work of your unit remains to be seen. There have been reports in Lyon of widespread bribery and protection of undesirables. That man knows something and is lying about it. What's his name, again?"
"Poissy, Sergeant Poissy. I repeat Inspector, Poissy is one my ablest men. He is devoted to the policies of the New France. He is a veteran with a notable war record."
Finckh smiled contemptuously. "Notable war record? Does that mean he did not run as quickly as other Frenchmen?"
Vendeur's face flushed in embarrassment. Finckh smirked. "If that man attempts to leave Privas whether on official Milice business or not, you will detain him and notify me immediately."
In the few days that Rochus had been in Privas, he had moved with dispatch and practiced thoroughness. He had made connections with fellow National Socialists in the regiment as well as the most reactionary elements within the Milice. Major Enke and *Leutnant* Dietl had promised him their full cooperation. Both officers were of the opinion that in the service of the Reich, standard army operating procedure could be superseded at the Party's discretion. Finckh was granted access to the soldiery of the 48th and necessary vehicles in the motor pool.
Just before noon on the day following the one he had encountered the Gestapo Inspector, Poissy announced to Vendeur his intent to patrol north of Privas. He was asked by the Captain to remain in the building for a briefing before leaving. In twenty minutes Finckh brusquely entered Milice headquarters with *Leutnant* Dietl and a full squad of panzergrenadiers.

Ensconced involuntarily beside the driver of the staff car that led the small convoy toward Couderouge, Poissy lightly probed the swelling on his lower lip with his fingers. Finckh and *Leutnant* Dietl sat to his rear. The staff car led a *Kubelwagen* and two, three-ton Opel German army trucks.

The vehicles carried the squad of panzergrenadiers most of whom were enthusiastic about this break from the tedium of garrison duty. However, their squad leader, *Feldwebel* Fritz Staiger, was not. The veteran knew the mission had to do with some dirty political business in which he would rather not take part.

Poissy was frightened. Finckh had struck him with his fist back at headquarters when his answers to the Nazi's interrogation were judged deliberately vague and insufficient. Poissy could not explain to Finckh's satisfaction his failure to follow up on what the August patrol report indicated were obvious and pertinent matters in the small French village. Particularly unsettling to Claude was the apparent absence of emotion on the part of the Gestapo man when he struck him and the remark, "You will cooperate fully, Poissy, or by day's end wish you had."

Poissy knew the convoy would eventually find its way to the Deschaines residence. The Meyers were sure to be taken into custody. Whether Marcus would be taken as well, he could not guess. Would the Deschaines be arrested for sheltering illegals and enemies of the New Order? He had heard that the Gestapo had conducted impromptu executions in the Lyon area.

Claude did not know what fate held in store for his friends and could not conceive of a way in which he could be helpful to them. He stared in anguished trepidation toward the floor mat. He did not notice his uncharacteristic lack of concern for himself. He reverted to a behavior which he had not experienced since he was a boy. He prayed for someone other than himself.

Anton Fedou passed wind in fright as he saw through his shop window a German convoy come to a halt in the main street of Couderouge. His cronies lost no time in hastily exiting his shop through the rear and disappearing into the bush bordering the village. Fedou watched anxiously as the soldiers spilled from the vehicles and formed up around the young officer in charge.

He withdrew from the window so as not to be seen and sat nervously on the stool behind the counter. He hoped that his vocal communist sympathies had not been reported to the authorities. His materialistic outlook tinged his fear-driven imaginings. "Yes," he thought, "such a thing could be done to me by almost anyone for money."

His sphincter spasmed when a man wearing a black fedora and taupe overcoat entered his shop accompanied by two soldiers. The man approached the counter. "Stand up," he ordered.

Fedou did as he was told. "Your name?"

"Anton Fedou," he croaked in fear.

"You will answer my questions directly and without hesitation. Do you understand?"

"Yes.........sir."

"Where is Michel Fleur?"

"Michel Fleur? I don't know a Michel Fleur?"

Fedou's head rocked from a blow to the side of his face. "Where is Michel Fleur?"

In absolute panic Fedous sought an answer. "Oh Monsieur, please, I don't know a Michel Fleur. I will be helpful but, believe me, I know no one by that name."

"A member of the Milice interviewed a man in this town by the name of Michel Fleur. I give you one more chance to cooperate. Where is he?"

Something occurred to Fedou. "Do you mean Maurice Fleury, Monsieur?"

"Maurice Fleury? Who is Maurice Fleury?"

"A young man who lives in our village. He has disappeared. He has been gone for several weeks."

"What do you man 'disappeared'?"

"Yes Monsieur, he has not been seen for quite some time."

Finckh stared at Fedou processing the information and calculating his next question. "Who are the Dechenes?"

"Dechenes? Do you mean Deschaines, Monsieur?"

"Who are they?"

"A landed family, actually, a couple who live outside of the village."

"Are there refugees there?"

Fedou, eyes wide in apprehension, nodded in the affirmative. "Yes Monsieur, I know of one. But I've heard there are others."

"How many?"

"Perhaps three or four in all. I don't know exactly."

"Jews?"

Fedou continued his obsequious nodding. "Yes, I think I've heard that there are illegal foreigners there."

"Have you seen them?"

"No, I've only heard of it."

"Where is the residence?"

"Out on Ormeau Road, a few kilometers, on the north side, a dark gray stone manse."

Fedou knew his safety lay in his helpfulness. "Stone pillars, black iron gate, circular driveway. Go down to the intersection and go left pass the church, maybe three kilometers."

"Is the house the only building?"

"No Monsieur, there is a large attached garage in the rear. There is also a cottage toward the back. I think one of the foreigners lives in it."

Finckh narrowed his eyes. "Is there anything else I should know?"

Fedou fished for something additional. "It is known that the foreigner who lives in the cottage can be a violent man."

Finckh snickered at the remark. "Violent, eh? We will see to the violent man."

The *Inspektor* scanned the shop, his eyes falling on several unopened crates of wine stacked by the door. "You," he said, indicating to the soldier on his left, "put those crates in the staff car."

The convoy roared onto the Deschaines estate and halted just at the front entrance. *Feldwebel* Staiger quickly exited the *Kubelwagen* and ordered the soldiers leaping from the back of the first truck toward the large oaken door. With a sweep of his arm he sent the men from the second truck running around toward the rear. He walked slowly after the second group, reluctant to follow young Dietl and that Gestapo bastard into some well-to-do Frenchman's private home.

A shoeless, middle-aged man was led at gunpoint from the quarters above the garage. The cottage was empty. "Sergeant," one of the men with the prisoner asked, "what do we do with him?"

"I don't know a goddamned thing, Riebenstahl, maybe they want him in the house. He doesn't look too dangerous to me. You men put your weapons down."

Staiger took the frightened man by the shoulder. "Come," he said curtly.

Auguste and Marcus were in the study when the soldiers burst into the house. Hearing the stomping and shouts of the intruders, Helene and Ruth came up from the kitchen and were rudely ushered into the study to join the men. Shortly thereafter, Zalman entered escorted by Staiger. The sergeant reported. "I think that's everyone, Lieutenant. The other buildings are empty. No one else is reported on the property."

"You will report to me, Sergeant," Finckh interjected.

Staiger looked to his officer. "Sir?"

"Do as he says," Dietl indicated.

Finckh moved around the desk to where Auguste was sitting. "Move out of there."

He took a chair and seated himself at Auguste's desk. He noticed the brass ship's bell. "Ah, you are the commander here and summon people to you with this, eh?"

Auguste made no response. Finckh snorted. "Commander Dechene, eh?"

"Deschaines," Auguste corrected.

Finckh smiled insidiously. "Pronunciation, yes. You are about to see how important pronunciation is."

Propping his elbows on the desk and intertwining his fingers, Finckh contemptuously eyed the five middle-aged people before him. "Of course you are all French citizens," he said caustically, "and none of you are Jews. Correct?"

"I'm not a Frenchman," Marcus said pointedly.

"Oh no? And where are you from?"

"I'm Irish. I've been in this country since the early twenties. Like you, I wasn't invited."

Finckh stared at Marcus attempting to cause unease and submission. The blue eyes looked defiantly back.

Finckh's gaze went to Zalman and Ruth but he directed his question to Auguste. "Monsieur Dechene, do you employ Jews here?"

"No."

"These two work for you?" He said, pointing at the nervous couple.

"Yes, they do."

"You two, what are your names?"

Ruth spoke up quickly. "Marcel and Renate Mineur."

Finckh grinned broadly. He pointed at Zalman. "What did she say, silent one?"

Zalman swallowed. "Uh, Marcel and Renate Mineur."

"Odd accent, Mezchir Miner," Finckh snickered, "it sounds somewhat German. Where are you from?"

"Strasbourg," Zalman said uneasily.

"Strahsborg, eh? Tell me, Mezchir Miner. Are you a Catholic?"

Zalman looked to Ruth. He swallowed again and weakly answered, "Uh, yes."

"Well Mezchir Miner, what is the name of the cathedral in Strasbourg?"

Zalman looked to the floor, "I can't remember."

"Really?" Finckh commented mordantly, "you can't remember the name of the cathedral in your hometown?"

The Nazi was now thoroughly enjoying himself. "You two," he said, indicating Zalman and Marcus, "stand in front of the desk."

They stood before him. He casually examined his fingernails. "Drop your trousers."

Neither man moved. "Sergeant," Finckh said, looking to Staiger.

The Sergeant looked to Dietl who remained impassive. He looked back to Finckh and asked uneasily, "You want these men to drop their, their trousers?"

"What did I say?" Finckh snapped.

Staiger groaned inaudibly, took an MP40 from one of his men and jabbed it into Zalman's back. "Trousers down," he ordered.

Zalman was bewildered. He looked about not knowing what to do. He went into a half crouch and hunched his shoulders. A hot primal wave of anger swept through Marcus. He knew with certainty the reason for Finckh's bizarre directive as well as what caused Zalman's dread and confusion. Marcus knew the Nazi wished to humiliate the Jew by exposing the fact of his circumcision and his bewildered friend was trying to comply with orders he only partially understood. Zalman understood the directive "down" but he did not know the French word for "trousers."

Marcus could not constrain himself. "Let the poor man be," he shouted.

There was suddenly silence in the room. Finckh reddened and slowly rose from the chair. He withdrew his pistol and walked around the desk to Marcus' side. He pushed the Walther up under the Irlandais' jawbone. Marcus felt no fear but only an odd curiosity about the vague familiarity of what was happening to him. He saw in memory the drunken Black and Tan outside Phoenix Park on that long ago, cold wintry day with Kate Jamieson. He remembered he had been saved by the intervention of the officer who came out of the lorry.

"Marcooz!" He heard Auguste cry out, "for God's sake, say nothing. Do as these people tell you. He'll kill you. Do you understand?"

With the pistol still jammed under his chin, Marcus turned toward his friend. He smiled and pursed his lips in his characteristic way. "You take your trousers down for these bastards if you like, Auguste, but I'll take the bullet before I do it. These turds will kill us anyway."

Finckh brought his face within inches of Marcus'. "Drop your trousers, *Irlander*, or I'll blow the top of your head off," he snarled.

Suddenly, Marcus planted himself and whipped his left arm quickly upward, knocking Finckh's gun hand toward the ceiling. The startled Nazi inadvertently squeezed the trigger and the shot shattered the glass in the overhead light. Marcus then brought a vicious uppercut from his waist, crunching his fist into Finckh's chin. The black fedora flew off as the Nazi's head snapped backward. His knees buckled and he fell backward into the desk before crumbling to the floor.

Feldwebel Staiger was as shocked as anyone in the room. He looked wide-eyed at Dietl waiting for the officer to react. Dietl pulled his Walther from his hip holster and come toward the desk. He knelt down to Finckh. "*Inspektor! Inspektor* Finckh! Are you all right?"

Finckh lay motionless on the wine-colored carpet. Blood trickled from his mouth. The completely disoriented and suddenly manic Dietl stood. "Sergeant Staiger, take this man out and shoot him," he shrieked hysterically.

"Yes sir," Staiger replied stiffly.

The Sergeant nudged Marcus in the stomach with the submachine gun and motioned him out of the room with its barrel. "Outside," he grunted.

Marcus paused briefly at the doorway making eye contact with Auguste and then Helene. He smiled wistfully and nodded his goodbye. Helene began sobbing as she held her hands to her face. Auguste tightly gripped his armrests in anguish and dropped his head to his chest. "Adieu, my dearest friend," he whispered inaudibly.

As Marcus walked out of the front entrance he heard Helene's plaintive, "Marcooz," wafting after him.

"You men, stay here. I'll take care of this," Staiger said gruffly to the young soldiers stationed outside. He pushed the weapon into the small of Marcus' back. "Out there, beyond those trees," he indicated.

Marcus walked stoically past the evergreens and cottage beyond, toward the woods. He looked at the disorderly pile of firewood at the tree line and had the thought that there would be no one about this fall to cut, split and stack it. The work was too heavy for Philibert.

The Sergeant was keeping a good distance behind Marcus. There was little chance that he could turn on the man or make a break for it. He wondered if the man would shoot him in the back. Probably not, he guessed.

They walked for several minutes through the hardwood trees, well beyond what Marcus expected. On impulse, Marcus turned around to look at his executioner. The Sergeant stopped, put the butt of his weapon on his hip and waved Marcus on. Marcus thought he detected a faint smile on the man's face.

Marcus reached inside his jacket and pulled out a cigarette. He lit it and drew on it deeply. Was the man allowing him a last smoke? He didn't know. He dragged deeply again and looked up through the canopy of leaves to the blue sky beyond. "*Irlander,*" he heard the Sergeant say.

The Sergeant was now smiling broadly. Suddenly, he pantomimed an upward punching motion. "Boom!" he ejaculated.

Marcus could not help but smile in agreement that indeed, he had given Finckh a good one. "Run," the Sergeant suddenly said.

"Run?"

Staiger made jerking motions with his thumb. "Run," he repeated.

Marcus hesitated, then took a deep breath, turned and bolted. Staiger watched him thinking that he ran well for an older man. Perhaps, the Sergeant thought, the *Irlander* is an ex-boxer. Young Panzergrenadier Fritz Staiger had been the Divisional Middleweight Champion in 1932.

The Sergeant pointed the weapon into the air. He fired two short bursts for the benefit of those back at the residence.

Despite a small measure of grim satisfaction upon hearing the gunfire, Finckh was humiliated and enraged. He sat at the desk holding a blood soaked hankerchief to his mouth. Periodically he picked small chips of tooth from the inside of his mouth. The I*nspektor* was waiting for the return of the two soldiers he had sent to the apartment above the garage to find the Jews' overcoats. The soldiers returned and brought the coats directly to him. His hands felt the linings searching for the telltale lumps of hardness. He discovered a gem immediately. He would have smiled in satisfaction had his mouth not hurt so much. "Put these coats in the staff car."

Finckh stood. "Dietl, put all of them on the trucks."

"All of them, *Inspektor*?" "What of him, the one in the wheelchair?"

Finckh went to Auguste and stood over him. "Well Commander Dechene, would you like a little truck ride or would you rather join your friend in the woods?"

For the second time in what Finckh thought would be an entertaining routine enterprise, his sense of personal invulnerability was shattered. Auguste lunged forward and gripped the *Inspektor's* coat, jerking him violently downward. Auguste's strong grip locked on the Nazi's throat and his thumbs dug deeply into his trachea. The panzergrenadier closest to the two men reacted quickly. He raised his rifle and struck with the butt end into the side of Auguste's head. The Frenchman's head rocked sideward and he released his grip. Gasping and sputtering, Finckh staggered backward. He glared at his assailant, now dazed and sitting helpless before him. "French swine," he growled.

Suddenly, screaming in fury, Helene flew at the startled soldier who had struck Auguste. She raked at his face with her fingernails. Finckh, reacting quickly, gripped her by the hair and threw her bodily across Auguste's desk. She thudded heavily into the wall just beyond and fell from view to the floor. Finckh, still sputtering, yelled in anger, "Put all of them on the trucks. Now. All of them."

Finckh strode from the room as Dietl barked orders and the soldiers complied by manhandling their prisoners toward the doorway. The *Leutnant* found Helene on her hands and knees behind the desk glaring up at him with incandescent eyes of anger. "You, get on the truck with the rest of them."

The young officer found something odd in the way the woman got quickly to her feet and walked almost purposefully from the study. There was not the least sign of submission in her movement. It was as if she were about to do something. He followed her as she went directly to the others at the back of the truck. It was she who helped the Meyers climb up and then appeared to supervise the soldiers lifting Auguste and his wheelchair. She then clambered up herself refusing the extended arm of a soldier. Dietl could not define his unease as he watched Helene sit erectly, pull her gray cardigan tightly around her and stare stoically straight ahead.

Riding southward along the main route to Privas, *Leutnant* Dietl could not dispel his mild angst. Now and again he turned to look back at the trucks following his lead vehicle. He scrutinized Finckh still dabbing at his mouth with the blood-soaked handkerchief. Should he have listened to Major Enke about going along with whatever the Gestapo man wanted to do? The Major had told him confidently that in the long run it would be in his best interest, especially with regard to his career in the *Wehrmacht*.

But there was something ugly and stupid in this enterprise. Those people back in the trucks had not hesitated to stand up to Finckh. Had not his squad been there exactly what kind of power would the Party man have had over them? They seemed like ordinary people. How were they a threat to the Occupation or the aims of the Reich? So, two of them were Jews and the French couple had given them refuge. It had been a long time since Dietl had heard a speech from an official justifying this kind of thing. Dietl remembered that his father had not liked the idea of his joining the Party. Papa had been in the Great War although he had refused to talk about it. He remembered his father's Jewish friend and business associate who had always treated him kindly.

Dietl remembered that after entering the house the men had looked to him for directions. Sergeant Staiger had, in fact, appealed to his authority when Finckh sought to humiliate those two men. He had unthinkingly deferred to Finckh and now wondered if he had lost respect from the squad.

Suddenly, the *Leutnant's* viscera knotted in panic. In his initial zeal and mindless participation in the mission to Couderouge, he had forgotten the Colonel, his commanding officer. Von Rugen had not authorized this.

As a matter of fact, he probably would never have authorized it. What, after all, was the military objective that would have required the use of his panzergrenadiers. Unfortunately, the Colonel held the Party man Enke in contempt and therefore the Major would be of no help to him. "*Mein Gott*," he thought, "I'm liable to be posted to some godforsaken place as a *Privat.*"

Dietl looked over again with contempt at the complacent cruel schemer who had gotten him into this. Finckh sat comfortably in his rear seat looking impassively over the French countryside. His hand lay protectively over the coats in his lap that had been confiscated from the Jewish couple. On the floor were the crates of wine taken from village vintner.

Yes, the *Leutnant* had listened to the Nazi rhetoric and on occasion had been intoxicated by it. But now, bumping along the highway to Privas, it was only conscience and instinct that were operating in the young officer. The former caused the clear realization that he had just taken part in a nakedly criminal enterprise. The latter caused the thudding in his chest as he imagined himself standing at attention before *Oberst* von Rugen.

Shortly after the German convoy had passed through the village on its return to Privas, Père Bassard set out on his bicycle for the Deschaines residence. Madame Boulerice and her daughter had reported to him that they had seen Helene and other civilians in the back of one of the trucks. Upon entering Auguste's study Bassard observed the shattered ceiling lamp and the objects from the desk strewn across the floor. There had been a struggle. He felt a cold dread thinking of the possibility that he might find the bullet-riddled body of a friend in the house or outside on the property. He went apprehensively throughout the house then walked the grounds crying out. As he was returning to the manse, he heard his name called out from the woods beyond the cottage. He knew who it was without turning. Marcus broke from the tree line followed closely by *Yaourt* and *Biscuit*. As he neared the priest he shook his head and grimaced. "They've taken them all, Paul, they've taken them all."

"You Marcooz, you managed to escape?"

"No. I bashed one of them and was taken out to the woods to be shot. For some reason only God knows, the man let me go. He let me run for it and fired into the trees."

"The others were seen on the trucks passing through the village to the south. Privas, no doubt."

Marcus stared forlornly off into space. "Do you think it was Poissy who gave us up? They might have beaten it out of him if they suspected he wasn't on the up-and-up with them."

Bassard shook his head. "No, I don't think so, Marcooz. They would have come directly to the residence if that were the case. They were some time bullying about in the village trying to intimidate townsfolk for information. They came here only after leaving Fedou's place."

"Fedou. Yes, he'd give us up all right. I'll deal with that bastard soon enough."

"Leave Fedou to me, Marcooz. I know what to do. The right people will be informed and things will be taken care of."

"You mean like Fleury?"

"Perhaps. But he will be dealt with."

Marcus paused, then nodded in assent.

The men went to sit in the kitchen where Marcus boiled water for tea. They sat in silence. In a plaintive voice just above a whisper, Marcus asked, "Do you think, Paul, there's any chance for them?"

Bassard resisted the impulse to give false hope. "We'll never see Zalman and Ruth again, Marcooz. They're foreign Jews. Perhaps Auguste and Helene will be imprisoned or sent to a work camp. But there's a better chance they will be executed. It was a Nazi operation, not local Milice, and those people habitually do that kind of thing to discourage others from helping Jewish refugees."

There was a morose moment of silence before Bassard repeated gravely, "They do that kind of thing."

Marcus' eyes welled with tears. "For helping refugees?"

"Jews, Marcooz, for helping Jews."

Marcus wept openly. "What in God's name is it all about, Paul? Why are these things done?"

The priest, who through years of self-discipline had taught himself to weep only in private, felt the hot sting beginning in his eyes. "There has never been an adequate explanation for evil, my friend. It is a mystery beyond our human comprehension. It is an unfathomable mystery and," Bassard paused, "it is upon us now."

Marcus slumped into the heavy, wooden kitchen chair. His head sagged to his chest as he brought his hands to his face. He moaned softly, "Oh, God help them. God help them all."

Paul extended his arm across the table to Marcus' shoulder. "You must leave now, my friend, it is not safe for you to remain."

"Leave? Leave and go where?"

"Return with me to the rectory. We'll think of something. Consider this, Marcooz, Auguste was a relatively wealthy man."

As he spoke Bassard noticed his own use of the word "was" with regard to Auguste. He continued, "The house contains artwork, valuables and whatnot. I've heard of many instances of looting. It is common with the Gestapo, even sometimes by officers of the German army and the Milice. They're liable to return here."

Marcus stared morosely down at the table. "I'm to run, is it? Escape to a new life. Paul, I have no life without them. I'd just as soon be with them now. I'd be satisfied if I could just get my hands on that bugger in civilian clothes who was in charge."

Bassard knew his friend well enough to now understand that Marcus would not flee. He was not interested in survival. He would choose to do something. It would be rash. He would die. Bassard wept openly now. "Our friend, my friend, the Irlandais."

Marcus looked across at Paul with a wry inscrutable smile and broke the old taboo. "Will you hear my confession, Father?"

After Bassard left, Marcus heated water, bathed and shaved. He went out to the cottage and changed into clean clothes and donned his favorite dark gray sportsman's cap. He returned to the main house and went upstairs to Helene's bedroom. A gold chain and medallion hung from the end of her mirror. Without examining the image on the medallion, he put it in his breast pocket.

Marcus went down to the study and rummaged through the drawers of Auguste's desk. He was looking for the old Lebel revolver that had seen service in the Great War. It was gone. He assumed it had been confiscated by the Germans along with the shotgun that had hung on the rack in the hallway.

He went out to the garage to find something among the tools. He finally opted for the short-handled spade and amused himself with the idea that he could walk the streets of Privas with it and arouse no suspicion. He remembered the grim old warrior he had seen with a spade when he was leaving the barracks yard at Aughris Head those many years ago. The old codger had said something about beheading a man at close quarters. Marcus found a metal rasp and set to work filing a blade edge.

By the sun, it was late afternoon when Marcus wired the spade to the handlebars of his bicycle and set out for Privas. With circling crows cawing derisively above the fields to the south, a hunched quixotic figure pedaled his bicycle down Ormeau Road on his way to challenge the might of the *Wehrmacht*. Now and then he put his hand to his breast pocket.

Upon return to Privas, the convoy stopped at *Le Cygne Noir*. Finckh ordered the four prisoners to be detained in a dusty, basement storage room as a deliberate slight to the Milice. He assigned two panzergrenadiers to guard duty. He briefly considered detaining Poissy but allowed the incompetent and inconsequential militiaman to return to his headquarters. He was hungry and wondered if the pain in his mouth and jaw would interfere with his evening meal.

When the convoy returned to the motor pool, Staiger checked with *Leutnant* Dietl before dismissing the squad. He returned the MP40 to the soldier from whom it had been borrowed, commenting, "Well Hans, this has been a glorious day for the *Wehrmacht*. One of our dreaded enemies is dead and four other combatants taken as prisoners of war."

Staiger made directly to the regimental headquarters. There he would tell his old comrade, First Sergeant Traub, the full details of what he knew was an unauthorized mission. Traub, he also knew, would report immediately to Captain Shinse. The Adjutant, of course, would go directly to Colonel von Rugen.

Feldwebel Staiger stood nervously before the Colonel's desk. With *Oberfeldwebel* Traub at his side he had reported, to the best of his recollection, the events of the day. Captain Shinse had interjected now and again with questions relating to specifics. Von Rugen had said nothing.

The Colonel stood with his back to the men looking out of the rear window. "I dismissed the men at the motor pool and reported directly to First Sergeant Traub," Staiger concluded.

Von Rugen began to pace back and forth, then turned and stared ominously at Staiger. "You disobeyed a direct order from *Leutnant* Dietl. Correct?"

Fear gripped Staiger. "Uh, *Oberst,* I uh, had doubts about the, uh, proper authorization for our mission. The man was unarmed. I, uh, didn't know what to do."

Shinse came to his aid. "And you were not quite sure that the order for his execution was initiated from the proper chain of command. Isn't that so, Staiger?"

"Uh, yes *Hauptman* Shinse, yes sir, that's it, that's it exactly."

Von Rugen looked at Shinse and smiled inwardly.

"Sergeant Staiger, is there anything else you can tell the Colonel, any other irregularities, any other thing out of the ordinary? Perhaps, even a personal observation," Shinse asked.

Staiger thought for a moment. "Well Sir, I thought it odd that the militiaman was treated as if he were in custody. He was told to remain in the back of the truck when our men entered the house. On the return I saw that he was weeping."

"He was weeping?"

"Yes Sir. It was as if he had some personal involvement in the affair. I can't say what it was."

"Is he in custody with the others?"

"No Sir, I think the Gestapo man let him go."

"Anything else, Staiger?"

"No Sir, that's about it."

"*Oberst?*"

Von Rugen shook his head, "Dismiss the men to their normal duties, Captain."

"*Hauptman* Shinse, Sir?"

"Yes, Traub?"

"The guards on the civilians, are they to remain there?"

Shinse looked to the Colonel for direction. After a moment, von Rugen said, "I'll take care of that situation."

Von Rugen's gaze went from one man to the other. He spoke gravely. "I want you three men to understand something perfectly. Listen carefully to me. You are soldiers under orders, my orders alone, no one else's. Should there ever be a question about that in the future, you will indicate that you acted under my orders alone, under orders from your superior officer, *Oberst* von Rugen. Do the three of you understand that clearly?"

The soldiers responded affirmatively. "Dismissed. Captain Shinse, remain."

When the sergeants had left the office, von Rugen began his pacing again. "We must move quickly. I will personally deal with Major Enke and *Leutnant* Dietl. Something then must be done about this man Franck."

"Excuse me, Colonel. I believe the man's name is Finchk."

"Finchk, eh? *Inspektor* Finchk of the illustrious *Geheimes Staatpolizei*. I must think about him. Shinse, I want to see that French militiaman. Find him and bring him to me."

"Now, *Oberst?*"

"Now, Shinse. You will inform those at Milice Headquarters that the Gestapo man is not to be informed of it. Put that in the form of a severe warning from me personally. I will underscore it with a telephone call before you arrive there."

"Yes, *Oberst*."

In his zeal for his work with the Gestapo and the Reich, Finckh was bound to make enemies. In his total disregard for army protocol in Privas he had made an implacable adversary of the hard-bitten Commander of the 48th Panzergrenadiers. *Inspektor* Finckh was not a formally educated man. He was ignorant of the psychology of the Junker military tradition. He did not know of the Prussian martial propensity for tactical craft, calculated ruthlessness and the inclination, when in contention, to go on the attack.

Although he was confused and anxious, nonetheless, Poissy had been given hope. The change in his morose state oddly began the moment Captain Shinse had entered Milice Headquarters and ordered Poissy to accompany him. When subsequently brought before the commanding presence at German Army Headquarters, he could not guess his fate.

Initially, he had difficulty believing the information given him. He was told that Marcus was alive and that Auguste, Helene and the Meyers were about to be taken into what the Adjutant called "protective custody". Their safety, as well as his, depended upon his full cooperation with the *Wehrmacht*.

"Do you understand?" Shinse asked brusquely.

"Yes Captain, I understand," Poissy replied glancing nervously at the disfigured ogre listening at his desk.

"You will go to that village under escort, what is it called? Find the man who escaped and bring him to us."

"It is called Couderouge."

"If you attempt duplicity of any kind, you will be shot immediately. Understand? We know you are connected in some way with those people. That, however, is a matter of indifference to us, complete indifference."

"Captain," Poissy asked, trying to fathom the real reason behind this late night summons, "the Gestapo, what of them?"

The Adjutant looked to the Colonel as if for direction. The blue eye gazed mercilessly at Poissy. "What does it matter to you, Frenchman, whether those swine shoot you or we do?"

There was something in the sarcasm of the Colonel's remark that suggested authenticity to Poissy. Somehow he knew the professional soldier's ultimate purpose was not directed toward him or his friends. He decided then to follow that instinct.

It was just after midnight when von Rugen got through to Divisional Headquarters in Paris. He spoke briefly with his friend *Generalleutnant* Loerner. The General did not ask the reasons for von Rugen's request.

First Sergeant Traub was sent to *Le Cygne Noir* with signed orders from von Rugen for Major Enke and *Leutnant* Dietl who were abed. They were to pack their belongings immediately and depart within the hour for immediate transfer to duty in Paris. The officers did not know that their stay in the French capital would be exceedingly brief. They were on their way to combat duty on the eastern front.

Helene, Ruth and Zalman sat huddled together in the total darkness of the musty, damp basement room. Zalman held both women protectively with his arms around their shoulders. No one spoke. Their attention was suddenly drawn to voices speaking in German in the corridor outside and the heavy clumping of boots approaching the door. They squinted when the room was flooded with light from the corridor as the door swung open revealing a young *Wermacht* officer staring in at them. He looked about the storeroom. "Where is the other?" He asked abruptly.

Zalman answered quietly. "We don't know."

The officer stepped back and turned to the guards. "Where is the other one?" He demanded.

"At the end of the hallway, *Hauptman* Shinse, in the small room by the wheelchair."

The Captain turned his attention back to Zalman. "Get up. You people are now in the custody of Colonel Dietrich von Rugen, Commander of the 48th Panzergrenadiers. You are to be transported to another location."

Shinse strode authoritatively down the corridor followed by the two guards. He opened the small door. After peering down on the crumpled figure on the floor he turned angrily to the soldier on his right. "Tischler, what in God's name happened here?"

"The Gestapo man, *Hauptman* Shinse, he spent some time in the room with him. We heard the sounds of the beating."

Shinse knelt down to Auguste. "Are you conscious, Frenchman?"

"Yes," Auguste croaked in reply.

Shinse stood. "Tischler, go out to the truck and get a few men. Carefully put this man in his wheelchair and get him on the truck with the others."

Helene came to the entrance of the small room and began to weep softly as she looked down on her bruised and bloodied husband.

"Don't cry, my love," Auguste whispered, "I'm a tough old bird. If I could have gotten my hands on him again, he'd be lying here next to me."

Helene stood by as the soldiers, under the scrutiny of Shinse, slowly and gently placed Auguste into a sitting position in his wheelchair. Although he grimaced now and then, he made no sound. Helene followed closely behind as they wheeled him down the corridor. She continued to maintain that peculiar posture of constantly holding her cardigan wrapped tightly around her.

The Deschaines and Meyers were billeted in two upstairs rooms at von Rugen's headquarters. The men were put in one room, the women in the other. The one soldier posted outside acted more the orderly than guard. A German Army doctor arrived to see to Auguste. After attending to Auguste's wounds, he informed him that the Colonel wished to see him at his earliest convenience. Ruth was the most hopeful of the group. She had felt no real hostility from the German soldiery since the appearance of Captain Shinse. For her, there now appeared a vague chance of survival and escape from the tentacles of the Third Reich. She said as much to Zalman who simply nodded gravely at her comments.

Oberfeldwebel Traub wheeled Auguste into von Rugen's office and placed him before the Colonel's desk. For an extended time the two of them eyed each other with something resembling wary inquisitiveness. Each concluded from his reserve and bearing that the other was a man of substance.

Von Rugen spoke first. "Your physical infirmities, are they the result of soldiering?"

"Yes, Verdun."

"Ja, Verdun, and how may I ask?"

"German mortar barrage."

"Attacking the German entrenchments?"

"No, running back to our lines after an idiotic reconnaissance patrol."

Von Rugen chortled, "My father was at Verdun. He told me of the lunacy of it."

"And you, Colonel, your disfigurement?"

"A Russian artillery shell on the Volga."

"You were no doubt, attacking, eh?"

"Ja, of course," von Rugen laughed, "but in that instance it was David throwing rocks at a host of Goliaths."

"Lunacy?"

"Ja, ja, but only in retrospect. At the time I thought myself invulnerable."

A silence ensued. Then August asked quietly, "And now Colonel, what is the situation?"

"Waiting, Monsieur Deschaines. Waiting for the Allied invasion and my regiment's participation in the destruction of the German Army. It is my duty to make that as difficult as possible."

"Yes, that would be the duty of a career soldier. But now, in Ardeche, what is your duty?"

"Preparedness."

"And that only?"

"You are alluding to the political business being conducted by the nonmilitary elements of the Third Reich, ja? I do not take action against anyone who does not threaten our military preparedness."

"We haven't done that."

"I know. I am now dealing with the unauthorized use of members of this unit in the collection of civilians. There will be repercussions."

"But not for the four of us."

"Five of you. I have good news, Monsieur Deschaines. Your man, what is he called? He was not executed in the woods by my sergeant. The Sergeant Staiger let him go. He is at large."

Tears of gratitude welled in Auguste's eyes. "Marcooz not dead? Colonel, forgive my emotions. That man is my closest friend. This is miraculous."

"A miracle, eh? I do not know about such things. You people are free to go home but I must warn you that the Gestapo man, Finckh, will no doubt organize something again, probably with the thugs in the Milice and come for you."

"That would assuredly be true. You're saying we're not out of danger."

"I'm afraid not. Perhaps you could go into hiding. Is there somewhere you could go?"

"My condition prevents that for me. I would be a burdensome risk for my people while on the move. I would prefer to stay home and deal with him and the others as they come through the door. But then, I'm sure my wife, Helene, would not leave without me and they would get to her. I'm afraid for the moment I have no solution."

"Monsieur Deschaines, let me make a small suggestion. Remain in custody for a few days and try to sort things out. Perhaps, the possibility of resolution will become manifest. Perhaps a miracle, eh?"

"Thank you Colonel. I appreciate your offer. Perhaps you and I will speak again."

In the short time they had been together von Rugen had come to admire the Frenchman. "Of course, Monsieur Deschaines."

Auguste began to wheel himself from the office, then stopped and turned again to face von Rugen. "Colonel, a personal question, if you don't mind?"

Von Rugen nodded. Auguste put it to him bluntly. "Have you thought about the fact that your command's presence provides the opportunity for the hoodlums to do their dirty work?"

"Ja, I've given that considerable thought but I have no solution. Any overt action against them puts the men of my regiment at risk. Additionally, it puts the very members of their immediate families at risk. I cannot allow that. A few months ago I attended a military conference of field grade officers where several of us discussed that very thing privately. The consensus was that nothing could be done. We are in the midst of a war for survival as a nation and that must receive the highest priority. It is Field Marshall von Runstedt's point of view. As one of his subordinates, I have adopted that policy. Schicklgruber and the National Socialists currently hold the reins of governmental power. There is murder and horror against innocents all across Europe. But perhaps that will change as the military situation deteriorates. I cannot say. The Fatherland is currently being attacked by powerful outside forces. It must defend itself despite being afflicted by an insidious internal infection."

Auguste nodded somberly, "I appreciate your candor, Colonel."

"Ja," von Rugen sighed.

Auguste wheeled about and left the office.

Sitting in the rear of the lead *Kubelwagen* coming north out of Tournon-sur-Rhone, Poissy looked out to the river on his right. He was thinking that the best place to start in the search for Marcus would be a visit to the priest at St. Gregoire's. Perhaps he could persuade Captain Shinse to remain in the village with the soldiers while he walked to the church alone. "No," he thought, "Shinse wouldn't allow that."

The priest would have no obvious reason to cooperate, Poissy reasoned, but perhaps he would send a message to Marcus. Maybe the Irlandais would come in if given the chance to see his friends again.

In the soft light of dusk, looking forward past the driver, Poissy noticed a cyclist approaching in the opposite lane. "That's him," he exclaimed, grabbing the driver by the shoulder, "Captain, that's him."

As the vehicle braked to a halt, Poissy leaped from the back of the vehicle onto the roadway. "Marcooz, my friend, you must come with us. Listen to me, please Marcooz, listen to me."

Marcus stood, straddling the bicycle, looking from Claude to the soldiers in the *Kubelwagen* and truck. "What the hell is this, Poissy? What are you doing with them?"

"Oh my friend, I can't explain everything to you. The Gestapo doesn't have the Deschaines and the Meyers anymore. The German army has them and their commander wants to talk to you. You must come with us. You must."

"The Commander wants to see me? What the hell does he want to see me about?"

"I don't know, my friend. I just know that he sent me to find you. He said that the Deschaines and the Meyers are not prisoners but are just being kept in custody as a guarantee for your coming to Privas. I am inclined to trust him although I can't say what he is up to."

Marcus noticed that the soldiers were remaining in their vehicles. Several of them were poking their heads out of the back of the truck. He looked at the officer in the *Kubelwagen*. "You," he said, pointing at Shinse, "what happens now if I make a run for it."

"I'm not quite sure, *Irlander*, I suppose I'll have him shot," Shinse responded in a light tone while pointing at Poissy.

Marcus smiled. "Well, we can't have that, can we? Will I put the bicycle up on the back of your truck?"

Shinse nodded.

Inspektor Finckh looked into the forbidding countenance across the desk. He held himself in psychological readiness without a trace of apprehension. He had initially been surprised and irritated to hear that the Colonel had taken his prisoners at the hotel into custody. He assumed the issue at hand would no doubt be one of propriety and jurisdiction. The Colonel was about to express his displeasure concerning Finckh's initiatives, conducted, as they were, without *Wehrmacht* approval and complicity. He was quite sure that the matter was about to be resolved. Of this, Rochus was confident. He was wrong.

The Colonel continued to stare at Finckh without speaking. In order to begin discussion and resolution of his current problem, Finckh began, "Colonel von Rugen, I ...."

"Be still," came the abrupt command.

Finckh waited, expecting the Colonel to begin speaking. The officer said nothing.

Minutes passed. The Colonel finally rose from his chair and stood with his back to Rochus looking out of the window into the night. He clasped his hands behind his back and began pacing back and forth. "You are to have no official contact with any soldier in the 48th Panzergrenadiers. I will warn you exactly once on that account. While speaking to me you will not make the least of assertions. Your speech will be in the form of answers to my questions. Do you understand?"

"Colonel, I think ...."

"Silence! You are making an assertion. I asked whether or not you have understood me. You will respond in the affirmative if you have understood what I have just said."

Rochus did not answer immediately but sought in his mind a reason for the officer's behavior. He could find none. The idea occurred to him that perhaps, as Major Enke had suggested, von Rugen was insane and if that were the case, at this very moment, his life might be in danger.

This day had been like no other in his career with the Gestapo. Twice he had been suddenly assaulted in a situation in which he thought he had been in complete control. Shockingly, his power and authority had disappeared and his confidence in benign providence had been shaken thoroughly. Sitting now before von Rugen, he felt stripped of that invulnerability he had always assumed for himself in pursuing the interests of the Reich. "Colonel, perhaps I ...."

"Silence! You will now answer yes or no. I will not repeat myself."

Finckh felt a cold shiver of anxiety. "Yes Colonel, I understand."

"You will now agree to these realities or choose not to. You will not, repeat not, attempt to engage me in conversation regarding the implications of your choice."

There was in the Colonel's tone an ill-defined transcendence that suggested to Finckh that the man who confronted him fell quite outside any considerations of human normalcy. He was being exposed to a raw elemental power that took no account of social identity or its implications. The Nazi was encountering a stark will greater than his own, a will that sought no compromise and threatened destruction to that which stood in its way.

Yet Rochus knew he was not being deliberately threatened. After all, he was intimately familiar with the practice of intimidation and forced submission. He realized that he was simply now in a position of choice. He would submit to the Colonel's will or be no more. An existential dread came upon him. His illusion of personal power was gone. The *Wehrmacht* had intervened to save him in Couderouge but there was nothing in this present situation that could help him. Nothing, that is, but submission. "Yes, Colonel, I understand and agree."

Von Rugen remained standing without turning around toward Rochus. "You will come again to this office if summoned."

"Yes, Colonel. Colonel, may I ask a question?" Finckh sniveled obsequiously.

"No, get out."

The *Inspektor*, stunned and unsettled, walked out of regimental headquarters into a light rain. He did not seek a ride back to the hotel from military personnel for fear that von Rugen would hear of it. He pulled the lapels of his overcoat snugly to his throat against the night chill and thought of the long walk in the darkness back to his lodgings.

Finckh would not, of course, report his difficulties to Gestapo Headquarters in Lyon. He certainly did not wish to appear the incompetent to his superiors, but more importantly, he suspected that the eerie frightening figure he had just encountered was a familiar of powerful men in the upper echelons of the Reich. Why else would that disfigured monstrosity totally disregard the aims of the Party and treat one of its agents as no more than an insect.

Rochus wished now only to get back to his warm bed at *Le Cygne Noir*. Tomorrow he would resume his audit with the Milice, complete it quickly and get out of Privas. He had the strange feeling that he was being stalked. A numinous menace was approaching him from an unknown quarter. His hand went involuntarily to the Walther in his shoulder holster. It felt hard and alien and gave him no comfort.

Shinse stood before the Colonel holding the spade he had taken from Marcus' bicycle. "*Oberst*, I thought you might be interested in this. When we collected the *Irlander* he had it wired to the handlebars of his bicycle."

"A spade?"

"Examine it, sir."

Von Rugen took the spade in his hands. He immediately noticed the filed edge and ran his thumb along it. Shinse had never heard the Colonel laugh. Von Rugen's face contorted into what appeared as a grimace. He made repeated coughing sounds not unlike the basal murmurings of a stallion. The Colonel, Shinse realized, was chortling. "This man, Shinse, what is his name?"

"I don't know, sir, the Frenchman referred to him as the Irlandais."

"*Irlander*, eh? He was working for the man who was arrested, correct?"

"Yes *Oberst,* according to the Frenchman they were long-time friends."

"Where do you have him?"

"I have him and the Frenchman under casual guard in the basement of the building, *Oberst.*"

"It is your impression that the *Irlander* and the militiaman are friends?"

"Yes sir, that is my impression."

"Bring them here."

Shinse led Marcus and Poissy into von Rugen's office. The Colonel motioned toward the chairs. "Sit," he ordered.

He studied Marcus briefly then probed. "You struck an official of the Reich. You can be shot."

Von Rugen found Marcus' calm reply interesting. "Am I supposed to be afraid now?"

"You are not afraid for your life?"

"We're all going to die, Colonel, but I'm not thinking about that just now. I'm here because you have my friends in custody. They're not a threat to you or anyone else but your people came and took them away. Your people took my friends, good and decent people. It was an evil thing, plain and simple."

Von Rugen smiled, "And you, *Irlander*, intend to do something about it with your broadax, eh?"

Poissy saw the muscles in Marcus' jaw tighten. "Colonel," he interjected, "is there some way these people can be released?"

"I will release those in custody right now and you two are free to go as well. I have no interest in civilians. Do you understand?"

Poissy looked to his friend, "He has no interest in civilians."

Marcus was puzzled. "Colonel, if you have no interest in civilians why did you send your people to Couderouge?"

"Listen carefully, *Irlander*, I will neither explain to you how the operation in Couderouge came about nor why you are free to go now. You will not be informed about that. You must do as you deem fit."

Poissy understood. "Colonel, if you don't mind, may I ask a few questions?"

"Be quick about it."

"Colonel, you have no interest in civilians?"

"Correct."

"You have no interest in, ah, politics?"

"Correct."

"You are concerned with military matters only?"

"Correct."

"You did not authorize the operation in Couderouge?"

"Correct."

"The people in custody are still at risk?"

The Colonel paused and looked directly at Marcus, "Correct."

"We must see to our own problem?"

"Correct."

"One last question, Colonel, is it possible that our problem can be solved without, ah, repercussions, without your, ah, further interest."

Von Rugen did not answer immediately. He rose from his chair and picked up the spade that was leaning against his desk. He walked around the desk and handed it to Marcus. "Are you familiar with your people's history?"

"I am," Marcus nodded.

"In their confrontation with English musketry their reliance on the pike and battleax was to no avail. Isn't that so?"

Marcus smiled grimly. "You're right, Colonel, that's all we had. But now and again we'd get close enough and if you get close enough, that's all you need. And right now, Colonel von Rugen, you're close enough."

Shinse's hand went to his hip holster. Von Rugen smiled, enjoying the sudden tension immensely. "Periodically, *Irlander*, I engage in saber practice with some of my soldiers. I am not unwilling to do that with you at some time. You may have that satisfaction if you like. Understand, however, that whatever the outcome of such an encounter, your people will remain at risk."

Poissy stood quickly. "Marcooz, it is not the German Army that is a threat to us. It is the Gestapo. The man who instigated the events in Couderouge remains the threat. He is the one we must deal with."

Marcus thought a moment. "But that means that Auguste, Helene and the Meyers will still be in danger if they go back home. The bugger is likely to come back, isn't he?" Marcus then nodded toward the officers, "Should we talk about it in front of these two?"

Shinse addressed the Colonel, "*Oberst,* is this interview at an end?"

"In a moment, Shinse. *Irlander,* it is not necessary that your people be released immediately. That, I've agreed, is up to them."

"Can I see them?"

"You can."

"Now?"

"*Ja.*"

"I want you to come with me. I want them to see us together."

"*Ja.*"

Ruth looked out into the night from a second story window in the regimental headquarters. She, like Helene, could not sleep. Her heart skipped a beat as the door from the corridor opened behind her. She gasped in horror as the uniformed golem appeared in the doorway. Her fear suddenly gave way to utter amazement as Marcus stepped past the German officer and entered the room. "Marcooz, Marcooz," Helene shrieked, leaping to her feet from her cot and running to embrace him.

"*Merci Dieu*, Marcooz, you're alive, you're alive."

"Helene," Marcus sighed, crushing her to him.

Ruth joined the pair in embrace. "We heard the gunshots, Marcus, we all thought you were dead."

"I thought I was a dead man too, Ruth, but the soldier let me go. He told me to run then fired into the air."

There was silence for a moment. "They caught you later?" Ruth asked, "that's why you're here?"

"No, it's not like that. We're all free to go home. The Colonel, here, will release us right now. But that's not a good thing. You see it was the Gestapo man who came to get us. It wasn't the German Army. The Colonel has no interest in us but the other bugger is sure to come back."

Helene looked at von Rugen still standing in the doorway. She lowered her voice to just above a whisper. "Can we talk in front of him?"

"Colonel," Marcus asked, "will you give us some privacy?"

"*Irlander,*" came the stern reply, "it makes no difference whether I hear what you speak of or not. You will solve your problem or you won't."

"What does he mean, Marcooz, when he says it makes no difference whether he hears or not?" Helene asked.

"He's saying, Helene, that we're on our own. He has no intention of acting against us or helping us. When he said that we're free to go, he meant it."

"Then, let's go. Let's run for it. Let's do it now before morning." Helene insisted.

"No, Helene. I'll go down the hall and speak with Auguste and Zalman. You four stay here. Claude and I will try to do something. I can't put it into words, but somehow I trust this German bastard. While you're here in his custody, nothing will happen to you. He's just that kind of a man. Poissy was saying that he doesn't believe this battered old warbird thinks much of the Nazis. He's just a soldier. That's what he thinks about and he's not much interested in rounding up civilians who haven't done anything. So, I think we can trust him. We can trust him to be himself."

Von Rugen looked vacantly off into space, "Are you finished here, *Irlander*? You will stay with these people until morning or you will leave now. If you remain until morning you will be put on a truck with them and returned to your home. You will not have the freedom to come and go at this headquarters."

"I'll go now, just after a short word with the men."

"Follow me," von Rugen said as he turned and left the doorway.

Marcus embraced each of the women. "I'll get you out of this. You'll all be safe, I promise."

Von Rugen was standing alone at the front door when Marcus was leaving. "Your friend has returned to Milice Headquarters. Perhaps it is not the right time to see him."

"Are you saying, Colonel, that the Nazi is there?"

The Colonel's gaze went out into the darkness. "I have no idea where *Inspektor* Finckh is."

"That's his name, is it?"

"Ja."

"Well, can you tell me where he is going to be tonight sometime or even tomorrow?"

"Everyone must sleep. The *Inspektor* does that at *Le Cygne Noir* hotel as do numerous *Wehrmacht* officers."

"Are you saying the place is heavily guarded?"

"All areas of *Wehrmacht* activity are secure. The hotel is no exception."

"You're not going to help me, are you Colonel?"

Von Rugen smiled sardonically. "Everyone must eat. I'm told Finckh does that at a restaurant near the hotel and, of course, he spends much time at that Milice dung heap which is also nearby."

"He'd be on the street sometime then."

"Ja, that would be so. You understand, don't you Irlander, there would always be armed men in close proximity?"

"I suppose so. Mostly your people, eh?"

"Ja. There is the chance that if you stalk well and are quick enough you can take your prey unaware. But I doubt you'll escape. You'll be gunned down or taken into custody. In the latter case, of course, I will have to have you executed."

"That would be nice and tidy, wouldn't it?"

Von Rugen grinned again. "Ja, that would work out quite well enough."

"I appreciate your candor," Marcus remarked sarcastically, reaching for a cigarette.

Von Rugen laughed, "Your friend, Monsieur Deschaines, said that very same thing to me."

Marcus offered the Colonel a cigarette. "No thank you, Irlander. You know, this kind of thing is best accomplished by a trained sniper from a distance. Do you know of someone with that skill? It is possible that I could arrange for one of our appropriate weapons to be missing for a short while."

Marcus shook his head. "No, I don't know anyone like that and I wouldn't try it myself for fear of botching the job. I've got to be certain it gets done properly, you know Colonel, for those people upstairs."

"I admire your loyalty and courage. I must say that. I remember years ago when I was in cadet training one of my instructors remarked that the historical success of the British army was founded on its Celtic soldiery."

Marcus smirked slightly. "So the ideal army has Irish, Scots and Welsh regiments led by Prussian officers, is that it?"

Von Rugen was thoroughly amused. "Of course," he replied and then came to a quick instinctive decision.

"Irlander, I will make you a solemn promise here. You have my word as an officer from an ancient and honorable tradition. If you fail in your attempt with Finckh, I will see to it personally. Neither he nor anyone else will harm your friends under my jurisdiction. While I am commander here they will remain in safety."

Marcus nodded. "That's good of you, Colonel. That takes a great weight off me. You're a decent man."

Marcus reached down and shook von Rugen's good hand. He shouldered his spade, turned and slowly walked down the stone steps and off into the night. Von Rugen watched him go feeling a quite unfamiliar emotion somewhere between admiration and pity.

His uniform and officious air got Poissy past the hotel's security as well as Finckh's room number from the elderly night clerk. He stood erect, took a deep breath and knocked authoritatively on Finckh's door. "*Ja?*" came the muffled reply from within.

"*Inspektor* Finckh, it is Sergeant Poissy. We must talk."

"Poissy? What is it you want?"

"I want to talk to you about the business up in Couderouge. There are things you don't know about, things of consequence."

"Are you alone, Poissy?"

"Yes."

Claude heard the door being unlocked. As the door opened, he continued, "I'm here on my own, *Inspektor*, and it is most important that you discuss our meeting with no one."

"What are you talking about?"

Finckh stood facing Poissy holding his Walther in his hand. He was barefooted, wearing only his suspendered trousers, undershirt and fedora. "Listen carefully to me, *Inspektor* Finckh, I have been doing this roundup business for over two years now and to put it bluntly it has proven quite profitable for me as well as others. You see, when foreign Jews and their protectors are taken into custody there always remains the question of their personal property. Most of these fugitives are from the middle classes and have converted their wealth to hard assets when they went into hiding. They generally have gold, silver and jewelry. Often those who hide them are people of considerable means as well. Also, as you are no doubt well aware, there are those sympathizers in France who have been quite willing to pay substantial sums of money as a kind of surety against molestation. You would, of course, understand from your work that this kind of thing is common, yes?"

Finckh squinted at Claude and nodded. "Yes, we are well aware of that. Go on."

"Because you are a man of considerable experience in interrogation, you detected that I was concealing something when you questioned me at headquarters the other day."

"Of course, I did. Go on."

Claude smiled. "As one professional to another would you care to tell me now what you think I was concealing?"

Finckh remained impassive. "No Frenchman, you just tell me what you were concealing, eh?"

"You suspected graft. But, *Inspektor* Finckh, the corruption that I was reluctant to talk about was not one involving me. I hesitated to speak of it because of concern for my own safety."

"Ja?" Finckh responded with a hint of sarcasm.

"It is quite simply the fact, *Inspektor*, that Monsieur Deschaines of Couderouge had been paying out large sums of money to insure that those staying at his residence would not be subject to collection."

"And you're about to say that you weren't the recipient of that payment, ja?"

"Don't be absurd, *Inspektor*, I'm but a mere Sergeant of Milice."

"Who then, Poissy?"

Poissy nonchalantly reached into his jacket for a cigarette. "*Inspektor*, where are the four people you took into custody? Are they in your custody now? Who has them?"

Claude lit his cigarette and watched as Finckh's expression changed. "You are saying, Sergeant, that it is Colonel von Rugen who has been accepting bribes. That is a very serious allegation against an officer of the Reich."

"Can you think of another explanation for the odd events since our return from Couderouge? *Inspektor*, what possible interest could a field grade officer in the *Wehrmacht* have in those four people? But he took them from you, didn't he? And he has them now, doesn't he? I am saying that he is simply protecting his investment, an investment that you unknowingly interfered in. An investment, I might add, that from his point of view should go on paying handsomely. Eh, *Inspektor?*"

Finckh sat on the edge of his bed and slid the Walther into the holster lying beside him. Poissy noticed the move and was encouraged in his deceit. "How is it you know of this, Poissy? I am not as yet convinced."

"You had a man shot for assaulting you at the Deschaines residence. That man happened to be one of my best contacts in Ardeche. He worked for Monsieur Deschaines and Deschaines used him to deliver payments to von Rugen. He and I became friends over a year ago. He was an Irishman who had absolutely no interest in the occupation, politics or welfare of refugees. However, he was quite interested in the support of his habitual drinking. I would pay him a small sum now and again for information. He used his obvious connection with Monsieur Deschaines to gain the confidence of those people helping refugees. I was able to make a number of arrests as a result of his information. I can only imagine that when he assaulted you, he was drunk and feared for his life."

"Have you any kind of proof of what you say?"

"The man who could verify what I am saying is dead. And because von Rugen has the Deschaines and the Jews you will not be able to extract the information from any of them."

"So, I am supposed to simply take your word for it, eh?"

"Well, *Inspektor,* consider my notes added to my report you found in the files during your audit."

"What of them?"

"They were not part of the formal report, correct? They were a kind of reminder to myself regarding the fact that another of my contacts had found out about the situation at Ormeau Road. Understand, I had no idea at the time that there would be a thorough audit by the Gestapo. Now, *Inspektor* Finckh, what is it that you discovered when you sought out Maurice Fleury in Couderouge? You found that he had been missing for several weeks. For some inexplicable reason, a lifelong resident of the village has vanished. Didn't you find that strange, *Inspektor?*"

"You are suggesting that he has been eliminated?"

Claude took a long drag on his cigarette and looked toward the ceiling. "Well, perhaps he had the sudden impulse to go on an extended vacation."

There was no reaction from Finckh to Claude's levity. "Well, what do you think happened to him, Sergeant Poissy?"

"I know this. I shared that information with the Irlandais. No doubt, he would have shared it with Monsieur Deschaines and it is probable he also mentioned it to von Rugen. Both of them, therefore, would have a reason to do something about Fleury. My guess is that it was the Colonel because in the inexplicable disappearance there is the element of sheer ruthlessness. I am told that Monsieur Deschaines is a gentleman from the old school, an ex-professor, a man of letters, of culture, of breeding. The cold elimination of an enemy would not come easily to him. On the other hand, von Rugen strikes me as a man who would squash an enemy as easily as he would a bug."

Although he gave no indication, Poissy's remarks struck a responsive chord in the Nazi. He merely nodded. "I must tell you, *Inspektor,* now that my Irlandais is gone and cannot act on my behalf I have the great fear that I will be found out as a man who simply knows too much. I have, after all, no relationship to the Colonel. I have absolutely nothing to offer to insure my own survival. The Colonel, I think, has set himself up in this area as a supreme potentate, answerable to no one. He does as he pleases and he will eliminate anyone he perceives as a threat."

Despite the vague convolutedness of Poissy's story, his last remarks regarding von Rugen struck Finckh as having the ring of authenticity. The Frenchman's thesis could, of course, explain the Colonel's actions as well as the rude treatment he had received in regimental headquarters. Yes, it was probably true. Von Rugen was using his considerable military power on behalf of himself alone. He was, in plainest terms, a traitor, an enemy of the Reich, an enemy of the Fuhrer himself.

Finckh began to think tactically. "Let us assume for the moment Poissy, that your concern for your safety and the interests of the Reich are what, compatible? Have you something concrete that I can give to my superiors?"

"You would like convincing evidence that von Rugen is the recipient of bribery. I believe I can give you that."

"You can? Well then, show it to me."

"What I have, *Inspektor*, is secured in a location known only to me. My problem is this. What guarantee do I have that you will not take the evidence and leave me hanging in the wind?"

"You have the word of an official of the Reich."

Poissy sighed. "I do not mean to be insulting, *Inspektor*, but you must understand I have no wish to have my life hanging on somebody's word. You see, the problem is considerably greater than the graft of a mere local commander. No, it reaches higher than that. No doubt it extends into the Vichy Government and perhaps even into the German general staff."

Finckh frowned. "What are you saying, Poissy?"

"*Inspektor*, just consider the roundup policy in the agreement between Vichy and your government."

"The roundup policy? What of it?"

"It specifically stipulates that French Jews are not to be molested by the security forces of the Reich or the Milice. They are French citizens and should not be included in roundups, correct?"

"Yes, and?"

"I have concrete evidence that von Rugen has tapped into an extensive network of French Jews and their sympathizers who are willing to pay for the hiding and support of refugees. Security men at our level, *Inspektor*, only deal with the small fish. The problem requires an authority higher than ours. Then too, I'm afraid I must require an authority higher than yours to insure my safety. You can understand that, eh?"

Finckh smiled. "So, you have information concerning others besides that man Deschaines who have business with von Rugen. Is that it?"

"Yes, I do. Didn't I tell you earlier that Deschaines' man gave me information? I have a rather extensive list of names and connections."

"And proof of von Rugen's involvement."

"Yes."

"But you will not show it to me."

"I will do that only when my safety is guaranteed."

Finckh mulled the possibilities. Could it be that providence had suddenly given him the opportunity to advance his career in the Party? His work in uncovering widespread corruption in Vichy and the *Wehrmacht* would not go unnoticed by his superiors. As for the Frenchman, well, he could be used or discarded as was necessary. Poissy was of no importance yet the situation at hand required a certain craft. "I will be finishing my work with your organization in a few days, Poissy, say by Friday. You can accompany me back to Lyon with your evidence."

"That is exactly what I had in mind, *Inspektor*."

"You understand, of course, I will be the one presenting your documentation to my superiors."

"Yes, of course."

"Well then, Poissy, it's late. I'll see you at your headquarters in the morning, eh?"

"There's just one other thing, *Inspektor*."

"One other thing? And what would that be?"

"Recompense for my information, *Inspektor*. I am entitled to fair payment as well as safety, am I not?"

Finckh smiled in understanding. "I suppose you are, Frenchman. You will be paid adequately enough in Lyon. I can guarantee that."

Poissy grinned as well. "I would prefer payment now."

"Now? I can give you nothing until we are in Lyon."

Poissy laughed lightly. "*Inspektor,* I believe you confiscated some items from the people in Couderouge. Those, I think, will be sufficient, eh?"

Although irritated, Rochus was impressed with the Frenchman's boldness. Had he underestimated him? In the Nazi's mind, Poissy's sudden canny demand tended to give added weight to his assertions concerning von Rugen. The *Inspektor* would do nothing to jeopardize his opportunity at this juncture.

Rochus went directly to his overcoat, withdrew a small package from the pocket and handed to Poissy without comment. "*Merci beaucoup, Inspektor,* this will do nicely I think. Good night then," Poissy lilted as he turned to the door.

After the Milicien had gone, Finckh sat on the edge of his bed considering various scenarios for his return to Lyon. The Frenchman would have the gems and evidence on him. His disappearance would be of concern to no one of importance.

In the street just outside the hotel, Claude walked briskly toward his flat in a state of considerable relief and surprise. The Nazi had really believed all that nonsense about von Rugen. Beneath his posturing and blatant viciousness, the *Inspektor* was evidently no more than a self-seeking moron. On the other hand, he, Claude Poissy, had apparently missed his true life's calling. No doubt in other circumstances, he would have made an excellent confidence man. A sudden sobering thought then occurred to Claude. He had not yet worked out all the details on how he was going to kill Finckh and get away with it.

The call came in at just after 3:00 AM. Fireman Cloutier, on night watch, took the information and logged in the particulars in pencil. The entry would later be amended to read 3:37. He rose from the desk and began ringing the large alarm bell by the office door. Upstairs, the *pompiers* rolled out of their cots and hurriedly began donning their rubberized gear and old-fashioned brass helmets.

Captain Briand, still buttoning his slicker, was the first to reach Cloutier. "Enough now, enough Cloutier. Where?"

"Milice Headquarters."

"Oh yes?" Briand commented, rubbing his chin.

He thought for a moment. "Tell the men to man the two small trucks. The main pumper's carburization problem hasn't been fixed yet."

"Something is wrong with the carburetor on Juliette?"

"Milice Headquarters, Cloutier, Milice Headquarters. Do you understand?"

Briand's point suddenly dawned on the fireman. He smiled impishly. "Oh yes, Captain, the main pumper's problem. I'll see to it as soon as you're gone."

After hearing of the location of the fire, most of the men on the trucks understood the leisurely pace through the dark streets of Privas. In order to maintain at least the suggestion of proper procedure, *Pompier* Campeur reluctantly cranked the siren now and again.

When the fire company arrived on the scene a large crowd in various stages of dress had already assembled in the street in front of the building. Knots of German soldiers stood watching together. Police and a few Miliciens were scattered about.

The first floor was engulfed in flames. Captain Briand stepped down from the lead truck and immediately declared the building a total loss.

He then directed the men to set the hose lines to protect against a spread of the conflagration by windblown sparks. The hoses were connected to the nearest hydrant and deployed to both sides of the inferno. Their spray was greatly reduced because of the ragged punctures that began to appear mysteriously along their length.

Inspektor Finckh stood next to three panzergrenadiers toward the front of the crowd of delighted spectators. He would have much rather remained in safety at the hotel. He nervously looked about for Poissy. He was anxiously hoping that the Frenchman had not secured his evidence of criminality and corruption at the now disintegrating headquarters.

Von Rugen had been awakened by his orderly and informed of the fire. He had given the soldier instructions that Captains Shinse and Bachofner should report immediately to his office. Within minutes, the officers were standing at attention before his desk. "Bachofner, the fire might well be a diversion by the Resistance," he began authoritatively, "make the rounds of our installations and put them on alert. Disregard the vicinity of the fire, including the officer's quarters at the hotel. You understand?"

"Ja, *mein Oberst*."

"Dismissed. Shinse remain."

When Bachofner was gone, von Rugen stared at Shinse for a time. "Shinse, listen carefully to my instructions and listen with understanding. *Inspektor* Finckh is presently in great danger. There is a good chance he will not survive this night. Take two squads of men. Be sure to take new men. Avoid taking veterans. Go south to just outside Privas. Encounter the *Maquis* in a secluded wooded area. Engage in a brief firefight. Foray a bit to make sure they have been driven off. Afterward, commend the men for their bravery under fire, especially the youngest ones. Report back to me after dawn. Any questions?"

"No sir, I think I can handle it."

"Shout at your men frequently. Display anger. Repeatedly direct their fire. Understand, Shinse?"

"Ja, Colonel."

"The young ones will see *Maquis*. Of that you can be certain."

Shinse allowed himself a small grin. "Should I take Sergeant Staiger, sir?"

"Sergeant Staiger?"

"Ja, Colonel. The Sergeant is good at shooting trees."

Von Rugen snapped, "You find something amusing, Captain?"

Shinse inhaled and swallowed. "No, mein Oberst."

"Get on with it."

Marcus had no difficulty when he had attempted to gain access to the basement of the quiet darkened Milice Headquarters. He assumed at least one of the uniformed thugs lay asleep upstairs. The rusted lock on the door at the base of the mossy stone steps was easily broken. He moved quietly into the darkness, feeling his way down the dank musty corridor. After bumping his head twice on the low uneven ceiling and feeling the delicate traces of spiderwebs on his face, he lit a match to get his bearings. He poked his head into the side rooms looking for ignition materials to suit his purpose. In a corner, a ribbed, green spouted can of about a fifty-liter volume caught his attention. He unscrewed the cap and sniffed. Kerosene. He had his means.

As he began his unhurried roundabout route toward the hotel, he turned to look back at his handiwork. Already, heavy dark smoke bathed in orange light was pouring from the basement entrance.

Marcus approached the hotel on the opposite side of the street and found his dark alcove from which he could observe the entrance to the lobby. He resisted the urge to light up a cigarette as he calculated the distance at no more than fifty meters before he would be upon Finckh. He was not nervous as he grasped the spade tightly in his right hand. One good full swing into the nape of the man's neck should do the job, he thought, then down the alleyway just beyond the hotel. Maybe he could get in more than one stroke. Maybe if someone shot at him, they'd miss. And maybe, yes oh Lord, maybe, this was the end of his life.

Marcus McQuillan was roused from his flowing imaginings by the shouts and general reverberant noise that came from the direction of the fire. A crowd was gathering. Two soldiers ran out of the hotel in that direction. Marcus waited, watching the small groups of soldiers and civilians exit the hotel. A few lingered in conversation. Then he saw Finckh.

As his quarry turned to walk toward the Milice building, Marcus tensed and made ready to charge. Suddenly, as if from out of the darkness behind him, yet somehow within him, he heard a familiar voice. "Wait."

The queerly nostalgic familiarity of the voice held him in place. Had he heard Avram? Ould Sean? His father? He had been told to wait by a loved one from the past. Wait? Wait for what?

The obvious then occurred to him. Yes, of course. It would be so much easier to get nearer Finckh from out of a crowd. Then strike and dash back into the crowd for escape. Marcus relaxed, exhaled and reached for a cigarette. He lit it and stepped out of the alcove.

As he approached the scene of his successful arson, Marcus was surprised by the size of the throng thoroughly enjoying this late night satisfaction. There was among the people in the fire-lit street a festive convivial air. A wizened old Frenchman, the image of Ould Sean Mulcahy, grinned at him with the gleam of deviltry in his eyes.

Marcus spotted the black fedora toward the front of the crowd. He noted the proximity of several soldiers. He entered the mass of animated noisy onlookers from the rear and began a winding stalk toward the front.

Obergrenadier Ritterlich stood in the middle of the street watching the orange-yellow flames now rising from the top of the building. His left thumb gripped the sling of his submachine gun as he turned to speak with Grenadier Kellner. Kellner was talking with the civilian in the black hat and trenchcoat who had positioned himself just behind them. Ritterlich had no idea who the man was, perhaps a local who knew some German. "Kellner, should we move these people back?"

Kellner shrugged. Ritterlich turned back to watch the conflagration. Suddenly, within the headquarters, the heavy framing collapsed with a roar sending a galaxy of bright sparks into the night sky above them. Ritterlich involuntarily lurched back as the inferno cracked and popped. It seemed the sound of small explosions was all about him. He felt a warm spray of liquid splatter on the back of his neck. He wiped at it then looked at his hand trying to understand what had just happened to him. He turned around and saw the hatless civilian now grotesquely sprawled out in the street, his face toward the cobblestones. A pool of dark blood was fanning out from under his head.

Ritterlich stared wide-eyed. From within the crowd someone shrieked. "The *Maquis!* The *Maquis!* They're on the roofs."

The Obergrenadier fearfully looked up at the tops of the buildings opposite the fire into billowing smoke and small glimmerings of sparkle. He saw movement. He saw rifle fire. Dropping to one knee, he quickly raised his MP40 and began firing bursts along the rooflines. At the sound of gunfire the spectators panicked. Several of them screamed in fright. Others jostled with one another and ran for cover. Soldiers dropped to the ground, ran for doorways or dove under the nearest vehicle. Some joined Ritterlich and began blasting away at the rooflines. Many of their rounds struck stone eaves and cornices, ricocheting back down into the street and twanging on the cobblestones. A young Frenchman took a spent slug in his buttocks. A middle-aged woman was hit just above her collarbone.

The heavy fusillade continued for several minutes then began to taper off. Captain Hebbel, who had come down from the hotel earlier, appraised the situation from under a fire truck and began calling out to the men to cease their firing. Except for the cracking of the fire, a short period of quiet ensued. Hebbel crawled out, got to his feet and warily looked about. While keeping his eyes on the tops of the buildings he walked uneasily over to the body in the middle of the street. *Leutnant* Alsdorfer came to his side. "Captain, isn't that the Gestapo man from the hotel? Frink or Frank or something like that?"

"Ja, I think it is."

"So, the Frenchies got him."

"Ja, they got him, all right."

Alsdorfer looked up and down the street at the extended rooflines. "One of them is an excellent marksman, eh?"

Hebbel looked up as well and commented dryly, "Ja, Alsdorfer, it would seem so."

Just after dawn, Poissy, in civilian garb, answered the pounding on the door to his flat. It was fellow Milicien Audette. The man was almost hysterical. "Claude, we must get out! They are going to come for us again! They got Finckh so easily! Some of the unit is missing. Perhaps they have been taken away to be tortured then killed. I'm told they struck at several places during the night. They even engaged the German Army. My God! None of us are safe."

Poissy lied calmly. "I'm not going anywhere. We still have our sworn duties, Audette. We'll set up somewhere else that is more secure. We'll get weaponry. We cannot let them do as they please. Have you no sense of honor, man? Are we to sit back and let these damned Communists destroy our New France?"

Audette's expression suddenly changed. It was now his turn to begin lying. He nodded solemnly, "Yes Claude, yes, you're right. I forgot myself for a moment. Yes, we have our sworn duties. We must go on for France."

"Indeed we must," Poissy commented, supressing a snort of cynical laughter. "Find Captain Vendeur. He'll begin the reorganization. He'll need every man. I'll join you as soon as I can."

Audette nodded in transparently false agreement. "I'll see you then, Claude, *au revoir*."

Poissy watched Audette as he quickly walked away knowing with certainty that the man was about to make a run for it. He could not resist having his bit of fun. "Audette!" He called out after him.

Audette turned. "Yes?"

"You'd best get out of that uniform, eh?"

Poissy returned to his preparations. He wouldn't take his rucksack. He'd wear what he had been wearing throughout the night although he still smelled of smoke. The large British Webley revolver he had been carrying inside his belt was beginning to chafe him. He switched it to the other side. Claude slipped his Milice identification papers and excellently forged documents into his inside breast pocket.

The packet of gems in his trouser pocket was a loan. If the Meyers survived this current madness, he'd find them and pay them back with interest. Maybe one day he would see Marcus and Auguste again and sit at the Deschaines' table reminiscing with them. The war could not last forever. In the meantime, Claude Poissy, a man convinced of his shrewdness and resourcefulness, was off to get lost in Marseille and become someone else.

Von Rugen received the report of the night's mayhem at Milice Headquarters while he was at breakfast. As he was wont to do, the Colonel did his own driving to the site with Shinse at his side. He dropped the Captain off at *Le Cygne Noir* with instructions to empty Finckh's room of anything of importance and then meet him at the scene.

The interior of the building had collapsed into the basement forming a radiant searing furnace of incandescent debris. Von Rugen stood at a comfortable distance taking Captain Hebbel's report. "Not one of our men was hit, correct?"

"Ja, *Oberst,* just the *Inspektor* and two civilians with flesh wounds."

Von Rugen looked up at the tops of the buildings. "Perhaps one marksman, ja?"

"Colonel, I think by the volume of fire there must have been several of them up there. They probably scurried off quickly when we immediately responded with our own heavier fire."

Von Rugen noted the bullet-scarred, projecting eaves and cornices. He knew where the rounds that hit the street originated. The fire trucks that his soldiers had used for cover hadn't been touched. The old officer laughed within himself. "Commend the men, Captain, now where is the body?"

Hebbel led the Colonel to Finckh's corpse now lying on the sidewalk. The upper half of the Nazi's body was covered by his trenchcoat.

"His head is severely damaged, sir, perhaps it was a dumdum round."

Von Rugen smiled in self-amusement. "Ja, maybe so, those things can cause a mess. Put that speculation in your written report. Captain Shinse will be handling the full report of the night's activity."

Von Rugen looked over to what he now thought would make an excellent incinerator and did something Captain Hebbel viewed as extremely odd. He knelt and went through Finckh's pockets taking papers, wallet and holstered pistol. "Captain, get some men, strip him and throw him on the fire," von Rugen ordered upon rising.

Hebbel's brow knit in perplexity. "Strip him, sir? Throw him on the fire?"

"Oh ja, of course, Captain. Strip him completely. His clothes and shoes are perfectly serviceable. After all, there are many indigent needy people in Privas. The cremation is an entirely appropriate procedure for an official of the Reich, wouldn't you agree?"

Hebbel assented automatically. "Of course, *mein Oberst.*"

As von Rugen wheeled about to return to his vehicle, he did a backward flick of his left hand toward the pyre and added lightly, "Have him thrown on with reverence, Hebbel."

Von Rugen returned to Regimental Headquarters with Shinse. At his desk he briefly instructed the young officer on what to include in the report that would go up to Division. He then sent a courier off with a handwritten note to the Gestapo at the Hotel Terminus in Lyon. It read: Your *Inspektor* Finckh has been assassinated by elements of the Resistance operating in the Ardeche area. Due to the Maquis' ubiquity, the 48th Panzergrenadiers cannot guarantee the safety of Gestapo personnel in the Ardeche environs for the foreseeable future. *Inspektor* Finckh's remains were disposed of in the traditional Nordic manner. D. von Rugen, commanding.

The receipt of the note in Lyon subsequently engendered a series of telephone conversations. Their themes centered on the inadvisability of political activity in Ardeche and the suspected derangement of the Colonel at the head of the 48th. Allusions to his powerful connections with the highest officers in the *Wehrmacht* were often made as well.

At the head of the long walkway leading to the entrance to regimental headquarters, the Deschaines and Meyers stood with Shinse and several soldiers. They were waiting for the truck and escort that would return them to Couderouge. They had been informed earlier by the Captain of their good fortune arising out of the events of the night. He had also conveyed to them the Colonel's personal assurance of their relative safety. Helene stood apart appearing somewhat wan and distracted. "Are you not feeling well, my love," Auguste asked solicitously.

"I did not sleep well. I was up several times during the night and wandered about out here waiting for the dawn."

Ruth put her arm around the woman. "Yes, I saw you come into our room at first light. You'll have a good rest after we get home. I'll make you a nice cup of that sleepy tea."

Helene managed a tired smile. "Where can Marcooz be? I'd really rather stay here and wait for him."

"I'm sorry, Madame Deschaines," Shinse interjected, "I have my orders from the Colonel. We'll be leaving presently."

The downshifting noisiness of a heavy vehicle turned their attention to the approaching small convoy. The soldiers went to Auguste's side and he was hoisted into the rear of the large Opel troop truck. The others were helped up and left to themselves as the grenadiers clambered aboard the other two vehicles.

The youthful face of a young German soldier suddenly appeared above the tailgate. He was breathing heavily as a result of running. "The Colonel wants a word with the woman."

"With me?" Helene asked in surprise.

"No, he wants to speak with her," the young man answered, pointing at Ruth.

Ruth's eyes widened. "He wants to speak to me?"

"Ja, He said 'Frau Meyer'."

Ruth anxiously rose, walked to the tailgate and was helped to the ground by the soldier. She saw von Rugen standing at the top of the steps to the front entrance. She walked toward him and stopped at the base of the steps looking apprehensively up at him. He appeared to her like the mythic figure from the netherworld she had seen in a Wagnerian opera as a young woman. "Yes Colonel von Rugen," she asked timidly.

He stared at her and she could discern nothing from his imposing posture and countenance. "Do you know the Driedl Song?" He asked abruptly.

"Driedl Song?"

"Ja, the song about the little spinning toy."

"Yes, Colonel, yes, I know it."

"When I was a boy, my governess would sing it for us during one of her holidays. I remember it was always near the Christmas season."

"That holiday is called Hanukkah."

"The old woman was taken not too long ago like you were taken. She did not survive."

"I'm sorry for you, Colonel von Rugen."

"Ja. Thank you, Frau Meyer. Will you do something for me, please."

"If I can, Colonel."

"At your holiday time will you sing that song in memory of her? I would very much appreciate that. She was a fine person and very good to us as children. She was part of our family."

"I will, Colonel. I will remember her at Hanukkah. I will sing the Driedl Song for her then."

Ruth looked into the disfigured face. A single tear ran down from the good eye. On impulse, she rose up the steps to him and astonished the observing soldiery. She embraced him and kissed him lightly on the cheek. "May God bless you. You are a righteous man, Colonel von Rugen," she whispered in his ear.

Dietrich von Rugen stood stoically, suffered the woman's affection then turned briskly and strode toward his office. "Shinse," he barked. Then he paused in mild embarrassment, remembering he'd sent the Captain to lead the convoy. "Traub!" He bellowed, regaining his equilibrium.

Marcus trudged wearily up the Deschaines driveway at dusk. He found everyone, including Bassard, in the kitchen. After embracing his friends, he took off his cap and flopped into a chair. He was exhausted. "Are you hungry, Marcus?" Ruth asked.

"Yes, Ruth, I am. I'll have a bite then I'm off to bed. I had a few short rides on the way back but had to walk a good bit of it. I haven't slept in days."

The kitchen was silent for a time. No one felt inclined to broach the subject of the past two days' happenings. They were simply grateful that their ordeal was over. The one concern that remained, particularly with Auguste and Marcus, was the fate of Poissy. "Goodnight all," Marcus said unexpectedly, rising and walking toward the back door, "I'm very tired. I'll have a good breakfast in the morning."

He turned from the door when he heard Auguste speak to him. "Marcooz, Poissy? Did you see him?"

"No, Auguste, I never saw him again after he left the Colonel's office," Marcus replied, and added as he opened the door, "aah, he'll be all right."

The reluctance to discuss the ugliness of their experience continued with the people on Ormeau Road. Each had their own memories and suppositions and felt no need to share them. Père Bassard, although terribly curious about what happened to them down in Privas, noted that disinclination and had the good manners not to inquire.

It took Helene several weeks to locate Madeleine who was living with a second cousin in Valence. After listening to Helene's sincere apology and pleading description of Marcus' thorough unhappiness without her, the Frenchwoman could do nothing but return to Couderouge. All were joyful with her reappearance in the kitchen, but no one more than the man in the little cottage.

Following the Allied invasion of Normandy in the late spring of the following year, von Rugen waited in eager anticipation for mobilization orders from higher headquarters. He was to be disappointed. The 48th was held in reserve in the German Army's anticipation of an additional Allied assault into southern France. Operation Anvil came in August 1944 with the American and French amphibious landings near Cannes.

As part of the understrength 19th German Army, von Rugen's unit could do little to impede the advance of three American Armored Divisions up the Rhone Valley. Their retreat was cut off near Montelimar in late August. Captain Shinse and Sergeants Traub and Staiger were among the 50,000 *Wehrmacht* soldiers taken prisoner.

Von Rugen did not choose a personal *Götterdämmerung*. He had learned something from the slaughter on the Volga. The Colonel's beloved regiment was not sacrificed to the lunacy of the dying Reich. He sat alone in his *Kubelwagen* watching a column of Sherman tanks approach him down a dirt track not far from the Rhone. The lead tank roared to a halt just before him as he stepped from the vehicle. New Yorker Corporal Mushie Abrams approached the Colonel with several other infantrymen accompanying the tankers. His Garand rifle was pointed at the Colonel's midsection. "Okay, Fritz, hand over the pistol."

Von Rugen pointed at his rank insignia and then at the double chevrons on Mushie's shirtsleeve. *"Offizier. Oberst von Rugen,"* he indicated.

Private Dixon, to Abram's right, snorted and said, "the Nazi wants to surrender to an officer."

Von Rugen understood Dixon's comment and became angry. *"Nicht Nazi! Nein! Wehrmacht! Wehrmacht!"*

"Easy Fritz, easy," Abrams interjected as he pointed toward the rear of the column, "officer that way."

Von Rugen nodded. *"Ja, offizier."*

The Colonel calmly got back into his vehicle and started the engine. He pointed imperiously with his thumb to the rear seat. Mushie smiled broadly and climbed into the back. He laid his rifle across his knees and stuck his chin up. "Home, Hans," he quipped.

Just after the war in Europe ended in May 1945, while Zalman and Ruth were away retrieving their children from the convent near the Swiss border, an American jeep rolled up the Deschaines' driveway. The driver, a staff sergeant, drove away after dropping off a nattily dressed civilian. Claude Poissy had come to see his friends and return the gemstones to the Meyers.

Everyone collected in the study where after embraces and handshakes, glasses of cognac were clinked in mutual toasting. Claude proudly gave them a description of his present circumstances. "Oh yes, I'm doing quite well in Marseille these days. I must return shortly with my business associate, Staff Sergeant Florio."

"The fellow who dropped you off?" Helene asked.

"Yes, him."

"You say 'business associate', Claude. He is an American soldier, isn't he?" She continued.

Poissy smiled broadly. "In our business venture, he is on the procurement side, I am on the sales and distribution end."

Auguste began laughing. "You're in the black market. Is that it, Claude?"

Poissy grinned. "No, no, Auguste. We steal nothing. We pay for all the goods and sell at profit. The Americans are very good at this kind of thing. We are simply businessmen. The war has created a demand for everything imaginable."

He looked about the room. "Is there anything I can get for anybody? Anything. Nylon stockings? Perfume? Cigars?"

Madeleine was very interested. Helene was not. Marcus thought of single malt scotch. "Claude Sticky," he joked, "a man who has finally found his niche in life."

Later, after the women went down to the kitchen to prepare the evening meal, Auguste, Marcus and Claude sat around the desk smoking and drinking. In their mild state of tipsiness, Auguste and Marcus were no longer reluctant to speak of the trouble in Privas. Poissy had never had such an aversion. He was saying, "After I saw the Nazi lying dead in the street and heard of the *Maquis* attacks around Privas, I knew it was time to get out."

"You say you intended to shoot Finckh that night?" Auguste asked.

"Yes, when I heard of the fire at Milice Headquarters I took it as an opportunity to meet with him, get him alone and kill him. I was thinking I could do it in his hotel room and slip quickly away."

"So, you were going after him that night too," Marcus quietly commented. "I was moving toward him through the crowd when the inside of the building went down and all hell broke loose. I didn't run with the others until I saw him stretched out there in his own blood. That was just after some woman was screaming about the *Maquis* and the gunfire started. I ran in the opposite direction from the hotel and threw the spade into an alleyway."

Poissy chuckled. "Oh yes, the spade. Von Rugen was impressed with that. Tell me, Marcooz, why didn't you just get a gun?"

Marcus shrugged. "Before I left here for Privas I went through Auguste's desk looking for his revolver but it was gone along with the shotgun. The soldiers must have searched around a bit and found it when they were taking everyone that day."

Auguste looked quizzically at Marcus. "You are mistaken, my friend. The revolver was here."

Deschaines pulled open a side drawer and withdrew his Lebel. He held the revolver up. "See? It was always here."

Marcus' eyes widened in puzzlement. "I'm telling you, man, that gun wasn't there when I looked for it."

Auguste clicked open the cylinder and smelled the weapon. He frowned. "I always keep it fully loaded and scrupulously clean. It seems one round has been fired."

Marcus insisted, "It wasn't there that day when I looked for it, Auguste. I'm certain of that."

Auguste hunched his shoulders and turned up his palms. "Perhaps, Bassard borrowed it for an animal pest or something and returned it. But then, it would be strange that he would do that without mentioning it to me."

Marcus had a grim thought. "Maybe for Fedou. He promised to do something about him."

"Our Père Bassard?" Auguste replied laughingly, "oh no, Marcooz, he'd never do something like that. He told me that Fedou was taken by a Communist cell of the Resistance. They just snatched him away one night and put him to work for them. He's alive but won't be allowed to return to Couderouge."

"It is a mystery, gentlemen," Poissy added, "and you know, it has also always seemed somewhat strange to me that the Maquis happened to strike at just the right time that night in Privas."

Marcus and Auguste nodded in agreement. Poissy raised his glass. "To the unknown gunman. *Merci beaucoup.*"

At dinner amid the lively chatter, Marcus continued to ruminate on the perplexity of the missing revolver and the enigmatic events of that long eerie night in Privas. For no conscious reason, his mind went to the day before Saint Valentine's Day, the previous February. He remembered he had purchased three small boxes of chocolates for Helene, Madeleine and Ruth. At the time, it had come to him that he had never returned the medallion he had taken from Helene's bedroom before setting out for Privas the day they had been taken. He had retrieved it from the breast pocket of the worsted jacket he had worn. Before dropping it among Helene's chocolates he had again studied the figure. Who was that woman wearing an outlandish hat? He sipped at his red wine. Hat? That was no hat. It was a helmet. He knew who it was! The medallion bore the image of the young woman who was perhaps the greatest warrior of all time. *La Pucelle,* the Maiden, who drove the enemy from those she loved. It bore the image of Saint Joan of Arc.

Marcus felt the beating of his heart as, in memory, he stalked Finckh through the crowd. He remembered the roaring sound from the building's collapse and then recollected for the first time the flash of light and sudden crack at the front of the throng. He recalled that it suddenly grew silent before he heard the woman shouting the warning. "The *Maquis!* The *Maquis!* They're on the roofs!"

Why was it only now that he recognized that resonant voice as familiar as his own? Tears welled in his eyes as he looked across the table at her. She was laughing lightly at one of Poissy's self-deprecating witticisms. She knew her Marcooz was out there alone that night. Yes, she knew he would try to deal with the Nazi but his determined guileless directness would most probably cost him his life. She could not allow that to happen. Helene had acted against her very nature for him. She did not shrink from taking on that alien ugliness in order to protect him. She loved him too much for that.

Helene looked across the table at him. She smiled tenderly and mouthed his name silently, extending her lips as if cooing on the second syllable. "Marcooz."

About the Author

Mr. McCann is a retired teacher who has spent considerable time abroad. He now resides in the Hudson Valley.

He has been published in several periodicals.

Printed in the United States
35924LVS00006B/1-66